Fractal Terminus

Fractal Terminus

A.Z. Rozkillis

Space Wizard Science Fantasy
Raleigh, NC
www.spacewizardsciencefantasy.com

Publisher's Note: This is a work of fiction. Names, characters, places, and incidents are a product of the author's imagination. Locales and public names are sometimes used for atmospheric purposes. Any resemblance to actual people, living or dead, or to businesses, companies, events, institutions, or locales is completely coincidental.

Cover art by MoorBooks
Editing by Courtney Brooks
Book Layout © 2015 BookDesignTemplates.com

Fractal Terminus/A.Z Rozkillis.— 1st ed.
ISBN 978-1-960247-56-8

To Dad

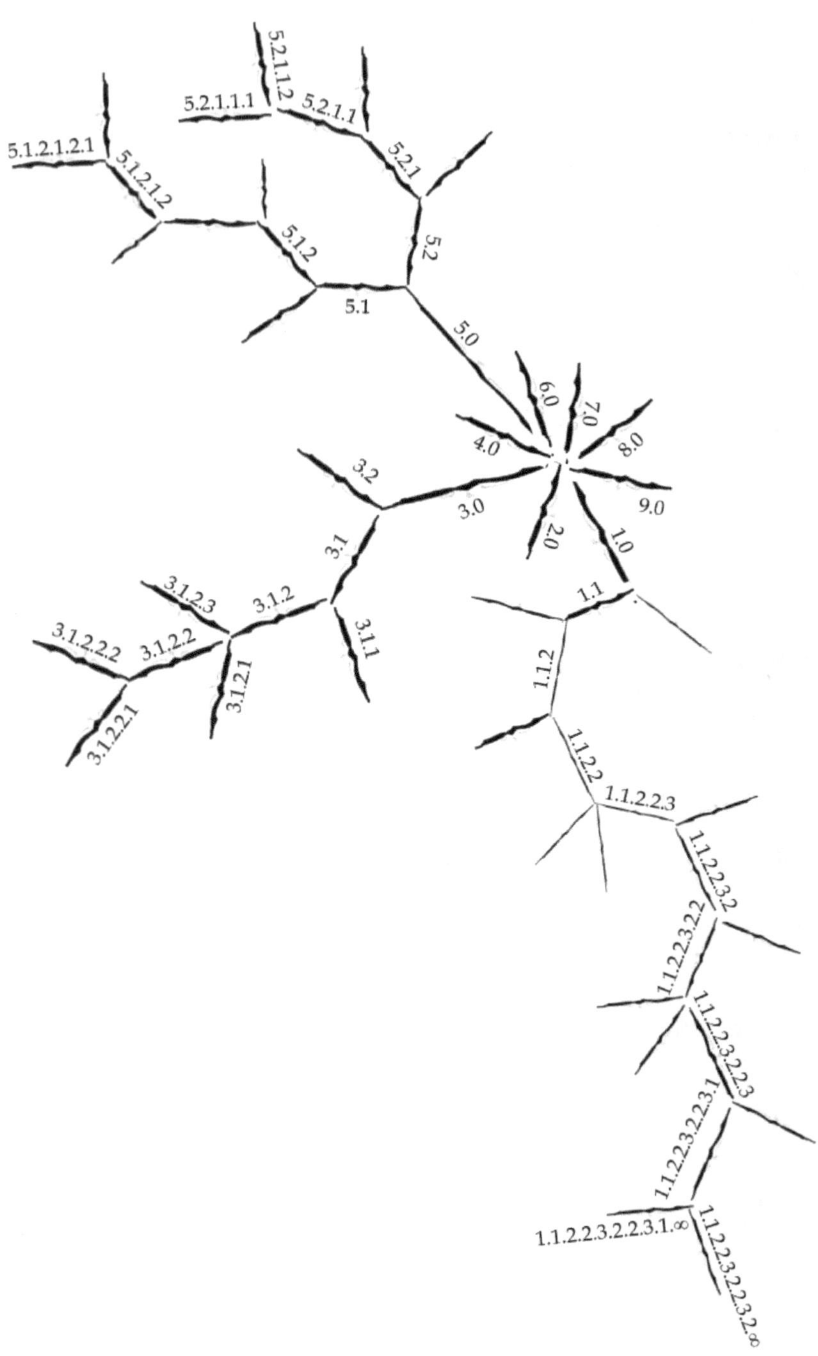

CONTENTS

1.O

Jax opened her eyes. The surroundings were strange and unfamiliar, and her back was fucking killing her. This was not her bunk. This was not anyone's bunk. This was not the core of her precious deep space waypoint Station.

She blinked. Her vision blurred then focused to allow Level 1 of the Station to swim into view. Sleeping on the first floor of her Space Station next to a compromised airlock was not an entirely normal occurrence in Jax's heretofore miserable life. Something was off. Jax went to sit up, stiff back protesting against whatever hard rivet from the corridor wall was boring into her shoulder blades, and was met with resistance. A motionless and weighted mass, solid like a boulder made of muscle, seemed to be anchoring Jax to the flooring. The boulder groaned from below Jax's arm, and she realized it was the still-sleeping form of Saunders, gripping the front of Jax's shirt like a life preserver in a storm swell.

Being presented with the reality that Jax was sprawled awkwardly in a hallway of a space station's outer ring, like the leftovers of a bad night out, wearing the company of a cute blond, made Jax's head feel absurdly heavy. She let her neck rock backward until her skull thudded mutely against the wall of the corridor again. It felt like the universe's most monumental effort to piece her memory back together, all of it circling the major singularity that was her only coworker's fists clinging so tightly to her front.

Desperate to clear the fog in her thoughts, Jax let her vision refocus through the scraggle of too-long black hair that had fallen from the mane down the center of her head into her face. Her sight landed on the porthole windows across from her. The Station's emergency lights cast a dim amber glow along the corridor, which allowed the faint pin pricks of stars to show more clearly through the inches-thick glass. The stars winked benignly back, giving Jax a moment of calm before recall hit her with the force of a very large wrench to the chest. A searing pain shot up the side of Jax's left leg and she spasmed. Panic rolled up and over her, in a rush of nausea and anxiety, as Jax arched her back against the dead weight pressed on top of her and scrambled against the wall. This woke Saunders up.

The Station Security Officer startled as if pulled from a nightmare, which conveniently prepared her for the realistic nightmare she would find in the waking world. Saunders always seemed a bit more put together in a crisis. This illusion was promptly dissolved by the urgency in the woman's voice as she scrambled awake.

"Jax!"

But Jax was already pushing herself upward, sliding against the wall for support, feet digging into the flooring as if to push her as far as possible from the portholes across from her. The Security Officer followed the cue and Saunders twisted herself around to look out the windows. Jax dimly realized she had reached out next to her to grab Saunders' arm as she struggled to upright herself.

Outside the windows, space winked back at them. Stars arced past in the ever-continuous rotation that generated the simulated gravity on Station. There was not, at least not readily visible, any indication of the massive tear in the spacetime fabric that had sucked them in. Jax would have considered it a collective nightmare, if it were not for the fact that she had just woken up in the Level 1 corridor with Saunders' face in her tits and what sounded like half of the Station residents surrounding them. Only maybe seventy percent of that scenario was a nightmare.

"We're...we're alive," Saunders mumbled next to her, as if she wasn't quite sure.

Jax broke her line of sight from the windows and looked up and down the corridor. At various intervals, and at accompanying levels of disarray, several residents were returning to consciousness. Some were in shock, others were still knocked out cold, but a few were up and moving, centering their focus on the expanse beyond the portholes.

"What *was* that?" Saunders sounded far more comprehending than Jax felt personally.

"I...I don't know." It was all Jax could manage after finding her voice, which sounded like she had swallowed a jug of coolant at some point. Talking seemed to make her head feel like it would split open, so Jax instead opted for sinking her face into her hands. She couldn't fathom how long she had been unconscious, nor whether she had even been awake before. It sure didn't seem possible, since she vaguely recalled spending her last waking moments fighting off zombie-space-bug-murder-freaks. Jax felt distinctly vomitous.

Next to her Saunders was shifting around.

"The residents, they need help..."

It was an uncharacteristically halfhearted statement.

Jax mustered the ability to groan some unintelligible response and suddenly there were tentative hands on her shoulders. Jax stilled. The feeling was alien to her, strange and out of place in her memory, yet not entirely unwelcome. Gentle fingers brushed over Jax's forehead into her hair, sweeping it from Jax's face and lifting her head so she could finally look at the Security Officer.

"Are you okay?"

Jax couldn't miss the deeply open, and concerned expression Saunders had etched into her normally cheerful features. Saunders searched Jax's face, her hands almost delicately tracing whatever bruises and scratches Jax had acquired in their recent struggle. Jax figured her own face looked some off shade of green, mixed with animalistic panic. But she also wanted to show Saunders the smothering relief she felt at their current survival; at the fact that Saunders was still here, in Jax's arms.

"Head hurts, from, whatever that was. How about you?" Jax's tongue felt thick in her mouth. She tentatively raised her hand toward Saunders' face before her nerves failed her and Saunders glanced away.

"Same. But I can't tell if the headache is from *that*..."—Saunders cocked her head toward the window—"whatever *that* was, or from sleeping on the floor...or just..."

"Security!" a voice called from outside Jax's field of vision. Saunders snapped her attention to the side, to see who was calling her. Jax looked around bewildered and noticed a resident nearby, struggling to make her way over.

"Rose," Saunders stated quietly, as if reminding herself who this person was. Jax had a flooding moment of recall about deep-space academics and research teams. She couldn't be sure if Rose had been with them when they had dropped through the rift. Or perhaps Rose has never been there, or wandered off... Jax *really* couldn't be sure how much time had passed.

"You are both alive." Rose sounded as if she herself was unsure. She surveyed both Jax and Saunders with a defeated expression. Since Jax was still trying to find the jumper cables to her brain, she appreciated someone who didn't feel the need to get chatty at the moment.

"Are the others okay?" Saunders asked, beside her. Rose looked about over her shoulders.

"Possibly. I cannot find my brother, but no one appears injured. Just...what actions could we conceivably take at this time?"

"I was hoping you could tell us," Jax muttered, which earned a look of alarm from both Rose and Saunders. "Kidding, who the fuck knows what just happened." The levity of her joke went sour on her own tongue.

"I think what Engineering is saying," Saunders trailed slowly, "is that we aren't sure what to do either. But we should probably find out if everyone is okay."

Jax felt grateful for the assist. She could tell it would be several cups of coffee before she could say anything effective.

Saunders turned her attention back to Jax, her injured shoulder nearly brushing Jax's arm, but just out of reach for Jax to feel the contact of the other woman.

"We should probably do that."

Jax startled from where she was staring at the bloody bandages on the soft skin of the Security Officer and looked at Saunders blankly.

"Get everyone together and make sure everyone is okay? Especially after last night," Saunders elaborated.

"Last night?" Jax was vaguely aware that the resident, Rose, had asked in unison.

"Or whatever time it was...before we...dropped? We came down here to give everyone answers and then...*that* happened..." Saunders trailed off, her face turned in profile to look down the arcing corridor, displaying the easy curve of her neck where it met her jawline. Jax willed her brain to catch up before she missed something important.

She didn't get the opportunity.

A scream echoed from around the curve of the Station, ripping their focus from their immediate dismay and off toward where the disruption reverberated from.

Saunders moved first, tearing herself from the wall at Jax's side. Jax felt the solidity of the other woman's presence depart her and grappled with a moment of feeling entirely adrift in the chaos, before Saunders grabbed her arm and pulled.

The band of them hauled off after the commotion, which had grown louder in the wake of the sudden outburst. Jax noted Rose struggling to run after them, and felt a wave of indignation at the added presence, which was quickly replaced with the searing scorch of humiliation as Jax tripped gracelessly over something on the flooring and landed hard on her knees. Saunders rushed onward and Jax rounded on whatever poor soul was the source of her demise, only to find her thirty-six-inch steel spud wrench, discarded from their earlier fray with hallucinations.

Jax glowered at her wayward armament and scrambled to get her feet back under her. A small hand grabbed at Jax's upper arm and hoisted. Before Jax could object, she was back on her feet and Rose was indicating they should continue toward the ruckus. There was no amusement in the smaller woman's features, and Jax felt mildly better about her fall. Wrench grasped at her chest, Jax followed after the noise, and the long since out-of-sight form of Saunders.

The group was frantic. Saunders had broken through the throng and was engaged on the other side. Jax pushed onward herself, shouldering through the forms of people she had never bothered to know. As the masses parted, it became clear they were not at all done with the horrors.

A man lay partially in the corridor, clearly dead. His eyes were sightless and open, staring into the infinite space between them all. Kneeling by his side were a group of residents who obviously knew him personally. Judging by the matching t-shirts, Jax assumed they were the Space Marines.

"Avery! Avery!" a woman shouted, her short dark-red hair plastered to her forehead with sweat. She tugged on his arm fruitlessly.

"Corine, *stop*!" Saunders barked. The woman frantically turned her attention to Saunders in response, but did not let go. Jax wished she would.

"Are we still in a nightmare?" The whisper at Jax's side startled her, and she tore her eyes from the sight and glanced at the short researcher beside her. Rose had a horrified, yet studious look to her face, as if she were collecting data on the terrible moments surrounding them.

Jax hoped it was still a nightmare. But the vision of Avery in front of them was not fading, not even with Jax's proximity to Saunders, or the fix she had imparted to her failing Station before the drop through that inexplicable rift in space.

Instead, Avery remained very real, and his body remained perfectly bisected at the middle by the solid metal of the corridor wall. It was as if he had fused with the side of the Station, his body being swallowed by a solid impassible barrier.

"Get him *out!*" Corine was screaming.

Saunders had knelt by the body as a crowd continued to gather, filling with wails and shrieks of distress as it grew. Something tugged at Jax's instincts just as Rose spoke again.

"Where is the rest of him?"

Jax lurched sideways, knocking through the gathered group and slamming painfully into the wall. The sounds of Saunders trying to control Corine behind her, while also fending off the growing crowd, were muted as Jax sought frantically for a weakness in the wall panel. If only this was a section where she had hidden an escape route, she could easily access behind the wall and *see*, really see for certain if he had been consumed by the Station or simply vanished.

"What is *happening*?" someone shouted behind Jax.

"Corine, *stop! STOP!*"

That last one was Saunders' voice, and it filled Jax with a sense of dread. Her hands slipped on the wall panel and she tumbled forward, knocking her head against the metal. Jax turned in time to see the distraught woman resume her fruitless yanking on her teammate, despite the attempted intervention of other residents. But it wasn't fruitless. Instead, Avery's body gave way, tearing from the wall.

There hadn't been blood before. It had just appeared as if the man had become part of the Station himself. Now there was a wave of gore as he separated from the wall. The woman pulling stumbled backward with a scream of horror and the crowd parted, some rushing from the scene altogether. Jax nearly slipped on the growing pool and lurched away. She found herself shielded behind the bracing muscular arms of Saunders, who had backed up, giving the space a wide berth.

"Nobody get near him!" Saunders barked.

A deafening silence fell over the crowd.

Jax felt a ringing in her ears and her vision narrowed to the point where Avery had been connected to the Station wall. A bloody smear remained against the dull luster of a very solid looking metal wall panel.

"We need to find everybody else," she heard a voice say.

Saunders spun and sized Jax up with a searing stare. It was only then, Jax realized she had been the one to say it, and she swallowed hard.

"I don't think this is over, Jax," Saunders whispered low in her throat, green eyes boring into Jax's soul. Oh, how Jax yearned for the opportunity to revel in that stare, but the horrors of the universe were still unfolding.

"What else do you believe is happening?" Rose re-emerged at their side like a shadow.

Jax tore her eyes from Saunders' glinting jade, glancing over Saunders' shoulder to survey the group surrounding them. The woman who had pulled at the dead man was being consoled by another Space Marine. Those who had fled seemed to realize they were trapped on a ring with no escape from whatever hell boiled around them. The scattered gathering stood in apprehension, unsure what next steps to take.

"Jax, get back up to Five. Make sure we're okay," Saunders hissed, her hands fisting in the front of Jax's filthy coveralls, dragging Jax's eyes back to her. Saunders then spun again, relinquishing her grip on Jax, and started barking orders.

"Okay no one touch him. We need to get a barrier around the body, work on cleaning this up. We need to find as many survivors as we can. If we find anyone else like Avery we need to secure the location, avoid another...mishap." She marched into the group pointing at residents and launching directions. The nausea of the mutilated body filled Jax with dread at the idea of separating from the energy of this woman.

"Saunders, I can't just leave you!" Jax growled after her, side-stepping the still spreading puddle of gore.

Saunders whipped around to face Jax, from where she was ordering an ashen faced pair of people to find cleaning supplies in a nearby locker.

"I'll be *fine* Jax, please, we still don't know what is going on around here, and you are the only one who knows how to control this station. Go!" Her dirty blond hair clung to her forehead in a new sheen of sweat.

"I'll accompany you," Rose interjected, quietly determinate. Jax shook her head as if in disbelief and scrutinized the other woman distractedly.

"What—I don't need some Martian to escort me. Saunders—"

Saunders had slipped away again, and Jax chased after her, through the chaos of reaction buzzing around them.

"Jax, take Rose with you, she can help," Saunders replied, distractedly.

Jax took pause. She stood in the corridor of her Station, next to half a man, and surrounded by the chaos of a group of humans torn from their own reality, as the woman she cared about spun away from her.

"I'm going with you too," said another voice. Jax snapped around to see a lanky, mousy-haired woman with broad shoulders and a sharp brow glaring at her.

"Who the fuck are you?" Jax barked.

"Eave." Saunders had appeared in front of Jax again with timely introductions.

Jax looked bewildered between the three women in front of her. Saunders strode forward and grabbed Jax by the coveralls. "They can help you. I'll find you, don't worry."

With that, the Station Security Officer kissed her and stepped back. Before Jax knew it, Saunders had melted into the roiling crowd battling their predicament.

"Engineering," drawled Eave. Jax swung around to look at her and Eave glared back, challengingly. "This guy isn't getting any deader. Let's go!"

Jax swallowed hard, glanced at where the half-man was swarmed with residents and then reassessed her escort. The two women stood expectantly.

"Okay, fine, let's go."

The stairwell to Level 5 was disturbingly empty. Jax felt a sinking feeling that it might not be easy to locate everyone they should have on Station. She hauled herself upward, as if fleeing the presence of her entourage, but the women who pursued her did not let up in their query.

"Engineering, did you not mention that you hypothetically solved the issues plaguing us prior to the anomaly?" came the clipped tones of the shorter woman, Rose. Jax didn't bother replying and the other woman interjected for her.

"Anomaly? I watched my roommate peel her own face off before flinging herself into a corridor full of gore, and now I just watched a man get ripped in half. I'd call this way more than a fucking anomaly," Eave snarled.

"I speak of the cosmic event that occurred, in which we seemed to pass through some unidentified passage—"

"That black hole?" Eave barked

"It wasn't a fucking black hole," Jax growled, unaware she was even saying it.

"I agree with Engineering, that was not a known cosmic event." Rose lagged behind, her shorter legs working hard and making her breathless.

"No shit," Eave hissed.

Jax rounded on them both. Somewhere below, Saunders was in triage mode, throwing herself into her role and controlling their populace through a nightmare that Jax had to leave her alone with. In a decade in space, Jax had never wanted the company of anyone but her own self-depreciating thoughts. But she wanted company now. Only, not the company of these two anonymous women flanking her. She wanted Saunders, who had summarily dismissed her.

"Just what, exactly, are you expecting by following me like this? Level 5 is inaccessible to residents!"

Eave stomped up a step and entered squarely into what Jax considered her personal space. The woman was as tall as Jax, which was notable in its own right. Her hazel eyes burned with animosity Jax felt might be just slightly misdirected.

"That's where your navigation computers are," she stated. It wasn't a question.

"I believe," Rose interjected, sharply, as she ascended to the same stair level as them, "what Miss Idenah means is that she has considerable navigation experience. And as for myself, I was studying an electromagnetic anomaly occurring in our lab instruments before this event occurred. I would also appreciate the opportunity to observe this station's navigational readouts."

Jax glared between the two of them, which was challenging given that Rose was at least a foot shorter than her. Eave glared back. Rose assessed them both with a benign appraisal that did not lend itself to their predicament of half a dead man on the first level and a Station in chaos.

"Fine," Jax exhaled through gritted teeth. "Just, don't touch anything." She whirled around and stomped up the remaining steps, her entourage in tow.

The two women tailing her behaved themselves only as long as it took to reach the entry doorframe to Power and Life Support on Level 5. As soon as Jax rolled the door open, Eave nudged past her and shouldered her way into the room. Jax keyed up a scathing admonishment, but the woman was already pulling up star tracker readouts and queueing databases.

"How, exactly, are you able to just bypass all the logins?" Jax objected, feeling aggravatingly more curious than flustered as this woman worked. Rose had also pushed past into the room. She was touring the numerous display screens and data centers Jax had kept at her sole disposal.

"Admin privilege," Eave replied, distractedly.

"I beg your fucking what?" Jax coughed, not sure what she had heard.

Eave looked up, her brows knit in annoyance.

"Admin privilege. I used to work for the network. I don't anymore, and the login codes are supposed to update annually. I had a bit of a hunch that hasn't happened on a station as...remote...as this. Quinn and I were routed for a different waypoint near the outer bands as replacements, looks like neither of us are going to get there any time soon..."

Jax was all at once incensed and ashamed. She made a mental note to update the entire system's security settings, then wondered why Saunders hadn't updated them herself. Eave moved to the scrolling star tracker readouts that Jax had set before they...fell...through whatever that rift had been.

"They're still cycling. I think the rift blocked out their key waypoints—" Jax tried to supply, as if in defense of her own ability to manage the Station's location in deep space. "They won't match with the star charts."

"You aren't even utilizing the Nav-hub?" Eave's incredulous voice cut her off.

"Why bother. I can personally vouch for the fact this Station hasn't moved in over ten years." Jax could at least be proud of that fact.

Eave looked up, eyes narrowed again.

"Station contracts are three years. Why the fuck have you been out here that long?"

Jax growled. "No one's fucking business, that's why."

Eave shrugged and went back to what looked like rebooting a system that Jax hadn't touched in ages.

"Well, *that* certainly tracks," the navigator said. And Jax couldn't tell if it was in regard to the computer, Jax's blithe response, or some little navigation in-joke.

Rose was still at her elbow and now the researcher spoke up.

"Engineering, is there any way I can also review some of the more recent data collected by the Station's operations center?"

Jax flinched. She needed to check the core, but the thought put her chest in an ice cold vice-like cinch. She didn't want to have anyone in her Station's core but herself, and Saunders.

"The core is off-limits."

Rose simply replied with the benign smile again.

"Certainly, Engineering. Just an inquiry. Additionally, how did you know I was from Mars?"

Jax blinked, caught off guard, then grit her teeth at her own slip-up.

"Only a planet founded entirely by academics talk like they are constantly delivering their thesis," Jax stated.

"That is a fair assessment," Rose hummed. Jax turned her shoulders to truly look at the woman. Short, with dark brown hair in tight curls, pulled into a knot at the back of her head. Rose had amber eyes that shone out of her tan face, skin the telltale color of someone with a darker tone who had not seen the light of a sun in a significant amount of time.

"You can read whatever data you need from here in Power and Life support. I need to get to the core." Jax put as much energy as she could into making it sound nothing like an invitation. Rose was busy studying her in return, and the act left Jax feeling stripped bare. Jax strode over to a console and jabbed at a report generator. She watched the readout tick past. No Station damage flagged itself in the data as it scrolled. She wouldn't find her answers here.

"Just, don't fucking *touch* anything," Jax repeated, leaving the report up for Rose to peruse as she backed out of the room where Eave was definitely touching everything. Rose watched her pass, almost inquisitively and Jax made a point to not say anything further.

The entrance to the core was daunting. Jax felt fear grip her as she stood at the base of the strut that led to the center of all Station operability.

"What happened to us, Station?" Jax whispered, her hands on the wrung. The dark interior loomed overhead, not nearly as much a comfort as it had been in all her years prior. Who knew what horrors might await her up there, coiled and ready to strike should she let her guard down? Human bodies were being fused with this Station's inner walls. Nightmares had leaked from every corner, and Jax had *thought* it was the Station's fault, then she had thought it was the massive rift in space they fell through. There was no telling if they were free from the madness yet. And all she wanted was a moment, again, with Saunders.

Jax took a deep breath and went to hoist herself up the ladder.

A navigation alert blared in her ears and the warning lights flashed ominously. That would teach her to leave complete strangers in the most critical section of the Station operations center. Jax swore colorfully and tore herself from her battle with braving the Station center. She stormed back around and into Power and Life Support in a near rage, ready to boot an ill-willed resident, only to find herself face to face with an irate-looking Eave braced against the main nav console, a feral look in her eye.

"Good," she snarled, as Jax stomped over to her, "that got your attention back."

"What the *hell* are you doing to my Station?" Jax growled at the so-called navigator, bearing down on her in challenge. But the mousy-haired woman didn't look so mousy anymore. She looked formidable, and she refused to back down.

"Do you *know* why the charts don't match?" she demanded. Jax shot a look at the main console over Eave's shoulder, which appeared to still be cycling.

"Do you—" the woman started again and Jax cut her off.

"Of course I don't know why the charts don't match, that's why I let you in here!" Jax spat through gritted teeth.

"The charts don't match because we are no longer in any recognizable space to match them to!" The look in Eave's eye was manic.

"I could have deduced as much," Jax sneered in reply.

"No, I don't think you get it!" Eave stalked forward as she jabbed a finger behind her at the useless console. They were less than an arms-length apart. "Those charts are a standardized and maintained four-dimensional database of the known immediate galactic neighborhood. They are the basis of all human space travel in the known fucking galaxy."

Jax glared back.

"So, what are you saying?"

"I'm saying," Eave breathed, "that the reason the star trackers will forever continue to cycle, the reason the charts don't match, is that we aren't even in our own damn galaxy anymore. We're not even close. Those stars out there, those are stars no human has laid eyes on *ever* before."

Jax's ears were ringing. She opened her mouth to speak, but there wasn't anything else she could think to say. So Eave said it.

"We're totally and utterly fucking lost."

2.O

The Station tipped forward, drawn in by the inexplicable magnetic draw of the tear in space. It wasn't gravity pulling them in, but a source more powerful. Extreme levels of current coursed through the metal structure, magnetizing it and polarizing it. The resultant electromagnetic field that was spawned drew with it the strongest slew of hallucinations, swarming the Station with a blanket of nightmares as it began to break up in space.

The Station was old. It had been in service for nearly sixty years. And while it had seen a loyal and effective team of staff to keep her running, concluded by the most diligent and capable Mechanical Engineer to grace its core in its final years, there was no way that an aging nuclear reactor could take the strain of passing through a rip in the very dimensional plane the Station existed in.

From some distance out—were an observer to have been there to witness it—it could be seen that the Station first warped, and bent under the extreme structural strain drawing it down. The steady rotation that maintained the artificial gravity onboard slowed and stopped, as the great disk bent like a coin on railroad tracks. The strain on the core resulted in a reply of a multitude of electrical arcs, streaming out like angry blue lightning across the surface of the ruptured Station interior.

The structural failure had compromised the exterior armor that kept the Station pressurized and capable of supporting human life. From great tears in its sides, it bled its inhabitants to the void surrounding it.

With a final jolt that could send waves through the entire localized fabric of space-time, the core imploded, rupturing the remaining structure surrounding it. The debris ignited and ripped the remaining structure to pieces.

The vacuum of space is infinite and unforgiving. The Station's interior, inverted to the merciless void surrounding it, winked out of existence, as if it had never mattered to the universe in the first place.

Elsewhere in the endless expanse, debris drifted through an opening somewhere, never to be found or identified again.

Space returned to a state of rest.

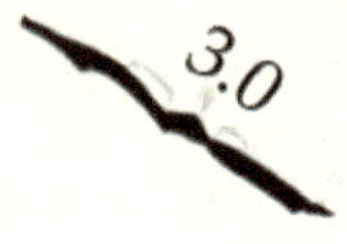

3.0

Jax pressed her hands so close to the thick glass of the Station porthole that if she could, she would phase through the dense material at a molecular level. The ethereal static of whatever they passed through started to fade as the Station dropped from one corner of the known universe into somewhere entirely unseen. A manic, giddy feeling bubbled inside Jax, though she distantly noticed if she focused too closely on it, it might just be panic or worse, the last dregs of her sanity slipping.

But then, all at once, as if blinking, the passage stopped.

Saunders still clung to Jax's side, the hall echoed with the wails of despair from all those on Station with them, but the rift that had swallowed them was gone, as if it had all been another hallucination.

It wasn't though. It couldn't have been. Because they were no longer alone in the depths of endless cosmos.

Beyond the porthole windows there loomed a daunting structure. It was a murky, almost mottled green, interspersed with an off-putting pale sand color. It was illuminated by the light of a suddenly much-too-close star, and in tight orbit around a clearly terrestrial, and atmosphere-rich planet. It was not a naturally occurring structure, as instead it appeared to be a ring, constructed to circumvent the entire planet within.

Along the ring there were distinct openings, gaps, not at all random, that gave way to an interior that was clearly illuminated, though not in a manner that was welcoming. There was method to it.

Humans had done a viable effort of spreading out across their own galaxy to further points of existence. Outer planetary systems had been identified and colonized. But they had remained confined to a single galaxy, and the universe is unfathomably infinite. Even at the furthest reaches, there is still an eternity to follow. Even if humanity reached the edge, it could only cross over to the edge of another, receding universe.

As such, humans had never yet crossed paths with any other intelligence, and any other intelligence had yet to cross paths with humans.

It would stand as no real surprise then that should humans suddenly appear, without answer or reason, amidst an astronomically advanced system of extra-terrestrial life, that it may not, exactly, go smoothly.

As Jax stared in awe and sinking dread at the undeniable proof that someone else was out here with them, another structure emerged in the viewing range of the porthole. This one was not attached to anything. It was oblong, with an uneven surface, but still a sense of symmetry and purpose to it. Beneath its strange topography, Jax could see mechanisms of unfathomable function at work. The engineer in her was thrilled at the concept of seeing purely alien mechanics. The human in her was wholly terrified.

That was a transport, and they were about to be boarded.

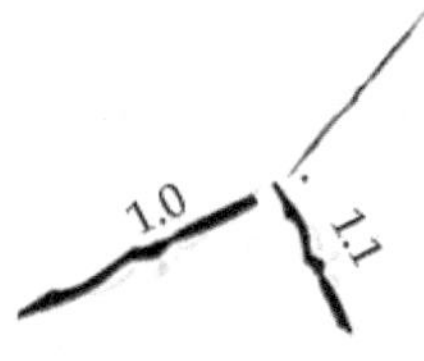

1.1

Jax stood frozen outside the entrance to Level 4: Berthing. Beyond the doors there could lie carnage, hedonism, destruction, or at the very least, an incredibly irate bitch of a navigator and a resolute researcher informing all survivors that they were adrift, somewhere in the infinite cosmos. Whatever reality awaited her beyond the threshold, Jax was not ready for it.

She had spat, bitterly, back at Eave, rejecting the navigator's remarks, only to find herself faced with the scrutiny of Rose and her interpretation of the data. Only once Eave had barreled past, in search of the remaining surviving residents, did Jax realize she needed to intercept this madness and gain the upper hand. But that impetus dissolved in the face of needing to follow Eave into Level 4.

There had been death here before. And there had already been death again. And where was Saunders? There was nowhere safe for Jax to retreat to any longer. She could not hide in her safe haven up on Five, not with such an unnerving reality formalizing around them.

The doors to Four were lit by only the interior corridor emergency lights. No movement was visible beyond them. Jax thought to call out to Saunders on comms, but this was where Eave and Rose had run, bearing their terrible news. Jax sucked in a breath until her lungs felt they might burst, and held it as she reached for the door latch panel to open her passage into the Meat Market, real or unrealized.

Her fingers barely hit the access pad before the doors rolled back on their own, and Jax screamed.

Sturdy arms shot out and grabbed at her shoulders to brace against Jax's instinctual flailing.

"JAX!" Saunders shouted as she gripped Jax in the stairwell. "Jax! Are you okay??"

Jax stuttered through her ebbing panic as she took stock of the shorter woman grasping at her.

"Me? Am *I* okay? Saunders!" Jax cried out, her breaths ragged. She didn't know how to continue any other thought in her head. Saunders seemed to pull her closer and their surroundings stilled. Impossibilities loomed just beyond where the two of them stood, but being in the presence of the Security Officer once again threw their predicament into sharper relief for Jax to cower before.

"Jax." Saunders' voice quieted. "Eave and Rose are talking to the group, saying things, I don't understand..."

"The group," Jax interjected. "Did you find everyone else?"

A complicated look flashed over Saunders' face. Her piercing green eyes had been boring into Jax where she held her, but now they flicked away.

"No, we haven't found everyone..."

"Did you find more..." Jax couldn't finish her thought. Bodies. Parts of bodies. Residents consumed by her Station. All things Jax didn't want to breathe truth into with anything so formal as words.

"No." Saunders' reply was forceful, and Jax winced. Then the other woman softened.

They had awoken, atop each other in the corridor of Level 1. They had traversed the rings from Level 5 down to Level 1, having saved their dying Station, only to find it being swallowed by the universe, and Saunders had held Jax tight as they had dropped. And upon awakening they had been torn apart again. Jax had held hope that they might forge forward as something new together, and now it all seemed to hang in a balance of uncertainty.

But Saunders sank her forehead to Jax's front, pulling her close. Jax wrapped her lanky arms around the firm, sturdy shoulders of the blond, and reveled in the quiet calm their proximity afforded her. She had yearned to hold this woman from the moment they had awoken, and it seemed the cosmos were still trying to drive them apart.

"Jax, what is happening? What are they trying to tell us in there? Is it true? Are we so far gone from it all?"

A heaviness landed on Jax's shoulders. She couldn't be the one to bear this burden, but there was little other choice.

"Is it okay in there?" Jax responded, jutting her chin at the open doors to Level 4.

Saunders tipped her head back again to study Jax's face.

"I gathered everyone in the far-side galley. It's clear. They're all talking about it now."

Jax exhaled a breath she didn't realize she was holding. Clearly no one else wanted to risk hanging out in the near-side galley and its ringing echoes of slaughtered screams.

Saunders pulled back from her embrace and held out a hand. Jax studied it. It had been only mere hours before that she had taken this hand to be led to their next fate. And here she was taking it again.

"Come with me, help us all understand," Saunders spoke as Jax reached for her.

The uproar could be heard well before they reached the gathering. Jax rounded the curve of Station flooring to see a sizable knot of residents, encircling a galley island. Clearly Eave had delivered her news as she was already seated, glowering at the counter while the storm raged around her.

"Enough of this bullshit! What we need to do is get on that stupid radio and start calling for all the universe to hear us!" A large man, with an unruly beard and matching hairstyle was crowing. He was utilizing his bulk to fill as much space in the group as possible. "And we need to scour every damned corner of this blasted tin can for our people—"

"Now hold on a minute!" Saunders barked, as she led Jax toward the group. Some instinct swept over Jax as faces turned to scrutinize their approach, and she let go of

Saunders' hand. The Security Officer swept forward instead, descending on the crowd and the man in the middle.

"No offense, *Security*, but I think this is a little out of your pay grade," the man countered, dismissively.

Saunders seemed to study him before turning to the group.

"Engineering and I had to take a lot of action before that…Drop? If that's what we're calling it? Anyway, to secure the safety of this station. It is not fit to have anyone simply wander off. We can't afford to lose more of us right now." Saunders tilted her head at the man as if she was explaining something ridiculously obvious, and the resident sneered. But he also backed off. Jax slunk around the back of the group to find a nook to lean in, just out of sight of the mob so she could watch.

"If what this navigator is telling us is true, what do we have to lose if we try to rally our resources?" a burly Space Marine called out.

Jax craned her neck, was surprised to see him, and nearly toppled from her perch where she watched, catching herself on the cabinet handle. It swung open to reveal a jar of dehydrated coffee crystals.

Saunders sighed and glanced over at the soldier.

"Okay, yes, we're in a bad place. We've lost people, unimaginable things are happening, I think it's a great idea to rally our group as best we can. I just want us to be smart about it, okay Zick?" She aimed this last sentence at the large man who had been stirring up orders, and not the Space Marine. Zick scoffed in reply, but slipped to the edges of the group where several others fell in ranks behind him. Jax tore her eyes from the crowd to pry a spoon from the drawer beneath her ass and scrabble at the coffee container's seal.

Saunders had found herself in the center of the group now. Jax had always figured the Security Officer was a crowd favorite, with her friendly disposition, and tendency to enthusiastically greet every new resident with warmth and care. Jax had known Saunders to spend her time among these people in a way Jax had never truly been comfortable with. But then, Jax had never really seen Saunders among her people.

Now, the Security Officer hung her head, looking exhausted and aged despite her almost impossibly young face.

"Tizik, I'm so sorry you have another casualty," Saunders called out forlornly to the Space Marine. The man set his mouth in a grim line and bowed his head in response. Saunders swept the group again. "Kiv, I'm sorry you had to find Paul like that." A vaguely familiar and reserved looking man seemed to shrink away from Saunders in reply. But the Security Officer continued.

"We're supposed to have fifty-five residents in addition to Engineering and myself, and I only see forty, forty-five of us? Zick and OS2 Bracken are right. If we don't know what has happened or where we are, we best get to work on gathering our resources. We just need to be smart about it."

"And what, exactly, would you have us do then?" the large man, Zick interjected.

Saunders glanced over at him with what Jax considered to be incredibly superior patience.

"Right, well, Zick, you have a big crew. If you break into search teams, and work *with* us, Engineering and I can give you a schematic of the Station and point you to better access routes that aren't locked off—"

At this, Jax inadvertently inhaled a spoonful of powdery caffeine and burst into a fit of hacking coughs. The combined scrutiny of the gathered group turned on her and she shrank from the surveillance as she desperately hacked up inhaled coffee. Saunders marched over, prying the can of crystals from Jax's claws and shoving a glass of water in her hand before pulling a sputtering Jax toward the gathered crowd.

"I'm doing what now?" Jax wheezed as she was dragged into a mess she wanted no part of.

"We're going to work as a team on this," Saunders barked to the whole group, nearly glaring at Jax who pitifully crunched on whatever crystals she hadn't forcefully spat on the flooring in disbelief.

"Tizik, you take your crew down to the Security quarters and start working the radios, like Zick mentioned. Obah"—Saunders glanced over at an older woman against the back wall—"can I trust you and your team to help me start an inventory?" The woman, holding tightly to an older man next to her, nodded resolutely.

"And Jax," Saunders rounded on her, and Jax flinched. "We need a place to put the *bodies*. Can you help us with this?"

Jax wanted to shake her head. She wanted to shout, to run, to say she wanted nothing to do with dead bodies in any way shape or form. But Saunders was right there, close enough to touch, pinning Jax with a fervent green stare that seemed to analyze Jax where she stood rooted to the spot in the center of gathered residents. Whatever moment of tenderness they had shared seemed to fade like a distant memory.

"Okay, fine," Jax croaked. She had no idea why, or how, but she didn't have it in her to say "no" to Saunders anymore. Oh, but she wanted to *talk* about this though. She and Saunders had only just created something between them, and the universe, in all its uncaring glory, had not seen fit to allow them to examine it yet.

As if on cue, Saunders' grip on Jax's arm relaxed, but then departed altogether. The Security Officer was off assigning task teams in a wave of authority that Jax would rather take the time to admire if it wasn't for the fact that she had just been ordered to play nice and give up all her toys. And yet, there was Saunders updating access cards for everyone so they could run amok in Jax's Station.

"Saunders, can we *talk* about this?" Jax surged after the blond as she weaved through the crowd, assigning tasks.

"About what, Jax?"

Jax gestured vaguely, desperately around them both, but Saunders' focus was elsewhere.

"About, I dunno, just releasing everyone? This isn't safe. You just *said* it isn't safe. I don't want them walking through my—"

"Jax," Saunders finally turned her attention to her. "We're walking a thin line here." The way she said it made Jax's stomach drop and a wheel of irrational fear spin in her head. "We need to get everyone on the same page, and early, or we can find ourselves in a real shitty mess with the people around us. I know you care about the station, and you are amazing about that. Let me do *my* job now." This was punctuated with an arched sandy eyebrow that forced Jax to shut her trap. Saunders then snapped her attention back to someone asking her a question and Jax found herself alone in the crowd once again.

Some hungry little monster of anxiety gnawed in Jax's gut. Bodies in her Station's walls, residents given free reign, and uncertainty at where she and Saunders lay. She needed to get moving, remove herself from the mix.

"Okay, I'm...going to get a head start. Down on two. I'll...make sure it's accessible, and set up a space for the, uh, bodies. Just...send them that way," Jax called after Saunders, almost pitifully. Saunders glanced up, gave a small, determined smile that did not reach her eyes and nodded. The gnawing in Jax's gut intensified, so she turned on her heel and strode off.

It was not until Jax stood on the landing outside Level 2: Supply, in which she realized her mistake.

"What the *fuck* was I thinking, this place doesn't need *more* corpses," Jax exhaled toward the dark and frosty glass of the Supply level doors. Beyond them lay the nearly desiccated and mutilated corpse of a woman who had suffered unspeakable things *before* the Drop, and the shadows of ghosts that haunted Jax from deep in her past.

Jax would just move this party to Level 1 and ping Saunders on the comms about it.

"Excuse me, Engineering?" A quiet voice caused Jax to shriek in panic and spin on the spot, hands raised in pitiful self-defense.

An older man, his face covered in graying stubble that stood in stark contrast to his skin tone stepped down from the upper-level stairs, his hands out in supplication. Jax had a sudden moment of panic telling her this was another ghost, but then she remembered seeing him next to that woman who agreed to run an inventory.

"My name is Gedry Habburn...Ged...Security mentioned you might need some help down here?"

Well fuck if old habits died hard. Even in the depths of Jax's discomfort at standing outside a haunted Station level, she still felt her mood sour.

"These are facility modifications. Not some craft project," Jax growled.

Ged seemed unphased by this.

"Of course not, Engineering, I assume you have it under control. I'm not exactly a trained station mechanic, just the foreman of my settler group. But I do have a decent set of trade skills. If anything I can help keep you company."

Jax wanted to tell him how little she cared for anyone's company. But then it would be a lie because right now Jax was one more jump scare from shitting herself and Saunders had made herself unpleasantly scarce. The man looked like the last person Jax would ever consider a tentative partnership with, but the chill dread of the half-dead Level 2 overrode her insufferable nature. Not breaking eye contact with Gedry, Jax reached out and keyed the latch, letting the door roll aside.

The man followed her through the darkness. The burst casings of the overhead LED tube lights crunched under foot, and Jax veered toward a nearby storage locker in the opposite direction of where her and Saunders had sought answers before The Drop. Jax cursed herself for leaving her tools behind as she felt sightlessly through the gloom of the locker. A shuffling to her side set her teeth on edge only to suddenly be blinded by the bright flash of a light streaking across her vision.

"Sorry, figured it would help," Ged stated, good naturedly. "What are we looking for in here?"

Jax opened her mouth and closed it several times as she assessed the man at her side. Several retorts about flashlight etiquette filled her brain but none of them spilled from her mouth. Instead she took a long, deep inhale and shoved inward to pick up some auxiliary lights on charged battery packs.

Ged didn't seem to mind the lack of reply. Instead, he held the light at a convenient height and hauled the equipment from the locker as Jax wordlessly passed it to him. Back in the corridor, with flood lights casting the arc of the flooring in eerie contrast, Ged toed at the crushed LED tubes under his feet.

"What happened here, Engineering?"

He followed as Jax strode further along the now-lit corridor. The silence was oppressive, so Jax found herself doing something entirely uncharacteristic of herself, and answered.

"We—uh, I, thought there was a massive electrical surge arcing from the Station core. I tried shutting it down, but not before it blew the lights," she offered, gruffly.

Ged had stowed his flashlight and strolled almost genially through the crushed glass.

"I figured. You take far better care of this place than any other station I've been on. You wouldn't just let a level go to hell like this. Must have been a hell of a power surge."

Jax glanced over her shoulder. She had no metric of how well she cared for her Station. She simply assumed no one loved their keep the way she did. There was something oddly, vindicating, about hearing it directly from someone else.

"Well, yeah, we thought it was causing all those hallucinations," Jax trailed off.

"So you all saw it too then," the man said. Jax turned to look at him. Ged had paused in his stroll and was studying Jax where she stood a degree or so further down the corridor.

"Yes," Jax said slowly and evenly. Ged gave a pensive smile in response. "I suppose that depends, though."

"Depends on what?" Ged pressed, continuing his stroll to pull up even with Jax.

"Depends on what you mean by 'it'," Jax mumbled, recalling the feeling of something inhuman curling tight around her body and refusing to let go; the vision of a marketplace splashed with the gore of dead residents on a chopping block. "Why, what did *you* see?"

At this Ged sighed and continued onward, though he no longer had any direction to head in, being uninformed of Jax's intended path.

"Just shadows, echoes... It was unnerving. From the sound of it, Obah and I didn't get the worst of it. Though to be honest I'm not sure I fully understand what drove those *particular* visions..." He paused and turned back to face Jax where she stood. "And *you*, Engineering?"

Jax realized she had pried past the acceptable limit. She tightened her shoulders and strode onward toward the storage locker she was aiming for.

"Just...ghosts," she replied, gruffly.

"Well then," Ged fell in step beside her. "Sounds like maybe we did see the same thing. So, where are we headed?"

Jax had figured she could convert one of the long-term stores into a place they could hold the bodies they uncovered. Most Stations just assumed if you had the misfortune of dying while on board, that you would just leave with your crew when the time came. But now Jax was tasked with overriding the already taxed environmental controls on a storage locker meant to hold food supplies, not corpses. They had been halfway through a resupply cycle, so, at the very least, this storage locker would be vacant.

Gedry proved a useful accomplice as Jax hauled the interior environment controls out and began splicing wires and crossing vents. They didn't need the dead air recirculating back into their own breathing without passing through added filters.

"Isn't this going to reduce the oxygen content in here? Make it hazardous for anyone entering?"

Jax closed off the last vent re-route and scrutinized Gedry from under a narrowed brow.

"Why would anyone need to be hanging out in here? It's going to be dead bodies..."

But Ged simply shrugged.

"I just figure people like to visit their dead. It helps them feel connected to something they have lost."

Jax hunched her shoulders again as if sealing herself off from the thought. But Ged was right. She couldn't leave a risk unattended like this when all these people were wandering around with free reign these days. The last thing Jax wanted was to add to their body counts.

"Okay, fine, I have a solution," Jax grumbled and stepped out into the hallway. Lying in wait were at least three Space Marines, looking livid.

"Engineering," barked the man in the lead. Jax flinched and shied away from the vanguard.

"What are you *doing* in here?" she hissed. Gedry had followed her back out into the corridor and stood by her shoulder as the group of drop-squad teammates flanked them. The man in the front looked bitter, but his reply was even.

"Security Officer Saunders told us we could find the body of Base Sentinel Lark in here."

Jax looked back at him.

"What?"

"The body of our teammate? Illy Lark?" the woman at his shoulder added, looking equal parts shell shocked and impatient. The blood on her clothes told Jax this was the same woman who had unsuccessfully ripped the man from the wall down below. "Excuse me?" the woman repeated, voice raising.

"Easy, Corine," the lead Space Marine interjected. He fixed Jax with a firm stare. "We're here to move her. Saunders told us you were setting up a place for holding casualties, is this it?"

Jax squeezed her eyes shut to avoid the scrutiny of the man in front of her and help her brain catch up. Right. There was a dead woman on this level waiting to be collected. There was a dead man upstairs on Level 4, impaled by a very large spud wrench. There was half a body down on the first level, the rest consumed by the Station walls. And there were undoubtedly more bodies they had missed.

"Right, yes, your, uh, teammate. She's around the corner, at the one hundred-seventy degree mark. Saunders covered her up. You can bring her…uh…in here." Jax turned and looked at Gedry. "Okay, you go help them move her, and get her in here, I'll go handle the environmental controls issue, okay?" Jax figured this was a glowing display of cooperation.

The older man glanced at the Space Marine and then back at Jax and gave her a curt nod and a small smile. He then strode off with the Space Marines in tow.

Jax exhaled.

She didn't want to be alone on this level, but she needed a moment to collect her thoughts. Residents would be running all over the place soon enough. She would need some form of control over her haven if she wanted to avoid it falling into chaos at the idle hands of transients.

Only they weren't transients anymore, were they?

Jax strode off in the opposite direction of the Space Marines, past Common Access. She and Ged had only set up flood lights on the arc they had entered, but as she walked she noticed more lights had been set up, arcing further around the curve away from where Jax had been working. Someone had already infiltrated her domain and started touching Jax's things.

She fixed her face with a scowl as she marched off toward her permanent stores bay, ready to accost whoever was making themselves at home.

Jax was five degrees from the storage bay she needed when she collided with a brick wall.

"Ah, fuck, sorry," the brick wall replied, as Jax shook her head to clear the swimming feeling from the impact. She then assessed the barrier she had walked smack into.

Jax may have been an antisocial recluse, who refused to make anyone's acquaintance, who struggled to fathom how Saunders seemed to know each and every last person on Station, but she had to give herself some small credit. She swore she would have noticed an absolute stack of a woman like the one who was standing in front of her, having clearly emerged from a storage locker she wasn't supposed to be in.

Maybe there *were* residents on this Station they didn't know about.

"How long have you *been* here?" Jax growled.

"Like, in the hallway?" the woman replied.

In that moment Jax didn't want to stir up some business about imaginary friends and people who don't exist, so she pivoted.

"No, here on this level."

"Ah, I guess an hour? Security said to fan out and start looking for more, uh, survivors, and I might have gotten split from the others. You're Engineering right?" The woman reached out and jabbed at the tape on Jax's coveralls that, sure enough, said "engineering."

"Well spotted," Jax grumbled, rubbing a sore spot on her wrist where they had slammed into each other.

Jax was tall and lanky. This woman was taller. And she was built like she hauled cargo by hand for a living. But her tan face was round and friendly looking under the shorn cap of her dark brown hair. "Was there something you were looking for in particular, uh..."

"Andee." The woman had a grin unbefitting the circus of death they were running through.

"Right. Andee. The group just came through here to get their dead person, do you need directions?" Jax asked as she sidestepped the massive form of the resident and angled herself toward the locker she had intended to visit. Clearly this was an invitation to follow, as Jax realized belatedly, and Andee turned to fall into step alongside Jax.

"Uh actually, you might know the answer to this!"

Jax was pretty certain she did know the answer, if it pertained to her storage that is. Andy continued.

"That massive airlock down on Level 1, does it connect to one of the storage bays up here?"

Jax gave Andee a sidelong glance as she reached the compartment she needed. She had to break the stare as she punched in the combo code.

"It's the storage lift. Like any other waypoint station," Jax replied, kneeling to leaf through the supplies inside.

"I mean I figured that much, but I haven't been on any waypoint stations before, so I wanted to be sure," Andee said from behind her. This conversation was losing any chance of being exciting. "And that other airlock, the one on this level, that leads to the tug hanger, doesn't it?"

Jax paused only slightly before regaining her composure and standing back up to face the woman.

"What of it?" she challenged. Andee did not look put off, even in the slightest.

"So, where's the tug?"

Jax rolled her eyes, closed the locker, and strode off back toward the other side of the level, Andee in tow. It dawned on her there wasn't going to be a simpler way to address the topic.

"It's in repairs. I have it stored in the hanger locker. The lift can service large stores and the tug if need be, but it's out of commission. That what you needed to know?" They kept walking.

"I can fix it!"

That stopped Jax in her tracks. She whirled on the massive form beside her.

"Look, I know we're suddenly playing 'let's get along and survive' and now everyone is just free grazing across my Station hunting for whatever body parts we can find, but I have kept this tin can running as smooth as can be for the past decade. If there's something that needs fixing here, that's my job. And if I haven't been able to fix that thing yet, I doubt anyone else can do better." She glared up at Andee, but the woman just cracked her grin.

"Yeah, well, what's wrong with her?"

Jax exhaled loudly, filling it with as much exasperation as she could. Then she pivoted and continued to stalk back to the other side of the ring. Andee, of course, followed.

"Cracked docking ring," Jax growled. It meant ordering a repair, but that had meant also ordering a visit from Station Management, so Jax had been tinkering on a work-around.

"Ha, see, I'm a welder."

Jax slowed her step only slightly. In truth, a welder was a perfectly reasonable work around. She didn't reply, but she knew Andee had seen her hesitate. Instead, she strode onward, Andee in step.

"So, what do you say I have a look at that tug—"

"Engineering, I need you up on Medical!" the comms panel directly to Jax's left blared, cutting Andee off and rocketing Jax away from the sudden noise. It was Saunders' voice, and it sounded urgent.

4.0

Jax bit her lip to keep quiet. She gripped the solid and dependable shape of her murder wrench close as she was forced to watch the woman across the corridor slowly peel her own face off. Jax had already been sick once, and had fought to keep more bile down. The only comfort was the idea that perhaps this was all just another hallucination.

Odds weren't great though.

Around her, the Station ached and groaned as nightmare after nightmare seeped from the walls. Outside, the windows were endlessly, crushingly black; devoid of stars and, anything known to humanity. There was no longer any telling what surrounded them. The existence of space within the rift seemed to consist of terror and oblivion.

Something clattered to Jax's left and she flinched. She turned to see what might be approaching, while still keeping an eye on the unfortunate victim she had been monitoring. Anyone who could commit such atrocious acts of self-mutilation might easily turn and inflict such acts on others surrounding them, and Jax had hoped to get up to Power and Life Support in one piece, face and all.

Nothing approached. Nothing visible, at least. And Jax paid for her distraction by losing sight of the ruinous resident giving herself a face-lift. The corridor was empty, save for a skid mark of blood and some accompanying gruesome handprints on the metal flooring. The gore trailed off to a darkened docking room off to the side of the Level 1 corridor, leaving the door frame to security clear of immediate, tangible threat.

Jax gripped her wrench and scurried across the corridor into the old security office. It would be dark in there.

There was no telling how long they had been in this rift, this void, this emptiness full of nightmares. It had been eternity and only a moment. For all Jax knew they were suspended here indefinitely. Saunders had retreated to Power and Life Support up on Level 5, burying herself within the fortress rings of Jax's Station, just as Jax had before the drop.

That was where Jax wanted to return. The shell of the woman who had claimed her affections sat huddled before the larger array of monitor panels and visual displays that foretold their fate in every corner of this spinning, dead disk. If nothing else, Jax yearned to return to her company; this connection all that grounded them and saved them from the onslaught of horrible visions. But there was a mission to attend to first.

Another clatter from the poorly lit corridor snapped Jax back to her present predicament, her focus sharpened and on edge. If she turned on the light someone would know she was in here, which might invite more terror than Jax was ready to deal with. So instead Jax drew on her intimate knowledge of Station layout, and bore her wrench like a shield to ward off any dangers from within the abandoned room.

There were radio communication tools in here.

It was futile, really.

There was nothing in this void. How could they expect radios to help them? But that glimmer of hope kept them grounded. Perhaps, even if there was no escape, a call of distress could be sent out into the cosmos, to echo for eternity until it fell on whatever ears could hear it. At least then someone, or some*thing* might know what had happened to them.

The comms were better on Level 1. So Jax needed to do her job as Station Engineer and dismantle the heart of the relay system then cobble it together 4 levels inward. It really just meant pulling the more powerful relays. Jax had managed to reroute the control wiring on a previous daring mission, but the primary relay board was still stashed under the main communications console.

Jax passed another furtive glance at the doorframe to the corridor. She debated closing the door before getting on her knees to un-bolt the relay panel covers, but then she might not have a quick escape route, should some horrible vision become reality.

Even *that* was absurd, Jax mused, as she worked quickly with her tools, glancing at her only exit as often as she could without slicing her hand on the sharp metal panels. These were still hallucinations, brought on by the magnitude of apparent electromagnetic field swarming through this interstellar phenomenon they found themselves wallowing in. Really, it was the piss-poor reactions of the terrified residents that had created the most threat. The bloodbath of those who had gone mad immediately, versus those who preferred to slowly lose their minds and body parts had certainly set the stage for their tortuous demise. But by this point, Jax was less afraid of some creepy crawly emerging from a dark corner than she was of some resident bursting out of a locker to murder her to death.

The dead CC footage screens that lived in this office seemed to stare back at her. Jax regarded them briefly as she felt under the main console for the disconnect lines. At least they still had access to the CC footage system upon Level 5. It had been able to highlight who was threat and what was imaginary. Nightmares don't show up on camera.

Jax felt the relays connection pop apart under the console panel as she hefted the clunky radio component out from its former hold. The corridor flickered beyond the door frame and Jax knew it was time to go. The lighting always wanted to fail just before things got really bad, and Jax had seen enough on this venture. It was time to return to Five, and hole up with the only person she could really trust. She took two steps toward the door and then paused. She shot her hand out and snagged a busted-looking music storage player off the nearby table. It certainly didn't look like it would ever work again, but maybe Jax could fix it. She used to be good at fixing things.

Saunders was still where Jax had left her. The former Security Officer was curled in on herself, hunched at a console somewhere in the middle of the Power and Life Support center of operations. The room wasn't large, but with Saunders so situated it seemed to yawn out from where she sat, eyes affixed to the multitude of screens in front of her. Jax thumbed the door latch to roll the door closed and the smaller woman seemed to jump as if she were spring loaded.

"Jax!"

Saunders' face was hollower than Jax remembered. Her cheeks were no longer round, and the jut of her chin seemed pointier. More than anything, her eyes, which had always been the brightest green, and full of wit and mischief, were now dull, and round with fear.

"I got the relay—" Jax began but Saunders cut her off.

"Did you see it?"

Jax swallowed her reply, hesitating. She had seen a lot of things.

"What, the resident? Yeah, I was trying not to though—"

"No, it was *following* you..." Saunders interrupted again. Jax cocked her head in confusion.

"What? No, no one was around after that resident slithered off, I kept my eye out."

"Slithered..." Saunders repeated, in a way that made Jax's spine flush cold. "It was right there. It got the resident, and then it was after you."

Jax huffed in annoyance. They had solved this problem before. It was hallucinations. The footage was right there. Saunders had been glued to it, deciphering every horrible thing Jax encountered on her infrequent excursions, just so they could both cling to sanity.

"Babe, fine. Show me." Jax sighed. Best to just get things over with. Sure, some grubby nutcase probably had been closer than Jax had realized.

Saunders shifted in her perch to reach for the controls. She moved as if her limbs were leaded, but she managed to toggle the video feed to show the corridor down on Level 1. There on the screen was Jax, standing vigil as she observed the horrible fate of the resident blocking the security office. There, Jax saw herself distracted by a sound, as the footage panned over toward where she was looking. Nothing. But off toward where the resident had been Jax saw the woman's lower half jerk suddenly, and her feet leave the corridor flooring in a flailing struggle before going limp and being dragged off screen. Unsettling.

"Wait, go back toward where she was," Jax interjected.

But Saunders ignored her. Instead, the footage stayed static, showing Jax entering the darkened security office. Jax was about to protest and ask for the younger woman to pan the camera to follow her when she saw it.

It wasn't human. It couldn't be. At least not anymore. *Slithered* was the operative word. A malformed body trunk, writhing across the floor, leaving a trail of blasphemous filth in its wake, encroached on the door frame which Jax had unsuspectingly passed through. The clattering sounds Jax had dismissed in her efforts to prize the relays from their nest had come from something indeed. Jax felt sick all over again as the form lurked, within inches of the door frame.

How had Jax missed this? And how was it real? The footage had always shown them the divide between fact and fabricated visions. Jax flinched as the thing extended an appendage; something that ended in unspeakable looking claws. It gripped the door frame as if to enter it, though instead it continued to linger.

The minutes ticked by, recounting a time that had only just passed for Jax, but now seemed agonizingly slower. Jax waited for the thing to move so she could emerge to the abandoned corridor and make her way home. But instead, to her horror, Jax saw herself step through the doorframe, wrench slung over one shoulder, relay and long-forgotten music player hefted in the other arm. She walked directly past the phantom creature, oblivious to its presence. And as she passed, the thing turned, and rather than make immediate pursuit, it looked directly at the camera.

Jax recoiled at its visage. Inhuman eyes in an inhuman face that melted into the body. But it held a very human, and very predatory intelligence in its features. Jax had already slipped off to the side of the footage screen and the thing lingered only a moment longer before slipping, *slithering,* after her.

"What—How?" Jax found herself at a loss for words, but not lacking in a frantic desire to sweep the outside corridor as she saw it: clear and secured up in their keep on Level 5.

"You didn't see it," Saunders stated with finality.

"Of course I didn't, but the hallucinations are supposed to be things we *see,* and the CC footage shows us they aren't there, not the other way around!" Jax cried, feeling panic rise around her. Had something really followed her? Was the footage part of the hallucination? She burst forward in a nearly violent thrash and pushed Saunders aside at the console.

There were years and years of CC footage, enough to cycle through for a lifetime even, but Jax was looking for just before their Drop.

There. Jax and Saunders fighting nothing in the corridors, looking like crazed maniacs in combat with shadows. It was supposed to mean they had been hallucinating, not actually fighting off monstrous zombie residents and unearthly interstellar insectoids. But as Jax watched the footage seeking comfort it instead flickered. One moment it was as expected, the next, it swapped for Jax swinging her wrench into the skull of a massive aggressor as swarms of skittering creatures surged around them.

"That can't be right," Jax said weakly. They had reviewed that scene before, to confirm the hallucinations. Jax scrabbled for another view. The unfortunate first victim, mauling herself on Level 2, only it wasn't another distraught and crazed resident who landed the killing blow, but something just as horrible as what had followed Jax, appearing in another shift of the lighting in the CC footage.

Clip after clip, Jax surfed through, feeling a growing shiver of dread with each stretch of video footage that showed first normalcy, then transformed to terror. Stretches of the abandoned medical level, empty save for Jax and Saunders on patrol, swarmed with chitinous insectoids. The dark and haunting supply level clear of carnage, flickering to a roiling sea of the dead. Sludge filled Jax's gut, rising in a surge of anxiety, and ended with the swing of a glinting meat cleaver, wielded by a maniacal butcher still restraining the headless body of a twitching resident on his chopping block.

"Does this—" Jax had to swallow hard, and her voice seemed wedged in her throat. "Does this mean the CC footage is part of the hallucination now too?" she managed.

"But that's what I've been up here studying," Saunders spoke quietly, as if she had already endured this despairing truth. Something clattered out in the empty hallway of Level 5. "Either the CC footage is part of the hallucination, or it's real, and the recordings lie."

5.0

5.0

The aggravated groan of the Station's structure shook Saunders awake. She looked up at the darkness around her. It was unfamiliar. It was not her bunk; it wasn't anyone's bunk. It was the corridor of Level 1.

Saunders pulled herself up into a sitting position to see she had been passed out on top of Jax's chest. She felt a wave of panic that Jax might be dead, reached her arms out to check, but then the mechanic moved and Saunders relaxed. They were both alive. She looked up and around her to try and get a better understanding of their surroundings.

The corridor was so *dark*. There should at least be hazard lights running along the base panels. Instead, the only light that shown was the small white glow every few degrees indicating that auxiliary power was still on.

They also weren't moving. Saunders could tell, because gravity was wrong. She wasn't the technical expert on the matter— that would be the woman passed out beneath her, brow knit in concentration like she was trying to solve the problem in her sleep. But the concept was pedestrian enough: the station was several concentric rings that spun around an axis generating centripetal force, which resulted in artificial gravity.

But Saunders and Jax were resting flat on the wall, the windows over their heads. What Saunders thought was the wall behind her was actually the floor. Gravity was pointing in the wrong direction. But there *was* gravity. They were just no longer spinning...in space.

"Jax. Jax wake *up!*" Saunders shook the woman next to her. Jax tossed her head from side to side as she came around, screwing her eyes up like she had a headache. She then sat up with a jolt, and Saunders put a cautionary hand on her shoulder.

"What? What happened?" Jax stammered, looking around in a panic, tangled mane of black hair obscuring part of her face. She flailed for a moment before realizing it was Saunders next to her. Jax's expression relaxed. "We're alive," she whispered.

Saunders understood the anxiety. The last thing she recalled was clinging to Jax as they dropped through an opening in space no one on the station seemed to have any explanation for. Prior to that, everything had been a nightmare, save for the company of the mechanic.

In front of her, Jax had started looking around again, this time in earnest.

"What.... What's wrong with the Station..." Jax had tilted her head back and noticed the windows in the wrong place. Saunders, instead, was studying the face of the woman she was hopelessly in love with. She saw the dawning realization on Jax's face in real time. "We aren't moving."

"Yeah, I came to the same conclusion," Saunders stated in a hushed tone. She followed Jax's line of sight. The mechanic was staring out the windows, looking for stars, looking for the rip in space that might describe the strange gravity they were all experiencing.

But there were no stars. Outside the windows there was nothing but infinite, inky, black.

The station groaned again, this time with a sound like a thousand fathoms of pressure straining to crush it in its grasp. This must have startled Jax, as she shot up from where she lay, tripping over the blank maintenance panel on the wall that was now their floor. Saunders also pulled herself up from where they lay, and Jax blindly reached down to hoist her along. It wasn't like Saunders really needed the help, and Jax was usually less coordinated than her, but it was welcome physical contact after a year of seeking it out. Saunders took the opportunity to stand close to the tall and lanky woman who had hoisted her to her feet.

"Jax, where are we?" Saunders mustered as steady a voice as she could manage. She was not a stranger to deep space. Jax may have had more years on station, more years across the stars, and more years on her, but Saunders had seen her own share of action off world. There was nothing familiar about this. She looked around them, at the strange orientation of the station, and the dim lighting casting shadows on the other residents who were also stirring.

The other residents! Seeing them stirring and waking at various intervals around the lopsided corridor brought a flood of relief that they had also survived. She sank against Jax for support at the thought of those she carried responsibility for. One resident was making her way over to them.

"Security, Engineering, I am relieved you are okay!" It was Rose. She looked a bit banged up, but otherwise she seemed fine. Saunders reached out to clasp her arm.

"Rose! Are you hurt? Where is your team?"

"I cannot find Collins, but I am not injured," Rose replied quietly. Jax didn't seem to notice they had company, which wasn't a surprise. The Mechanical Engineer seemed far more prone to paying attention to machinery rather than those around her. She was still craning her neck up at the misplaced windows overhead.

"We need to get people accounted for." Saunders returned to Rose, who was also watching Jax in her thrall. "Do you think you can help us round up everyone?"

Rose had only been on station for a few days, but she seemed to have the same comfort in taking action Saunders had. Saunders usually got along swimmingly with everyone on the spot, but every now and then she met someone she liked on instinct. She had even already discussed leaving the station with Rose's crew, when she thought Jax was a lost cause.

Saunders winced at the awkward line of thinking. Rose looked back over at her.

"Your shoulder—"

Snapped from her recent memories, Saunders looked down at her right shoulder. The bandages had peeled back, and they were blood stained. Underneath, her shoulder ached with a deep bruise surrounding a healing stab wound. Saunders winced.

"I'll be fine, it's been an...interesting few days," she replied.

Jax's hand shot out and grabbed her other arm, making her jump.

"Ow, Jax what—"

"Shhh!" Jax was gripping her forearm, knuckles white, and staring upward now, frozen in place. Saunders also turned to look, and next to her Rose followed.

The station levels were wide enough for a central corridor, and rooms along the sides. Level 1 housed all of the engine wells, and windows were present on both sides, depending on what part of the station you were walking through. This part was near the Common Access stairwell that would lead them to the inner levels, and so it only had windows on the one side. The corridor was wide enough for the glass portholes to be a good fifteen feet above Saunders' head, causing her to crane her neck.

"Something is wrong," Jax whispered next to her. Saunders waited, barely breathing next to Jax's still frame.

Outside of the station, through the thick glass windows, something moved.

"What the FUCK!" Jax jolted backward. Saunders grabbed hold of her to keep her from tripping back over the wall panels. Jax pressed herself to the flooring which was now a wall. "Did you *see* that?" Jax shot her attention to the two faces in front of her. Saunders wasn't sure what she saw, but she had seen *something*.

"What the hell is out there?" Saunders asked, grimly. Rose had stepped back again to look out. Next to her, Jax edged herself away from the wall/floor again. They all waited, breath caught in their chests.

There it was again. A pale flash of movement, unable to be fully comprehended. There was something *moving* around outside of the station.

"Hallucinations again?" Saunders whispered. They had worked so hard to fight off the horror that had enveloped the station. Jax had nearly fried herself alive in the core trying to fix things. It was disheartening to think it had all been in vain.

"Power is almost completely off. What could be causing them..." Jax trailed off, probably continuing the conversation in her own head. Saunders didn't have an answer. Jax knew the systems like her own hands, so Saunders had no real choice but to accept the response.

Saunders reached for Jax in the dark, aching for the contact, but Jax had skirted away down the level. Saunders turned to look after her, watched the mechanic pick her way along, splitting her attention between the windows overhead and the traps awaiting her on the misplaced wall. Jax reached a recessed panel and kicked it with the heel of her boot.

"Jax. *Jax,*" Saunders hissed from where she and Rose were still huddled. Jax waved her off. What the hell was she doing? They needed to get moving, to find everyone and figure out what they were up against. Jax kicked at the floor...wall...a few more times and Saunders heard the panel finally crunch inward. She squinted in the darkness as Jax's lanky figure hunched over, searching for something.

"Security, shall I start rounding everyone up—" Rose asked, but Saunders just held out a hand.

"Wait, I want to see what she's doing."

Jax was returning, slowly picking her way over wall gratings and support struts. Saunders waited for an explanation, which, of course was not forthcoming. But Jax had always used her words sparingly.

Jax turned on a small flashlight, keeping the beam tight to her frame. She busied herself examining the wall they had been sleeping near, or was it the corridor floor? Saunders felt entirely disoriented. Jax was fully engrossed, running her fingers gently, lovingly over her station. She paused, and pressed her hand to the metal.

"Hold this." Jax thrust the flashlight toward Rose, who accepted the task with a questioning glance at Saunders, and trained the light on where Jax had paused. Saunders shrugged and cocked her head back to whatever Jax was up to. In the gloom surrounding her, voices were starting to echo.

Jax had produced a screwdriver from her coveralls and jammed it into a gap Saunders had not noticed. The mechanic then started wedging with the handle of the screwdriver like a lever. Saunders had a brief thought that absurd wrench would have been a better tool. Jax started grunting in her efforts, and a small gap emerged in the flooring to reward her.

"Saunders, I sure hope your arm is strong enough for this. Help me pull," Jax panted at her.

Saunders' shoulder hurt like a bitch, but she swung it once to check and it felt functional enough. She flexed both her forearms to loosen them up, then set her hips.

"What, exactly, are we doing?" Saunders paused, hands half-raised to help Jax without question.

"It's the engine well. I can climb the hatch if we pry it far enough open. I need to get *up* there." Jax's voice was tense.

Saunders only had more questions, but the eerie dark was creeping in on her senses and the shadows cast by the small light were setting Saunders' teeth on edge. So she leveraged her good arm, and shouldered herself into the gap between Jax's chest and the flooring. Saunders felt Jax flex and her pushing in the same direction. The crack in the flooring split open wider, with a metallic strain, leaving a gap of about a foot wide, leading into an even darker cavern.

The empty engine well. Saunders had only seen Jax work in these once before.

"That's enough," Jax grunted in her ear. The beam of light from Rose cast briefly inside, showing the well to be empty. Of course, Saunders thought, the engine would still be out on the Station's external circumference, though it probably wasn't operating anymore.

Saunders was too preoccupied with the empty engine well to notice Jax had started climbing. A flash of a grungy work boot, straps loose, passing her shoulder, drew her attention. Saunders instinctively reached out and paced a hand on the back of Jax's left leg to stay the mechanic. Jax flinched in response and Saunders let go, realizing she had grabbed at the injury from their fight against hallucinated space bugs. The scratch they thought had, impossibly, been a bug bite. Jax twisted and looked back down at her, face shrouded by the ridiculous shank of hair down the center of her head.

"Sorry, but, Jax what are you trying to do?" Saunders asked, her arm still extended. Saunders generally thought Jax was brilliant, but the woman was a bit off-script sometimes, and now wasn't a great opportunity to get injured.

"I need to see out of the windows." Jax's voice sounded strained and earnest. Saunders paused for a moment, considering the scenario, then relented. Rose stepped closer to them both, keeping the light trained small on the flooring. Saunders reached her hand back out to squeeze the toe of Jax's work boot.

"Just don't do anything stupid Jax, I just got you back." Saunders hoped her chuckle hinted at a confidence she was certainly *not* feeling presently. But the jokes usually helped her get a handle on her environment. And Jax smiled in response. She had rarely ever seen Jax smile, and it usually was more disconcerting than friendly, but the weak flash of a grin that Jax showed her made her heart soar. Then it was gone, as Jax twisted back and returned to her climb.

Saunders watched with unease as Jax ascended, now nearly ten feet off the ground. She saw the woman cautiously choose her footing, and recalled with a sick worry that the airlock had emergency releases placed inside it. Saunders doubted they needed an accidental airlock breach in this moment. Jax had reached an apex on the engine well door, and paused to turn. Saunders coiled in anxiety.

"I need the light," Jax called. Saunders looked down and over at Rose, still clutching the pin-prick of a beam, then back up at Jax.

"Would have been a bright idea to bring that, yep," Saunders quipped back. Of course she would forget the damned light. A few other residents were gathering around them.

"*Saunders*," hissed the easily irritable mechanic from overhead.

"What's going on?" Ged Habburn approached, his wife, Obah, holding on to him for support as she limped on a busted ankle.

"Engineering is trying to illuminate us on our current predicament," Saunders replied, looking over at them. The situation was dire and horrific, so of course she could only do one thing.

"*Would you cool it with the damned jokes and just help me?*" Jax was growling back down again. Saunders glanced up, then back around the group. Familiar faces were emerging from the gloom to surround them.

Saunders knew everyone on this station. She had personally seen to their entrance and wellbeing to the best of her ability. But, once again, something had gone horribly wrong. And now it wasn't that Saunders worried she would see unfamiliar faces, but that she would see more familiar faces than she wanted to.

"*Saunders, come on!*" Jax called again, and shuffled from her new perch.

Rose didn't look like she had any interest in climbing, so Saunders resigned herself and hefted her injured shoulder again. If she was going to start seeing faces she knew in the crowd, she wanted to be fifteen feet above them all.

"I guess I'll help her shed some light on this," Saunders offered, taking solace in her levity, reaching for the flashlight, and ignoring any further complaint from above. Rose handed it to her with a grim smile. They may be in a nightmare, but at least Saunders could provide the comedic relief. It always made her feel better about the situation, and once she was on a roll, it was hard to stop. She flicked off the tiny light, jammed it in her security belt, and reached for the gap in the wall.

Saunders picked her way up, trying to follow the same careful path Jax had laid out for her, keen on not letting her boots trip any of the mechanisms inside the engine well. She stopped just past Jax's boots, wedging herself against a horizontal ladder embedded in the well wall, and the gap in the door. Saunders pulled the flashlight from her security belt and hoisted it up to Jax's extended hand. It was lucky the woman was so lanky, her reach made up the difference. Saunders made a point of not looking down.

Jax was looking down. In the near pitch black of the corridor, a crowd of the station populace gathered below, Saunders caught the dark eyes of the station Mechanical Engineer; the woman she had spent a year falling head over heels for from afar, who she had thought would never be within her reach. And now Jax was reaching for her, reaching out to her, a look on her face that read as complex and longing, despite the annoyance at Saunders' earlier jokes. Saunders felt a tight curl in her chest. Then she reached out and grasped Jax's extended arm and let herself be pulled up the rest of the way.

With Saunders wedged high above the crowd below, pressed against Jax for support and security, Jax flicked on the light and held it up to the glass, trained into the featureless void around them. The station creaked again.

Time seemed to stand still. Saunders realized she was holding her breath and she didn't dare change that fact. Next to her she could tell Jax was doing the same. She felt Jax's hand grip her good arm, pulling her close; heard her heartbeat through the thin fabric of the coveralls she always wore. The light shone out into whatever lay beyond, casting a beam in a manner that was impossible in the void of space. Motion darted past again.

"That's fucking impossible," Jax muttered, so quietly that only Saunders could hear it from their vantage point.

Saunders felt the unease of the situation grow around them, the silence oppressive.

"What is? Jax talk to me, please," Saunders whispered.

Jax pulled the flashlight down and cast the light over the crowd that had gathered on the back wall of the Station. She had a tight, terrified, trapped look on her face, as she scanned their surroundings, and Saunders felt her heart sink. Then Jax's dark, seeking eyes found Saunders, and they bore into her in a way that made her feel raw. Jax cleared her throat.

"We're under fucking *water*."

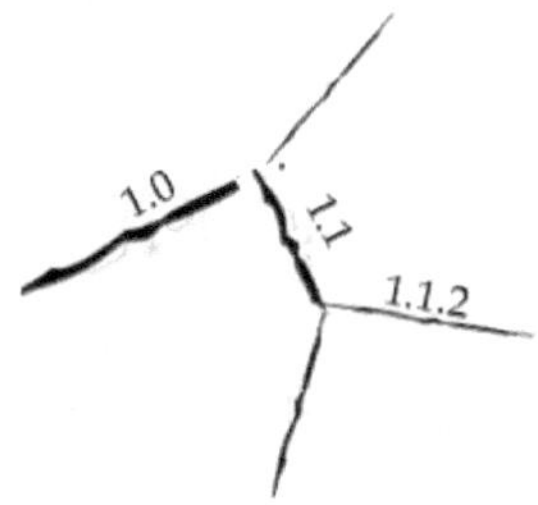

1.1.2

Jax took off at a sprint toward the stairwell. She heard calls of protest behind her from the Space Marines returning with their fallen teammate, but she was already halfway up the first set of stairs. Still in lockstep with her was the welder, Andee, running right behind her.

"Where the hell do you think you're going??" Jax roared as they bounded up to Level 3.

"We were having a conversation, I didn't think it was over." Andee barely seeming to be out of breath. Jax grunted in frustration and hauled herself upward.

"This is really not the, huff, *time*!" Jax wheezed, throwing herself through the open doors to the medical level.

But the welder tailed her all the way through and around the bend to where Saunders was actively placing herself between two irate looking residents.

Saunders was a brawler, but she was still short. Jax was long and lanky, but she was the furthest thing from a fighter. And now neither of them were properly armed or equipped to handle a riot.

The man barricaded behind Saunders made a lunge around her, bashing into Saunders' bandaged shoulder in an effort to get his hands on the other resident. Saunders barked out in pain and crumpled sideways from the altercation. Jax took two steps forward and then realized she had no idea how to handle the situation. The target of the onslaught raised his own fists and hammered back at his assailant. Jax sidestepped the flailing fists and had only a moment to feel the brush as someone passed her. She witnessed Andee the Welder stride forward, hoist the first man clean off his feet and drag him three steps back from the fight.

Jax realized her jaw was hanging slack just as the man in Andee's arms flailed in shocked surprise.

"Put me fucking down you freak!"

Saunders had eased over to near where Jax stood, nursing her injured shoulder. Jax leaned over and whispered.

"You see her, right? The giant?"

Saunders wheeled around and glared up at Jax who shrank away.

"Yeah, that's Andee. Are you telling me you only *just* noticed her?" Saunders looked incredulous.

"Ease off, Enith, you asshat," Andee rumbled, right on queue. Saunders strode back over to the pair where the man not suspended by a massive welder was nursing a broken nose.

"Put him down, Andee," Sauders directed.

"Whatever you say, Security—fuck is that a body?"

Jax whirled around in a panic, but she was the only one. Saunders hung her head dejectedly. The brawling residents looked surly in response.

"Catching on, are we?" the asshat named Enith replied, getting his own feet underneath him. "This shitstain is telling me this guy has been dead for longer than a day. Last I checked, our weird little trip knocked us out for only eighteen hours. So this fucker is nuts," he snarled, jabbing a finger at the other guy.

Jax crept around the squabbling pair, leaving any more swinging fists for Andee to sort out, and knelt next to where Saunders studied the body.

The man looked stiff, his face etched in what looked like pain or distress.

"Jax," Saunders whispered from where she crouched. "He's right, this is Koty Higgs, but he has been dead for days," she stated.

"Another victim of the Butcher?" Jax asked. Paul's body would probably still be a level up on Four, unless someone had already hauled him down to the new storage locker for Dead Residents.

Saunders turned to face Jax, her green eyes looking wide and shining with something sharp.

"Jax, you and I inspected this level. Twice. We didn't find any bodies in here!"

She was right. Jax and Saunders had fought off swarms of space bugs, but no dead bodies. Jax studied the form prone on the flooring.

"So somebody moved him here?" she asked dumbly. This was the closest she had been to Saunders in hours, and some longing pulled at her to close the distance. But some equal and opposite force kept her at bay, watching the Security Officer.

"There's more, Jax," Saunders replied, glancing furtively over her shoulder, back at where Andee was performing an admirable service as a wall between them and the shitty guy named Enith.

"More than a body?" Jax uneasily scanned the immediate area for any manner of horrific addition.

"Koty isn't on my manifests," Saunders replied, her voice small. Jax glanced back up at her.

"Okay, so you missed—"

"No!" This time the reply was forceful and accompanied by the piercing green of Saunders' stare. Jax flinched under its gaze.

"I mean," Saunders continued, her voice dropping even lower to a whisper, "I remember him. It makes sense he is here, but I also know for a fact he was...never here."

Jax scrunched her brow in confusion.

"It's like, a shadow of a memory. He's supposed to be here, but...not. And now he's dead."

"Saunders, nothing you are saying makes any sense..." Jax trailed off. Saunders glared at the body before them, as if it was his fault. Then she glanced back up at Jax with something that looked like pleading. In that moment, Jax desperately wanted to reach out to her. They had been so close, so near to something and now it seemed too distant. Jax had admitted how deeply she wanted them to be something more, and for a brief moment, they had been. Now they were just standing apart from each other, two coworkers looking at a dead body where it shouldn't be, an impasse growing between them. Jax could close the distance. But in that moment, she wasn't sure Saunders wanted it.

The opportunity faded. Saunders replied, her features closing her off from Jax.

"You just asked if I had ever seen Andee before. Of course I have, and she's on the manifests. But...you haven't seen her. That's the feeling I'm having right now."

Jax spun her head around to check to see if the hulking form of this new person was still filling the space between her and the irate resident. Instead, she saw a growing number of new faces filling in around them.

"Uh..." Jax replied, eloquently.

Saunders whirled on the spot to address the residents who congregated around them, several already engaging heatedly with Enith about the dead man at their feet.

"I need to get this under control," Saunders breathed, the statement made more to herself than to Jax. But Jax felt it ache deep in her, somewhere she wasn't comfortable with. Why couldn't they have just been able to save the day, and fly off together into something warm and new?

"Well what the fuck happened to him? I only saw him last night!" Someone was shouting into the crowd. Another person shouldered past and suddenly Jax was shoved aside as more living bodies crowded around the dead one at their feet.

"Okay everyone, listen up!" bellowed a commanding voice.

Jax stumbled from where she had been shoved and wheeled around in near alarm.

Saunders took another deep inhale and called out, again, in a voice that carried far more authority than Jax had ever afforded her before.

"I NEED EVERYONE TO STOP!"

The crowd stilled and turned to assess the short, buff blond where she stood opposite Jax. The impasse yawned.

"We knew going into this search that we would find bodies. I know it doesn't make any sense!" she interjected, cutting off a retort from the large man with the frizzy beard who had commanded the conversation up on Four previously. "But right now, the important thing is that we maintain some forward-thinking action. We have a place to keep the bodies of our teammates who we find, right, Engineering?"

The formal title buzzed Jax from her stupor. She glanced up at Saunders, made eye contact with searing green, and nodded mutely.

"Right." Saunders carried on, as if she had hoped for more but knew she wouldn't get it. "So, Zick, you and Enith can take your man down there. Then I think we need rest!"

"Rest? We've been knocked out cold for eighteen hours, you think we need rest?" Zick snapped back. "What about the other missing people?"

Saunders stuck out a hand as if to head off any further dissent.

"I need everyone who is a foreman or team lead to take stock of your own roster. Tomorrow we can compare against my Station records and manifests. We need to be systematic about this, and then strategize our approach."

"Who, exactly, put you in charge of this?" Zick snarled, standing astride his dead teammate and knocking shoulders with Enith to form a wall.

Saunders narrowed her eyes. "I'm not trying to be in charge, I'm simp—"

"Rogle, she's the head of goddamn security, why wouldn't she be in charge?" rumbled the deep voice of the lead Space Marine, who strode up to the group from the far side of the corridor.

Zick Rogle spun on the spot, his wall of meat crumbling with the surprise flank.

"Really, OS2 Braken? Aren't you the ranking officer here? You really just gonna hand it off to this discount cop?" Rogle snarled.

Jax looked back over at Saunders. Her face seemed to burn with some emotion between discomfort and aggravation.

"Not an officer, first off. And besides, she was the same rank as I am. This isn't *my* job, it's her's." Braken spoke as if there wasn't any other argument.

The Space Marine had fully joined the group now, which stood in a semi-circle, as if standing vigil over the fallen resident at Zick's feet.

"I just need you to help me account for your people, Zick," Saunders finally spoke up, avoiding any form of acknowledgement of Braken's endorsement. But Jax had felt the air shift in the group. Nods of concurrence, concession, and acceptance started to dissolve the tense standoff. Zick still seethed over the remains of Koty Higgs, but Enith put a hand on his shoulder and whispered something in his ear. The irate man glared at Saunders, then spun to pin Jax with the same foul assessment. Jax flinched.

"I didn't come here to find my death dictated by a pair of shitty station janitors. This is my team. And in the end, what I say about them, is what goes with them. You hear? Keep them out of your fucked up little honeymoon." And with that, he crouched over the body beneath him and started positioning it for a lift alongside Enith.

"I'll help you, I know where they are putting the bodies," Space Marine Bracken offered. Zick swatted him away.

"Worry about your own fucking people, this place is killing them quick enough as is!" And with that, he hoisted Koty's body and shuffled off with Enith.

Jax felt rooted to the spot. Zick's words echoed in her ears, drowning out the commotion around them.

"Jax!" Saunders' voice cut through the static that was in her head. Jax snapped her attention to Saunders who stood in front of her now, looking strained.

"Yes?" Jax muttered, holding herself at a stiff arms-length from the Security Officer. This wasn't her idea of a honeymoon either.

"I don't think they are going to want to put Koty down on Level 2 yet."

"We're just going to let them horde a dead body like that?" Alarm prickled at Jax as she watched the two men carting their fallen teammate off down the corridor.

"I'll deal with that later," Saunders insisted.

Jax looked helplessly after the receding trio then back at Saunders.

"And the rest of us?"

"We need rest. Real rest," Saunders stated.

"I doubt you'll be able to get them all to agree on that," Bracken added, striding up. Saunders glanced up at the guy and sighed, the tension in her shoulders releasing just enough for Jax to feel jealous. She wanted to be the reason Saunders relaxed.

"I know Tiz, but I can't hope to control that. If they choose to stay up and wander, then that's on them. But I need rest. My shoulder needs rest. We need to look at this strategically in a new light tomorrow."

Jax felt like an awkward addition to the group. Here Saunders' familiarity with these people was shining through. As if to solidify it, Tizik Braken put a heavy hand on Saunders' uninjured shoulder.

"We can keep an eye on things. Are you going to be okay?" He asked with an uncertainty that made Jax bristle. There was no way any of them could be certain of that anymore.

"I'm fine. Just keep up the comms sweeps, okay?" Saunders replied. The Space Marine nodded and then turned to stride off.

Jax scanned the corridor of Medical. It was empty, not even a sign of Andee.

In front of her, Saunders put her face in her hands and buckled over, her knees hitting the floor.

"Saunders?" Jax hissed in alarm, sinking in a crouch beside her.

"What am I *doing*, Jax?" the other woman cried, muffled, into her hands. She peeled them back from her face and stared up at Jax with a deep jade glint in her eyes. Jax could only look back, confused.

"I can't lead these people! I'm barely able to keep track of who comes and goes, and they are going to look to me for answers? Or worse, not want answers from me at all?"

Jax lifted a hand, as if to place it on Saunders' shoulder, but it was the shoulder that still bled with a stab wound, and so Jax let her fingertips drop again to her side.

"Who else would lead us?" Jax asked, stupidly. Saunders glared at her in response and Jax swallowed hard, shifting her line of sight to the sterile walls of Medical that surrounded her.

"There's so many dead. *So many*, Jax! And none of it makes sense! Dead in the walls? Long dead, but fresh? Missing but still here? I can hardly hold my own grip on reality and now I'm in charge?" Saunders heaved a sob, or a gasp for air. Jax mostly felt the air leave her lungs.

"If I had any guess, it's probably not over."

Saunders had slumped off her knees and now sat on the flooring, hands in her lap, defeated.

"What's not over?" she asked, voice small.

"Whatever is happening to us. Or maybe it isn't something that ends? Maybe this is just the nature of the universe now? That Drop was something out of nightmares. Fuck if I know what's happening, and I doubt any of us will figure it out *now*. You've had the right idea so far: focus on the survival..."

"It's not *supposed* to be about survival—"

"And my Sation was never *supposed* to take this many lives," Jax insisted. "I feel like we are all off the map now. Literally and figuratively. But Saunders"—Jax returned her eyes to the woman who sat despondently in the corridor— "No one knows this group as well as you do, I can't think of anyone else in a better position to direct this!" Jax hoped her words carried enough sincerity to ease the distress blooming from the other woman in front of her.

Saunders regarded Jax from where she sat, her forearms on the tattered knees of her filthy security pants. They were both a mess: blood from each other, blood from the residents, the dirt and grime of fighting the Station is its death throes.

"Jax, I came out here to get away from conflict, not get elbow deep in it..." she said, forlornly.

In that moment Jax desperately wanted to clean herself off, to reset, to fall into a deep sleep and awaken to the universe making sense again.

"You picked the wrong fucking Station if you wanted to avoid conflict, Saunders."

Saunders huffed a dejected laugh. She pulled herself to her feet and looked down at where Jax remained on the flooring. Saunders didn't say anything, just jutted her head back along the length of the corridor toward Common Access.

Jax hefted herself upward and trailed after.

"I'll have them all trace their group numbers, then I'll compare against the manifests. The ones who are traveling solo can work with me directly. It's not gonna help if we find another mystery, but maybe we can at least figure out if anyone else is truly missing."

Saunders continued to mutter quietly as they made their way back to the stairwell.

Jax nodded along silently. In her head she assessed her own need to verify the core functionality, assure the structural damage of the Station wouldn't kill them, check the operation of the outboard rotational engines...even with all the gruesome mysteries, something else nagged at the back of her mind.

They were stranded.

Their sinking ship had found itself wrecked on the shores of a distant space and time where no rescue would ever be able to find them. The idea of sitting here among their dead, waiting for a hope that didn't exist, curdled the fear tightly inside Jax's gut.

They had reached the stairwell. Jax turned to see Saunders head down to her quarters on Level 1, half wondering if she could follow. But instead, Saunders took a step upward, toward level 4. A thrill shot through Jax, eclipsing the dread she was nursing.

"Where?" she asked before she could stop herself. Saunders glanced down as she ascended.

"I gave Tizik and his crew my berthing. They want to run constant comms sweeps. So I moved my stuff," Saunders replied.

Jax realized the other woman was nearly at the next landing above, and she scrambled after, feeling as if she were wheeling on the edge of the chasm that had grown between them when they had awoken in this mess.

"Where, uh, where's your stuff?" Jax aimed for nonchalant and failed.

As if in answer, Saunders stepped up to the threshold of Level Four, and a twisting, sickening swoop filled Jax's stomach.

"I figured there was plenty of room, and it would be easier to be close to people for once. It's not like anyone is coming or going anytime soon down there, anyways." Saunders added the last part as if it were a bitter afterthought.

Jax could only stand, mouth agape. This moment seemed to define something, just beyond their grasp, yet still unattainable. She wanted to say something, but no words came.

As if in reply, Saunders took her hand from the threshold of the doorframe to Berthing and stepped closer to Jax, who felt her breath hitch.

"I knew this detail wouldn't be lost on you," she said, quietly. She took another step closer and Jax felt a strange thrill shoot up her spine. The distance closed further, and Saunders hesitated just shy of Jax's lips. The shorter woman flickered her line of sight from Jax's mouth up to her eyes and back again. Jax realized she was holding her breath, brain having gone blank of every aspect of their predicament. Then Saunders closed the space between them with a chaste kiss.

The moment passed before Jax could react and the impasse yawned again. Saunders gave a lingering glance over her shoulder and then she was gone, through the doorway to Level 4: Berthing, and out of Jax's sight.

Stuck standing alone in the Common Access stairwell, Jax was left with little in the way of options. There hadn't really been an invitation to follow. There were dead people hidden in the walls of her Station, and they were so far lost to the void that their own death might not matter anymore. Considering a path, Jax spun around, before slumping her head low and stalking back up to Level 5. There were residents moving about the Station still, and Jax had no control over the matter anymore. The only place left for her to go was her own quarters.

Up on Five, Jax could find nothing better to do with herself than stand, destitute, in the center of the cluttered nest she called her own, and barter with the rising anxiety. At some point in the last several hours Saunders had held her hand, filled her arms, even kissed her in the Common Access stairwell. Jax felt foolish for even feeling this surge of unease. They had only just patched whatever this was between them, and then found themselves flung into additional madness. There should be no reason for her to be lamenting Saunders' new choice of quarters, aside from Jax's usual reservations about Level 4. But those reservations had ebbed in recent cycles. And had Saunders not shown herself singularly unique to those circumstances?

But it was hard to shake the idea that something had not quite gone as planned between them.

She shook her head to clear her thoughts. In reality, Jax needed to focus on their new predicament of being really fucking lost to the endless consuming maw of deep space. *That* had certainly not been part of any plan.

Jax felt the hair on her neck bristle. The grime on her arms and legs made her skin itch. In a fit of pent-up rage and confusion, Jax ripped at her clothing, tossing it to any corner of her room and flung herself into the coffin like confines of her shower where she let her discomfort in her own skin be matched in heated fury by the scalding water she used to scrub at her own existence. She stayed until the steam made her cough and the warning light indicated water shutoff. It wouldn't be enough to drown out the incessant buzzing panic in Jax's head.

She exited the lavatory to a knock on the door, and Jax tensed.

For the first time in her entire tenure on Station there were residents infiltrating all levels of her Station, *including* the walls. They had boldly swept into her sanctuary and refused to leave, dead or alive. Who was it to say they were not bold enough to sweep into her berthing as well? After all, Saunders had given up her own space for the sake of their new reality. Perhaps this was that prickly navigator come to claim Jax's space so she could stay close to a navigation console she had no right to claim as her own. Jax was not ready to find herself in a lonely Level 4 berthing anytime soon.

But the knock was persistent. Jax threw on a t-shirt and snatched up some undershorts from the clean pile on one of the chairs. She knew better, from experience, than to ever answer the door in just a towel ever again. She pinched her face in aggressive annoyance and strode over to the door to thumb the latch. The door slid back to reveal Saunders standing with a large grey duffle bag slung over her shoulder and a tight, almost strained look on her face.

Jax felt the mask of her own aggravation wipe free and she regarded the woman on her doorstep.

"Jax." Saunders regarded her back. "Can I come in?"

Jax felt the words die in her mouth and only managed to make her body move, stepping back into the space behind her to make room for the Security Officer. Saunders crossed the threshold and the door slid shut behind her.

Some additional eternity yawned between them as they stood in the cramped space. Jax distantly recalled that she should be self-conscious of the mess surrounding her, and her distinct lack of clothing, but instead she found herself assessing the figure in front of her. Saunders' hair was also damp from a shower, and it was tucked behind her ears where softer tendrils, already dry, were starting to fly away from the others. She wore grey security pants and a clean tank top, rather than the bloody mess of the distant-feeling past. Some fresh bandages were wrapped around her shoulder injury. The duffle on her other shoulder bore a faded and frayed name tag labeled "MS2 Saunders, J." with some military looking symbol patched next to it. But Jax kept getting drawn back to the look on Saunders' face.

"Is this okay?" Saunders' voice was quiet, tense, eyes vivid green and boring into Jax's soul.

Jax could only nod.

The duffle dropped to the flooring with a muffled thud and Saunders was in her arms and on her lips. Jax pulled Saunders' body tight against her, right arm snaking around her waist, and left reaching up to tangle in the soft hair at the base of Saunder's neck. Saunders seemed to strain upward, hands grasping at Jax's face, and pressing her mouth, open and needy against Jax's own, striving to accommodate the difference in their height. Jax felt a pressure at her hips and realized she was being pushed, gently, firmly backward. Her bare feet hit the storage compartment built into the base of her bunk and she lost her balance, tipping over backward on to the thin mattress and its pile of blankets.

Jax thought she should be distantly concerned for the wellbeing of Saunders' injured shoulder, but Saunders, for her part, was absolutely feral. She had already rid herself of the tank top, and, while sat astride Jax on the bunk, had pushed Jax's t-shirt up her torso. Jax obliged in shrugging the rest of the way out of the garment before Saunders moved to further occupy the space closest to her skin. The woman broke their kiss and breathed in the minute space between them.

"Saunders?" Jax managed, tentatively.

"I want you to call me 'Jillian' in here," Saunders replied. Jax let out a strangled groan and pulled Saunders back to her.

And in that moment they could have been a million years away, or lost within their own universe, but Jax was fully intent on being exactly where they were right then.

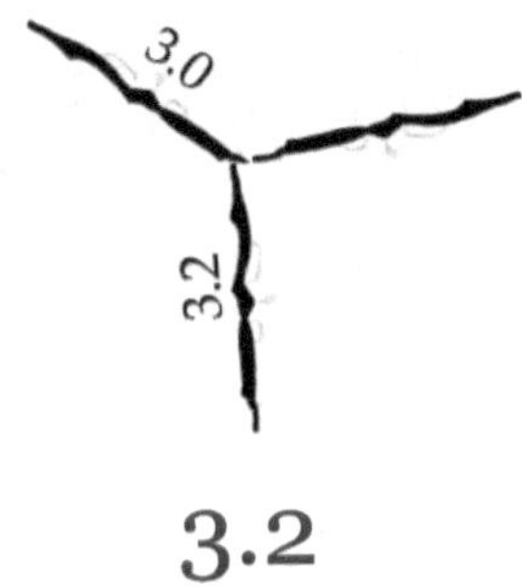

3.2

A blast powerful enough to breach the exterior rocked the Station. Jax braced against the wall of the Level 1 corridor. Outside, she saw an alien craft arc past the sluggish spin of the Station. A flash showed the destruction of one of the outboard rotational engines, and debris passed by the portholes.

"PULL BACK!"

Jax heard orders bellowed by the man in charge of the small military squad that had taken up residence with them. From her vantage point on the wall, she saw a few of them bolt for far cover near Common Access.

The exterior wall of the Station, barring them from the merciless void of space, shimmered almost on the edge of Jax's vision. Then it seemed to part like a curtain. Jax was frozen in place, as if she had forgotten a large quantity of carnivorous alien plants were after her. She watched in horror as a new set of nightmares poured through the suddenly permeable wall of the Station.

These creatures squirmed through like massive centipedes, nearly twenty feet long, carried along by fringe-like appendages. In their centers, at the midsection of their gleaming segmented and shelled bodies, there looked to be a cluster of eyes, like those on a crustacean. As the first few cleared the Station wall they rose at the middle, eye clusters at the apex, folding in half to stand as some nine foot tall being of frills and terror.

Jax watched as three soldiers who found themselves cornered by the newcomers backed away against the

Common Access door frame. The lead creature bore down on them, imposing in its height and demeanor. The air crackled with the anticipation of attack. The foremost soldier, still in whatever workout gear he had been wearing before the Station dropped into this corner of hell, relaxed his shoulders. It was as if he either accepted a fate, or the hope that maybe there was a moment of understanding that may lead to peace.

The motion was faster than Jax could comprehend. She could not tell what part of the creature had moved, but an audible *crack* sounded like a whip between where she crouched, and the fated squad-mates. The foremost soldier fell in two, as if cleaved in half from forehead through parted legs. He spilled to either side, a mess of gore, splashing on the two surviving members, who followed immediately similar fates.

Jax had to bite through her fist to keep from screaming. She forced herself to back up from the incoming swarm. She would take her chances with the carnivorous plants. She had already seen one take a woman's head clean off, but the woman had at least had a chance to put up a fight.

"Please be hallucinations, please!" Jax hissed as she threw herself back down the corridor, trying to not slip on blood. She passed the body of one of the research team, which seemed to be covered in some form of black, shiny fungal growth. To her sickening horror she noticed the substance was eating through the flesh of the body, dissolving it like acid. As she crept past, it seemed to shift, and then in a fresh wave of terror, it tracked her, bubbling in her direction.

Where the fuck *were* they? Jax tripped over something as she tried to avoid the surge of dark, seemingly sentient goo. She crashed to the floor, ready to meet her end at the bloodthirsty whim of tentacles, fangs, acid and nightmares. She scrambled to see what she had tripped over. It was her wrench.

Jax scrambled to gain purchase, grabbed the three-foot, steel spud wrench, and felt a strange sticky feeling, as if her foot was being sucked into quicksand. She looked down to see a glob of the black fungus envelope her boot. She screamed.

A blur of motion impacted her hard from the side. The shape was human, and Jax realized it was one of the residents; a man Jax had never actually met. He pulled her from the grip of the seeking gunk on her boot, though a burning in her shin told her it had already set on her.

"Follow me, Engineering," he hissed, and Jax limped after him. He held his arm close to his chest, and as he turned, she noticed his hand was missing, his bleeding arm bound tightly with a bloody fabric scrap. He kicked open a panel and Jax followed him inside. It was a back access well, but at this point she didn't care who knew it existed. They were under siege.

The man slowed as they ascended, his back pressed to the wall, his remaining hand out to slow Jax. His sight was pinned to the steps above, as if he were unsure of what they might come across.

"Where is Security? Where's Saunders?" he asked, not taking his eyes off the route ahead of them. Jax kept her sight trained downward. She didn't bother wondering why he thought to ask her about the Station Security Officer.

"We split up. I went to the core to check the reactor, and she was supposed to round up the residents. I don't think things went to plan, but I haven't seen her since," Jax admitted. She did not admit the extreme grip of terror she felt at Saunders meeting a similar fate to those she had seen out in corridors of the Station.

"She did come find some of us. Then she took off to look for you. I haven't seen her since. My name is Ged Habburn, by the way, I don't think we've ever really met."

Of course they had never met. Jax had made sure, leading up to the moment of Station Drop, to avoid every resident as if they were out for her blood. Funny enough, now something *was* out for her blood, and knowing the residents might have been useful.

"Well, it's lovely to meet you, but right now isn't the most convenient time for afternoon tea," Jax hissed. Habburn glanced down at her as he crept forward up the stairwell, his pace slowing with every step.

"Hmm, I see what she likes about you."

Jax flushed, despite the horror surrounding them. The man in front of her, with his gruesome injury, and clear acknowledgement of their predicament, seemed to prove these nightmares were real. And he knew Saunders, at least well enough, it seemed.

"Sorry," Jax said gruffly. "I'm a bit...nervous, about where she is," she trailed off. Something clunked the stairwell wall down below them.

"She's a combat vet. I think you need to trust her right now. You and I, on the other hand, need to move." Habburn surged upward, as a crash below indicated their holding place had been infiltrated. Jax threw herself after him.

They burst through a doorway on Level 4, and Jax found herself back in the Meat Market. This time, there was less blood and gore here than on the rest of the Station, but it still looked like a war zone.

Habburn led her down the corridor and she saw several residents prone against the walls, some getting helped, others left to their fate. She passed one of the research scientists, with acid burns on their left shoulder, trying to tie off the leg of a woman who looked to have gotten too close to one of the centipede-shrimp creatures. Her leg ended above her knee, the wound as clean a cut as if it had been done with a laser. She looked to be in shock.

Jax found herself scanning the sides for Saunders, either as a body, or as a responder. The woman was a combat medic, her training would probably have drawn her out to save her people. As Jax followed Habburn to one of the common gallies on Level 4, she hoped to catch a glimpse of short, muscular, blond Security Officer, but all she saw was carnage.

"I found Engineering," Habburn said, ahead of her. He was addressing another woman that Jax didn't recognize, but she felt a pinch of embarrassment when he greeted her with an embrace and a kiss. "Seen Saunders at all?"

"She passed through, but that was a while ago. It's hard to keep track of time right now," the woman replied. Habburn turned back to Jax.

"Engineering, this is my wife, Obah. Saunders left her to cover medical services here on Four."

"Wife?" Jax asked stupidly. It had never really dawned on her that residents were anything other than young, horny, transient degenerates. This pair looked old enough to be Jax's parents, if Jax had parents still.

"Engineering, Saunders was looking for you." The woman sounded kind and calm, with the same sort of tone used to deliver very bad news. "But she has a feeling of duty to her role here, and I think she set back out again to try to find casualties."

Jax hugged her wrench tight to herself. The last time she had stood in this galley it had been stacked with the bloody corpses of the Station residents, laid out on a chopping block for market sale. It had been a maddening hallucination, brought on by the failing Station, and calmed only by Saunders' presence. This, however, was all very real, and Saunders was nowhere to be seen.

"I understand," Jax mumbled. She looked around. Obah had started cleaning and tending to Habburn's destroyed arm. On a far wall, someone hoisted up a slumped body with potentially fatal facial wounds. Clearly no one thought it necessary to bring the pieces of soldier she had witnessed being flayed from below.

"Engineering? Engineering!"

Jax snapped her attention back to the woman, Obah, who had apparently been talking to her.

"What?" Jax seemed unable to string together more than two words at a time.

"I asked about the core? Ged told me you went to check on the station, that's why you and Saunders split up."

"The core was fine. It was still working, but then the first blast hit, so I came back down to look for her. She didn't want to separate, she had wanted to go with me, and I told her we had jobs to do, that we needed to focus on that, that she needed to help everyone, and I left her to check on the core and the core was fine."

And Jax cracked. She crumbled to her boots, curled against a cabinet in the corner of this galley, turned butchers block, turned galley, turned field hospital. She couldn't cry, that wasn't the emotion breaking through her. Instead she hyperventilated, her vision narrowing to a pin prick and a wave of panic washing over her. She wanted to cry. Crying would be easier.

A sharp sting reverberated across Jax's face. The sudden and surprising pain snapped her vision into focus. The woman, the wife of the man who had saved her from downstairs, was crouched in front of her. From the sting in Jax's face, she must have slapped her. Jax wanted to be offended, but she was more shocked. She was shocked further when the woman pivoted to slide down the wall next to her and put a motherly arm around her. Jax had never known this kind of attention. She regarded Obah with suspicion and concern, but did not move away.

"Jax—I'm going to call you Jax, even though we haven't really met—I understand. When Ged used to get called out on deployments I would have to really fight off the despair. But we don't have that luxury right now. There are things coming through these doors to kill us. Right now, we need to focus. I know you miss her. And I know there's nothing she probably wants more than to know that you are okay. You'll find her. But you need to put a game face on," Obah said, soothingly. Jax regarded her, and Ged behind her, cradling his ruined stump of a hand.

"I'll find her," Jax repeated. She would head back out, look for survivors, and try to help get them back up to Level 4. If Saunders was out there doing her job, Jax could help, and she would find her.

"You have two legs and two hands, and that's doing a hell of a lot better than I am right now," Habburn rumbled from above her. In the light of this level his face looked a lot more sickly pale than seemed right. He was in more serious pain than he was letting on. The acid burn on Jax's shin stung.

"Okay, I need to look for her. I'll try to send as many people up this way as I can while I look," Jax stammered, attempting to scramble to her feet.

"Easy does it, kid," Habburn put a hand on her shoulder to steady her. Jax resented the "kid" comment. She was in her thirties.

"We can't have everyone just sprint off, we'll all get lost." Obah also rose to her feet beside them. Somewhere on the far side of the Station another blast rocked through. Jax felt the gravity drop. Her outboard rotationals were being gutted.

"But I need to find—"

"Right, so we go in pairs," Habburn interjected. "That way if something happens, you rally back to here to report so we don't think you're still out there."

"You were on your own when you found me," Jax argued.

"Because my partner had just gotten his face chewed off by some fungus. You tripped over him."

Jax shut her mouth.

"Okay, love, are you sure you can handle heading back out there?" Obah asked her husband. Jax looked at the older man's face. He looked like he was hurting, but he also looked like he was dead set on going.

"I'll be fine. I have Engineering with me now. She knows this place pretty well. Besides, she had a wrench. What can go wrong?" He kissed his wife and backed out into the corridor. Jax stood rooted to the spot watching them both. Obah turned to her and put a kind hand on her shoulder.

"Go. Find your girl. It's about time you two actually finally found each other. Keep an eye on him for me."

Jax wasn't sure how to process the message, so she grimaced a smile and stepped out after Habburn. She gave one last, fleeting look over her shoulder at Obah as they marched back down the corridor toward Common Access. The older woman was already hopping into action to help someone who looked like they were missing half their right side.

* * *

They crept out back into Common Access. Jax followed Ged Habburn closely.

"I think we need to pick a level and go for it," he said.

"Yeah, but what is the plan if we run into those things? Are we fighting them? I watched them walk straight through our walls, can we even stop them?" Jax was desperately trying not to be hysterical.

"I think the idea is to get everyone to Level 4, pull back and take a defensive position, but we were all over the place when this struck."

"You were a soldier?" Jax asked, wanting to better understand her surroundings.

"A long time ago. These days, I was just supposed to be a settler on a new world. Looks like the new world's found us instead," Habburn replied.

"Medical," Jax stated. He looked at her. "I want to search Medical. Saunders is a medic. She might be in there using the equipment."

Down in the stairwell a blood-curdling scream echoed upward.

"Okay, better move fast," Habburn barked. Jax spun toward the steps and willed herself to descend toward the sounds of someone being ripped limb from limb.

On the landing outside Medical, the door was nearly ripped open, as if it had been blasted. It did not bode well. The screams from below had gurgled to a halt, but there were other noises now. Jax realized they were too close to whatever was ascending to backtrack. Their options were the ominously destroyed entrance of the Medical level, and whatever nightmare slithered up from below.

Jax backpedaled away from the stairs and threw herself through the remnants of the Medical doors. Habburn followed her, not bothering to see what might follow him. Inside the level, Jax looked from left to right, wondering what direction to take. The left looked brighter, so off she went.

Habburn took up the rear, and she assumed he would keep an eye on whatever might pursue them. But Jax was growing more and more desperate to seek out Saunders, and her focus had narrowed again.

They slunk quietly along the corridor, keeping close to the walls, and training their ears to any sounds that might alert them to the arrival of murderous extra-terrestrials.

At the twenty-five degree mark they found someone. A woman, prone, but lacking any massive traumatic injuries. Jax took a furtive guard post, clutching her wrench, while Habburn knelt down to check on her. The sudden contact caused the woman to jolt awake and scream.

"Shhhh," Habburn hissed, putting his one remaining hand on the woman's shoulder to hold her down. Jax glanced down at them. "We are trying to get everyone up to Level 4."

"They're coming through the walls!" the woman wailed, hysterical. Jax looked around alarmed, assuming this was a current threat, but she saw nothing. She knew what the woman meant. She had seen it herself not half an hour ago.

And not but eighteen hours before that Jax had been right here on this level, shoulder to shoulder with Saunders, fighting off the surge of horrors they thought were just a dream, and realizing how much she needed the Security Officer in her life. The Security Officer that was still missing.

"We need to go," Jax whispered urgently. Habburn tried moving the woman, but she recoiled.

"Eave, don't stay here, please come with us," the older man grunted. But "Eave" refused. She instead shoved herself further into the wall. Jax half wanted to ask if she had at least seen the Security Officer, but from the look of it, Eave was too far gone to be able to reply.

"Ged, let's *go*!" Jax hissed. Habburn looked up at her in disappointment. Jax felt a pang of guilt. She supposed if she was a better person, she would drop Saunders from her mind and put everything into whatever it took to get Eave off the floor and up to Obah on Level 4.

A crash echoed behind them, near the entrance to Common Access. They all jumped in terror. Jax made last-moment eye contact with Habburn and reached down at the same time he did to grab one of Eave's arms. They both pulled. Eave screamed.

"No, don't take me! Don't let them take me!" she wailed. The noise from behind them seemed to zero in on her lament.

"Habburn, we need to GO!" Jax spat, under her breath, huffing from the exertion of pulling along the struggling woman. Eave gave a final, massive struggle which wrenched her arm free of Habburn, who swore in pain. Jax nearly toppled over with the full weight of the struggling woman, and she let go in an effort to not fall. Eave scrambled back to her place on the floor.

"Fuck this, let her stay!" Jax was done trying. She set off down the corridor away from Eave, and away from whatever might come down the hall from Common Access. Habburn followed.

"We are supposed to be finding survivors, Engineering. Anyone, not just the ones we want!" he growled after her. But Jax wasn't listening. She saw something.

Up the bend, discarded against the wall, was a security belt. It looked to be damaged by either acid or burns, but the distinct lack of Saunders accompanying it meant that it had been purposely discarded.

"She's here, I know it." Jax broke into a run.

"JAX!" Habburn called after her, but right at that moment they both heard Eave scream in terror. Whatever had entered through Common Access had made its way to her. The sounds of the woman dying echoed off the walls. Habburn, clearly giving up on the rescue, followed on Jax's heels.

They only made it a few degrees further when one of the side access routes they had taken earlier burst open. A collection of horrors poured out, including several of the carnivorous plantlike creatures with the grasping tendrils of vine, and one of the centipede shrimp things. Horrifyingly, the plant creature's surface shimmered with the seemingly sentient acidic black mold. It immediately slithered off in rippling, sludge-like waves.

Jax had only just made it past the access entrance, but Habburn had been in the way. One of the plant-like creatures, moving rapidly on flagella, knocked into him, throwing him to the far wall. The creatures descended on him and his screams went from shock and surprise to terror and pain before Jax had found a way to move.

One of the carnivorous plants seemed to catch sight of her, though it had no recognizable eyes, or front. She saw it shift its weight in a way that seemed to target her. Jax swung her wrench and it collided with its head, crushing it. It let out despicable sound that seemed to relay information to its peers, because a few pulled themselves from the body of Habburn and pursued her.

Jax turned and ran. She didn't think there was a way to outrun something with that many legs and the ability to phase through walls, but she tried. She rounded the curve of the level, passing several bodies, both alive and dead. Jax heard some of the pursuers peel off and dispatch anyone in her wake, but she knew they wanted her. She had killed one of their own.

As Jax skidded around the apex of the level, she saw, for the briefest instant, the most beautiful sight she never expected to ever see again.

At the apex one-hundred-and-eighty-degree mark, Saunders was crouched over someone, checking on their injury, and applying a bandage. She had clearly been working through the corridor, with all the commitment and resolve of a seasoned combat medic, who was rising to the occasion of her vocation. Jax saw the sudden flash of recognition on the other woman's face as Saunders caught sight of her. Jax knew Saunders was witnessing a vision of herself, arriving in character, wrench at the ready.

The pair of them, reunited again, each in their place, as Engineering and Security, fulfilling their duty until the last possible moment here on Medical.

It hung there, for a breath: the sight of them both. Saunders managed to make it to her feet, and Jax nearly closed the gap between them. But her pursuers were closing in. A massive rumbling shook the entirety of the Station, another blast from whatever ship was bearing down on them.

Jax felt a heat tear through her shoulder like being punched by a molten hot steel slug. The force knocked her forward onto her face, the wrench in her hand flying forward with the rest of her arm. There were already slimy flagella tentacles winding their way up her legs, and a burning sensation growing from her feet. She looked up, dazed.

Saunders had probably been shouting her name, but Jax couldn't hear it. She saw the other woman take a step toward her, and thought, briefly, that she instead needed to get away, to save herself. Jax didn't get the chance to respond, as a bloody protrusion emerged from Saunders' middle, hoisting her off the corridor floor. One of the massive centipede-things had risen behind her, and skewered Saunders with its extendable, whip-like appendage. It ripped the appendage out, taking a decent portion of Saunders' ribcage with it, and dropped her to the corridor flooring again.

The sounds of the surrounding survivors that Saunders had so clearly been trying to save filled the corridor, as the invaders made quick work of dispatching them all. Jax felt herself fading. She couldn't even feel pain anymore. She was certain the acidic mold had started in on whatever it had begun on her leg down on Level 1. She managed enough energy to look up at the body of Saunders across her. She imagined they made eye contact.

The invaders moved, floor by floor, eliminating the threat. Humans did not exist out here. And then, for a brief moment, they had. Then, humans no longer existed out here.

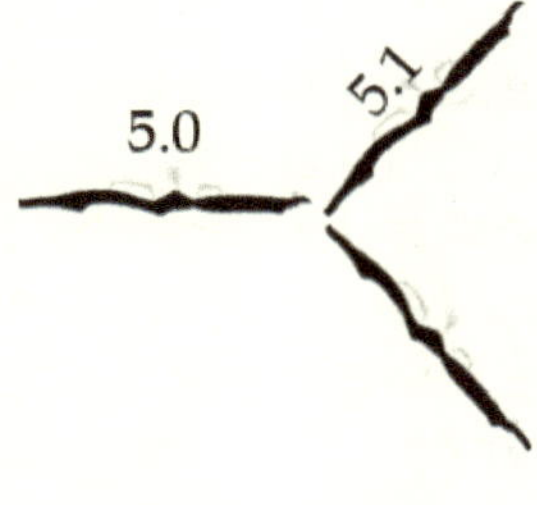

5.1

"Is this...everyone?" Saunders felt a sickening jolt to her stomach as she looked around the sparse gathering of residents. They had moved to Level 4, if only so they could be sure anyone left in Berthing could find them. It had not been easy navigating the station on its side.

"We'll try checking the back ninety degrees, but they might be flooded," Tizik's squadmate, Corine, replied.

Saunders wrapped her arms around herself. She had practically memorized the manifests. She had met every resident and knew them by first name. There had been fifty-five. Paul Hower had died before they dropped. And Illy Lark had passed away on Level 2 after succumbing to psychosis from the hallucinations. But here, in this haunted house of a ruined space station, Saunders counted less than twenty-four residents. That meant more than thirty were, well, missing at the very least. Any number of them might still emerge from the shadows. Any number of them may never emerge again.

Who Saunders *really* didn't want to see, was Tess. And that's who had shown up.

There was a dank chill in the air, which seemed stagnant and almost overbearing. Saunders squeezed her eyes shut and scrubbed at her face with her hands. But Tess was still there, leaning quietly against the curve of the station flooring near a bulkhead. The dim glow from the small pin pricks of various flashlights flickered occasionally over the woman's face, and Saunders diligently sought to look anywhere else.

Another light flashed from around the bend of the station, reflecting off the metallic flooring. This had to be someone else approaching. And if Tess was already here, Saunders only hoped it was someone who could quell her madness.

Saunders thought of herself as a levelheaded individual, who could maintain composure in the face of absolutely fucked up circumstances. But the silhouette of the lanky Station Mechanical Engineer picking her way back over to the small group of survivors was enough to rip an emotional rush of breath from her lungs.

"Jax!" Saunders managed to call the mechanic's name without, hopefully, sounding too desperate. Sure they had their moment before this all had gone to hell, but she was still uneasy about what was happening between them. And of course the last thing she needed was Tess ruining this now that Saunders had finally gotten through to the mechanic.

Jax picked her way over to Saunders in the darkness, skirting even the few residents present. It seemed almost absurd that, despite the monumentally impossible nature of their situation, Jax still seemed full of continued social anxiety. Her brow was furrowed and the curtain of hair covered her already dark eyes, which looked fathoms darker than Saunders could recall.

"Is this the whole group?" Jax asked when she got close enough, reigniting the surge of panic and unease in Saunders, who turned her back to where Tess leaned.

"We need to keep looking. Corine said there might be more on the back ninety."

Jax looked genuinely troubled, which was a look Saunders could not recall ever seeing on the woman in the fourteen months she had been on the station. The prickle of her own anxiety surged, just as a few more residents joined the small group surrounding them.

"What's the verdict?" someone asked.

Saunders swallowed her growing distress.

"Right, Jax, you checked the systems?"

Jax hadn't heard her, though. She was looking around at the numbers gathered.

With all the furniture bolted to the flooring, the couches and galley counters all rested some five to ten feet up what now was essentially a wall. It was disorienting. The survivors huddled together in bunches. Jax had hoisted herself up to sit on a vent sticking out from the ceiling panels, and surveyed the group from her perch.

Saunders needed to act. She shored up her nerves, rubbed at her face and strode over to where Jax seemed to want to melt into the darkness.

"Jax, please."

The mechanic looked at her as if seeing Saunders for the first time. Saunders braced for a scathing remark but instead Jax only jumped, as if only realizing she still had something to do.

"Right, so, from what I can tell the core reactor is still running. It's nuclear after all, but yeah, pretty much every system but ventilation is shut down," Jax updated loudly for the gathered group.

"What about water?" someone asked. Saunders knew what they meant, she really did, but the surging adrenaline of panic and the discomfort of reality boiled over.

"I'd say there's no shortage of *that,*" she responded, then winced.

"Saunders?" the mechanic whispered quietly.

"Sorry. Fine. I don't actually know how that system works." Saunders swallowed hard to derail the urge to make a joke about how moist everything was about to get. Somewhere in the darkness the sound of a drip echoed ominously. This was horrifying. Next to her, Jax faltered, squinted at her, forcing Saunders to blatantly avoid the eye contact, and then continued.

"Yeah, so the water filtration is mostly mechanically driven, with little electrical interface. We still have running water and filtration. The systems are on a tiered structure. Anything that requires power gets ranked on criticality. Oxygen is last. Water is second-last. And from the frosty nature of things, it's clear the third to last of 'temperature controls' has also bit the dust, so the speak," Jax reported, and to Saunders' surprise, the mechanic actually sounded personable. Or, as personable as one could sound as they were faced with drowning in the depths of an alien abyss.

Saunders flinched. There was a sound like rushing water and she braced for the deluge that would wash them all away until she realized it was just rushing in her ears: her heart racing. She took a few steps to the side, hoping to not get flooded with questions she barely had the answers to. Tess had moved from her dark corner and stood just outside the small ring of light they all shared, as if daring Saunders to look at her. Saunders grit her teeth and scraped the wet hair from her face. She couldn't crack, not here, not now. These people needed her. So many people needed her, and she could be that person. She could be there for them this time.

Saunders glanced sideways at the mechanic who, while folded in on herself, was addressing questions from terrified residents. She sounded grumpy, but she was being forthright in what was asked of her.

"How are you doing, Jillian?" came a voice from Saunders' side that made her jump, but then instantly relax. Obah Habburn had stepped up next to her and held out a blanket. The woman had been an absolute sweetheart over her extended stay on station with them all, and Saunders had grown fond of this person she was supposed to say a permanent farewell to when her settler group finally departed for their posting. Saunders shook her head to clear the thought that no one would be making it to their intended destination.

"I'm as fine as possible, Obah, thank you," Saunders lied. "How about you?"

A shadow cast over Obah's face, and she lowered her eyes.

"We can't find Bergan. I'm worried..."

As if taking an order, Tess picked up her bag and turned to stride off around the sideways corridor into the encroaching darkness. Saunders allowed herself to watch the woman go, before turning to put a hand on Obah's shoulder.

Saunders hated to admit it, but Tess was probably right. They needed to find the rest of their people. Saunders latched onto the opportunity for initiative and made an energetic scan of the group she had already memorized the entirety of. She raised her voice to cut off Jax and grab everyone's attention. "I think we need to take some distinct actions."

Jax looked relieved to no longer be conversing with strangers, not that they *should* have been strangers. Saunders squared her shoulders and clenched her jaw until some marginal level of control returned.

"Okay, let's break out into task groups." She could do this. Break down the mission, assign roles, get people moving. Saunders had never been in any command, but field medics were trained to triage, trained to burst into any emergency and know how to act. Rank and position meant nothing when you were bleeding out. She had trained for this; had only ever had to use it once...

She pushed the thoughts out. They were in danger. They needed food, insulation, to look for survivors, to make sure the station would hold—

"Jax." Saunders stepped to where Jax was huddled on the vent housing, past the group tasked with stripping bedding from the unused berthings. The mechanic looked up from where she was studying a portion of the ceiling panel closely.

"Yeah?" Jax answered, in her typically guarded, but still clearly curious, tone.

"You checked power and life support, do we need to check the core?" Saunders asked.

Jax visibly paled. And she was already pale to begin with since she clearly never spent long enough under the UV-LEDs. But the look of unease on her face told Saunders there was more too it.

"I mean, I can tell the reactor is still running from life support..."

"What's wrong?" Saunders pressed. If she could focus on Jax's needs, she could keep her own panic from winning over.

Jax so frequently looked uncomfortable around any form of human interaction that her squirm looked normal to

Saunders. But they had gotten so much more comfortable around each other. Saunders stepped closer, and Jax cast a wary eye around at the few silhouettes in the vicinity. Looking over her shoulder at their surroundings, Saunders cocked her head back at Jax, questing for an answer.

"It's just...really far...away," Jax grumbled, and flicked her eyes back to Saunders from where she had been scanning the group. "I didn't want to leave you that long while I checked. It took forever to make it just to Power and Life Support." At this, Jax leaned forward, closing the distance between them.

Saunders felt a surge of affection and the slightest pull of a smile at the edge of her mouth. Let Tess come back and size her up from the shadows, Saunders' heart belonged to the lanky woman in front of her.

"I don't really want you leaving that long either," she admitted, and felt a small spike of relief at the smile wanting to escape the sullen mechanic's features. "There's a group who want to run a search for survivors, but I can peel a few off if we need to assemble a group to help you check for damage?"

Jax mulled over the idea for longer than Saunders expected. To be honest, Saunders hadn't expected Jax to consider the offer at all. But ultimately Jax pushed herself off the vent box and rose to her full height. Saunders waited for Jax to tell her she didn't need help, that she was perfectly capable on her own. But instead Jax nodded.

"You know them all. Is there anyone you trust to be an actual help in there?"

Something surged in Saunders, and she cast her gaze around the dark common area again. "Ged can probably help—"

Jax had closed the distance between them while Saunders had been looking away, and a hand caressing the side of her face, refocused her. Jax seemed to be studying the shape of her face, rather than the shadows that enveloped them. Water drizzled beside them, as if trying desperately to remind them both that there were greater realities looming. But it seemed like a distant thought.

Saunders turned into the space between them, while not wanting to push Jax away with the display. But Jax leaned in. A swell of emotion coursed through Saunders as the mechanic kissed her. It was the calming moment she needed; the comfort she didn't know she sought. And then it was too much. She wanted to break, to crumble where she stood, held up only by the lanky form of Jax the Mechanical Engineer.

As if sensing the precipice, Jax let go and stepped back, searching for the person Saunders had promised would help. Saunders faltered, then drew a heavy breath. She needed to regain her footing. Right on cue, another stream of water broke free of whatever barrier had held it and dripped between them.

"Careful Jax, you'll get us all wet," Saunders muttered.

The mechanic froze, minutely, in her search for Ged, and looked back at Saunders in what appeared to be alarm.

"Are you fucking *kidding* me right now?" Jax whispered, her brow narrowing slightly in disbelief.

Saunders smirked, feeling a bit steadier already. "Come on, I'll introduce you to Ged, he can help you in the core."

Saunders watched as Jax disappeared into the gloom again, with Obah's husband in tow. Behind her, a group had already departed on a search along the ring for survivors, following whatever path Tess had laid out. Another band of residents were scavenging in the nearby berthings, hoisting themselves in from the sideways corridors, or dropping in to the doorways beneath their feet. The corridor cleared, and Saunders found herself not quite alone, but alone enough.

She sank to her knees, head in her hands. This was too close, too familiar. There were already dead bodies, and there would be more. It didn't seem to matter where they were or what might have caused it. There were always violence and destruction in the end, whether intelligent or simply the will of the universe. Saunders raked her hands through her hair and looked across the warped corridor and common area.

A shadow cast by a dim light told her someone else was nearby. There was nothing Saunders wanted less than to have to confront Tess head on, but she needed to maintain some semblance of functionality. So instead, Saunders cautiously tip-toed around the detritus on the wall they used as flooring and maneuvered herself to see who it was. She sucked in a breath of apprehension, then exhaled.

On the other side of a couch dislodged from its bolt pattern during the Drop, sat Rose. She was wrapped in a thin blanket from one of the nearby berthings, staring into the middle distance. In the minimal light cast from an emergency beam, Saunders could see she had been crying.

"Rose?" Saunders asked, gently. The smaller woman started, then relaxed and returned to her pensive act. Saunders hazarded the opportunity to sit next to her, and the researcher did not react.

The silence continued between them, as somewhere, distant in the darkness, the sound of rivulets of water trickling and dripping provided a constant reminder they were not where they should be.

"There would not have been a way to save him," Rose finally spoke, drawing the blanket tighter around her shoulders. Saunders suppressed a spike of adrenaline, wanting to flee these conversations, but she was already here.

"There would have been no way to guard against such an astronomical event," the researcher continued.

From just around the bend, Saunders could make out the rough shape of a body, wrapped partially in another blanket. Collins was too tall to be covered by just a single shroud. She didn't want to inspect the bodies, but she knew it was inevitable. Obah could help—she was a capable nurse with her crew—but she had sustained her own injuries, and Saunders still had the most qualifications.

Still, Rose was right. Nothing would have saved her brother. Not when it seemed like the weight of the entire station had crushed him. Saunders sat in growing dread of who else they would find in such conditions.

"Security," Rose spoke, so softly Saunders was startled to hear it. "It was not a normal series of events that led us here."

Saunders shook her head vehemently at that understatement.

"But we were all experiencing it differently, were we not?"

"I don't know, I only know what I was seeing, what Jax..." Saunders trailed off.

"What did you experience?" Rose pressed, anchoring Saunders with a flat stare.

Saunders shifted uncomfortably. It was hard putting it all in words.

"Well...at first it was just...unnerving. I thought I saw things that weren't there, shadows...My tea—*someone* I recognized just up ahead but out of reach...then it got worse. Bugs, zombie residents, there was a whole thing about the galley on the far side of the station that I just do *not* want to get into," Saunders replied. Then curiosity got the better of her. "What *did* you all see here?"

Rose broke her gaze and focused on the far side of the lopsided space.

"This level certainly had some disturbing imagery. I know many of us simply hid in our quarters to avoid it. It seemed to stay out of the quarters, but I heard awful things, Security; people begging for their *lives.*"

Saunders shuddered. The butcher shop had been a vision, it had to have been. It had disappeared when Saunders held Jax close to pull her from that nightmare. It had disappeared with the achingly familiar contact of the mechanic's warm body grounding her to reality.

"But you didn't see anything?" Saunders ventured, cautiously.

"I did not," Rose replied, with a trail of apprehension.

"What?" Saunders could find no better way to eloquently ask for more information.

"Collins and I have been attached at the hip our entire lives, even once he hit a growth spurt and I did not," Rose replied. "From primary education, through dissertation, we have been two halves of one brain, unable to proceed without the other's input or approval."

Sounded kinda nice, which meant this was heartbreaking.

"So when visions started happening for others' it was as if the opposite occurred for me," Rose continued, glancing forlornly at the body of her brother. "Collins started to disappear. I would see him, then he would vanish. I would chase after him and he would suddenly be somewhere else. It was if the universe was telling me he was no longer to be a part of my life." The researcher's voice wavered.

They sat in silence, Saunders feeling it best to simply let Rose come to her own conclusions.

"I found him, alive, right before the drop. And I thought we were fine then. Clearly, I was mistaken," Rose continued, eventually. "Please understand, we are capable of being entirely self-sufficient adults. It just is different when you have shared every moment of your life with someone from cradle to...grave."

Saunders' heart ached. She had so little left behind on Earth, the closest thing she could think of in comparison had been her TSF team. And now, maybe, Jax.

A crash echoed strangely off the warped walls of the sunken station. Saunders shot to her feet, alert to the noise and its location. Shouts rose in a panic from the ninety-degree bend of the level. Saunders scrabbled at the comms port on her security belt she only just realized she was still wearing, and tried raising Jax on the comms, but the device was dead.

The noise escalated and Saunders was torn between the need to assist and the wrenching desire to have Jax with her. Leaving Rose to her grief, Saunders bolted for Common Access, hurdling over the awkward surface of the wall. She was running away from the problem, and it ate at her with every step, but if there was something falling apart, Jax would be the one to know how to fix it.

The Common Access entry was a dark tunnel beneath her feet. Saunders lay on her stomach and tipped her head and shoulders into the darkness below, angling herself toward

Level 5. Jax would be more than a simple level up. She would be in the core, a space the same distance from the ring of Level 5 as Level 5 was from Level 1. An oppressive distance.

"JAX!" Saunders cried into the darkness. Her voice echoed strangely, but she hoped it would carry. "JAX, COME BACK!" she tried again.

The noise radiated from behind her. Saunders' people needed her. She could not afford the luxury of finding the woman she loved in all this. She scrambled to her feet and sprinted around the corridor, no longer arcing ever upward, but curving constantly to the left.

In what felt like a marathon's worth of time Saunders rounded the corridor enough to see the group who had left to seek survivors. She also saw the sheets of water pouring from the overhead berthings.

"Security, we need to reseal them!"

The berthing door had clearly been pried open in some effort to see who was inside, but as the water rained down, it would be impossible to clamp closed again. The deluge would threaten the station stability, and the concept of being crushed inside this behemoth tin can shot Saunders into action.

"Try to get another point of leverage!" Saunders hollered over the roar of the water. The other residents in the group had tried to break into the various nearby maintenance lockers in search of tools. They had constructed a mountain of objects allowing them to scale the distance from what had been one wall, to what had been the other, across a height of nearly fifteen feet. But the distance was preventing them from gaining any footing to re-seal the door.

Once again, Saunders laid eyes on Tess, who was circling the tower, peering upward at the source of the pouring water as she moved, glancing judgmentally at Saunders every few steps.

"Just sit back and watch like always," Saunders growled to herself, then instantly felt the crush of grief that followed. Tess slunk around the back of the tower as if she had heard.

This was bringing back all the bad memories for Saunders, so instead, she threw herself at the problem.

"We need to move this tower out of the main water stream!" she barked. Several hands were already dismantling the various berthing furnishings, resident possessions and containers, but the added effort caused the tower to topple. The water seemed to increase in flow.

Saunders swiped her soaked hair from her eyes, missing the simplicity of the short cut she had worn through her service, and put her weight behind shoving a large container of what looked like resident personal storage. Pain shot through her shoulder. She slid to the side, shouting through her agony to dissipate the pain.

The water was rising beneath their feet, but not as fast as expected, clearly draining down to somewhere else. But the temperature was dropping, as if the flowing water was also draining any remaining heat with it. Saunders' heavy breath misted in front of her, reflecting in the dim glow of someone's flashlight.

Andoria Tehani surged past where Saunders cradled her injury, to put her muscle into moving the detritus aside so someone else could scale it to reach the leak. It still didn't matter. Any effort to close the gap would only lead to toppling the arrangement, even with Andee using her bulk to anchor it.

Saunders struggled out of the way, tripping on the submerged wall and its many contours. She backpedaled over the edge of a door frame to what could have been the gym, but then she tripped on something not nearly as solid as the metal framework of the station.

She went down hard, nearly spraining her wrist on top of the aching shoulder injury. In the pale light she sought the tangle at her feet and saw limbs. A grey arm had risen from the murky water, bobbing just in sight below the roiling bubbles of the continuous waterfall. Alarm coursed through Saunders and she pushed herself up and away from the corpse, clambering through the water, praying the body wouldn't be wearing Tess' face, or the face of anyone she recognized, for that matter. Whoever it was, they clearly had not made it through the Drop.

Another noise resonated through the pouring water and chaos. A bang echoed again from a panel overhead, roughly three degrees from where they struggled. Saunders watched it in rising horror. With another firm bang the panel burst off, but no water flowed through.

Instead, Jax lowered herself through, held tight as if to contemplate the distance of the drop, then let herself fall to into the knee-deep water below. She landed awkwardly and tumbled to her left, submerging momentarily before scrambling to her feet.

Saunders could hardly recall ever feeling so relieved. It was short lived as the mechanic charged through the water at them.

"What happened?" Jax roared over the noise.

"Sprung a leak, Engineering," Andee barked from where she anchored the makeshift ladder.

Jax waded past Saunders, then twisted to catch sight of her, braced away from the bobbing dead bodies and the impossible task. Jax took two laborious strides toward her and closed a hand around Saunders' forearm.

Saunders used the leverage to pull herself to her feet. Jax didn't say anything, just put a hand on Saunders' shoulder as she pushed past to the edge of the floor panel partially submerged in the water.

The mechanic jammed her fist into the tool belt she always wore and pulled out the same large screwdriver she had produced down on Level 1. Jax rammed the flat head of the screwdriver into the flooring, denting the panel, but not doing much else.

"Jax?" Saunders managed to shout over the roar of the water and the shouts of the residents.

"Just get them away from the opening up there," Jax shouted back, ramming the screwdriver again. It punctured the flooring, or possibly just penetrated a gap in the panels. Jax pried at the gap, leveraging against the slippery surface below the water pouring into the recess she opened. With another shove the panel swung free.

Saunders stepped back from where Jax worked and waded over to the group of residents, making sure to avoid the floating body as she went.

"Andee, get them down from there, Jax is working on a fix," Saunders called to the welder.

"She better have a plan or we're all about to drown," Andee rumbled and called up to the residents still atop the pile.

Saunders looked back through the curtains of water to see Jax had procured a wrench, that, while not nearly as formidable as the absurd one she had been swinging around the day prior, was still decently sized. Jax jammed the wrench into the recess she had opened and pushed her weight forward to turn it.

Over her shoulder she heard a shout from the residents who were still perched above the water line on the pile of items.

"Looks like it's closing!"

Saunders and waded back over to Jax. The mechanic was grunting with the effort of cranking the gears controlling the door mechanism.

"Jax, what can I do?" She realized after the fact that it was a useless question. The mechanic wore a resolute look, and a grimace that only betrayed the effort of turning the unpowered mechanism.

"Just—need to—turn the—gears!" Jax grunted. She shifted the wrench from where it was to a new location for more leverage.

Saunders looked back over at the gap where the water poured. It was a distinctly smaller opening now, and the water was streaming through in an aggressive spurt as it forced through the smaller space.

Jax growled out a strained noise. Saunders turned back to her to see her struggling to crank the wrench against the pressure build-up of the water. The mechanic's boots were slipping in the swirling water below and the mounting pressure was turning the wrench back against her. Saunders pushed her shoulder into Jax's back as she struggled to regain control of the wrench.

"Get that...massive chick...over here," Jax grunted.

Saunders had already tangled herself trying to help the mechanic without hurting either of them but she extricated herself enough to call over to Andee.

"Andoria! get over here!"

Loud splashing announced the arrival of the welder, who assessed the situation in a glance and shifted to grab the wrench. She put her weight into pulling it as Jax reset her stance and pushed. The three of them strained and a shout from the corridor told Saunders it was working.

The berthing door closed, Jax gave the wrench an added shove to ensure it was sealed tight. From what Saunders could tell, the whole bank of resident quarters was probably flooded. Splashing from around the curve of the corridor told Saunders the other residents were coming to see what had happened.

"You only get to call me that in an emergency, Security, and you only get *one* emergency," Andee growled from Saunders' shoulder.

"Sorry Andee, knew it would get your attention though," Saunders huffed.

"Bergan! No!" Obah wailed from somewhere to the right of them all.

Saunders craned her neck around Andee's bulk to see what the older woman was responding to. Somehow Ged had also managed to join them, and regrouped with his wife who had limped over to examine the surrounding flood waters.

Another body had emerged with the calming of the falling water. But unlike the corpse that Saunders had tripped over, this one was severely damaged. His clothing was torn, and large raw patches of flesh showed through, as if chunks had been snagged and ripped away. The body was cold and bloodless; not a recent death. Obah didn't care about the horrendous state of the victim, as she clutched the body, kneeling in the water.

An arm curled gently at Saunders' back and she turned to see Jax next to her, studying the scene.

"Did you hear me calling you?" Saunders asked softly. Jax didn't respond. She was engrossed in the chaos. Saunders didn't want to focus on it.

"We need to gather everyone up again, make sure we don't mess with anything that could lead to another incident like that." Jax turned to look at Saunders. "I should have gone with them. I could have told them that compartment was flooded."

Gedry Habburn broke free from where his wife was wailing, and approached tentatively, sloshing through the water. It presented Saunders with an opportunity to pour focus into caring for her people. "Ged, I'm so sorry—"

"He was really all we had. Obah isn't going to take this well. Neither will I, for that matter. Bergan was like a son to us..." The man trailed off, clearing his throat to keep his voice from breaking. Saunders felt the absolute crushing reality of his words. Ged adjusted his face and regarded Saunders, this time with concern.

"Security, there weren't...children...on station, right?"

The question was baffling, so much so that Saunders had to process what he had asked her. Next to her, Jax reacted quicker.

"Protocol is that no one travels beyond static gravity until they reach twenty Earth cycles. Why would there be children on Station?" the mechanic sounded incredulous.

Ged's face scrunched and he scrubbed at his beard. He regarded Jax, then shifted back to Saunders, as if Jax had not spoken.

"We...had a tough time, before this drop. Obah was hearing things. Bergan was a comfort in that. I can't believe I am living in this moment. I suppose there's not much else to say other than to provide you what perspective I can. Where can I take my nephew's body?"

Saunders glanced back over at the group surrounding Obah. She needed to get a grip. She didn't have time for the simmering panic she felt building, or the shadows of her past that kept wanting to haunt her. This wasn't the same. This time they knew there was a threat. She knew what could happen and no amount of bureaucratic bullshit would keep her from doing her job effectively.

Ged awaited her reply.

* * *

The residents peeled off from the galley to fill the nearest vacant berthings, verified to be watertight. So few of them were still alive it was hardly a squeeze. Besides, Saunders noted groups joining up to huddle together. It made sense with the dropping cold that seeped through whatever cracks the water could not.

"We'll have to be smart about how to split up efforts tomorrow," Saunders said to Jax. The mechanic was huddled on an overturned island, prized from the floor of the galley. "Who knows who else we'll find, like Bergan. Like Collins." Like Tess.

"Let's hope we know when it is 'tomorrow'," Jax contributed, as she shook a canister near the pale glow of her utility light. Saunders slumped down next to her, trying to divert as much of her attention as possible from Obah, who was crying softly over her nephew in the corner with Ged. There would be time over the next few days where they would need to devise a plan for the deceased. Leaving them festering in stagnant water was not an option.

"What are you...making?" Saunders eyed Jax's activity. They had broken out whatever palatable rations could be eaten without heat or rehydration. No one seemed keen on adding *more* water to their surroundings.

"Here." Jax offered Saunders the canister. Saunders glared at the offering. Jax was not one to play pranks, or, do *anything,* for that matter, to endanger anyone. But Saunders still felt suspicious. Jax rolled her eyes and chugged from the container. Then she held it back out.

Saunders put on a brave face and snagged the canister. She peered inside, but that was pointless. Casting a wary glance back at Jax she took a swig and retched at the taste of cold, gritty coffee. She coughed and sputtered and shoved the drink back at Jax.

"Don't, *ever*, make coffee suggestions to me again," Saunders wheezed out before snorting with laughter. It certainly had snapped her out of the dark mood she had been nursing.

"Didn't think you'd actually like it, but it will probably help," Jax chuckled dryly.

Saunders coughed again to get the bitter taste out of her mouth.

"Why the fuck would *that* help?" Saunders wheezed. "We're all going to bed anyway."

Jax shrugged and sat back against the blocky surface of the dislodged countertop, taking another casual swig of her awful swill. She rubbed absentmindedly at her calf before reaching over gingerly to the hideous bandages on Saunders' shoulder.

"We should probably clean that up, right?"

Saunders looked down at the ragged wound peeking from beneath the gauze. The bleeding had stopped, so the clotting agent had worked, and the cold was numbing every part of her, but the ever-present damp would absolutely bring infection. Level 3 was so far away though, and *dark*. And despite the rancid coffee sludge Jax had just fed her, Saunders felt exhaustion in every part of her freezing frame.

"We should, but I don't know if I have the energy," Saunders admitted, shivering in the freezing, damp air.

Jax huffed out a laugh full of mist, as if she understood, but then slid from her seat and stretched. Saunders watched her closely.

"Come on." Jax held out a hand. "I have a first aid kit in my quarters. It's closer than yours. And warmer."

Saunders looked at the hand and wondered if she had ever truly believed the mechanic would have made her such an offer. She let Jax pull her gently from her seat and lead her, around the corridor, down into the abyssal tunnel that was once a stairwell, and along to the opening in the surface beneath their feet that was the entrance to Jax's buried quarters. Tess didn't follow, and Saunders felt relief despite their mounting dread.

Jax lowered herself into her room from the lip of the doorframe and made a space for Saunders to follow. She saw one of the wall lockers had dislodged to create a platform for them to climb down from. The quarters were as dark as anywhere else on the dead station, but it was clear Jax had already been in them since they had awakened on Level 1. Her bedding was pulled from the tossed bunk, and laid out on the new floor. The entire room looked ravaged, and Saunders had a passing curiosity as to how different it would have looked had they not fallen through a rip in space only to emerge under unknown fathoms of water.

"You're going to have to walk me through this again." Jax emerged from a crooked locker with a first aid kit that looked like it hadn't been field inspected in over a decade.

Saunders shivered as Jax put the finishing touches on the new bandage.

"You said it was warmer here?" she wheezed, wrapping her arms around herself.

Jax shifted backward on an overturned chair and shrugged out of her soaked coveralls. Saunders froze in place, though not from the temperature.

"Well, first of all, you need to get out of the gross clothes. Sitting in them is not gonna help," Jax countered. She was already stripped down to her underwear, and she crawled across the haphazard bedding with its tangled nest of blankets.

Saunders watched as Jax pulled several blankets over her shoulders and then held them back, indicating a space for her to join. And then it made sense. Saunders fumbled out of her wet clothes as fast as the numbness in her fingertips would let her and sank down under the blankets Jax offered. The mechanic pulled her close and the flush of body heat against her back made Saunders feel the first moment of comfort in what seemed like eternity.

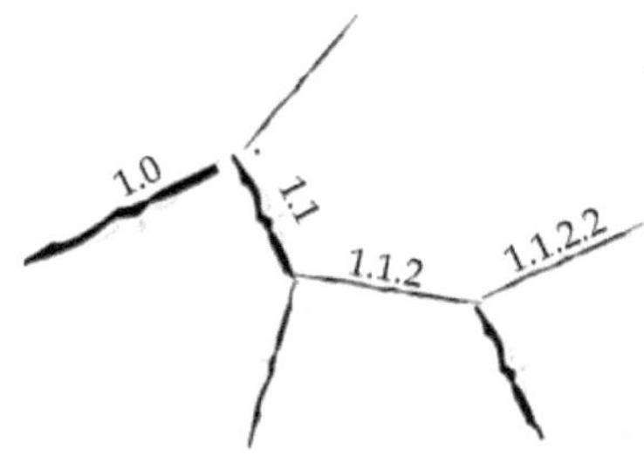

1.1.2.2

The first thing Jax noticed when she awoke was the cold emptiness. The window to her berthing looked out on the closest route to the core and the unforgiving void of deep space, but that was a common sight; it had once even been comforting to Jax.

But the emptiness was behind her. She had sworn she had felt the warmth of another body at her back all night. It had been foreign, but the most welcome feeling in the universe. Now, as Jax turned in her tangle of blankets, she found herself alone in her berthing, devoid of Saunders' company.

A twisting knot of unease flooded her, filling with thoughts that Saunders had run out on her the same way Jax had once run out on Saunders. It would be a karmic full circle, but twice as brutal given their new fate. Jax furtively scanned the cramped interior of the bunk space and her eyes landed on the large grey duffle bag bearing Saunders' former military rank and unit details. The panic ebbed. If Saunders had walked out on her she wouldn't have left her bag behind. She had just woken up early and left Jax to sleep.

Jax stretched tired limbs and lay back to stare at the curved ceiling overhead. Her thoughts drifted backward, reliving the feeling of her hips being pushed firmly into the thin mattress beneath her under Saunders' insistent grind. She felt the ache of bitten bruises on her shoulder and the lingering memory of sweat and burning need.

They hadn't talked about it. They probably should have. But at the moment, Jax mostly wanted Saunders back in her arms to pick up where they had both left off, before passing out from exhaustion.

As if hearing her thoughts, the door rolled back with a hiss and Jax dragged the blankets over her to shield against the intrusion.

Saunders stood in the door frame, sweaty and gleaming in an entirely appealing way, clearly having enough energy to spare for a workout.

"Good, you're awake." Her tone didn't indicate she had returned to relive their night before. It spoke of business. Saunders reached out and flicked the light switch throwing the state of Jax's quarters into uncaring glare. Jax hissed and drew the covers over her face.

"Why is the *light* on?"

Saunders strode into the small room and rummaged in her duffle on the floor.

"Something tells me that if this light was on more your rack wouldn't look this way," she replied.

Jax instinctively crossed her arms over her chest, uncovering her face to the searingly bright light.

"What's wrong with my rack?" she asked, tentatively.

Saunders stood up and leaned over the bunk, arms on either side of Jax's head.

"I meant your quarters. It's a mess." She leaned down and kissed Jax, chasing away some of the apprehension that had bloomed in Jax awakening to Saunders' absence. Before it could turn to more, the shorter woman rose and crossed the room toward the lavatory to turn the shower on.

"I might have to clean up around here if I'm moving in," she stated, popping her head out to eye Jax where she still lay.

Jax had been watching the other woman move, but her brain seemed to have short circuited.

"Moving in..." she repeated, quietly to herself. But not quietly enough.

"I can always stay down on Level 4 instead." Saunders' voice wafted from the lavatory like steam.

"No!" Jax barked, jolting upright. Saunders poked her head out one more time, and gave Jax a small, glinting smile, with a wink.

"Figured." Then the short blond disappeared into the shower.

Jax laboriously dragged herself to the edge of the bunk to rest her feet on the floor and rake her hands through the mane of hair down the center of her head. She scrubbed at her face, kneaded at her eyes, and willed herself to wake. She scanned the immediate area and noted the piles of dirty laundry, the greasy tools, and the detritus from her only plant, Ralph. She would need at least three cups of coffee to handle this mess, never mind what horrors awaited them below on a Station of free roaming residents at the end of the universe.

"Are you always this energetic in the morning?" Jax called, her voice scratchy.

Saunders poked her head out from the condensed wash station.

"If you let me stick around, you'll find out."

Jax held her eyes for a moment, her own brooding dark against this vibrant, green spark.

"Fine, you can try your hand at interior decorating. Just...no throw pillows," Jax growled, finally rising herself from the bedding to seek her own personal effects.

The water shut off. Saunders emerged from the cramped lavatory drying her hair and wearing distractingly little else. Jax swallowed hard, and craned her neck to look at the withering leaves of Ralph.

"You were up...early," she stammered, and glanced back at Saunders, making sure to avert her eyes from anything but the glinting green looking back at her.

Saunders smirked, dropped the towel and stepped closer, pressing the whole length of her short, muscular, naked body against Jax's own bare skin. She stretched upward until her lips ghosted as close to Jax as she could reach without Jax bending down to close the distance.

"You'll just have to work harder at wearing me out if you want me to stay in bed longer," she whispered.

Jax felt her breath hitch and some uncontrollable force drew her face closer to Saunders. The shorter woman lunged, gave a quick, chaste kiss and backed away to rummage in her duffel.

"Later though. We need to get moving."

Jax exhaled forcefully and started hunting for her own coveralls.

"So, uh, did they...find anyone? While we were, uh, asleep?" Jax asked, tentatively.

"Excellent change of topic, Jax. But, no, thank fuck," Saunders muttered, with a sigh. She pulled her head through a t-shirt and turned to look at Jax again.

"I did manage to get Zick's team to move Koty's body to your morgue downstairs through. We should probably put up some warnings or something in case people start wandering in there..."

Jax wanted to retort about how no one should be wandering anywhere, but it seemed irrelevant in the grand scheme of things.

"I meant to put some oxygen masks out front, but honestly, whatever keeps them out is preferable," she conceded. Saunders nodded, as if in thought and returned to dressing herself.

Jax intended to stick to her hidden routes and avoid people, but five steps past Common Access and she found her path once again blocked by Andee.

"What are you *doing* up here?" Jax hissed.

"Eave brought me up here?" Andee replied, as if it were an obvious answer. Jax wanted to snarl that the navigator had no business inviting strangers up to Level 5, but then she realized it meant the navigator herself was up here. Sure enough, there sat the prickly bitch, posted at a console like she owned the place. Jax huffed with indignance.

"I mean, mostly I came looking for Security," Andee replied with a sigh from over Jax's shoulder where she seethed at the windows into Power and Life Support. Jax snapped her head around and glared at the behemoth welder.

"Saunders is still getting dressed. How did *you* know she was up here and not down on Level 1?" Jax appraised the welder where she stood, benignly observing Eave through the windows as well. Andee heaved another heavy sigh and cast a glance down at Jax.

"I didn't know. You just told me. You, uh, *also* just told me she's in a state of undress... Think you can get her to head down to Four? There's an argument brewing."

With that, Andee strode into Power and Life Support like it wasn't the most secure control center on the entire Station, leaving Jax seething at her own stupidity in the door frame, ears burning with embarrassment.

"What did I miss?" came Saunders' voice from Jax's shoulder. Jax jumped at the sound and looked down at the Security Officer as she strode up, wearing a trim-fitting pullover sweatshirt that said "Security" down the sleeve. Jax took a miniscule step back to put some discrete distance between them and glared back at the two figures inside Power and Life Support. Andee turned and waved with a grin, dispelling any possible chance that she didn't know exactly what Jax and Saunders had been up to all night.

"Nothing, just, that welder said there's an argument down on Level 4," Jax replied.

"Wait, what?" Saunders was already striding across the corridor to the stairwell. Jax shuffled quickly after her.

The argument had spilled from the Berthing level into Common Access.

"I'm saying, I can solve the food situation if given the time and resources, you can't just make demands like this, Rogle!" a very weary sounding, strained voice was stating.

"And *I'm* saying this kumbaya shit it just going to get us killed. That lady said her inventory of food stores is only going to last us three years. Less if we're stupid. More if only a select few of us are *particularly stupid!*" came an aggravatingly familiar snarl.

"Then why aren't you going to help us get a renewable resource up and running—"

"*You're* the biodiversity doctor, *you* figure it out without fucking with the little bit of lifeline we have out here!"

As Jax followed Saunders down and around the corner, Zick came into view. He glared at the two of them as they approached. Another man, this one long, lanky and pale, with thinning sandy hair going a steady mix of grey and a pair of wire rimmed glasses stood opposite, looking aggravated and uncomfortable.

"Rogle, Bezley, what seems to be the issue—"

"Can it, Security. You already pulled a fast one on us getting Zarro and Torren to move Koty's body this morning. I'm not in the mood for your inputs," Zick spat, and he strode off down to the levels below.

Saunders watched him leave, then glanced up at the other man. He sighed.

"I was simply suggesting that he review his settler's supplies for resources with the potential to germinate. I can work with some of the common packaged rehydratables if we can set up a viable grow station—"

"What are you talking about, Dorian? Why does this matter?" Saunders interrupted.

The man, Dorian Bezley, turned his impatience on Saunders.

"Obah ran an inventory last night. Even with several of the storage bays on Level 2 locked down, we estimate we only have supplies on station to last us three years before we starve." The man then turned his scrutiny on Jax, who returned it in kind.

"Engineering, I assume our water recycling and air scrubbers would outlast that?"

Jax studied the man. He seemed prickly. She appreciated it.

"Sure, they only need refurbishment every ten years or so," she remarked, avoiding the detail that she herself had seen it done twice in her tenure on Station.

Bezley turned his attention back to Saunders.

"If we're as stranded as it sounds, I certainly am not interested in finding out what happens when we run out of food. I have some skills, but I'm not magic," he said, his voice silky and impatient.

Saunders nodded in thought.

"Theres a defunct biofiltration room upstairs," Jax mentioned offhandedly, before she herself realized it. The man swung his face around to look at her again, pushing his glasses up as they slipped down his nose.

"That is news. I thought I heard mention of such. You say it is defunct?"

Jax shrugged uneasily. She didn't want more people upstairs.

"Nothing survived living in there, is what I meant. Nothing except...well..."

"Well?" Bezley pressed. But Jax didn't want to reply.

"Jax, isn't that where that plant of yours came from?" Saunders piped up, inconveniently.

"Yes..." Jax replied through tight lips.

"Well, could someone please grant me access to this...facility? If we all want to last longer than three years, I'd sure like to have the best of what's available." Bezley looked impatient that such an offer had not already been made.

Saunders pinned Jax with a stare.

"I *need* to go inspect the engines, that is *critical*," Jax growled.

A huff of frustration from the shorter woman and Saunders piped up.

"I'll show you, Dorian."

The man nodded curtly. Jax opened her mouth to object, but the Security Officer was already leading him off to remove yet another layer of Jax's security up on Level 5.

Conveniently, Andee chose this moment to stroll down the stairs and toward Jax.

"Did I miss anything fun?" the welder chuckled, glancing over her shoulder at the receding pair.

Jax glowered, ignoring the massive form of Andee, and stomping past the entrance to Level 4.

Of course, Andee followed.

"I was wondering how these things worked," the welder said as Jax seethed in her work boots the whole way down. "I hear we only have a few years left to live, are they gonna make it that long?"

Jax glared up at Andee as she punched the codes to draw the engine inside its own airlock for maintenance.

"These engines run off a solid-state fuel reserve that reacts with the scrubbed carbon dioxide from the air filters to generate ionizable gas," she stated. Andee whistled through her teeth.

"Ah, gotcha. Well, no need to dumb it down for someone like me," she replied, and dropped herself on the sidelines to let her legs dangle into the engine well.

The engine rose up on its own rail support system, the void of space closed off via a port door frame. Jax was already wandering the base of it, scrutinizing any discoloration or unaccountable markings.

"That just means they don't need frequent refueling. But don't worry, there's extra fuel caches stashed externally. Plenty to keep us spinning for far longer than three years," Jax replied, letting her focus on the machinery distract her. Instead, she felt herself wavering. What would happen after three years? A Station spinning, full of corpses.

"This looks fascinating," came a voice from the opposite side of the engine well, pulling Jax from her spiraling nightmare into a bleak future. She startled.

"Hey Ged, Engineering is just explaining some rocket science to me, right?" Andee chirped from her perch.

Jax glanced up at the work boots of Gedry, standing next to the short form of Rose, the researcher.

"We just returned from assessing the rosters of our respective teams," Rose provided, though no one had asked. Jax squinted up at them, wondering if they were on the verge of asking anything particularly relevant to her, or whether they were just there to encroach on her time alone with the engines. And apparently Andee.

Gedry smiled back down at her in return and then, horrifyingly, dropped himself down into the engine well alongside Jax, who felt scandalized at the proximity to her precious hardware.

"These are certainly an older tech." Ged was examining the engine Jax had retrieved.

Jax wanted to argue, but the older man had crouched and prodded at a few spots Jax had only glanced at.

"You had several engine failures prior to that Drop, were you worried they had taken further damage after an ordeal like that?"

Caught in the opportunity to talk technically about her work, Jax found herself placing the scandal aside and kneeling next to the older man.

"I need to assess their ability to withstand extended use," Jax replied. Ged shifted around to the back half of the engine.

"Are these able to gimbal?" he asked from under a mass of wires and fuel feed lines.

"That would be convenient," Rose piped up from where she still stood at the edge of the engine well. Jax glanced up and saw her, face haloed in the frame of the nearest window at her back. Jax stood, lost for a second in the sight that seemed to tell her she was looking at one of the answers to the universe. The moment passed.

"...No, they're installed in predetermined locations. We wouldn't have a need to gimbal them. They can counter rotate though..." Jax trailed off.

A massive thud resonated within the engine chamber, setting Jax's teeth on edge. From the opposite side of corridor Andee had decided to drop down into the well with them both, and landed with all the grace of a falling stone.

Jax glared back at her, but the welder was already examining the engine construction up close.

"EB weld, common schedule," Andee murmured to herself.

Jax ignored her and crossed around to where Ged was still looking at the interface. The rail system was piston driven, hydraulic load bearing, and robust enough to handle the weight of the engines at top rotational speed, with margin. It was a solid mechanism.

"Why would you say it's convenient if they gimballed?" Jax squinted up at Rose, allowing curiosity to get the better of her.

The researcher shrugged and instead of answering, she turned about to glance out of the porthole at the arcing unfamiliar pin pricks of light.

"There are a lot of stars out there," she stated, her voice ringing clearly over the lip of the engine well. Jax could hardly see the top of her head from her place crouched at the bottom. She rolled her eyes. She didn't particularly have time or interest in an academic grandstanding.

"My team was conjecturing about the viability of a parcel of space like this. We have no idea what is out there. It could be anything, or nothing. But a chance as this, to explore, so far from anything any human has ever seen. It is exhilarating," Rose continued.

"Not to burst your bubble Dr. Jahar, but that sounds terrifying," Andee rumbled from where she leaned against the inner wall of the engine well.

Jax also thought it was terrifying. Just not nearly as scary as the sheer number of residents crowding her very own personal space. Sure, she'd love for them to explore. Mostly somewhere that wasn't her engine well.

But the idea of distant travel was, strangely, comforting.

Now Jax was also studying the mechanism of her engines. A six-bolt star pattern interface secured the rail system frame mechanism to the engine itself, with the necessary hydraulics then converting to the four-bar system that would engage to invert the engine. There were less connections than she would have assumed, though. Looking at the interface it looked plenty robust enough.

If she were to, say, clock the six-bolt pattern, just one or two bolt holes counterclockwise, it would vector the engine in a way that would disrupt the Station's flat spin. Then they would be rotating on more than one axis, which would be bad for all on board.

But if Jax were to do the same on numerous engines, say one every thirty degrees, so they were equidistantly spaced, they might instead impart a total vectored force on top of their (albeit reduced) rotation ability.

"They could rotate," Jax said softly, as if to herself.

Of course, Gedry heard.

"I think you're right, Engineering!"

"Why would we *do* that?" Andee asked. Her legs were long enough that her workboots stuck out into where Jax was still crouched.

Rose returned from her pilgrimage to the windows.

"We could go somewhere," she said brightly.

Jax snapped her attention to the pint-sized doctorate. Somewhere along the ring there was a contingency of Space Marines calling out into the void on radios that would never reach any human ears. There was nothing out there coming for them, not by a long shot. And Rose was looking right back at her, amber eyes piercing and intent.

"Uh, go where? We slipped through a crack in hell, it's not like there's something out there for us anymore," Andee shot back.

But Rose was grinning. Jax felt a surge in her chest.

"There is opportunity out there," Rose replied.

Ged had stood up to come to Jax's shoulder and look up at the short woman.

"Alright, well, that's cool and all, but I mostly followed Engineering down here to try to get a look at that tug up on Level 2." Andee grunted as she hoisted herself back to her feet. She eased herself around the edge of the engine where it sat and sidled up alongside Jax who watched her approach out of the corner of her eye. Rose beamed down at the three of them.

Where Jax stood now, her line of sight came even with Andee's shoulder. Gedry fell some height shorter than Jax. It was tight quarters, and Jax was done sharing her personal space with anyone but Saunders. She grabbed the edge of the engine well and hoisted herself out to stand face to face with Rose Jahar. The researcher took advantage of the closer quarters.

"Come by our lab equipment around the bend if you want to know what I think we have discovered," she whispered conspiratorially.

Jax felt a shock of adrenaline. Lab equipment laid out on Level 1, discoveries on a Station where bodies merged with the walls... She opened her mouth to reply, but the hulking form of the welder pulled herself from the engine well in Jax's wake and the opportunity passed. Rose simply smiled and turned to stroll back down the corridor.

"What do you say, Engineering? Take me for a spin?" Andee rumbled.

Jax scoffed in distaste and glared up at the welder.

"Oh, come on, not like that!" Andee chuckled and jabbed an elbow at Jax's side

"Ow," Jax huffed.

"You go on ahead, I can put 'er back for you!" Ged called up from where he still stood in the well.

Jax opened her mouth to argue that she wasn't leaving her precious engine with someone she had just met, but then she closed it. There was nothing good to come from hoarding it all anymore. And Ged had proven capable of helping her before. She leveled him with as stern a stare as she could muster.

"Don't let anyone else in there. When you're done, just hit the yellow relatch button on the panel. I'm serious!" Jax barked, as the man gave her a sturdy two-finger salute.

"Ah, yeah, that's it Engineering, let's go!" Andee chuckled, smacking the back of her hand into Jax's sternum, driving the breath from Jax's chest, and striding off toward Common Access.

Jax took a moment to get over being winded, looked longingly over her shoulder at the engine and who she left it with, then she tailed after the welder.

The tug hanger was, of course, entirely in disarray. It was, however, devoid of anyone unexpected, living or dead. Jax had worried the vanguard of residents left to roam free the night before had infiltrated even the most reserved corners of the Station. But rather it simply looked like the contents had never been strapped down properly.

Andee didn't waste any time getting up close to the hunk of junk stashed in its hanger, and not out in use like most other stations' tugs. She ran hands over the joints, nudged a toe against the scrap metal on the floor, perused the enclosed workstation and ducked her head inside the open docking port.

"Solid starting point, but a definite oxidation on that main connection there," she called out, punctuated by an affectionate kick to the hull.

"Careful, she's an antique," Jax replied instinctually, as if she too hadn't aimed a well-meaning boot at some portion of the tug over the last several years.

"It's not a simple fix," Andee continued, ignoring anything Jax had said, and perusing the area once again, "but I like a good project, especially to keep my mind off of all this bullshit." Andee had come up short in front of Jax, wearing a grin.

Jax waited for more, but the welder just stood there, as if listening for the starting bell that would let her snap into action. Jax contemplated the benefit of a Station of people busy with something other than sex, squabbles, and discovering their dead friends half absorbed into the structural elements. Maybe Saunders was onto something with her efforts to get them all working.

Jax snorted through a brief smirk.

"Ah, there you go, Engineering, you get it!" Andee piped up, clapping a massive shovel of a hand on Jax's shoulder, nearly knocking Jax from her feet.

"Yeah, whatever, give me your access card and I'll code you in," Jax responded gruffly. Andee grinned wider and held the card up between two fingers, just within Jax's reach. Jax growled and snatched it, using her momentum from the motion to take her clear to the nearest panel readout. "What do you do, bench press steel girders before you weld them? That felt like a sledgehammer," Jax called over her aching shoulder as she waited for the access to update.

"Huh? Oh, nah, just runs in the family," Andee replied, already back examining the tug. "I don't get much into those workouts the jarheads and your girl do."

Jax's brain short circuited. She stood, rooted to the spot, hand holding the access card halfway between pulling it from the panel and returning it to Andee.

"My *what?*" Jax managed to choke out in a hoarse whisper.

The card vanished from her loose grip and Andee was studying it beside her before Jax knew what was going on.

"Sorry, I meant Security Officer Saunders," Andee corrected herself, shoving the card back in a pocket, a benign look on her round face. Jax still hadn't moved.

Andee dipped her shoulders down to look Jax in the eye and waved a hand in front of her face to break the thousand-yard stare Jax had adopted.

"You okay, Engineering?"

Jax flinched and stepped back.

"What did you say?"

"What, about Saunders? You guys are a thing, right? I mean, I'd hope so, what with you knowing what state of dress she's in all the time..." Andee replied, sounding incredulous.

Jax put her burning face in her hands and hunched her shoulders before letting her arms relax back down at her sides. She fixed Andee with a narrowed brow and a challenging glare. "Okay, yeah, sure. I think."

"You *think?*"

"Yes! Okay?" Jax snipped, feeling entirely exposed.

Andee just rumbled a laugh and shook her head. "Ah, yeah, I get it. Don't worry Engineering, you're good." Andee went to the hanger door and neglected to illuminate Jax on what exactly she was good at. "I'm gonna go get my weld kit, you staying?"

Jax ran a hand through her mane of hair, tilted her head back to inhale a deep breath of hanger particulate and grime, and blinked upward to the ceiling above as if willing the universe to give her strength. Then she strode right through the hanger door past the welder and into the corridor. Andee chuckled and followed, throwing a heavy arm over Jax's shoulders.

"See, I knew we'd be friends!" Andee rumbled and she strode off, dragging Jax in tow.

"Just, don't do anything stupid in there. That thing might be our last hope," Jax growled in response, extricating herself from the steel beam that was Andee's arm.

"You think?" the welder replied, offhandedly. Jax shrugged. The tug was close range, and had been stashed inside to prevent an imbalance in the Station rotation for nearly half a decade. Nothing about it told her it could play any part in bringing them back to humanity.

"This all sit right with you, Engineering?" Andee asked, breaking through Jax's inner thoughts.

"What, letting people into my space?" Jax replied, genuinely confused.

"Huh? No, though I heard you don't play nice..." Andee chuckled. But the humor was gone from her tone. "Nah, I meant the shit happening. People missing like this? I wasn't out here with anyone, but I got to know a few faces...its freaky knowing they just disappeared."

"Who disappeared??" Jax whirled on the welder, a knot of nerves erupting.

Andee glanced down at her. "Nah, no one I know. Just saying, is all. Did you hear that one guy was found half coming out of the wall? Haven't found anyone else like that yet, right?"

Jax swallowed hard.

"Yeah. Yeah, I heard. No one else like that who we've found yet..." she trailed off.

"I mean, it's not like they're alive anymore, right?" Andee responded, swinging her arm to tap against the wall panels as she passed them.

"Who?"

"The people missing. They're dead right? It's not like they're all hiding out somewhere alive, right?"

There wasn't an answer to that, but Jax didn't want to think about it. Andee was probably right, and they were just waiting to find the remains of anyone who might still be missing. Something had happened to them all when they had Dropped. Or it was still happening. Jax shuddered at the thought there might still be more gruesome finds in their future.

Jax split from the welder near Common Access. Andee parted with a sledgehammer fist bump to Jax's shoulder and then strode off toward some goal of hers up on Level 4. Jax took the moment of solitude to return to the storage locker around the bend.

Her relief in being alone only lasted as long as it took her to realize she was standing in front of several bodies. The locker was frigid, and the air was already thin. Four lumps lay, covered by Kevlar tarps. A pile of disposable oxygen masks had made their way to the corner without Jax's assistance. She pulled one on and crossed the small space to the smallest lump. Steeling herself against the gory sight she planned on observing, Jax pulled the covering back to show the severed midsection of Avery.

She didn't want to have to look at this. She didn't need to see the cross-sectional carnage of the man's ribcage and innards. But Jax needed to understand how a human body could intersect so completely with the metal panels of the Station. She crouched closer, holding her breath, even if the ox mask would cover up the smell.

But Jax wasn't a medical expert. The closest they probably had was Saunders, and there wasn't a need to bring her into this. Jax just needed to understand.

The ragged edge of the man's body gave no clues. It simply looked like he had been torn in half. The feeling of bile rising in Jax's throat cut her observation short. She covered Avery again and dragged herself from the chilling confines of the locker. Back in the corridor, Jax sealed the locker behind her and paused. There *were* going to be more bodies. Andee was right. There was no hidden section of the Station full of survivors.

Jax strode over to the wall panel and jammed an elbow into a recessed nook to pop out a hidden control console. Jax had already altered the storage climate controls. Most of the food and medical supplies were dehydrated, it should be clear that this housed something other than supplies. But Jax wanted to be crystal clear about what they were dealing with. She typed in a text command that would display on the screen, deterring any nefarious residents from thinking the storage locker held food:

"Morgue."

The other half of this puzzle would be downstairs on Level 1. If Avery's body wouldn't tell her anything, then Jax needed to look at the wall panel again.

The engine well was closed by the time Jax returned to the first level. She could only hope that Gedry had taken the right steps to close it properly. Jax felt the urge to check herself, but knew if she lingered it would only draw more attention. She skirted past the door to the Security Office that was packed with the Space Marine squad and their hopeless attempts at communicating with the void.

Around the back half of the ring, Jax slunk up toward the patch of wall where Avery had been found. It wasn't hard to locate. A t-shirt with some stylized creature posing aggressively above a banner indicated a shrine had been placed in recognition of a fellow fallen soldier. As Jax got closer she could see someone had used marker or paint to etch an epitaph in the wall panel of her Station.

"To Avery, who fell in the plunge."

"Great, now I need to worry about graffiti around here," Jax grumbled. She crouched by the wall panel. It had been cleaned in the last day. She was sure if she had the right lighting she could see the bloody residue, but to the naked eye, it as was if Avery had never been here at all.

Jax was struck by the horrifically tempting thought that if she punctured the metal panel it might bleed. Her Station had done so well keeping her all these years, and vice versa. And now it had tasted blood.

"What *happened* to us?" Jax heard herself whisper. What absurd anomaly had they encountered out in the middle of nowhere?

"It was strange, was it not?" came a voice, causing Jax to jump.

"*Fuck*!" Jax swore, and spun on the spot, her heart racing. Rose had materialized from around the curve of the corridor.

"Sorry, no, I am not particularly interested," Rose replied, serenely.

Jax shook her head to clear it and glared at the researcher.

"No, I mean...don't sneak up on people like that!" Jax growled. She glanced back at the wall panel and stepped away.

"My apologies Engineering, I did not expect to startle you. I assumed you had returned to seek my consultation?" Rose glanced up at Jax, her eyes calculating.

"About what the hell kind of deep-space anomaly we encountered?" Jax replied before she could stop herself. She wasn't particularly interested in getting schooled by a perma-academic elite.

Rose's expression shifted from one of ruthless calculation, to one of fleeting insecurity. But it was gone in an instant.

"On the contrary, Engineering, I had possibly hoped to discuss that matter with *you*."

Jax rose from her crouch, to tower over the resident, who regarded Jax in return with an almost defiant expression.

"What in hell would you expect out of me? It's not like...whatever that was...a rift? A rip? Never saw one of those before..." Jax trailed off.

Rose contemplated the answer, then angled herself off down the corridor, indicating Jax should follow. There was little else for Jax to do.

"One such as myself possibly spends their lifetime hoping to witness true secrets of the universe unfold," Rose contemplated as she led Jax around the ring of her own Station.

"You think that was a secret of the universe?" Jax was uncertain where the researcher was going with this.

"Are you telling me that is a frequent feature of your station's location in space? A wormhole of sorts?" Rose sounded genuinely curious.

"Not a wormhole," Jax practically replied to herself. It couldn't have been. She had been through wormholes, natural and artificial. They had known ingress and egress coordinates. This had been different. "Perhaps a fold of dark matter, over stressed? A relic of a black hole we never thought to consider? Or something altogether unknown?" All thoughts that Jax had fought to expel from her half waking brain in the early hours as she lay beneath Saunders' solid sleeping form.

Rose was studying her. The researcher regarded Jax where she slunk alongside her, and Jax felt the scrutiny burn the tips of her ears.

"Do you think there may have been any...intelligence in this event, Engineering?"

The question sent an uncomfortable shiver down Jax's spine.

"No...not intelligent," Jax replied slowly, eyeing the researcher from her peripheral. Rose seemed to be taking detailed mental notes of every aspect of this exchange.

"Random?"

"Very."

Jax turned herself sideways to study the short woman in return, their meandering paused.

"Chaotic. Like most things in nature," Rose stated.

"Why are you asking me this? You're a deep-space researcher, aren't you?"

"Indeed. Aurelia University tenure."

"Yeah? Well, *I'm* just a mechanic," Jax growled, feeling her hackles raise.

Instead of answering, Rose smiled gravely, turned and continued her stroll. Jax's pure curiosity dragged her from her discomfort and bid her to follow.

"I would postulate," Rose continued as she walked, "that any infinite number of outcomes could have been generated from our passage. That transportation was only one possible option."

"So, what, we rolled the dice and fate picked this hellscape for us?" Jax snorted, letting her long legs close the gap between them so she was once again not being led around the corridor of her own Station.

"Oh, I would not be so poetic...it may very well be more than that. It would quite probably require decades of research for us to understand, if only we had the data to study on it."

"Didn't you have equipment running while we were...falling?" Jax asked.

"Our laboratory equipment was not equipped to handle such an event. It was calibrated for a deep-space gravity signature, and did not have an accurate four-dimensional baseline prior to our Drop. That rift was nothing like any event we have ever studied. What we encountered, I don't think there is an academic description for. Something truly anomalous, chaotic, and terrifying. The nature of the universe exposed," Rose stated.

"Now who's being poetic," Jax grumbled.

Rose came to a stop. They had come up short at the foretold lab equipment, splayed out across the corridor of Level 1's back ninety degrees.

"Well, it is no matter. Not in the face of our current fate. Engineering, I believe we should discuss my team's findings."

"Your findings? You were pretty vague." Jax scanned the arranged equipment uneasily. Memories of her distant past were flooding back in, making her neck itch. At least now the hot chick she was sleeping with wasn't planning on stealing her research and blacklisting her career.

Rose sighed as if she could hear Jax's thoughts. And for a terrifying moment Jax felt like maybe she *could*. Like falling through the rip in space-time gave this pintsized academic some absurd superpower. But instead, Rose reached out and adjusted a dial on the nearest instrument.

"Tell me, Jax, what do you know about exo-planets?" Rose asked.

"What, do you mean conversationally, or scientifically?" Jax felt relieved that maybe the space anomalies *weren't* granting superpowers to unassuming post-docs.

Rose glanced up at her. "Let us assume we do not have time to be conversational. Collins?" The incredibly tall, lanky form of a man who had the same face as Rose emerged from behind a portable data display and glanced down at the pair.

"How about you show Engineering what we have found?"

Jax cast her gaze between the pair, nearly dumbstruck.

"You...we haven't *been* here long enough, you *found* something?"

Rose grinned and it was a sharkish, predatory expression. Jax felt flushed with adrenaline, and the mysteries of the rift were instantly forgotten.

"Show me!"

Jax's hands were sweating almost too much for her to thumb the door latch to her quarters. when the door finally rolled back to show Saunders, sitting in the tangle of blankets on their shared bunk, the overflowing surge of information bubbled up from within her.

"Saunders! Saunders I was talking to Rose and Collins and—"

Saunders looked pale. She startled as Jax tore into the small room and Jax backpedaled to regain control of herself. The news died in her throat.

"Saunders? Jillian? What happened?" Jax strode over to the bunk and dropped herself at the foot of it.

Saunders scrubbed at her face, her lap littered with paper printouts and her old tablet.

"That thing has got to be useless, right?" Jax stated absentmindedly.

"It might as well be," Saunders replied. She sighed and dropped her hands back to her lap. "Jax, nothing makes sense!"

Jax blinked, slowly and regarded Saunders across from her.

"Yeah...that's been a running theme lately..."

"No, I mean, I had all the teams run inventory on who is missing, and who should be here. But their lists don't match *my* lists. It's like...there's more people than there should be, but we can't actually tell who is missing?" Saunders looked exhausted.

"What, can't we just round everyone up and see who is just not here?" Jax asked.

Saunders tossed the papers in her lap and glared out the window, before fixing Jax with a withering side eye.

"Jax that's what I'm *saying*. We *tried* that. We still can't tell who is and is not supposed to be here...hell I can't even tell if they are even on this fucking station anymore. *Fuck* what are we even *doing* here?" Saunders tore at her hair again and gave a muffled roar of aggravation into her hands.

Jax let her fingers stretch, tentatively, toward the woman in her bed. She half expected Saunders to shy away from the touch, but instead she leaned into it, grabbing Jax by the wrist and pulled her along as Saunders leaned back. Jax had no choice but to follow, until she rested above Saunders, braced on her forearms on either side of the other woman's head.

Saunders gripped Jax by the front of her coveralls and buried her face in Jax's chest.

"What can I do to help?" Jax asked, her neck craned to see the top of Saunders' head.

"This is a good start," came the muffled response. The hands gripping Jax's clothing started to relax, started to wander.

"Uh," Jax replied, wondering what it was she had come storming in here for. Saunders started to squirm beneath her and the hands had managed to infiltrate the zipper on Jax's coveralls. Lips found the place where her neck met her shoulder and a shiver ran down Jax's spine. She was only just starting to wonder how exactly Saunders could handle the distress they were dealing with when the other woman froze.

Jax glanced down at Saunders.

"What did you come running in here about?" Saunders asked.

Jax lay there, sprawled atop the lithe and muscular form of Saunders in her disheveled bedding, the shoulders of her coveralls already slipping down and her breath already coming in short pants.

"I, uh, I think we found a way out of here."

Saunders' face was impassive for a heartbeat, then she jolted upward, nearly knocking Jax off.

"WHAT?!?"

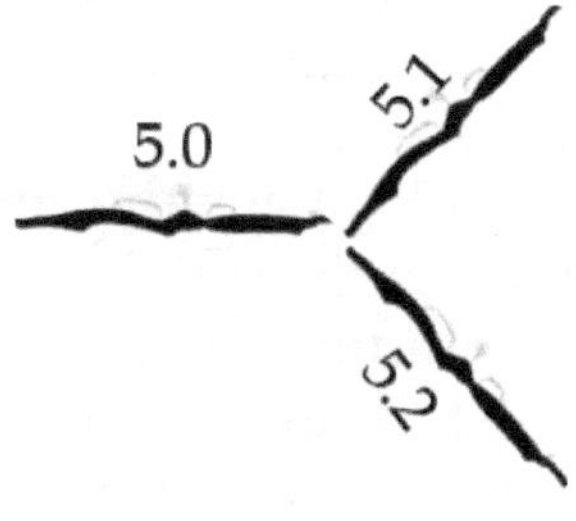

5.2

Something smashed against the station.

Saunders awoke with a jolt to oppressive darkness and damp cold. Jax's quarters were on the side of the station resting on some sea-bed surface, and the single window was pitch black beneath them. Saunders scrambled for a light and found only Jax's utility flashlight. She shone it at the glass, but only saw its reflection.

Again, something smashed into the station. It sounded large, and close by. Being on Level 5 meant the station exterior was just beyond the arcing ceiling panels, but the station skin was thick, designed to withstand the impact of space debris. Something would have to be relentless and massive to make noise reverberate through to the quarters within.

The inches-thick glass of the window shuddered with another impact. Saunders flinched, and scanned the dark glass for any signs of damage.

"Jax!" Saunders hissed.

The Mechanical Engineer was still fast asleep beside her, filling the freezing cold quarters with a warm place Saunders desperately wanted to return to. She scanned the interior of the quarters. The external assault had stopped. Jax had not even reacted. Maybe she had imagined it.

She curled back down under the blankets, pressing her face close to the soft curves of Jax's chest, feeling the heat radiating off of her and hearing her heart beating. Jax was almost feverishly warm, and Saunders wanted to wrap herself in as much of the other woman as she could. Even in sleep, Jax curled her lanky form around Saunders, cocooning her, and driving back the shadows.

But, in spite of the comforting heat of Jax's unconscious embrace Saunders could not fall asleep. Her mind churned, reviewing every moment they had endured.

And Tess. She only showed up when things were *really* bad. Saunders had half suspected it was Tess' shadow she was chasing around the curve of the station as it failed before the Drop. She had seen someone in tactical gear, just ahead of the curve, and she had been unable to catch up to them. For a blissful moment Saunders thought it had just been a hallucination from the core, from the rift, and not the same haunting that stayed with her soul day after day, even all these years later. But there were more than just shadows down here. And this was one shadow Saunders really didn't want to keep with her.

An unbearable weight pressed down on Saunders, making her want to throw the blankets off and seek the freedom of movement beyond, but the chill kept her where she lay.

Bodies. There were bodies of people she was supposed to keep safe. In every path, every route she took, the destination was the same, and it was always her, left to oversee the carnage she alone could escape in cowardice.

Saunders *knew* it wasn't her fault. She *knew* there wasn't something to be done but grieve. But the weight only increased, and her breathing turned rapid and shallow. The distant drip of water turned to a rushing sound in her ears, as if their dark nest would flood at any moment. Saunders clung to the lanky and scorching form of the woman next to her and willed herself to calm.

Another loud noise slammed against their quarters, and this time Jax did wake. The mechanic flailed from the blankets to assess the intrusion just as the hammering came from the half open doorway overhead. Jax shot to her feet and picked her way over to the tipped locker, as Saunders pulled the blankets back around herself, hoping they would maintain the mechanic's warmth.

"Engineering!"

It was Andee's voice.

From somewhere in the darkness there was a thud, followed by a string of expletives as Jax knocked into something painful, and then a small light sparked in the gloom.

"Engineering, I need to talk to you and Security," Andee called again.

Saunders sat up, fully awake with a shrill spike of anxiety.

"Who the fuck are you?" Jax growled up at the opening overhead. "And how the fuck did you know Saunders was in here too?"

Silence.

"I mean, I only had a hunch, but thanks for confirming that, Engineering. Can I come in? It's freaky up here."

Jax shot Saunders a look that was a mix of alarm and frustration. Saunders shrugged out of the blankets to see if she could make eye contact with Andee. The welder's round face peered in from the gloom.

"Yeah Andee, hang on a second, okay?" Saunders called.

Jax was looking at her with a "what the fuck" expression, but Saunders tossed another blanket at her.

"Wrap up, babe, let her in."

Jax looked stunned for a moment, then grumbled "*wrap up babe*" under her breath as she pulled the blanket over her mostly bare form.

"Sure, uh, Andee. Come on in," Jax growled to the woman crouched above them.

The welder lowered herself down easily, and landed just shy of their bedding. She sat down heavily and stuck her wet work boots out, barely avoiding the blankets. She hadn't changed out of the soaked clothes from earlier, but seemed too focused to notice.

"Sorry guys, I didn't want to interrupt the honeymoon or anything—"

"Fucking *what?*" Jax hissed, but Andee ignored her.

" —but I wanted to talk about the tug you have stored on Level 2."

"Sorry, fucking *what??*" Jax repeated, still standing awkwardly under the opening to the corridor above.

Andee glanced up at Jax. "Chill *out* dude, everyone knows you guys have the hots for each other. We're shipwrecked, not fucking blind. This is *important.*"

Saunders wrapped the blanket tighter around herself and pointedly did *not* look at Jax. It was not a convenient time for them to all discuss how much Saunders had spent the last however many months on station telling every passing resident her unrequited love story. It had been entertaining for them. Now it might be a *slight* bit awkward.

Jax landed heavily on her knees next to Saunders on the mattress.

"No, not that, goddammit—okay we can get back to that later —-but what the fuck did you say about the tug? How did you know that was on Level 2?" the mechanic hissed.

"That psycho Paul Hower was muttering about it, *before* he got stab-happy. He must've seen it when he dropped off the stores he had saved down there," Andee shrugged. "And I saw the Level 2 hanger door when I docked with this place a few weeks ago."

"And that means we have some scrap-metal space tug stashed there?" Jax barked incredulously.

Saunders peered at Jax. The station *should* have a tug, but when Saunders had arrived, there had not been one in sight, nor had WSTN Station Management thought it critical enough to reply to her inquiries. She had only noticed its presence on Level 2 as part of her past manifest reviews, after her only coworker had gruffly informed her that it was "out of commission."

"Eave told me each station has one, and that they tend to stash it for maintenance so it doesn't screw up the rotation," Andee replied, as if this solved the whole matter.

"Who is—you know what, nevermind," Jax waved her hand between them. "Fine, yes it's on Level 2. What does that matter?"

"I want to fix it," Andee replied, simply.

"And what makes you think such a fun little project is a good idea right *now*?" Jax growled.

Andee mostly just cracked a smirk. Saunders could see the connection.

"Can we use it to escape?"

"See, there you go Security, knew it would be best if I had this conversation with the both of you. Sorry for the intrusion on your *personal* time." Andee winked.

Saunders hazarded a look at Jax who looked like she was about to combust.

"That is a hell of a long shot," Jax stated, formidably.

"Do you have any conveniently shorter shots laying around?" Andee asked casually.

"What, exactly, makes you think you can fix it?" Jax countered. "It's been down for half a decade, and I can't get it working. And if I can't get it working, good luck—"

"Can you weld?" Andee grinned confidently.

At this Jax looked taken aback. Saunders studied the lanky woman next to her, then appraised the hulking woman across from her.

"Okay," Jax stated, evenly.

Andee raised an eyebrow.

"Wow, that's it? That's the whole fight? You got it *good* Security," the welder chuckled.

Saunders felt the flush on her face, but knew neither of the other two could see it.

"I *mean*," Jax hissed, "okay, we can go look at it. Tomorrow."

"Hey, it's not like I got anything better going on," Andee replied cheerfully. She hoisted herself to her feet and stretched her muscular arms. "I'll let you guys get back to it then."

"Oh for fuck's *sake*," Jax bemoaned, tossing her head back in agony.

The welder stepped nimbly on the downed locker and launched herself up to grab the ledge of the door frame, then easily hoisted herself up and out of the quarters.

"See you two in whatever passes for 'morning' these days," Andee called down, but her features were already dissolving into the endless cold black above.

Saunders and Jax were once again left alone. Jax groaned and tossed herself face-first into the bedding, taking the blanket with her. Saunders merely looked over her blanket shrouded shoulder at where the other woman lay.

"You had that thing in there the whole time. Why wasn't it operational?"

"Busted docking ring," Jax mumbled into the pillow.

"And *why* didn't Station Management do anything about it?" Saunders pressed.

Silence.

"Because I figured I could teach myself to weld and fix it on my own time," Jax replied to the blankets surrounding them.

"Dammit, Jax," Saunders moaned, and let herself land back down on the bedding next to the other woman.

"I'm not going to be able to get back to sleep." Jax's voice was muffled by the bedding.

Saunders shivered at the recollection of what had been keeping her awake as well, and how she yearned for the deep, dreamless void of sleep. But instead, she simply replied, "me neither."

"Good, then you can explain to me why that welder knew so much about...whatever this is." Jax stuck a finger in the air to wave haphazardly between them.

Saunders felt her ears burn, despite the cold. She needed the bravado, the confidence, whatever she could get to make it through the day ahead of them. And she, too, needed to know exactly what "this" was. But that was a conversation, and Saunders didn't *want* a conversation. And it wasn't as if they weren't already *mostly* undressed.

Saunders pulled the blanket off herself and let the cold air prickle at her skin. She then made the conscious choice to pull off whatever else she was wearing. Jax raised her head at the sound of the motion beside her and her eyes went wide as she registered what was happening.

"Point is, Jax, they already know, so we might as well do something about it."

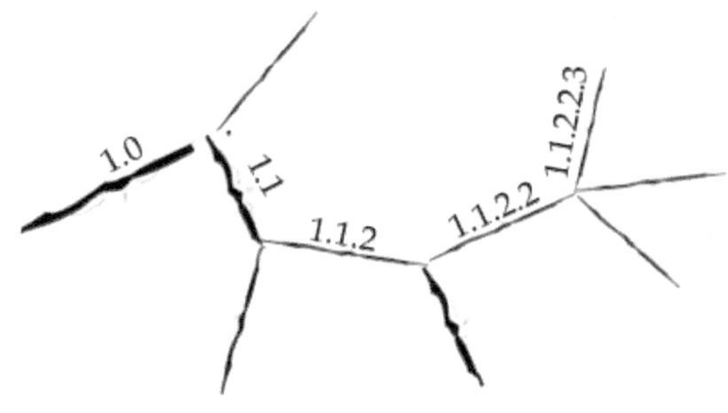

1.1.2.2.3

"Incoming!" Andee bellowed.

Jax jolted and slammed the back of her head into the underside of the engine she was modifying. Next to her, Gedry scrambled from the engine well and up over the side. Jax shook away the stars that swam in her vision and rubbed at the back of her skull to make sure she wasn't bleeding, then grabbed for the lip of the well.

The altercation had already started. Enith took a swing at Andee in an effort to bypass the welder and make it to the engine well, but Andee swatted him off balance and the man tumbled into the doorway of a nearby airlock.

"Is it true?" roared Zick barreling in from behind. Ged barely was able to turn in time to cut off the resident's path.

"Now listen here, Rogle, I have people on this station too, you aren't the only one here with a responsibility!" Ged insisted, hands out to hold off the onslaught.

"You have half the people I do, and you hardly know where any of them are!" Zick barked. "How dare you all make a plan to send us careening off across the stars! Haven't you heard that when you're lost, its best to just stay fucking put??"

Jax hoisted herself up finally, banking on the fact that Andee and Ged formed an adequate barrier between Jax and the prospect of getting her ass handed to her.

"But rescue isn't *coming* here!" Jax growled. Zick glared over Gedry's shoulder.

"How do you fucking know that, huh? Who said you could just make this choice for the rest of us??"

The commotion was drawing a crowd. And for all Jax knew, this was what Zick had planned. A few Space Marines emerged from the nearby Security Office. Some of Rose's team emerged from the curve of the Station corridor.

"Because the next transport was due here two days ago!" Jax spat back.

"What's happening?" asked a Space Marine.

Jax opened her mouth to provide the answer Saunders had coached her through, but Enith interrupted from across the tight space they all crowded in.

"These assholes are rotating the engines, they want to fly us out of here, into *nothing*. Its certain death!"

Jax glared at the man, but the damage was done.

"What the *fuck?*" the Space Marine shouted, and rounded on OS2 Tizik Bracken, who had joined her along with the rest of his crew.

The crowd grew larger. The shouting grew louder.

"Alright calm *DOWN*!" bellowed Saunders' voice from the Common Access Stairwell. She strode through the roiling crowd toward where Jax stood, apprehensively, on the edge of her engine well, lamenting that the wrench she needed was down below and the one she clutched in her greasy claws was just far too small for all this.

"Don't fucking tell me to calm down!" Zick snarled. "How many times do I have to say it, you aren't in charge around here!"

"Then who fucking is? You?" someone intelligent called out.

"I'd be doing a damned better job than this sorry excuse here." Zick jabbed a finger at where Saunders stood. "And I wouldn't be sending us on a fatal fool's errand. You have *no* idea what might possibly be out there for us!"

"But we do!" Rose emerged through the wall of residents who had gathered. "We have several viable targets which we believe are in range!"

Zick looked furious.

"But, that's insane. This is insane, right Tiz?" the Space Marine asked.

"It's better than just sitting here, Corine," Tizik replied.

"So you're just letting them make decisions for us? Where's your fucking spine, Tiz?"

"You can voice your opposition as much as you like, Base Sentinel Boralis, but watch the fucking insubordination!"

"Look, the only decisions being made here are to rotate thirty percent of the engines, and since they are still *my* responsibility, it's no one else's fucking business!" Jax snarled into the group. Saunders shot a hand out to Jax's forearm as if to hold her back.

"No one else's business until you fire them up and send us to our deaths across an alien universe!" Enith crowed.

"Oh come on, these two are too busy screwing each other to care what happens to the rest of us! We're trapped here, but they're having a *great* time!" Corine bellowed over the group, gaining a nod of approval from Zick.

The group fell quiet. Jax felt her face burn, her ears unfathomably hot. She instinctually stepped slightly to the side to put distance between her and Saunders. But the illusion was pointless. Everyone knew where Saunders spent her nights now. And they were even close enough to hear how. They were always going to be a united pair against a growing riot.

"No one is going anywhere," Saunders said evenly into the hushed silence, her face defiant and shameless. "But it's damned time we took some action. OS2 Bracken and his squad have been making comms sweeps for two weeks. The nearest relay point was half a parsec away before the Drop. We would have heard something by now."

Someone barked a nondescript argument, but Saunders carried onward. "If we stay here, we just get to wait until the clock runs out. If we go, it is a massive risk, with infinite outcomes, too many of which could be bad. But Dr. Jahar and her brother have a target in mind. I don't know about all of you, but I'll take even a glimmer of hope over no hope at all."

As far as Jax could tell, this was everyone alive on Station. Now was as good a time as any to be caught. The group was quiet, contemplative; a collection of spacefaring people who had already made their peace with being owned by the interwoven depths of space-time.

"*Fine*," Zick hissed. "Go on your little adventure. But leave that cargo tug here, with me and my crew. Don't drag us into it."

"Now *hold on* a minute asshat, that tug doesn't work yet!" Andee had swung around from where she had been corralling Enith.

"You cannot just drag us into this madness, it's *insane!*" Zick squealed, sounding more frantic as the moments passed.

"Rogle, be reasonable," Ged interjected, earning a glare from the other foreman. "That craft only seats six. You have nearly twenty people. Who were *you* planning on leaving behind?"

At this, Zick looked like he was ready to lash out. Andee strode forward a step, and Jax felt the grip on her tools grow tighter.

"This—this is mutiny!" Zick wailed. His words sounded pathetic, as if he had finally realized this was happening outside his control.

"Are you really letting this happen?" the insubordinate Space Marine asked Tizik again. But Saunders and Tizik Bracken had discussed this. Rose and her brother Collins had walked them through the options. And as Jax glanced around the group, she saw more nods of acceptance and approval than argument.

"Leave Engineering to her work. We have three more day-cycles to rotate the remaining engines. Every moment counts. Theres a long way to go in three years, it's time to move." Saunders announced.

* * *

Jax hated how the helmet of the pressure suit warped her vision of the stars arcing past. Her body maintained the relative momentum it had picked up from being inside the Station, so the stars continued to spin. It was something she was used to inside the Station, but outside it all seemed so much more vast.

"Are you gonna to hurl?" Andee's voice cracked over the comms port in the helmet.

"Just keep an eye on the fucking tether so we can get this over with," Jax growled.

"Hey I offered to go, but that suit wasn't in my size."

Jax pulled herself along the handholds as she navigated the narrow walkway to the nearest fuel reserve. The engines had rotated just fine, but the fuel reserves were proving finicky. Most could be monitored and adjusted from inside, but this one in particular refused to acknowledge the rotated engine was still functional. So now Jax was wandering beyond the walls of her Station, on some ridiculous mission to manually disengage the fail-safes.

Sure, she could have done this later, when they were in need of the surplus fuel. But Jax wanted to know her system was in top functionality. They didn't need any more arguments tearing the resident's resolve apart. They were going to leave this particularly desolate corner of the universe, and Jax was going to make damn sure of it.

"Why are you on my comms anyway, I asked Ged to walk me through this," Jax shot back as she pulled herself toward the fuel cache. A tether was clipped to her harness, and anchored inside the airlock nearest the problem she aimed to fix. An auxiliary redundant tether was clipped into the anchor points along the way as a failsafe.

"He's here, he's just making sure Security is breathing into the paper bag the right way," Andee replied, sounding far too entertained by this fact.

Jax paused on a handhold.

"*What* is Saunders *doing* in there? She was supposed to be on Medical."

"I dunno dude, but she—" The comms crackled.

"Andee?" Jax growled, resuming her path on the Station exterior.

"She wants me to tell you to never dare to leave this station without her knowing ever again?" Andee returned, static interspersing the second-degree threat.

"If she had stayed on Medical she wouldn't have known," Jax grumbled.

"Your mic is hot Engineering."

The fuel cache was within reach, flush to the side of Station and situated just above the outboard rotational sporting its fetching thirty-degree rotation. The narrow walkway would take her most of the way there, but the cache itself would require her to pull herself along on the handholds alone. Jax made a reach for the nearest handhold and missed, slipping off the narrow catwalk and leaving her to dangle into deep space, gripping the railing in her other hand like a lifeline. As the Station continued to rotate Jax would continue to feel the pull of the centripetal force simulating gravity, but this far out from the Station's center, the effect was stronger than normal Earth gravity. She clung to the handhold she still gripped as the Station desperately tried to fling her off.

"Fuck," Jax swore under her breath.

"Secur—" Andee's voice sparked and then faded in what sounded like a scuffle.

"Jax, when was the last time you even *did* something like this?" Saunders sounded downright panicky.

"Probably before you got on Station," Jax replied, having managed to regain her footing.

"Of course it was before I got here, I would remember being this pissed off at you," Saunders replied.

"Hey Ged, it's hard to focus on not drifting into eternity out here, can you give the Security Officer her taser back or something so she can stay otherwise occupied?"

Some loud comms feedback and background chatter on a hot mic ensued and then Ged's calm voice returned.

"Obah is dragging her back up to Medical. Are you there at the fuel cache?"

Jax strained her arm, wishing she maybe did just a little more workout, and hoisted herself again. She managed to latch on this time, and pulled herself over to the boxy containment unit where she could clip and use both hands. The Station still tried to toss her off, but the sturdy harness around her waist, and her boots pressed against the hull allowed her to stay wedged close to the surface.

"Yeah, I'm secure. You have the schematic up?"

"Right, you need to look for the fore and aft manual release markers, they should be red, and along the edge of the cache."

Jax scanned the surface of the Station. It had always been dark on its exterior since it had never orbited any star or planet to feed off its light source. Rather, the Station had utilized a series of bright external beacon lights to notify approaching transports of its location. But the surface had little light to illuminate it. Now they were even further from any source of light. The dull grey of the Station exterior mutely reflected the glow of Jax's helmet headlamp.

She worked by touch, relying on the feedback via comms. The status of her progress could be monitored by Andee on the internal engine maintenance panel, and Ged had the old schematics open. Jax grudgingly admitted there was no way in the universe she could have managed this task alone. Not even with just Saunders' help. *Particularly* without Saunders' help if the Security Officer was having a panic attack just thinking about Jax being free floating.

The only other source of light in this void was the dim glow pouring from the thick portholes of the Station and the light of the open airlock beckoning Jax home after a hard day's task in endless deep space. Neither managed to help illuminate her work, but it kept things from feeling so dark it was hopeless. That and the sound of Andee and Ged bickering good naturedly over the comms.

With the manual release latches activated, Jax was able to slide the fuel cache down into place for immediate refill. Eighteen of the thirty-six engines would run on near constant operation to maximize initial thrust as they kicked off their journey. The other eighteen were still in nominal orientation to maintain Station rotation until it was time to kick over to the new engines and move. It would make gravity a little weird in the corridors, with a slight thirty-degree acceleration in one corner, in addition to the continued rotation which would be slightly lower with the angled engines.

But they would have a constant fuel feed to last them well past the point of no return on their other supplies. And at least they would have tried.

The task done, Jax was eager to get back into the Station and provide the calming relief Saunders desperately seemed to need. She turned to unclasp her harness and head back, but saw a new source of light reflect in her helmet.

Somewhere, just beyond the immediate curve of the Station outer hull, an object floated, illuminated by a source of light too bright to only be a porthole. Jax tried turning to get a better look, but the angle, and the curve of her face mask made details almost impossible to see.

"Engineering, are you on your way back in? Andee can get the tether wound up," Ged's voice crackled over the comms.

"Wait a minute."

"What was that, Engineering?"

Jax punched the comms button to make sure the connection went through. "There's something floating out here, I want to check on it."

"Floating?"

Jax could only slightly register the alarm in the reply through the static of the close proximity comms. But she was already pulling herself over to the next set of handholds and the next engine's fuel cache.

The tether pulled taught. It had only enough give to let her reach the work location she needed, from the nearest airlock. But the object was moving with some slight original velocity vector and if she didn't get closer, it would be gone before she ever knew what it was.

Jax clipped her tether to the Station exterior, and switched to her auxiliary tether. She then released the main connection to swing anchored to only the single point. Only one inhibit: redundancy was gone. But Jax had the freedom of motion to laboriously hopscotch along the handholds to the next engine. All while fighting the Station's attempt to buck free of her.

"What is she doing?" Saunders had clearly broken containment and returned. "Jax? Jax why is your tether off?"

"I thought you were back on Medical with Obah," Jax replied with a huff of exertion. Her arms would be sore from the vice grip she was maintaining on the handholds.

"The hell I am, we finished up just in time for me to see your tether is clipped off, what the fuck are you doing?" Saunders growled into the comms.

Jax clipped the tether midpoint so she could undo the anchor. It wasn't a quick traverse, and her target was getting further way by the minute. She pulled the main anchor around to latch onto another handhold and then repeated the process with the mid-point anchor. She needed to swing herself over the bulk of the next engines fuel cache before she could get a better view.

"Saunders, there's something out here. I need to see what it is before I return," Jax tried to reason.

"The hell you do, there is nothing in this universe worth unclipping from your primary tether for."

Jax swung herself from the engine cache and around to the further handhold, and dragged the auxiliary tether's anchor with her. She clipped in and turned her whole core to ensure her helmet moved and provided the best field of view.

The body floated some thirty meters away from the Station. It had rotated slightly to show the basic form: two arms, two legs, a head. No pressure suit. The light that had illuminated it was gone.

Airlock.

"Saunders," Jax piped over the comms.

"Don't even start with me, you can sleep in the engine well tonight—"

"Saunders shut up and listen to me," Jax hissed urgently. "I need you and Andee to head counterclockwise. Go forty degrees, the small transport airlock, quickly!"

"What? What's going on? We need to get you inside if something is wrong!"

"I'm going to meet you there, just GO! Someone ejected a body out of the airlock!"

Jax swung herself another rung over, dragging the flying end of her tether. She paused at the anchor point she clipped into, near a porthole. She saw Saunders run past then pause and run up to the window and place her hand on the glass. Jax responded in kind before jabbing her thumb urgently in the direction of the airlock. Saunders turned her head, shouted something, and ran. Jax resumed her slow path along the exterior.

There was one airlock between Jax and the one they were targeting. She managed to clip the tether midpoint to the anchor at the doorframe and punch the access button. A low-level vibration could be felt through the handhold as the pumps drew the atmosphere out of the airlock and into the reserves to prevent any loss of oxygen from the system.

With a hiss the airlock rolled open and Jax pulled herself inside, straining with the need to hoist herself against the centripetal force pushing her outward. She braced against the airlock interior and punched the door closure latch.

Jax fidgeted anxiously in her pressure suit in the tight confines of the airlock while she waited for the module to repressurize and turn green for Station access. Saunders was already around the curve of the Station, and no one was answering her comms calls.

"Saunders! I'm in airlock forty-eight, what's going on?"

Silence.

"Saunders!" Jax snarled into the comms pounding a fist on the inner door.

Andee's face appeared in the window and the door indicator turned green. Jax burst through the door as it rolled back, yanking at her helmet and stumbling in the decreased gravity of the Station interior. Her feet were already sprinting down the corridor, carrying her body with them.

"What's going on?" Jax roared as she finally managed to unclip the helmet and pull it off, throwing it behind her in her wake.

"Our favorite people," Andee huffed out as she jogged next to Jax.

They rounded to corner and there Saunders stood, nightstick raised, facing Zick and three other residents. They stood with their backs to the inner airlock door, looking defiant.

"Who was that?" Saunders snarled at the group.

"Don't worry Engineering, they were already dead," Zick replied, ignoring Saunders and addressing Jax as she jogged up.

"'*Don't worry'?*" Saunders repeated jabbing her nightstick closer.

"Easy there, let's not add battery to your other list of issues, miss Space Cop," the guy to Zick's left sneered.

Saunders swished the nightstick down and away.

"It is not *your* call to just send the bodies of our residents out of the airlock!" Saunders growled back at them.

"But it's my crewmate," Zick replied, casually. "And it wasn't your call to send us on this trip, but here we are. You get to alter your station how you see fit. I get to dispose of my people the way I see fit."

Jax was already moving. The pressure suit was bulky and ungainly in the gravity of Level 1, but she wasn't a stranger to wearing one, so she hefted the weight of it around her shoulders and made for Common Access. But the suit was ungainly enough that Saunders gained the lead. Zick passed Jax with a shove that flared an unholy rage within her.

By the time Jax made it up to Level 2, the storage locker had been opened and the select few stood, as if standing vigil to its interior. Jax pushed through, using the bulk of the suit to displace Andee and the left henchman of Zick. Freezing air wafted from the compartment.

Saunders grabbed an oxygen mask and yanked it on as she strode forward into the dark storage space. She pulled back the Kevlar tarps over each corpse. One by one, the frozen faces of former residents appeared. Paul Hower, the butcher of Level 4, Illy Lark, his potential victim, succumbed to madness, half of Avery, Quinn, a woman they had found in her quarters, clearly another victim of Paul. And sure enough, Koty Higgs was missing.

Saunders looked up at Zick with a glare. She proceeded to re-cover each body, careful to ensure they were properly wrapped, and stalked out of the morgue.

"So *that's* how you treat your dead?" Saunders seethed at Zick.

"It's none of your business how I treat my dead," Zick replied, simply.

Saunders wasn't having it.

"Everyone on this station is my responsibility. The moment we start ejecting bodies out of the airlock, without warning, is the moment this place starts to fall apart!" she stepped forward, mere inches from the settler foreman. Jax itched to step into place and push the two back, but even the suit wouldn't protect her from the searing glare Saunders was wearing.

"This place is already falling apart." Zick rolled his eyes. He also took a pointed step back from Saunders' fury. "There's not really a point to keeping him on board."

Zick then turned to the rest of them. "You can check with my team. No one is going to take issue with this. But there's something more to it." He paused, as if for effect. "You all have chosen to leave. And it leaves *my* people with little choice but to join you all. You won't let us stay behind in the tug, so we have left Higgs behind instead. Let his body remain here as a message to anyone who may follow us. We were here. And then, we left."

At this, Zick turned and strode off down the corridor toward Common Access with his friends in tow. This left

Ged, Andee, Saunders and Jax, in her pressure suit, standing near the open morgue.

"So do we need to retrieve the body or something?" Andee broke the silence.

Jax had no idea how they would even begin an operation like that, but it seemed like an absurd waste of resources. Saunders hung her head.

"No. If he wants to eject his dead crew out of the airlock, I suppose we can't really stop him."

"Uh, I sure fucking *can* stop them," Jax growled. "I can pull the airlock system offline entirely. They can't launch people from the airlocks if they can't open the airlocks."

At this Saunders rounded on Jax and grabbed her by the helmet lock ring of the pressure suit that was around her neck.

"What the *fuck* did you think you were doing out there?" Saunders snarled, pulling Jax's face down the inches it took so they were nearly eye level.

"Ow, what? Babe, its *fine,*" Jax hissed, glancing at Andee and Ged, who had busied themselves with vacating the immediate area.

"It's *not* fine," Saunders shot back, and she looked strained. "I'm losing people left and right, I am *not* ready to lose you too."

Jax wanted to launch a rebuttal about how she was perfectly capable of doing exterior work, but Saunders looked ready to snap. So instead Jax put her hands, in the stiff suit gloves, on Saunders' hips and pulled her closer.

"No, you don't—" Saunders protested feebly before she let herself get pulled against the rough exterior of the suit.

"Sorry," Jax mumbled into the soft blond hair.

"Don't *do* that," Saunders groaned into the suit fabric.

"I know. But you won't, Jillian." Jax sighed.

Saunders pulled back sharply to glare at Jax for the moniker but then shifted her expression. She looked exhausted now, and confused.

"I won't what?" she replied, cautious.

"Lose me. I mean," Jax paused, intent on not making promises she could not keep out here in the distant void. "Not if I can help it that is. I love you too much—"

Jax froze, aware her brain was slowly catching up to the words leaving her lips. Saunders' expression was also frozen, as if she hadn't quite been sure what she had heard. Jax swallowed hard and craned her neck down to see past the hard metal ring of the pressure suit that Saunders still gripped.

Then, as if in slow motion, Saunders' face split into a bright shining grin. She tightened her grip and pulled Jax down further into a deep, forceful kiss.

"Jax," Saunders breathed, parting finally to let them refill their lungs. "I have been stupidly, maddeningly in love with you for far too long." Her sparkling green eyes were searching for something in Jax's face.

And then Jax felt the ache in her chest spill over and she breathed out a half laugh, half sigh of unknown relief. A grin broke her face in a way she had forgotten was possible. Saunders pulled her in for another kiss and Jax knew, come whatever hell they found along the way, she had the right person by her side.

The engines were rotated. The fuel was primed. Those on board were as ready as they would ever be. It was time to leave.

As the newly rotated engines kicked on, transferring rotation from the primary string, Jax and the rest of those on board felt the faint acceleration shift inside. Slowly, steadily, the Station started to accelerate away. They were off toward something, anything, as long as it was a faint glimmer of hope. In their wake there remained a single frozen corpse, standing as a marker that someone, anyone, had ever been present. In a month it would be just a distant memory behind them.

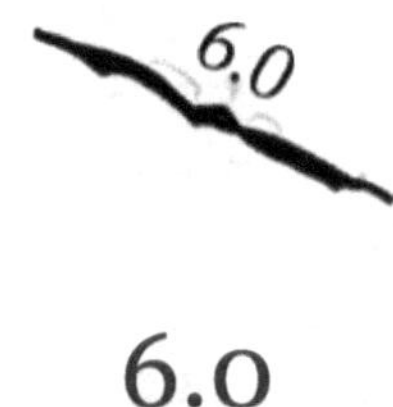

6.0

This page left intentionally blank

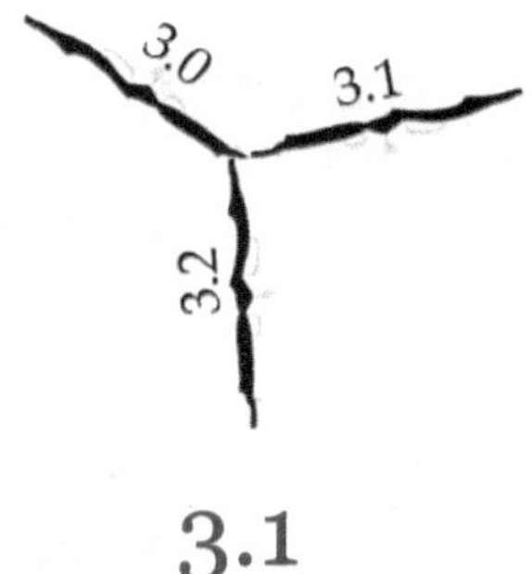

3.1

"We've gotta *go*, Engineering!"

The clambering echo reverberated around the confined space of the engine well, causing Jax to jolt. She jumped upright and smacked her head on the underside of the synthesis drive she had been working on while waiting. She swore, squinted through the pain, and thrashed in panic as she hoisted herself out from under the tug, her tool belt scraping on the formed coral bio-form of the orbital ring they were docked in.

"Are the aliens killing us again?!"

Saunders strode past her enroute through the tug docking hatch. Jax had to scramble up after her, casting a furtive glance in Saunders' wake as the shorter woman shot straight for the pilot's chair in the cockpit.

"No, not quite."

The panic faded and was replaced by a dull throb in the skull where Jax had made contact with the inhuman technology she had stolen.

"'Not *quite?*' Then what the *fuck* is the rush?" Jax growled through the pain in her head. "We're *always* 'not quite' safe from being killed. Didn't they give us clear passage this time?"

"In theory, but after all they've done to us, do you *really* trust that?" Saunders replied over her shoulder, dropping into the pilot's seat and drawing up the navigation charts.

Jax stomped over to Saunders and slapped her shoulder. "Out!" she commanded. Saunders put her hands up to show herself unarmed, and swapped seats to the copilot chair. Jax dropped her lanky frame into the seat Saunders had just vacated, still nursing the growing bruise on her forehead.

"Of course I don't trust them. Where are we going?"

"You think you can fly with a headache?" asked Saunders, courteously.

"My headache is short, blond, and buff," Jax grumbled, queueing up the last trajectory they took.

"Please don't tell me I rate higher than our hosts." Saunders pulled the seat restraints over her shoulders.

"Certainly not 'higher,' I did say *short.*"

"Not 'short,' just 'standard issued'," Saunders shot back. Then, "Is the synth-drive synced up?"

"Close enough—"

Saunders shot her hand out on top of Jax's to stop her from engaging the engine system.

"—What?"

"Please tell me we'll make it this time," Saunders pressed.

"*In theory,*" Jax replied. Saunders glared at her. "Do you want me to tell you we'll make it or do you want us to move?"

Saunders scowled at Jax in study for an extra breath, then, inhaled deeply, turned to look at the yawning maw of the docking bay's exit, and replied "punch it."

Jax jammed a switch on her right that initiated a light sequence and the synthesis drive hummed in response. The tug shifted, as if awakening from a hibernation to crawl toward the light of an unseen star. They slid from the opening on the ring to drop into the surrounding deep space and the accompanying microgravity. The transition was immediate, but at least by now Jax had stopped vomiting in reaction.

Saunders still looked green though.

The tug slid out and away, leaving the looming and massive ring that circumnavigated the planet. The mottled greenish grey of the structure only stood out against the dense vegetation of the planet's surface as it existed well beyond the upper layers of atmosphere, which coiled thick below.

"Alright look, if you're gonna hurl, do it in the back, I don't want to hit top synth-speed and have that floating around again," Jax ordered.

"I'm not gonna hurl, Jax," Saunders objected. "I'm honestly just a bit freaked out."

The tug was sliding past the hulking and twisted remains of a familiar structure. It loomed in the stark starlight, looking like a damaged and dismantled massive wheel. Jax felt a pang of longing for her Station, but knew if she set foot in there it would probably mean the death of any remaining humans. Passing its dead, inevitable bulk always sent a shiver down Jax's spine. She rubbed at the clean-shaven sides of her head and under the haphazard braid of her hair down the center of her skull and the back of her neck.

"Freaked out about what? You said they weren't after us." Jax whispered both in hushed respect for the death of her Station, and in nervous apprehension of what Saunders had to say. They wouldn't be able to fully engage the synth drive until they cleared the Ring, and the Station in its orbital grasp.

"We need to get over to the Tripple Point Moon. I think that Legs is up to something," Saunders added.

"Since when is Legs, 'leader of the killer space shrimp,' *not* up to something? They hate us."

"They don't *understand* us," Saunders corrected, uselessly.

"They understood us enough to know they could *stop* slaughtering us. They understand us enough to know they needed to try to communicate with you."

They had passed the bulk of the Station, and the tug fell dark as they entered its unmoving shadow. It would never rotate again. In the gloom, illuminated by only the lights on the tug control panel, Saunders looked over at Jax.

"And right now I think they understand us to be a threat."

The tug cleared the debris field and Jax punched the sequence into the synth-drive. An unavoidable hypersonic sound started up, and the inhuman technology strapped to the underside of the tug bloomed to life, drawing some unmeasurable power from the nearby starlight and using it to drag the tug rapidly across the star system.

"Well," Jax replied, watching the navigation readout to make sure they were targeting the right moon, "that was certainly cryptic."

Saunders looked up from her notes.

"What do we have on board with us?"

Jax looked over in confusion, and suspicion.

"We have...some basics...whatever we thought we needed for a few day cycles on the ring. Why?"

The look on Saunders' face was uneasy.

"There is a real possibility this might turn into a longer trip," she admitted.

"What?" Jax drew the remark out in her surprise.

"Seriously, Jax," Saunders insisted. "I'm unsure what exactly is going on right now, but we might have to system hop."

"*System?* To the damn Bat-Lizards?" Jax felt her body tense.

"If you call them that this is going to be a really ineffective trip," Saunders scolded.

"Oh, sure, don't call the bat-lizard-looking aliens something simple," Jax muttered to herself. "Why are we risking a peak synth-run? I can't guarantee I patched in the power cycle the right way, and it doesn't always want to read the photons at those speeds." They were twenty minutes from their destination on Tripple-Point Moon, which was just long enough for Jax to etch out some answers.

Saunders had unlooped her seat restraints and shoved herself toward the back of the tug to check the stores. It would be sparse back there. It wasn't like there was an excess of, well, *enjoyable*, food anymore. The ones who held their lives in balance didn't exactly eat scrambled eggs for breakfast.

Jax unbuckled herself and pushed aft to join Saunders.

"Hey," Jax said quietly, as she grabbed a hand hold to stop herself from colliding with the other woman. Her hips swung forward and it was all she could do to only catch Saunder's waist with her knees to keep them from both tumbling further aft. Saunders was holding another handhold with a sturdy grip, which let them both hang there, near a mostly empty logistics locker.

"You didn't answer me?" Jax insisted.

Saunders, despite having absorbed the impact of Jax joining her, looked up like she hadn't even realized Jax was there.

"Do we really only have the one hedger?"

Jax rolled her eyes and glanced down at the illicit weapon.

"I only ever *made* one babe. You still haven't told me what's going on. Can you cue me in please?" Jax released the handhold and threaded her fingers into the short hair on the back of Saunders' neck.

"Right, sorry love." Saunders closed the logistics locker and looked back at Jax. "That meeting didn't go well. Legs seemed really...well...off-putting. Moreso than usual," Saunders amended, given the look Jax gave her. "I tried finding a communication work around to settle things a bit, but I was still trying to barter a way to get us out of Foliage control. When we left the surface, I gave Rose a complete packet of all the comms breakthroughs I think we have had, but for some reason, when we got to the Coral Ring, Legs was being hostile."

Jax's face contorted in alarm. But Saunders just shook her head, leaned in and kissed her, then pushed gently on Jax's hips to move her back toward the cockpit.

"You still have your limbs, and your skin, of which I am thoroughly grateful, but what the hell do you mean 'hostile'?" Jax replied, as she let Saunders push her back to the pilot's seat.

"I think Legs plans to send a message via Tripple-Point Moon. They have their little summit there in a half-turn, or whatever they call a full Pentagram System rotation...anyway, I think they want to get the whole Malacost/Foliage bio-symbiety to unify and declare us as a danger they need to finish eradicating." Saunders had lowered herself back into the co-pilot's seat. Outside the cockpit Jax could see the swirl of Tripple-Point's horizon looming up.

"Ah yeah definitely not a fan of that phrase," Jax sighed, flipping a few switches to meter the synth-drive to allow them to slip quietly through the thick atmosphere. "I hate Tripple-Point," she added, as she switched out of autopilot and into manual for the drop sequence. "It feels like walking through giant coral and it's crawling with those fucking shrimp."

"We really need to figure out what they actually call themselves. We are going to make a mistake with all these fake names we have for them."

"I thought 'Malacost' was pretty good, until they killed Bezley," Jax replied. "Besides, half the problem is that they only communicate in the UV spectrum. How the hell are they going to know what we are calling them?"

The soupy atmosphere swept up around the tug as it descended. Jax flipped on the counter thrusters; something she had managed to cobble together using some old outboard rotationals salvaged before Station surrender. The tug dropped in speed.

"One hundred feet," Saunders called out from the co-pilot seat. The surface was thick with mist, as usual.

"Brace!" Jax barked from her controls. The old tug, made new again, dropped the last several feet onto the moon surface. They were lucky the gravity was low on this body.

"Ox masks are charged," Jax updated, as Saunders hauled herself from her seat. She grabbed a screen from the wall and pulled it over her face. Jax followed suit.

At the back access door of the tug, they paused, as Jax pulled the sleeves of her cover-all back over her arms. The atmosphere had enough pressure, and there was oxygen, but the thick vapor made breathing hard, and Jax hated the clammy feeling on her skin. Even Saunders zipped up her jacket.

"So, what do the Bat-Liz—Sorry, *Skraawl* have to do with Legs hating us so much?" Jax asked as they surveyed the alien landscape in front of them.

"Because Legs wants them to agree we are dangerous, which means we have no friends out here. And I dunno about you, but I am pretty sure we need some kind of lucky break."

"And what if we missed the signal?" Jax asked, her voice constrained by the mask over her face.

"Then we have a *much* longer trip."

"Wait, should I stay with the tug?" Jax paused.

"No, stick with me first, but if need be, I might need you to split and get things fired up." Saunders flicked the worn power button on a battered flashlight hanging from her old security belt.

"I had to fall in love with the only hope our species has in interstellar, inter-species, deep-space, public relations," Jax sighed.

Saunders was already moving in a crouched run, and Jax had to haul herself after in the swirling mist.

The tug had luckily set down in a thick patch of murky vegetation, so it was rather obscured. Jax still scanned the perimeter for Foliage. It wouldn't help them at all to return to a tug fully occupied by something sentient, inhuman, and bearing too many questing vines. But the damp ground muffled their footfalls, and thankfully they ran into no other life before reaching City Edge.

Out of the misty gloom, the massive spires of an alien city rose up, looking like the tubes of some deep-sea dwelling coral structure. The glass of the oxygen mask warped her vision, but Jax could make out the motion of Malacost roiling across the surface, extruding the material to build the spires even higher.

Jax and Saunders darted to a tunnel entrance and entered the main structure. Jax had been here before with Saunders, in the last several months since they had arrived. Perhaps it had already been a year. Years didn't exist here though. Time was counted in half-turns, full-turns, and orbit cycles. Jax figured they were lucky time was counted at all. Even the cycles of hair had fallen apart.

"I hate this place, it creeps me out," Jax repeated. She didn't know if her whispering was necessary. These species didn't seem to deal in the auditory spectrum, just the ultra-violet, but she didn't want to get caught pissing on their architecture at a time when they were hanging in such a balance.

"Just keep track of our route. I don't want us to get lost in a rush to get out of here," Saunders hissed back.

Jax had taken up a position directly to Saunders' back, covering her blind spot and moving sideways to keep an eye on the space behind her, a hand out gripping Saunder's belt for reassurance. Saunders' dirty blond hair was cropped short again, to combat the trips in zero gravity, and it stuck up behind the ox mask in sporadic directions as if rebelling against the moisture of the atmosphere. Her muscular shoulders were tense as they weaved through corridors.

They took a turn and Jax nearly knocked full-force into Saunders from behind, managing to brace herself by clutching blindly at Saunders' shoulders.

In front of them, one of the Malacost moved past, scurrying like a centipede, the four eye spots squarely in the center point of the long body as it slunk by.

"I think that is a member of the summit," Saunders whispered, Jax barely even able to hear her.

"So, we follow?"

"Wait first, then follow."

"How did you convince these guys to stop shooting first and asking questions later?" Jax breathed, having realized she had been holding a lungful until the Malacost passed.

"I still think they are ready to shoot, all questions aside," Saunders replied, ever still the soldier. "But mostly I think it was the fact they found that plant of yours in your berthing. Told them you might be worth keeping, seeing as their biggest allies are, well, also plants."

Jax wanted to remind her that Ralph wasn't sentient, but Saunders was already moving. She motioned for them to pursue the slithering creature that reminded Jax far too much of a distant memory of a hallucination on a dying space station.

"Somehow, in all this, they still marked you as our benevolent leader. And me as your loyal court jester." Jax huffed as they moved.

"Oh Jax, you're way more important than my court jester, you're my courtesan!"

Jax wanted to aim a well-placed retort in the face of their impending doom, but they rounded a corner, and Saunders paused again. Jax was paying better attention now and she pulled up short, avoiding tackling the body in front of her. In a distant corner of a chamber room, looking like the inside of some massive crustacean, the Malacost stood up. The long body folded in half, the four eye spots rising in the middle to a height nearly a foot taller than Jax. The mandibles that surrounded the middle flicked in and out, creating flashes as the creature "talked." Saunders had deciphered some basics of the light flash words, but neither of them could see in the UV spectrum, so they were missing entire layers of communication.

"Jax," Saunders said carefully.

"Yes?" Jax felt a cold chill, that probably was not associated with the damp air.

"Get back to the tug."

"What?" Jax stepped back to get a better look at the back of the woman she loved. She was entirely resistant to wanting to leave her behind anywhere, much less this infernal place.

"I need to make sure I caught the pattern right, but I think it's too late. Get the tug ready, and I'll be right behind you. Move easy, I don't want to alarm anyone."

"And in what universe do I want to leave you here like this?" Jax objected, louder than she wanted to. She flinched at the sound of her own voice and looked around nervously. Saunders did not move to even look at her.

"I love you, but I need you to trust me. Five minutes. I'll be moving before you even get back," she replied.

"Please, do *not* get your body split in half. I only ever need to see that happen to someone once," Jax moaned. She reached out her hand and let it brush, barely, between

Saunders' shoulder blades. The shorter woman did not react. So Jax took a deep breath, stepped back and turned.

"Five minutes," Jax said. She had to choke it back because three more Malacost were maneuvering down the hall. She knew they could see her. "On your six, love," Jax whispered. She felt, rather than saw, Saunders glance over her shoulder at the approaching delegates.

Jax flashed her hands in the only communication she knew, letting the light reflect off her palms twice. They had learned the signal was like saying hello in an absolutely atrocious accent. The Malacost did not respond to her, and passed them both to enter the chamber.

Behind her, Jax felt Saunders' absence, and knew she had followed them in. Jax took off.

She kept herself low to the ground. A tall, walking Malacost was out of place and disturbing, so a low, crouched Jax was less conspicuous. She counted the turns tracing her eyes along the route they had taken.

She took a wrong turn. It was one spiraling coral tube too many and she rounded a corner far more quickly than she had control over her body. Jax managed to skid her boots to a halt before stepping on the forward moving body of a low slunk Malacost.

"Oh shit!" she yelped, and was not comforted when she saw the creature flinch at the loud sound.

Maybe they *could* hear. Jax didn't have long to think on this as the creature drew itself up to its full height, folding at the middle to look like a cloaked crustacean with multitudinous blank eyes and sharp mandibles at the head. This was a position that could allow for commerce, diplomacy, or murder. Jax didn't want to stick around to find out which she might be subjected to.

"Time to go!" Jax announced, backpedaling, flashing her hands twice and bolting for the main tube she had come from.

She did a half run, sideways, trying to see if the Malacost followed her. If it did, she was fucked, because they were far faster than a human in their low, elongated form.

Jax burst from City Edge and hauled for the tug in its hidden shroud of mist. Thankfully it was still there. She smashed into the cockpit and hit the power sequence that booted up the synth-drive to get them off the surface. Then she bolted for the logistics rack and hauled out the hedger. She shouldered the misshapen weapon and dragged it to the back door to keep an eye out for Saunders.

She reached the access door just in time to see Saunders' figure break from the City Edge, moving as fast as she probably felt comfortable. Jax also caught the sight of three more Malacost and some Foliage, cloaked in the shimmering black mold, closing in from the side.

"Shit."

The Foliage were from Prime Planet and its moon, the fourth and fifth points of this blasted pentagram. They were the jailers currently holding the rest of the Station's residents on their infernal jungle of a planet, where even the leaves wanted to eat you. They shrouded themselves in acidic, psychic mold, and had no issue dissolving the limbs clean off anyone they didn't like. Jax suspected Saunders was correct that they only stopped the slaughtering when they convinced Jax's pet plant Ralph to defect to their side. And Ralph's diplomacy skills were questionable.

Jax revved the hedger, ready to carve off whatever vine snaked its way into Saunders' path. The Foliage was already splitting its petals, revealing the carnivorous spines within, and that was invitation enough to know this wasn't a welcome party.

"MOVE, SAUNDERS!" Jax bellowed. The former space marine got the message and swapped to a sprint. Jax posted herself by the door to provide coverage. The shimmering black coverings on the Foliage started to shift the space around them, and time was running short. The hedger revved to life, sounding like it was regretting its existence. It was probably good for a hack or two, but that would be it.

Saunders cleared the threshold the moment the Malacost were close enough to draw to full height. Jax slammed the door control latch, forcing it closed. She scrambled back, waiting for the material of the outer hull to dissolve and let the Foliage in.

"I'll take *this*," Saunders panted, snagging the hedger from Jax, where she had nearly flung the running weapon while trying to avoid being psychically dragged through solid matter into the ravenous mouth of a sentient pitcher plant.

Jax relinquished the weapon and bolted for the cockpit to slam the ignition sequence on the synth-drive. Let them see that she had shamelessly stolen their technology, Jax was a goddamn mechanical engineering master.

The tug lurched into the atmosphere and pulled them away from the surface. Nothing followed them.

Jax ripped her oxygen mask off, as Saunders hauled herself back into the copilot's seat.

"Cutting it close," she hissed.

"It's hard to run in this gravity."

"Did you see our little welcome party?" Jax asked, as she smashed the navigation screen readouts.

"Yes, that was enlightening."

"Why do I just know you're about to tell me we are in for a trek," Jax moaned.

"Because you are intelligent, and perceptive when you need to be, even if you are oblivious the rest of the time," came Saunders' response.

They broke into orbit. Jax didn't see any intercepting ships. Whatever poor fate they had run across, it hadn't followed them to space yet.

"We'll circle back to 'oblivious', did you preset the course to Creea?"

"It's in the database," Saunders replied, pulling up the last several trips they had made, even if they had been somewhat a forced measure by the Malacost.

"They're in, is that Synth going to work? Now is *not* the time to get stranded in intersystem space," Saunders called.

"Well, if we do, at least we'll get some alone time for a change," Jax mumbled, charging up the synth drive.

"Jax."

"Come on, I need a silver lining here." Jax glanced over at Saunders briefly before punching the drive. The tug's bastardized alien tech whined hypersonically, and they dropped into a realm of subspace darker than before.

* * *

With photosynthesis-drive subspace, it would take at least a few hours to reach the next planet system. Jax considered it a better deal than the months-long excursion with a three-week stopover on a desolate space station that it normally took. She wished she had more time to take one apart and study it. Then again, she was a mechanical engineer, not a biomechanical engineer. Dorian Bezley would come in handy right about now.

"You know I've spent more than one night lying awake wondering if I can reverse engineer the synth-drive to take us back home?" Jax asked to the spreading subspace before them.

"If that's what's keeping you awake at night, I'm not doing a good enough job wearing you out," Saunders replied, from where she was studying the navigation readouts again.

"It's a little hard to *really* get in the mood when the vines that make up our holding cell want to start joining in..." Jax mused. That got a rise out of the woman next to her.

"And here I thought you were into that."

Jax snorted a laugh. "I miss Ralph, but...not like that..." She cinched down her shoulder straps to give herself the illusion of security in the lack of gravity. At least with her hawk of hair braided, it didn't float into her face.

"So, what *happened* back there?" Jax asked, once she was certain the synth-drive wouldn't flicker out and deposit them far from any source of light, or survival.

"That was some sentinel from Legs that we followed. I discerned from whatever they were saying that a message had already been sent."

"And when you followed that slithery bastard into that probable little death chamber?" The whole idea of Saunders willingly entering that enclosed space full of those creatures made her shiver.

"I managed to get a few words back and forth. I was given the impression they thought it was a justified challenge."

"Challenge?!" Jax felt alarm now.

"Like a task, or trial," Saunders amended. "To prove ourselves? It's not a perfect translation."

Great. The former Security Officer, now "Speaker for the Humans" thrived on competition. Jax had learned this over the past year. Jax had also discovered she liked this fact in most cases, but sometimes it was hard to break through to Saunders when she was possessed of a mission.

"I would really like to think they aren't playing games with our lives. I suppose that vanguard we saw were just waving the 'go' flag?"

"I have no idea what that was, but they didn't follow us," Saunders replied.

The tug was back on auto pilot so Jax could pull her attention from the task of getting them the fuck away from Tripple Point. She squeezed her eyes shut, taking a mental inventory.

"If this takes as long as you expect, how will the residents know we are gone?"

"I briefed Rose before we left three cycles ago. She knows what to do," Saunders reported, not looking up from her tablet readout of schematics, or coordinates or whatever was more engrossing than Jax stewing in their current calamity.

"But, like, what if we're gone for...a *really* long time?" Jax stumbled over converting the time measures and gave up. Saunders would know what she meant. The other woman reached out and took Jax's free floating hand as if to confirm this.

"Jax, babe, its Rose. She's the only person I know who might be smarter than you," Saunders said softly.

"Bullshit, I'm a fucking dunce. That's a low bar to cross."

"I told her we might have something delay us. And we went over the contingency. She knows what has to happen if we never come back. That's been a plan since we first set foot on the Prime."

Jax released a long and exhausted groan. This was not how she had hoped to spend her remaining days; sprinting across the alien galaxy being chased by vindictive centipede fucks and their pitcher plant henchmen, toward the questionable comfort of a brutal warrior race. She had recently found a particularly soft section of vegetation-based jail cell with some vines that seemed disinterested in biblical familiarity, and were rather inclined to let her sleep. Jax had hoped for a break.

Instead, she unclipped her harness and floated from her seat.

Saunders glanced up at the motion.

"Where are you going?"

"To double check inventory. Just to be sure we even *have* enough to make it to the Skraawl and back."

With that, Jax pushed herself through zero gravity down the short length of the cargo tug she had outfitted under duress: slapped together extras they managed to retain before the Station was fully pirated by the locals. On one side, they had ripped out the extra seats and built in a pulldown bunk. Across from it was the logistics locker with minimal food and supply storage that bookended the access to the original engine wells. At the far wall near the access hatch there hung two pressure suits, Jax's tool belt, the only range weapon they possessed—the hedger—and her dearly beloved, massive, battered, thirty-six-inch spud wrench.

Their limited possessions were sparse, and the inventory was short. From the back of the tug Jax could see the endless dark of subspace streak past outside. She was never quite sure what speed the Synth-drive moved them at, but she knew it closed the gaps fast out here. It had dawned on her that perhaps the rift had acted just like a natural synth drive, but there was no way they would ever know. Even Rose had lost her lab equipment when the Malacost swept in. Still, it was oddly thrilling to be experiencing true alien technology.

Jax still missed the gentle arc of her Station though, with the curve of the stars as they had rotated around the core. So much had changed in so many ways they had never imagined.

For one thing, she was nursing a hell of a caffeine headache.

"There's not much in terms of food back there," Jax mumbled as she pulled herself back into the pilot's seat.

Saunders hardly looked up. "Skraawl probably have food."

Jax tried not to retch, but it came out as a cough. Saunders glanced up at that.

"Hey, it's better than eating each other…"

"Hardly," Jax muttered.

The quiet settled. The stars streaked past.

"The *Skraawl*," Jax repeated, to the quiet around them, making sure to emphasize the name. "Is it weird that I am almost just as unnerved by them as the Malacost and the stupid Foliage?"

"At least they have a face."

"A freaky looking face," Jax added under her breath.

Silence again.

"Saunders?"

"Hmm?"

"Do you ever miss it?"

"There are several things I miss and several things I sure as fuck do not," came the matter-of-fact response. Jax huffed to herself. Saunders had a point.

"There's just some days I wish I could evaporate from all of this with you," Jax offered to the void.

"Days don't exist out here love, its cycles of dread, remember?" Saunders replied looking up and over at Jax, who was lost to the sight of deep space slipping past their silent little tug.

"Fine, every other existential crisis, I wish we could just go back to your quarters, on Level 1, with your cheap, contraband alcohol, and your terrible cover bands, and do things right for a change."

"So I can watch you run out and leave me heartbroken again?" Saunders replied. That snapped Jax from her meditation. She looked back at the other woman.

"That would be the last thing in the universe I want to do."

Saunders regarded Jax for a moment, then reached out and grasped at Jax's forearm where it gripped her shoulder restraints, tugged until Jax let go and reached her own arm out to clasp their hands. Saunders squeezed, an earnest look in her eyes.

"This is the life we need to lead right now, so we can survive."

"I know." Jax swallowed an inexplicably painful lump in her throat, tearing her eyes from Saunders' to look out at the passing void beyond. "You can't fault me for wishing things were simpler."

"People like you and I walked away from simple a long time ago. You could even say that's why I knew I wanted you, Jax. Who else would understand that about me?" Saunders whispered.

Jax knew she was right. Jax had made a life for herself that, even when it centered around the endless upkeep of a deep field waypoint space station, was not exactly what anyone would call pedestrian. By nature, she had sought the most complicated manner in which to be simple. And she had found Saunders there too.

"Tell me something." Jax finally regained enough composure to look back over at the love of her life. "What were you doing on a deep-field space station with that much contraband alcohol?"

Of course, Saunders smirked.

"Well, really, it was just habit from my days in the service. But if I'm being entirely honest, I figured 'if I want to get to know her, get to liquor'."

Jax let out a low, anguished groan.

"Careful, I like that sound," Saunders interjected.

"That was just...so bad."

"*Defense mechanism*," Saunders stressed. "But don't worry, I have something that will make it all better." She let go of Jax's hand and punched a button on the tug controls console.

Jax's fraught objections were drowned out by the first power chords of a band that had existed centuries ago, on the opposite side of the universe. The tug streaked through deep space, enroute to its target destination, and a message that desperately needed to be intercepted.

* * *

The landing proximity alert blared from the cockpit console. Jax shook the dregs of the first real sleep she had gotten in what felt like light years and focused on dragging them out of synth-space. The first time she had tried this she had found herself overshot from her destination, certain she would never see another human, much less the gloriously aggravating woman next to her, ever again. She eased off the throttle and dropped the power transfer down to something more recognizable for low orbit control. The horizon of Creea, the primary Skraawl planet, loomed ahead.

"I suppose I'm looking forward to communicating in something other than jazz hands for a change," Jax yawned. "Unless they decide to cut off my jazz hands," she added as an afterthought.

"They aren't going to cut off your...hands," Saunders assured her. The woman probably hadn't bothered sleeping, but Jax had fallen asleep halfway through Saunders' third drum solo and air guitar act. For all she knew, Saunders had spent the time studiously reviewing the navigation readouts and lip-synching to cover bands of cover bands.

"They cut off each other's hands, it's practically how they say 'hello.' Don't make promises you can't keep, *Senator*," Jax replied, absent mindedly rubbing her wrist where she hoped to keep her hand attached.

The gravity grew around them the closer they got to the surface, and Saunders let her head tip back against the seat behind her. Sleep or not, she looked exhausted.

"You're over there being nostalgic for a time we never had"—Saunders interrupted Jax's thoughts—"and a Station that was never supposed to be forever. I'm over here wondering how we got so comfortable with the idea of aliens whose entire culture revolves around psychic slime mold, or brutal dismemberment because their limbs regenerate. I—" at this Saunders faltered and it caught Jax's attention. "I didn't think *I* would be so...immune."

Jax didn't have the chance to reply. The proximity alert that they were within landing range rang out. She dropped the tug down to the surface of the sprawling world in a dense crop of deep vegetation. She hoped none of it was carnivorous.

"I'd park closer, but we don't know if they want to murder us yet," Jax stated. Saunders was peering out of the cockpit, the humid world outside shimmering through the thick glass. Creea was at least warmer than Tripple, being slightly closer to the system's star.

"Just keep track of the location. If we need to bolt again, I don't want to get lost, or strung up in something's dinner trap."

"I say this with extreme affection, but I would ever-loving fuck-up anything that decided to make you dinner at the expense of my own feet," Jax declared.

"Glad I'm worth your feet. The feeling is mutual. We should get moving. This is time critical."

They made their way to the back of the tug. This planet didn't really require breathing apparatuses to keep them alive. They still paused at the back door.

"Saunders," Jax hesitated. "What do we do if we're already too late?"

"Run like hell."

"Yeah, but, run where?"

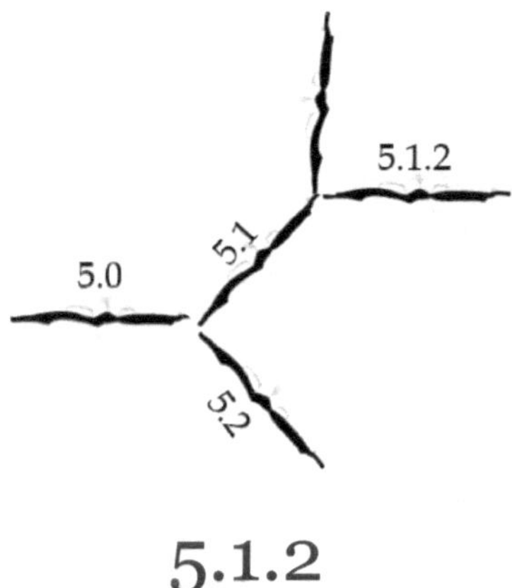

5.1.2

Water drizzled down past Saunders' shoulder and she shivered.

"Well, this is lovely," she hummed in the awful darkness, as Jax led Andee around the service tug Saunders was setting eyes on for the first time in over a year on station.

"How did you manage to bust this ring so badly?" Andee was asking Jax, who, despite the gloom, looked like she was grumpy about having to explain herself. On second thought, Saunders figured "grumpy" was simply Jax's default. It only made it more enjoyable when she could get the mechanic to crack a smile.

"I was trying a few...maneuvers...it didn't work out," Jax grumbled in reply.

Despite the horrible cold and damp, Andee rumbled with laughter. Saunders appreciated that about the welder.

"Maneuvers? You joy riding this thing, Engineering?" Andee barked a laugh, and Jax's uneasy look was certainly endearing. Or maybe she just looked sick to her stomach. Saunders couldn't tell in the dim light.

"I don't know how you think we're going to get this out of here," Jax responded, clearly trying to redirect the conversation.

"Isn't this room fitted with its own airlock?" Saunders hoped to sound like she was competent enough to know basic functionality of the station, even if Jax was the default expert.

The mechanic quirked a less than ecstatic smile her way that was gone in an instant. Jax's leg buckled in a limp as she stepped over toward Saunders. She noticed, but Saunders wasn't sure anyone else had.

"Saun—Security, with the power off...and the mechanisms probably all flooded, we'd never open it..." Jax replied, smoothing over the more informal title. Saunders rolled her eyes. It was going to take some time and effort to get Jax comfortable with the rest of the residents seeing a more human side of her. Effort Saunders had, time they did not.

"Yes, babe, I gathered. From all the water," Saunders responded, and reveled in the look of burning panic on Jax's face. Kicking and screaming.

She strode past the mechanic who was staring at her pointedly, mouthing the word "babe" back at her, and punctuated her passage with a tender hand on Jax's arm.

"So how else can we get out of here?" Saunders looked up at the cramped ceiling of the tug hanger.

"We could blast our way out," Andee supplied.

Saunders turned to her and grinned. "Going out with a bang?"

"Nah, that's between you and Engineering," Andee shot back. Yeah, Saunders always liked her.

"Okay, just going to STOP that line of conversation," Jax barked. Andee was already fist-bumping Saunders, but they both looked over to the Mechanical Engineer.

"You are *not* blowing holes in my *Station!*" Jax growled. She always had a way of saying "station" that made it sound like the massive metal rings had a personality. On second thought, Saunders wouldn't be the least surprised that Jax considered the station to have its own personality. "For starters, *what* in hell do you expect to use to combust with? We aren't allowed flammable substances, and Saunders already got me shit drunk on her contraband alcohol!"

Silence.

"Nice," Andee replied.

Jax was huffing deep breaths. Saunders could see a glint in her dark eyes. It took her a moment to register this was Jax fully committing to the bit.

"Worth it," Saunders mumbled, suppressing the desire to grin.

"Not that I mind being dragged through memory lane of young love with you all, but we do have a limit on how long we can survive down here," Obah interjected. She limped around the tug from where she had been standing with Gedry. Her ankle was a clean break, and Saunders had tried to reset it. It probably wouldn't heal correctly. Her heart was not a clean break, and there was little anyone could do about it. But Obah was resolute, and had insisted on putting her energy into their survival, keeping the memory of her nephew alive in her pursuit of living. Saunders respected that.

Jax glowered as she herself circumnavigated the tug, sitting at a precarious angle, clearly having tumbled in the descent into this particular pit of hell. At least it wasn't entirely sideways. As Jax passed, her own limp more distinct the closer she got, she cast a sidelong glance at Saunders, and Saunders swore she saw the mechanic give the hint of that smile again.

Definitely worth it.

"Okay, if I entertain this absurdity...just barely," Jax spoke up as she walked. "I don't need to combust anything. We would need to weaken the walls mechanically, and then we can time it with a pressure differential."

"Speak human, Engineering. Some of us just melt metal for a living," Andee replied.

Jax reappeared to size up the welder, which Saunders was incredibly amused by. Jax was tall, with legs Saunders wanted to keep wrapped around herself, and while Jax perpetually carried herself like she was ready for someone to bite her head off, the mechanic could be lithe and nimble when needed. But Jax was not muscular in the slightest. Strong, sure: it was hard not to be after a decade of manual labor. But Jax didn't have the muscle mass Saunders had worked to maintain since her days on contract. And Andee put them both to shame, in height and biceps. Jax seemed to constantly be calculating whether she could throw down with whoever was across from her. Andee could probably break Jax in half, but Saunders knew the welder wouldn't even want to think that way, much less act on it.

"Melting metal is exactly what I am saying you should do," Jax replied, stiffly.

"Yes, speaking my language," Andee chuckled. "Now, the rest of that bullshit you just said?"

Jax sighed.

"I can calculate external water pressure, get you to weaken the hull in the right places. Then we can set a pressure point...time it..." Jax had spun off on her plans, joining team "destroy the station" without further argument.

Saunders smirked to herself and let the two continue their conversation. Jax would deny it, but Saunders had spent enough time around people to tell: they might be fathoms in the deep on an alien planet, but those two could be friends.

The tug hanger was a tight fit. Saunders could see where the rails, clearly useless at this angle, fed into the cargo lift. The lift should be secured on this level, but it, too would be scrap metal with the station on its side. It was a wonder the tug hanger wasn't flooded. It was a relief, really.

She wandered the perimeter, picking her way over tossed detritus, and only half listening to the growing conversation between the hearty welder and the mechanic. The side of the tug hanger that ran parallel to the lift included some oddly-spaced wall panels Saunders recognized as accommodation for the vertical nature of the lift. As Saunders got closer, she could see a few areas that looked modified.

Figured.

Jax had stashed several dozen little passages throughout this station, customizing it to allow her to depart one level and reappear elsewhere far faster than anyone could have guessed. It had made Saunders' early pursuit of the mechanic a far more interesting game than she had anticipated. Fun, for a while, until Saunders realized she was desperately in love with Jax. And then it had gotten complicated. Hot, but really fucking complicated.

It was freezing right now. Saunders wrapped her sweatshirt clad arms around herself and crouched to examine what looked like an entrance to Jax's hideaway. A clanging sound reverberated off the other side of the metal panel.

Saunders fell over backward trying to step away. The sound of her falling alerted the rest of the group and Jax, limp and all, appeared at her side almost instantaneously.

"You okay, Saunders?" the mechanic asked softly.

Saunders pushed past Jax to get her ear closer to the surface in front of her.

The clanging sounded again, this time accompanied by a scratching sound that was all-too-human.

"There's someone trapped in there!" Saunders shouted, a rising panic filling her chest.

"What—" Jax replied, but Saunders was already running her hands around the exterior of the passage entrance, looking for a way in. It seemed jammed shut and it was clear Jax had designed these spaces so they couldn't be found on accident or infiltrated.

"How would they have even gotten in there?" Jax had hoisted herself up to put an ear to the panel and turned to beckon the others over.

Andee strode the distance in a few long steps. Obah and Gedry picked their way over in the welder's wake.

"Andee, set your grinder here," Jax was barking, and the welder didn't even hesitate.

Saunders found herself pushed aside as sparks started to cascade around them. Andee squinted against the bright hot metal shavings, clearly not equipped with her goggles in such a quick emergency. Jax had managed to produce that abominable wrench again, this time at least having cleaned the dried gore from it. The mechanic jammed the pointy end of the wrench into a crease Saunders hadn't noticed and used her weight as leverage. Saunders could help there.

She grabbed the upper portion of the battered tool and added her own heft to the effort. A sparking metal shaving landed on her bare hand, but the cold of the dark hanger was almost as painful as the spark of heat.

Andee shifted her grinder and the panel suddenly burst back, shooting an avalanche of roiling water. The burst dam knocked Saunders down and under, enveloping her in freezing, drowning depths. Saunders couldn't see, the only sound in her ears the roaring rush of the flood.

Steady hands grabbed her and Saunders' face breached the surface. She gasped for air to fill her lungs and scrambled to pull herself upright in the deluge of frigid water. Obah was hammering a hand on her back as Saunders coughed out whatever fluid she had inhaled, staggering.

Jax and Andee had shifted from trying to pry the panel open to trying to weld it closed again. Ged was shouldering the metal in place alongside Jax as Andee arced her weld pack and tried tacking the corners closed. With every inch welded, more water pushed through elsewhere, dislodging the gap and starting the process all over again. They would lose the tug hanger at this rate, and possibly even the whole station.

The Mechanical Engineer waded across the hanger to the far side. In the meantime, the water forced Ged backward and Saunders jumped from where Obah was holding her so she, too, could help. The torrents cascaded around their futile attempts to hold the deeps at bay. As Saunders braced her shoulder against the force, something slipped through the crack, squirming into the rising waters around their feet.

Jax stomped back, dragging a piece of what looked like scrap metal. She grunted at Saunders and Ged to get them to move and slammed the material in place. Saunders only distantly noted Jax had hinged the metal on a portion of the lift shaft, as the mechanic put all her weight into leveraging the unhinged end against the flow. Ged threw his weight into the blockage again, and Saunders followed suit.

With the blockage braced as it was, the water hissed through in high pressure bursts, but Andee got the bead going and tacked the material in place well enough to let her finish the job. The deluge contained, now just small rivulets of water dribbling down, as if to join the other minor leaks.

"That can't be a breach to the exterior, we wouldn't have been able to hold it off," Jax panted, the exertion having clearly worn her out.

"Let's just not open any more sealed compartments, how about that?" Andee shot back, also sounding exhausted.

Saunders wanted to reply that the sound of trapped survivors had driven her efforts, but she saw motion dart away in the water at their feet.

"Hey, did you see that?" she muttered, tracing the direction the ripples had flowed in. It was small, like a fish, but she hadn't seen any details to be sure.

"Uh, Security," someone said from behind her.

Saunders was on the hunt. She saw another flash of movement and darted after it.

"Saunders," Jax called.

"Hang on, there's something in the water!" Saunders snagged an overturned metal canister floating in the detritus. She waded after the small ripples that disappeared as soon as she caught sight of them. Then, near her boot she saw the flash and she dove, nearly putting herself under again. When she surfaced, sputtering and coughing, she peered into the canister. Something vaguely reflective darted and shimmered back.

"Gotcha!" she whispered, feeling the thrill of the conquest.

"Jillian," Jax called again.

"I told you, only in bed—" Saunders stopped as she turned to address the group behind her.

Jax was standing between her and the others, holding a hand out like she was trying to hold off an argument. Behind the mechanic, Ged and Andee were holding the mutilated body of Tizik Bracken.

* * *

Andee and Gedry deposited Bracken on the floor of one of the med-bays on Level 2. Nearby Jax feverishly hacked away at the bolted connections keeping a med-bay table connected to the vertical flooring, and Obah was tossing any reachable lockers for supplies. Tess had taken up a section of wall, laying with her back against a floor panel, and a mute, judgmental look on her ashen face.

"It's not like there's anything we can do to save him," Saunders heard herself guffaw, incredulous. She wasn't sure where her voice had come from. No one replied.

Andee evaporated from the area and Saunders suspected she had returned to the tug hanger. Meanwhile, a crash, accompanied by some particularly crass obscenities, indicated Jax had managed to remove the med-bay table from the wall.

Saunders couldn't look away. The Operations Specialist was wearing his unit moral t-shirt, not unlike one she had in her own duffle bag, submerged somewhere on Level 1; a shirt she rarely ever chose to look at. Tizik's shirt had a faded, stylized land animal on the left breast, and Saunders could almost make out horns. Either it was a throwback to some earth-bound creature, or some play on mythological legends. These Terrestrial Surface Force units liked reminding everyone that despite the stars calling, they still spent a lot of time in the dirt.

Below the stylized icon, the shirt was shredded. Beneath was raw open flesh, and jagged bone. Something had torn chunks from the man, and Saunders couldn't tell if it had been after he had drowned, or before. She sank to her knees next to him as if getting closer would make a difference. The other body they had found was also a mess. Like something found them, here under the fathoms, and decided to chew on them all.

A hand on her shoulder made Saunders jump. Jax flinched in reaction, and withdrew slightly.

"Sorry, Saunders, just, let's try to move him," the mechanic said softly.

"Why?" Saunders heard herself reply.

Jax looked confused, and she leaned back on the table she had re-arranged to study Saunders. It was an uncomfortable look, and Saunders decided she didn't like it. Sure, she liked everything about the mechanic she could get her hands on, but the thought of being seen, of being studied the way Jax was watching her now, set Saunders on edge.

"We should just set them all in here. Like a morgue. Collins, Bergan, Tiz, there's going to be more. It's not like I was ever going to be able to save them," she stated. Tess gave a silent snort of incredulous laughter and Saunders shot a withering look at the dark corner she lounged in.

"Sure, Saunders, we can move them all in here," Jax replied with a wince. She reached down and rubbed at her calf in the soaked coveralls she still wore. In the dim light, Jax looked almost pale and sickly. Saunders figured the mechanic might not quite be cut out for the intricacies of battlefield mutilations. She hadn't exactly done well in that nightmare on Level 4 pre-Drop.

"Then we should move this gurney to another room. Something tells me we're going to need a clean medical space, and I don't want to work over dead bodies," Obah replied.

Jax looked over her shoulder at the older woman and nodded.

As the Mechanical Engineer huffed and wheezed through dragging the metal table to the next bay over, Saunders looked down into the canister she held. Something inside flashed again. Saunders looked up to see Jax laboring under the direction of Obah and her broken ankle. With the canister of water and its single mysterious inhabitant, Saunder rose to her feet, stepped around the battered body of Tizik Bracken and picked her way out of medical toward Level 1, Tess in tow.

Dorian Bezley had taken to haunting the corridor where they had all awakened, just outside the entry to Common Access. The engine well Jax had pried open remained: a dark column of lightless void beckoning all who walked past it to either slip inside or ascend to see the wonders beyond them.

And thus, Dorian perched, having dragged a set of bedding materials up to the top of the yawning bay door.

"Bez, are you up there?" Saunders called into the gloom. There wasn't a reply, not at first. Then a rustle and the silhouette of the pale biodiversity researcher's form appeared.

"Security," the man said. It wasn't a question. He had the tendency to be as reserved as Jax. "Did you need something?"

Saunders looked down at the container that held the squirming aquatic creature. Then she thought of the dead bodies that were surfacing as they picked their way through the pieces of their lives down here. Tess leaned silently against the yawning door frame and Saunders thought of bodies littering a rocky field; people she was supposed to keep safe... She remembered Jax, ripping the med-bay tables off the flooring and the pinched feeling in her chest eased. She turned her back on Tess and glanced up again.

"I have something to show you," she called.

"You're welcome to climb," the researcher replied. Saunders exhaled to save her patience.

"Dorian, get down here."

An exasperated sigh responded, but the rustle indicated the man was descending.

Saunders stepped back to make room for Bezley to join her and Tess on the station wall. Tess shifted, looking disgruntled, and slid over, adjusting her field armor as she slipped into shadow.

"Yes, Security?" Bezley asked, adjusting his glasses on his face, snapping Saunders' attention from where she watched Tess dissolve into the surrounding gloom.

Shaking her head to clear it, Saunders handed him the container. He looked at it, impatiently.

"Thank you," he replied, clipped. "But I'm not thirsty."

"No! Dorian, I *found* something. In the water." Saunders gestured at the container. Bezley scrunched his face and peered into the murky water. Then his expression changed.

"This came from out there?" his voice filled with a level of awe Saunders thrilled to hear.

"Well, it's not like we had them onboard the station," Saunders replied, feeling a bit of self-satisfaction. The scientist glanced up with a look that said he disliked the sarcasm. Eh, she couldn't charm them all. "So do you recognize it?" she pressed.

He once again peered into the container.

"This isn't exactly the best setup for species identification, but the odds are, given the sheer uncertainty we have encountered lately, that no, I do *not* know what this is." He craned his neck to look at the top of the engine-well door he had been sitting on. "But this might be what I keep seeing flash past the windows out there. It is impossible to know how deep we are."

"Jax said she might be able to calculate depth based on station structure," Saunders offered.

Bezley looked back at her with a confused expression.

"Isn't she just the mechanic?"

Saunders gave him a once over.

"Jax? She is not 'just the mechanic.'"

Bezley shrugged. "Do you have a place I might be able to set up some equipment? My quarters weren't flooded, but they are too cramped."

"Sure, you can head to Level 3—" No, there were dead bodies littering Level 3. Saunders choked on the words and the scientist glanced back up at her inquisitively. "I think you can set up on Level 5. There's that old biofiltration room I think remained relatively dry... Just...honestly, wherever works. Let me know if you need a light," Saunders finished.

"I'll go and get my equipment then," Bezley replied, and he strode past her, peering into the container.

Saunders was alone in the pitch black of the empty level. Her pitiful flashlight was only barely able to keep her from tripping over the uneven surface of the wall.

There were things outside the station. Things that wanted to get in. Things that hammered at the walls as they slept. And inside, there were dead bodies. And every one they found was worse than the last. The dark felt oppressive. This station was supposed to be her place away from the memories, but it had dragged her back down into the abyss with them. She was never supposed to see Tess again. There was a moment in her life when that was heartbreaking. Now it was all she yearned for.

How. How the *fuck* had they gotten here.

"There you are."

Saunders flinched at the voice and spun around, but Jax had already stepped close enough for her to grasp.

"Easy, Saunders," the mechanic replied, holding her arms out. They were both still wearing clothes that had been soaked through, and were sluggish to dry in the cold, damp station interior. Saunders shivered and instinctually pushed into Jax's chest to chase the soft warmth from her.

"Sorry, I had to come find Bezley." Saunders' voice muffled into the wet fabric of Jax's coveralls.

"Who?"

Saunders rolled her eyes and reached up to unzip the coveralls, in hope of climbing in closer to Jax.

"Just, one of the residents. I found a sample he might be interested in."

"A sample?" At this proximity Saunders could hear Jax's voice echoing in her rib cage. Saunders wanted to chase the feeling of being wrapped up in the mechanic.

"Just...something living...in the water that got in...Fuck," Saunders exhaled into the damp fabric covering Jax's chest. "Jax, how is this even *possible?* How the hell are we able to go from being the last stop on the way to the outer bands of the galaxy to being submerged under water? Tell me I'm dreaming!"

Jax didn't tell her she was dreaming. But Saunders was already seeing Tess in the shadows, and hearing things in the walls, and for all she knew she had never woken up. But the mechanic held her tighter and some distant thought told Saunders it wasn't *all* bad.

"I have no idea what brought us here. That...uh rift? I don't think anyone has ever seen anything like it before.

Some unknown mystery of the universe, just…right outside us all long."

"And it brought us here?" Saunders groaned.

"I think there were any number of infinite possible options that could have happened. And here we are?" Jax sounded like she was making it up. And Saunders couldn't fault her. Here they were, stuck under fathoms of water, with their own ghosts to keep them company until their time ran out.

"Listen," Jax continued, clearly oblivious to whatever existential dread she had sown, "we set up a few med-bays, and cordoned off one of the far ones for the, uh, the bodies." There was a pause. Saunders pulled her face back to look up at Jax. The mechanic looked back and in the dim light her features looked strained, and a sheen of sweat coated her forehead.

"What?" Saunders asked.

Jax glanced to the side.

"We found some more. They aren't in good shape."

Saunders felt her gut plummet. There couldn't possibly be survivors anymore.

"Who are they?" she asked, feeling herself dip further into the echoes of painfully familiar feelings.

"I—you know I don't know anyone," Jax replied.

"Of course," Saunders muttered. She sank her forehead back down to Jax's sternum.

"But, I can take you to them, so you can see—"

"No."

Saunders looked up at Jax again and the dark eyes of the mechanic, curtained under that absurdly attractive long mohawk, darkened with confusion.

"Jax, I don't want to see any more dead bodies. I don't want to think about what's out there, or how long we have in here. I can't." The torrent of words jumbled from her mouth.

"Okay…" Jax started but Saunders cut her off. She fisted a hand in the shock of long hair at the base of Jax's neck to pull her down into a pointed kiss.

"I want you to make me forget about it," she breathed to the space between them. Having this with Jax, no matter how fraught it had been, meant everything in this nightmare they lived in. "Just, take me back to your quarters," Saunders pleaded. Let this tall, brooding, deeply committed woman she loved take her before Tess, or the shadows, or whatever sought entrance from beyond these station walls, could return for Saunders and take her instead.

"Is that really a good idea right now?" Jax stuttered.

Saunder gripped the front of those blasted coveralls like they were a lifeline.

"I don't care what is or isn't a good idea right now Jax, I just want you naked and on top of me."

Jax didn't reply, and Saunders pulled her tighter. Then the Mechanical Engineer wrapped arms around Saunders' shoulders and pulled her in close.

"Yeah, okay."

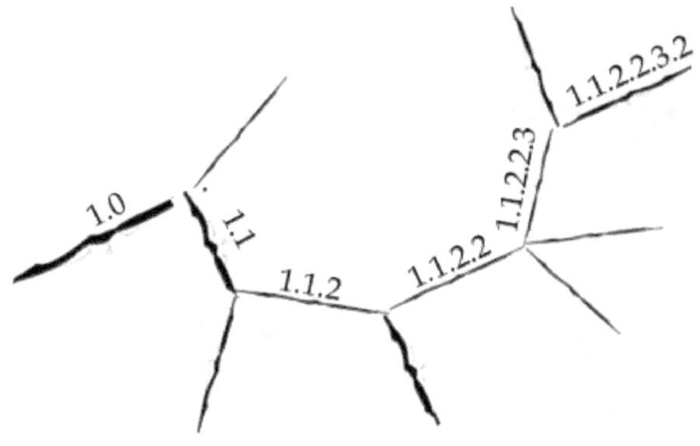

1.1.2.2.3.2

Jax had come back to her quarters for something, but what it was, she couldn't recall. Not since Saunders had greeted her when the door opened and pulled her desperately, hungrily into the tangle of blankets on their bedding. Now Jax's mind was elsewhere, caught between the strain of her wrist as she worked her fingers, the cant of her hips, and the look of Saunders' head thrown back against the pillows, the smooth column of her neck bare and inviting to Jax's lips.

The walls of their small quarters echoed with the all-to-familiar sounds of their rhythm. Jax could only hope the corridor beyond their door was clear. Saunders' body tensed, back arching, her voice crying out to leak into the unforgiving void of space beyond the window that framed their bed. Strong arms wound tight around Jax, pulling her closer, encouraging the pressure between them as Saunders' fingers tangled in the hawk of hair down Jax's head.

It wasn't until they both lay still again, panting and physically spent, that Jax tried to recall why she had bothered trying to return to their bunk in the first place. It wasn't as if she had been caught by surprise by Saunders' presence, more that she had sought the Security Officer out.

"How long have you been hanging out in here?" Jax breathed heavily into Saunders' cleavage where she lay.

Saunders didn't immediately answer, and Jax stared out from her resting place to take in the disarray of their quarters. The interior decorating hadn't really progressed.

"How long did it take you to come looking for me? Making me wait?" Saunders huffed with a breathy chuckle.

Jax gave an exhausted snort and shook her head. But she *had* come looking for Saunders. Because Saunders hadn't been easy to find. Jax's glance landed on the battered tablet tucked into Saunders' grey duffle bag. She lifted her head to get a better look.

"Are you *still* looking at that thing?" Jax asked, curious.

Saunders glanced over from where she lay and shook her head.

"Just some old backups on there, don't worry about it. Did you need me for something?"

Jax looked back at the woman sprawled naked beneath her.

"Something *else*?" Saunders cracked a mischievous smirk.

"Just, Obah was looking for you. Something about inventory," Jax reported, squinting into the distance to induce better recall following their prior distraction.

Saunders rolled her eyes, then rolled out from under Jax to put her feet on the floor. She started pulling her clothing back on.

"We just talked about this. We've only been adrift for a month cycle, if they scrutinize rations this early it's going to be a shitty three years."

Jax had sat back on the bedding, letting the sheets tangle around her naked hips.

"Wait, wouldn't we *want* to keep good track of our limited supplies? I mean, I need to make my coffee supplies last, but also, we don't want to have to resort to eating each other alive or something..." Jax said it like a joke, but there was a tiny, real, horrific pinch of fear. It was like a bright pinprick of light in a dark room that hurt to glance at if she looked too closely.

Saunders scoffed, and yanked on the laces of her boots.

"First off, the only person allowed to eat me alive on this station is you."

Jax groaned in reply and buried her face in her hands.

Saunders had hopped up from the bed, clearly energized from their activity, or just the opportunity for innuendo. Jax felt the press of soft lips to the bare skin of her shoulder and glanced up to see the other woman hopscotch over the clothes on the floor to reach the exit.

"But yes, we should be careful. I just don't know if I'm going to have the energy to track every crumb and band aid for the next thirty-eight months until we either die or we reach our one-in-a-trillion target."

Saunders reached for the door latch, then paused.

"Come on Jax, you better get covered up. Things to do other than me, you know...The busted laundry machine perhaps?" Saunders indicated the growing piles of dirty laundry littering their shared quarters. Then she very much did not wait for Jax to cover up before thumbing the door latch.

Jax dove for cover as Saunders exited with a cheerful wave.

"Jillian!" Jax roared. But the door had already rolled closed again.

She *did* have things to do. Repairs to make. The time between when they had fallen through a rift and the exact current instance in time yawned ever wider, leaving the anomaly in their wake as they pressed on through the stars. The engines wouldn't be fast. But they would pick up a respectable speed over the next year, and then...they would have to predict when they would need to start slowing down so they could arrive. "Arrive where" was still very much a question that hung over their necks.

But they had made this choice. Jax wasn't sure if there was even an alternative. And so, every day cycle Jax awoke to the endless, infinite void of unfamiliar space, and she went about caring for her Station. She had spent so long living this life already that she hardly could tell a difference. Well, the sex was different. That hadn't been part of her life before. Nor had she been able to recognize so many faces. Too many people felt familiar to her now. Okay, so Andee was alright. So was Ged, more or less. And Rose wasn't too bad either…

Jax stretched to ease the pleasant burn from their earlier activity and sought whatever corner her clothing had landed in. She certainly hadn't expected a relationship with Saunders to be so aggressively physical. Not that she was complaining. Jax probably shouldn't have been surprised by it, but it was new, and her monotonous days were suddenly filled with a different thrill. At least it took her mind off their slim odds out here.

The same couldn't be said for the residents. The typically salacious transients had begun to realize they were not quite so transient anymore. Jax felt only slightly vindicated that they had to start dealing with the fallout of their casual encounters up front and personal. But really, the entire populace had started to degrade into some well of depression and isolation. Jax could only relate harder to it, and figured it was a net-positive all around. But the feeling threatened to spill over into something worse, and she could tell there would be a limit to how much despair could be held in the confines of her Station's walls.

For one, Jax was intimately aware of how little coffee she had left in her own microcosm.

Today's duties included most unfortunate plumbing activity, and so, massive three-foot spud wrench slung over her shoulder, Jax strode past the galley on Level 5, where she horded her emergency stash, and made the bold decision to descend to Level 4, to pillage. One galley seemed permanently off limits to everyone, and Jax was certain it had been liberated of its stores to ensure no one had reason to linger there longer than it took to remember the horrendous visions of slaughter. So Jax slunk toward the galley on the back ninety degrees.

To her chagrin, there were people already occupying the space. But the coffee pot was in use and sported some surplus Jax figured she could snag. It was a small amount of luck that the residents present were Rose, her towering brother Collins, and the beefy lead Space Marine, Tizik, who nodded at Jax as she snuck around the back of the group to find a mug.

"Look, you have my support. I gave that to you fully when we made this choice. I didn't want to sit around waiting to die either, but that doesn't mean I *understand* this."

Tizik had clearly been engaging Rose on some topic prior to Jax's arrival, since the researcher sighed as if she had already been explaining something. Unnervingly, and without even turning to look at her, Rose addressed Jax instead.

"Engineering, perhaps you could provide some perspective here for our Operations Specialist Second Class Bracken?"

Jax, caught with a mug of illicitly procured coffee halfway to her lips, froze in her path and glanced around at the three faces trained on her.

"Uh, about what?"

Rose took a deep breath as if she were addressing a lecture hall.

"We were trying to discuss the probability of obtaining our target. Operations Specialist—"

"You guys call me Tizik all the time, you can stick to that," the Space Marine interjected.

"Tizik was asking about how we know where we are going." Collins' voice rolled down from his height like thunder off a mountain.

"So, what good am I in this conversation? I just run the engines." Jax wasn't a deep-space astrophysics researcher. Not anymore at least.

Rose studied her for a moment. Jax felt the scrutiny in her soul. Once again, here was Rose, putting Jax's limited academics on display, seeking some sort of feedback loop Jax wasn't sure she could provide.

"In fact, we were banking on you for a better layman's explanation," Rose said, finally, after a long moment of peeling back Jax's whole being with her eyes. "Since clearly you understand this challenge, yourself. Being...of course, *just* a mechanic."

Jax slumped her shoulders in resignation and sidled up to the galley island where the group stood. Fine. She could show off her rustier skills, like a side-show act. It was a fitting use for Jax's sordid past with academia.

"The equipment you guys have is *extremely* limited. Usually, it takes absolute ages to find an exoplanet—"

"Planets that are not within humanity's origin solar system," Rose provided helpfully. Tizik nodded.

"Right, so these guys have the ability to sense some orbital mechanics of a distant star. It used to take forever, studying portions of the sky—and it's a big-ass sky, finding a star that wobbled—"

"See this is where you lose me," Tizik interrupted. Jax looked plaintively at Rose and then glanced up at where Collins towered. They *had* to be twins. The low gravity on Mars wouldn't allow for someone as small as Rose if it wasn't that she had shared a womb with someone who took up far more space.

Rose simply conceded the floor to Jax, who felt like she was back in graduate school giving her oral exam. Or, well, one of her oral exams...

"Gravity. It's all about gravity," Jax leveled with Tizik. "Gravity is generated by mass. We all have mass, so we enact a gravitational pull on each other. Usually there is something far larger to distract that pull, like a planet or star, this Station even, so we aren't stuck orbiting each other. Every planet has a gravitational impact on the star it orbits. With every orbit around that star, it tugs the star toward it. And to us, from very far away, it looks like a wobble."

Rose's smile was a dead-ringer for one Jax had seen in her past telling her she had passed with full marks. It made for a strangely uncomfortable twist in Jax's gut.

"So, you guys looked out at these billions of strange new stars and immediately saw them wobbling?" Tizik sounded precisely as incredulous as he had every right to be. It *was* an improbability.

"We did," Collins replied. He crouched so that he could trace his finger across the countertop. "It was advantageous that we had the machinery set up prior to the Drop, as it was already scanning for gravitational signatures. We happened upon these readouts rather quickly, which is anomalous in itself, but yet, provided us an option."

Tizik shook his head aggressively and leveled Jax with a stare.

"But we had the *entire sphere* of space surrounding us. How the hell could you have been certain you found something we could reach? The best option? This all just sounds so infinitely impossible!"

"No, you're right," Jax answered, taking a searingly hot gulp of coffee to wash down the anxiety that drifted up every time she spared a thought about it. "There's probably no way of us ever knowing if there might have been a better option. We could have spent a lifetime in that one spot, searching, and still never been sure."

"So, we are taking this on faith?"

"Unfortunately, yes," Rose concluded. "In a strike of infinite luck, we found something promising. I had one of my post-doctoral candidates run a rudimentary sweep on the spectrum and we saw enough data to believe this is in reasonable reach for us. Perhaps we have been so lucky as to have landed in a place in the universe teeming with potential worlds."

"Or maybe we are on our way to nowhere," Tizik countered.

At this, Jax assumed her contributions were no longer needed, and the high of her midday romp with Saunders was wearing off too fast for her to be able to sustain this conversation. She bowed her head and pushed off from the counter, leaving the empty coffee cup behind, and reached for her wrench where it leaned against the far counter.

The other three, delving deeper into their conversation, were distracted from her departure, and she only just caught Tizik's follow-up question as she strode off down the corridor.

"Teeming with potential planets. What are the odds that means teeming with intelligent life?"

Jax shuddered. *That* was a thought she was definitely not ready to examine too closely. Maybe in some other universe, but she sure as fuck hoped that wouldn't be the case with this one.

The laundry machine was a daunting task. Jax was fresh out of coveralls, and the fact she had to get elbows deep in possibly stagnant dirty water in just a long-sleeved shirt and work pants made her grumpy.

This whole adventure would tax the hell out of her Station. They had been two months past their most recent resupply. Jax's systems were efficient, but three years was plenty of time to burn out the oxygen scrubbers, push the water recycler to a limit, overload the waste storage, and put them all at odds with survival. It was easier to just not think about it.

But, Saunders' manifests had estimated fifty-five residents on a Station with capacity for over two hundred, with factors of safety to cover everyone's asses twice, so they weren't hopeless. It didn't stop people from over working the fucking laundry machine, leaving them all in the choicest of emergency fashion statements.

Well, they *had* fifty-five residents. But ten had simply vanished (or maybe eleven?), and at least five had died, and honestly, as callous as it was, it meant longer odds for the rest of them. Jax hadn't asked, but she knew Saunders took it to heart to figure out who they had lost, even if they hadn't found anyone since Kotey Higgs' departure. There wasn't a possibility of finding anyone alive after this much time. Jax wanted Saunders to make her peace with that, and hence refused to bring it up.

Maybe the worst part of their little adventure would be this stupid laundry machine. Jax tossed a discarded and abandoned dirty garment (gross) into the vacuum entry on one end and hit the start button. It should only take about five minutes for a small load to pass through, but nothing exited the other side. She knelt to examine the water intake and flow meter and noted that flow was minimal. So water was being drawn into the machine, but at low rates. The outlet looked dry. That meant it was a blockage.

There were any manner of reasons the laundry machine could be blocked and all of them were disgusting. Jax glowered as she locked out the power source to the control box on the conveyor and hoisted her wrench to her shoulder to pry the main housing off. She gained leverage near the conveyor tube, which would pull clothing through the rapid wash cycle. The problem she sought was somewhere before the water reclamation basin, and before flash-heat auto dry.

The chassis was stubborn. Jax rolled up the sleeves of the waffle-knit shirt she wore, and unbuttoned what buttons she had at her neck. She hefted her tool belt around her hips and stepped up to put her whole weight into prying the chassis off.

"Here, let me help you with that," Ged called out from the entrance.

Jax let her frustration at the stubborn machinery fuel her glare, but the man seemed immune to her charm. He strode inward and grabbed a prybar from Jax's auxiliary tools. With two points of contact, and the added leverage, the chassis groaned, and the outer shell popped off its clips to fall forward on its hinges.

The smell would have immediately sent Jax roaring off about the poor hygiene of the residents, if it weren't for the mottled grey hand that flopped forward with the outer casing.

Ged also stepped back in alarm, his own immediate act of revulsion telling Jax it was okay for her to desperately want to flee the area.

"Oh, this is not good."

"S-Security," Jax croaked into the comms port clipped to her collar.

"Call Obah too," Ged ordered, as he stepped gingerly forward to examine what was in front of them.

"Security!" Jax barked into the comms, forcefully this time.

A beat. Silence. Jax stared at the arm the hand was connected to. It looked like it had been in the laundry recycler a long time.

"This is Security, Jax is that you?"

"Yes, it's me," Jax replied, and opened her mouth to say more. Nothing came out.

"What is it, Engineering?" Saunders pressed. Jax was distantly aware that several sets of ears might hear this call.

Ged had returned to Jax's side and he gently reached out and pulled the comms port from under her fingers and off her collar.

"Security, this is Gedry. Can you and Obah join us in the laundry system access room?" he spoke calmly into the port.

"On our way." The comms went quiet.

Jax stepped closer to see what she was looking at.

"Easy there, Engineering," Ged warned.

The arm belonged to a body. The body was wrapped around the vacuum conveyer tube, as if to fill the entirety of the space within the chassis. This was supposed to be how the water recycling passed through the system, but the body was blocking it, keeping whatever water was present stagnant. The flesh was mottled from the decay and the exposure to the wet environment. For an instant, Jax was horrified they could have been all drinking corpse water, if it were not for the fact that Laundry was a long way off in the recycle process before anything returned for human consumption.

There was no natural way this body could have gotten into this space. From its position, Jax could not make out who it might be. She stepped back, arm over her nose. Then Saunders entered the room.

"What exactly is going on—" Saunders saw the body.

Both Saunders and the woman in her wake swept forward to examine the situation. Jax was distantly aware of Ged offering his wife a summary of what happened, but she was watching Saunders as she sought answers within the machine.

"How—, how did he even get *in* here?" Saunders asked, voice quiet and filled with bewilderment. But Jax could only think: Rift.

"Saunders, who *is* that?" she asked, stepping closer again. Saunders stood up and put her hand over her mouth, either to quell the scent of decay, or to cover her distress. Jax put a tentative hand on her shoulder and Saunders did not react.

"I think...It has to be—but that doesn't make *sense,*" Saunders replied, hushed.

"How many people are *still* missing??" Jax hissed, alarmed.

Saunders' shoulder stiffened under her hand and the shorter woman shrugged out from under the touch. She turned to look at Jax.

"I don't *know* Jax," she replied, voice tight.

"Okay, so *who* is that?" Jax glanced over her shoulder as Ged's wife examined the body.

"His name is Corley. But, he's not supposed to *be* here," Saunders muttered.

Jax opened her mouth with so many comments and questions they jammed up at her lips all at once. The commotion in the laundry room had drawn more attention and Tizik appeared at the door.

"Is that..." He trailed off.

"Tiz, not yet," Saunders called out thickly, but the Space Marine and Ged were already working on extricating the man from his resting place. The body's decay had advanced enough that even just starting to move him threatened to have him fall apart.

"We haven't found anyone in weeks, why now?" Obah lamented, watching from the sidelines.

"Do we know if he was someone missing, or someone new?" Tizik growled as he pried at the machinery to release the man's body without it dissolving into its constituent parts.

Jax shoved forward and shoulder checked the massive soldier to prevent him from breaking her machinery. Tizik simply shifted to another location and continued to try to prize the corpse free. Jax brushed the rubbery skin and nearly retched on contact, backing away again to watch helplessly as her laundry machine was dismantled.

The smell was overwhelming, and Jax gave her hardware up for loss. She would let Ged and Tizik break the damned thing. Jax could go back and fix it later when it was corpse-free. Jax pushed out of the room into the corridor and took a welcome breath of stale Station air.

To her surprise, Saunders was the one to follow her out.

"Aren't you gonna, I dunno, stay with, uh, the..." Jax stalled.

"The body?" Saunders finished for her. She looked angry. Jax wasn't sure whether such fury was directed at her or at the simple fact she had found another casualty.

"Sorry, I just figured." Jax wasn't actually sure what she had figured. The site of a decaying resident in the laundry system was plenty enough to occupy her thoughts for a moment.

"Jax, I distinctly remember Corley, but I also have no records of him being on station. It's like my entire ability to track our people is a gaslit joke. Nothing matches, and I can't be sure *who* is missing."

Jax was waving a few curious residents back from the facilities, hoping to avoid any form of additional commotion.

"Yeah well, it was madness right before the Drop, maybe we hallucinated some people."

"Hallucinated people who are back again?" Saunders sounded incredulous. "That's a real man in there."

"Okay, so then you're shitty at your job," Jax snipped offhandedly, the strain of the day getting to her already. She immediately regretted it. Saunders leveled her with a glare fueled by pure green flame.

"Fuck you," Saunders seethed.

Jax threw her hands out in supplication.

"No, c'mon I didn't *mean* that! You are fucking great at your job!" Jax cried in objection to her own stupidity.

"Oh, sure. The only person who's more of a shitshow on this station is you!" Saunders snarled.

Jax felt something like a punch to the gut and had to shake her head to string together words.

"Excuse me?" she barked, incredulous. "Are you fucking kidding me?"

"Sorry, no offense," Saunders replied, with a sneer.

"No, I deserve that entirely. Saunders, I was being *sarcastic. You* are the force holding this place together, not me!" Jax felt panicky. There was a dead guy in her laundry machine and she was royally fucking up the role of being literally any form of partner to Saunders.

The short blond was burning a hole through Jax with her heated glare still.

"Jax you have a lot to fucking learn about *people*, you fucking gremlin."

It stung, but Jax figured she earned every barb.

"You *know* my background. You've *seen* how terrible my nightmares can be," Saunders continued.

"Yeah, but you're over all that," Jax replied in a spectacular final display of stupidly.

Saunders snapped upright and took a distinct step backward.

"You *would* think that, Jax, wouldn't you," she snarled. Saunders then turned sharply and stomped back into the laundry room.

Jax remained where she stood, stunned, then slammed the heel of her fist into her forehead in frustration.

"Fuck!" she roared, and stomped off down the corridor. They could drag that dead guy down to the morgue on their own. She stormed down the back access to Level 1, putting as much distance between herself and the madness above her.

Level 1 had always been the only other level with full access available to the residents. Jax usually avoided it in an effort to dodge human interaction. But these days most residents were holed up in their quarters in their little depression pit. The corridor was abandoned.

Some number of degrees to Jax's right, clockwise to Station rotation, Rose's team would be manning their equipment, steadily trained on their distant target. On the far side of the ring, the Space Marines would be holed up in the Security Office, calling fruitlessly into the void. To Jax's left, a dark patch of corridor loomed.

She wasn't sure if residents had knocked the lights out or if they had gone out on their own, but she let her feet carry her into the darkness.

Several degrees along, Jax noticed someone had blocked the security lighting on the flooring and the segment of ring dipped into pitch black. The only light spilled from the distant corridor lights still working at the fringes of the segment. She nearly collided with the edge of a couch someone had dragged into the corridor, and Jax realized several pieces of furniture had been relocated. She wanted to be mad about it, but they were positioned to allow occupants to stare out the more prominent windows of Level 1 into the distant cosmos in which they were flying toward. In the lack of interior lighting, Jax could make out the faint color of distant cosmic dust. They really were moving.

The magnetism of the yawning infinite space beyond pulled her toward the windows. She pressed her hands to them so she could gaze outward.

"You know what I find so very funny," a voice said, drifting over from the couch.

Jax clearly had been unnerved by the dead guy encounter because she did not make a dignified noise in response to the jolt of adrenaline the voice generated in her. She spun to try to get a better look, but the darkness was pressing and the speaker was just out of sight. She pressed her back against the windows, straining to make out any shape, but whoever it was, they had melded into the hulking forms of the furniture. She took a tentative step closer.

"It's that, while the rest of us were thrust so violently into the very depths of hell, the only two employees of this cursed place instead found themselves on their honeymoon," the voice continued.

Jax froze. She then angled herself to creep along the windows, aiming for a better line of sight of the nearest couch. Zick lounged across it, his feet up on the far arm, his head below the near arm. Jax felt instantly grumpy at the interruption of her reverence of the coming infinite.

"What, exactly, is your fucking problem, Rogle?" she huffed out in frustration. Her recent argument with Saunders was anything but a "honeymoon."

"My problem?" Zick turned on the couch, his body more stiff as he assailed Jax where she stood. "My problem is that while the rest of us suffer through this nightmare, the two of you are just having the sweetest time, aren't you?"

The thought of Saunders, four levels up, and in a shit mood, begged to differ. Jax scowled.

"That's not it," Jax replied, keeping her voice even. Zick remained half risen, his eyes narrowed at Jax. "You had a problem the moment this all started. The moment we dropped. Maybe before that. Before Saunders and I were even a thing. So it can't be that."

Zick slumped back down on the couch to look at the ceiling.

"You don't even know what the rest of us were going through before that drop. You and Security weren't the only ones battling horrors. We all were struggling."

Jax took the opportunity to boldly turn her back on him so she could look out of the portholes at infinity spiraling toward them.

"So if you all were struggling, then that makes none of us 'special' in this universe, does it?"

Zick shuffled behind her and she hazarded a glance at the barest reflection of him in the porthole glass, but the stars outshone any detail.

"Oh, we agree on that, Engineering. What I don't understand is why the two of you then continue to act like some sort of authority."

"Were you just pissed you weren't going to get to be in charge? Too used to being the boss?" Jax theorized. Silence. "Maybe you just hate this place. I know you aren't alone in that."

"You can't possibly relate to how anyone might hate this place," Zick replied. His voice was a more careful timbre. It didn't contain the constant sneer, just an edge of distrust.

"Much like most people can't relate to how much I had to hate myself to stay out here as long as I have," Jax offered.

Silence. Jax hazarded a glance over her shoulder but all she could make out was Zick's faint silhouette.

"You know the odds we would have been rescued by now are higher than anyone might want to admit."

"You don't know that," Jax countered.

"And you don't know that I'm wrong. You just have to live with the fact that you two won that little dispute, and here we are: flying toward our inevitable death. What exactly do you think is out there, Engineering?"

Jax paused. She didn't know the answer, and that was the point. But she didn't know how else to tell *him* that.

"What, exactly, do you want us to do about it now? Go back?"

"Not a bad start."

"And what does that get us? What if there is no rescue?" Jax rounded on the man and stood across from him, begging an answer.

Zick swung his feet down from the couch and planted them on the floor.

"Are you asking me, Engineering, would I rather continue a fool's errand into the void or take my chances that rescue awaits us if we return? Because I never took you for an idiot. Mostly I just took you for whipped." He stood.

Jax had no words. She only glared at the outline of his figure as her eyes accustomed to the lack of lighting.

"I'm not trying to take over, Engineering," Zick continued. He had turned as if to leave. "I'm just trying to make sure enough of us are alive at the end of all this to know, we should have stayed."

With that, he strode off.

Jax spun on the spot to glare back out as the yawning void beckoning them onward. Her eyes had fully adjusted to the darkness and the rest of the corridor came into better view.

Another three degrees down, a faint green light glowed in the gloom.

As she approached, she realized it was the same airlock they had battled OS2 Bracken's squadmate over. That guy, Pento Ricken, had survived the Drop just fine, lashed to the back wall where Saunders had secured him. For all Jax knew, he was holed up in the old security office, paying his penance for beating her Station to a bloody pulp with the fruitless task of scanning the opposite end of the universe for radio waves.

But the light was green. And Jax was damned sure it hadn't been in the last several months. She strode over and pulled up the access logs, thumbing through the data readout of the last several actuation cycles.

Saunders wasn't in their room when Jax finally made it back to Level 5, and she couldn't be sure the Security Officer wanted to be found. She figured they would have a lot more to discuss besides the mere fact that the airlocks seemed to be cycling more than she could account for. Some sick dread in Jax's gut told her she carried too much hope that this wasn't related to the missing residents in any way. The reminder of Koty Higgs forever floating in the distant cosmos seemed to haunt her more than she was willing to admit.

She wasn't sure when she had passed out, but Jax was somewhere between sleep and wakefulness when the solid weight of Saunders filled the space behind her. Strong arms wrapped around her waist, and lips pressed to the base of her neck. The warm feeling of a body behind her made Jax involuntarily shift to press her back against Saunders. The bed may be narrow but with them finding a way to stay as close as humanly possible, they had little need for more room.

Saunders' hands shifted, trailing upward to Jax's shoulder so she could pull it back, allowing her own head to fall forward over Jax's ear. A kiss, and the slight graze of teeth on Jax's shoulder pulled Jax further from sleep.

"I thought we weren't talking," Jax muttered, halfway still dreaming.

"We don't need to talk," Saunders whispered right by her ear.

"Probably should," Jax replied, shivering under the lips that had returned to her shoulder.

"Honestly wasn't aware we had stopped." The lips trailed down her shoulder.

Jax knew, distantly, they needed to do this right and address their argument, or, at the very least, apologize. But insistent fingers traced down her side and snaked down beneath the blanket, indicating that maybe Jax was already forgiven. Sure, they needed to work out their little spat, but, Jax wasn't exactly opposed to this either. And the questing fingertips of Saunders' eager hands assuaged some of the concerns Jax had gathered about where they stood.

"Are we okay?" Jax heard herself ask.

Saunders' hands had slipped below Jax's waistband, and she hardly had the conscious ability to register the reply.

"Of course Jax, we're okay."

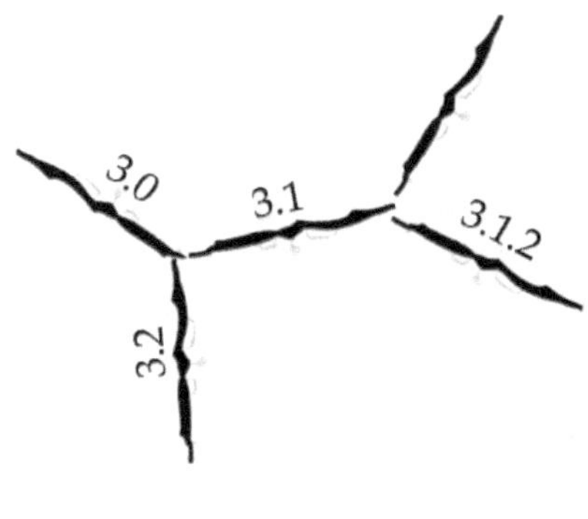

3.1.2

The hot, dense foliage of Creea, home planet of the Skraawl, proved a challenging course. Jax estimated they had only made it several yards before she regretted landing the shuttle so far from the entrance to the Skraawl Citadel.

"We're never going to get there in time with this mess to kick through," Jax huffed in frustration, kicking the base of some vegetation.

The moist atmosphere made her leg hurt. The scratch she had sustained ages ago looked healed, but every now and then it flared up, making her leg burn and itch. She usually forgot about it until they were dragged to some painfully moist planet surface that assaulted her lung capacity and aggravated her former injuries. Maybe she was just getting old.

"Jax, careful, I haven't figured out enough about their culture to know what you can and cannot *kick*," Saunders hissed from behind her, ducking under branches and vines that easily assaulted Jax in the face.

"Are we even going to be able to communicate with them?" Jax mused aloud, dodging another branch the other woman could tilt her head to avoid. Something alive in the foliage keened out a call, and Jax hoped it wasn't hungry for mechanics.

The Skraawl mostly used screeching and dismemberment for conversation, and Jax had only really met them once. Maybe there had been some language in there, but she hadn't ever heard it. Screech, she could do. The dismemberment? Not so much.

"I think I can get us by with enough. I had hoped for a bit longer to prepare, but Legs has sort of forced our schedule to shorten up."

Jax looked over her shoulder to see Saunders deftly sidestep a seeking tendril of vine. Too many things on this planet seemed sentient, and devoid of *boundaries*.

"I suppose revolutions rarely stick to a timely plan," Jax mused. "Uh, babe?"

"Yes?" Saunders stopped up short, hands on her hips, as if indicating they had important places to be, and no time for sightseeing.

"You're sure you can brush off those language skills, right?" Jax pointedly ignored Saunders' expression of impatience.

"Jax, I just said—" but Saunders caught on.

From the foliage, several sharp, obsidian blades emerged. Each menacing weapon was fused to a length of spear, and gripped in the claws of a creature that blended with the greenery surrounding them. Strong, sturdy forelegs sank into the ground like tree trunks. A swiftly arcing spine brought the aft legs up and over with dexterous feet that could grip the weaponry with vicious looking needle-sharp talons.

"Shit."

"Excellent diplomacy Jillian, I commend you," Jax muttered in reply.

"Shut *up*." Saunders had spun around to face the gathering that had encircled them.

A face emerged, following the spear encroaching on what Jax foolishly assumed was her personal space. The spear, and its bearer, did not care. The vampire-bat-like face scrunched up to bare its sinister fangs. A barbed tongue swept out past the teeth.

"Anything more productive to say before they start taking parts?" Jax hissed.

"I can't tell if Nos is here, I don't recognize anyone," Saunders growled back. More faces had emerged.

One of the Skraawl took a decisive and thundering step forward on the heavy forelegs and thrust its spear. But the Skraawl beside it swayed sideways as if it was off balance and knocked into the one breaking ranks. A screech and a hiss and Jax saw claws bared. Another Skraawl from the other side of the pair bellowed and stomped forward, adding to the stirring unrest. The newcomer flapped its fur cape and roared again, causing the mutinous Skraawl to turn and hiss a reply in solidarity. The caped leader kicked out with the right foreleg and knocked the original perpetrator to the ground, before swinging its glinting black blade around and promptly slicing the spear-wielding arm of the other Skraawl clean off.

The amputee squealed some horrible reply, and nursed the injury, but faded back into the group.

Jax felt Saunders bump into her from behind.

"Time to run yet?" Jax squeaked. From around them she spotted a few other Skraawl sporting limbs in various stages of regrowth. That victim's limb would be back in probably half a cycle.

A hand reached back to touch Jax on the thigh ever so slightly. Saunders was going to try to talk to them. Jax squeezed at her wrist again in growing anticipation.

"We come to speak to, uh, *EEikkaa...*" Saunders made a sound that was reminiscent of nails on a chalkboard at a death metal concert and Jax had to stifle a bark of laughter amidst threat of loss of limb.

The roiling mass of Creea Natives shifted around them.

"*EEiiittaaaaay,*" one of the Skraawl snarled in response. And Jax instantly missed Saunders' more dulcet tones of screech. The outburst from one Skraawl elicited several hisses in response from the others.

"What, did you pronounce it wrong or something?" Jax muttered, shifting her gaze from one to the other as the creatures bobbed around them.

Then another Skraawl, also wrapped in a thin fur cloak, strode forward, brandishing its blade. The point jabbed at them both and Saunders took a step away from it. The first cloaked leader had turned and was barking some form of orders to the others. A gap in the ranks opened and the leader strode through. The Skraawl at their back pushed them again, the horrific blades inching closer and closer.

"I think we need to follow them," Saunders replied, pushing Jax forward.

Jax's feet betrayed her.

"But how do we know if they got the message or not?"

"We don't," Saunders replied.

The band of Skraawl led them through the dense wooded area of their home planet, emerging at the base of a massive carved stone structure. Jax suspected it had once been caves, but it was clearly more than that. The procession had settled into a formation flanking them from either side, with the cloaked Skraawl taking post at the front and back.

While a few other Skraawl also sported cloaks, the rest were without any clothing. Jax wasn't quite sure what passed for fashion out here, other than fur scraps. As they approached the stone monolith, Jax felt a twisting mix of horror and fascination. A Skraawl to her left appeared to have an argument with its garments. It flailed in entanglement and its cloak flapped around it in objection before dislodging and taking to the sky like a large single bat wing. It fluttered and glided upward as if on a thermal to disappear into a cave entrance overhead, while its prior occupant let out a chilling screech.

"Did you fucking *see* that?" Jax snarled toward Saunders who had her head down and her eyes locked on the shape of the Skraawl in front.

"See what?" Saunders replied, not breaking her stare.

"That one's clothes just...flew away?" Jax felt at a loss for what to say.

"Jax, the Cloaks are a symbiotic parasite. How did you miss that?"

"Must have been paying attention to literally all the other shit we are dealing with," Jax muttered.

"That's weird though," Saunders continued, not breaking her line of site with the creature ahead. "The pairing is supposed to be permanent. I wonder why it left."

"Oh, sure, *that's* the weird part..." Jax hissed, watching her footing. The rock face looming ahead was surrounded by vines and roots that looked treacherous.

"Yeah, well, keep it down, I don't know what they do or do not understand. But I'm pretty sure that's Cul in front of us. I didn't recognize them."

Jax glanced up at what she suspected to be the Skraawl second-in-command. The Skraawl's Cloak, now that Jax could see it, was latched to the neck of the creature. There was no fastener. It simply looked like it was fused to the skin there, where it fluttered slightly. Jax realized it was a mouth, sucking at the back of the neck of the creature. Along the length of each of the Skraawl's aft legs, the Cloak appeared to be gripping into the flesh with pin-sharp dewclaws. Jax shuddered at the sight.

Cul lead them through a cavernous entrance carved directly into the cliffside. Inside the cave, light emanated from hidden sources Jax couldn't quite see. The walls looked hewn, as if they had been carved generations ago, rather than simply formed.

"Okay, I'm still figuring out the pentagram tech, I know it's all biosynthicate, and their technology relies heavily on the psychic surge from the mold, but what exactly do these guys have in terms of tech advancement? Or are they just stealing the same stuff we are?" Jax asked, from the side of her mouth. It wasn't enough. A Skraawl nearest her shrieked some ungodly pitch in her ear.

Saunders didn't bother replying. Another turn showed a room off to the side with what looked like screens displaying images. Jax felt a thrill at the idea these creatures might have actual tech and not some bastardized biological options. But the group dragged them onward.

A massive meeting room opened up around them with a large, ring-shaped slab in the middle. At the far end another Skraawl stood, Cloaked and menacing, as Jax and Saunders were escorted closer.

"Nos," Saunders said quietly.

Nos was larger than any of the other Skraawl surrounding them. They also had what looked like double-aft limbs, giving an insectile look to an otherwise hodgepodged body plan. The Cloak ruffled around Nos' forelegs.

The procession had stopped and the lead Skraawl lumbered forward. Jax noted the glinting obsidian in each of the leader's four manipulative legs: small blades, perfect for slicing. Nos circled them heavily before stopping in front of Saunders. The barbed tongue snaked out past the insidious needle teeth, but stopped short of getting intimate with Jax's Security Officer.

"SkeeeeEEEEKAAAAAH" Nos bellowed, drawing its tongue back in and whirling toward the stone slab. As Jax watched the center illuminated and small specks of light moved to generate shapes and images. If there were letters or language in there, Jax couldn't read it, but a flickering pattern told her it was Pentagram language being transcribed.

"Shit, whatever message Legs sent them, they got it," Saunders whispered beside her.

"Oh...so we are *fucked*," Jax hummed in reply.

Nos spun on them as if to ask "are you seeing this? This proof that we know?" and Jax flinched. The glowing image stopped moving and flickering, pausing in space. It was a perfect three-dimensional rendering of their Station. The image started moving again. Something cycled in the corner and Jax realized it was a counter of sorts.

"None of this looks good," she muttered. The image continued.

"YyyyEEEeeeekkeeee" Nos amended. Jax felt she had nothing more to add so she simply nodded. Before she knew it a greyish-green blur had knocked her off her feet, landing her square on her back, her head ringing against slick stone flooring. A sinister obsidian blade was pressed menacingly against her left kneecap.

"Watch it, you bat-lizard," Jax grit out through clenched teeth, fighting to overcome the wind being knocked out of her. "Mine don't grow back!"

Saunders was suddenly on top of her, hand shoving the blade back and shouting something unintelligible back at Nos. Cul's blade pushed past Saunders again and stabbed at Jax, easily slicing the fabric of her pants. She felt the razor thin edge of obsidian stop just short of breaking the skin. Cul snarled and put more pressure on top of Jax, pinning her below.

"EEEEeekkaaaaa!" Saunders was shouting again.

"SrreeeeeeekEEEEAA," Nos snarled from somewhere else in the room.

It was a tight little micro-universe: Jax on the hard stone flooring, Cul pressing menacingly close, bracing her with limbs in all the wrong places, Saunders trying to pry them apart while shrieking, and that sickly blade threatening without a reason. Jax screwed her eyes shut, just waiting for the blinding pain that would remove the only left leg she had ever been given in life.

"Sorry if I said something wrong," Jax hissed under pressure.

The biting pressure at her limb released. Jax opened her eyes. Saunders was still pressed on top of her possessively, but the Security Officer was looking over at the images displayed on the stone slab. Cul had receded with a snarl. Jax glanced past the blond's shoulder to see for herself.

Superimposed over the static image of the Station, there were words Jax recognized.

"I TRIED SAUNDERS I TRIED TO SAVE HER"

"What?" Jax asked, filled with utter confusion.

Nos took a lumbering step around the slab, and jabbed with a double leg for emphasis. The words changed.

"I DON'T KNOW WHY I HAVE TO TELL YOU THIS BUT YOU ARE WORTH MORE THAN THIS STATION"

Saunders swung around toward Jax, searching for an answer or question she could not put into words. She looked back over her shoulder at Nos, then Cul, then tried her best.

"EeeeAAAkAAaaaas?"

The words changed once again.

"ALRIGHT BITCH LETS TRY THIS DANCE AGAIN"

Jax barked out a laugh, then doubled up in hysterics, despite the recent threat of dismemberment. Saunders crawled off her in alarm, and the massive aliens surrounding them backed away in whatever passed for concern.

"You—Aheheheh—You fuckers, you brilliant fucking weirdos—*cough*—" Jax tried catching her breath. "You cracked into the Station's servers, didn't you?" Jax lost it in a fit of giggles again.

"What the fuck are you talking about?" Saunders asked from the side of her mouth, still eyeing the words floating between her and the leader of the Skraawl.

"I SUPPOSED ITS TIME TO RUN OFF TO SOMETHING ELSE" the words rearranged.

"I take it back, you can have my left leg if you let me see how this thing works!" Jax ducked her head under the slab to look. There weren't any answers waiting for her beneath, but Nos had hoisted themselves up onto the slab as if to sit. Saunders had risen to her feet.

"Are you saying they hacked our records? Where are these words coming from?" she asked, sounding incredulous.

"These are the last things we said in the Station core...the core records everything. Oh man, you guys know *everything* I ever said in there." Jax felt her face flush.

"I didn't know those records existed!" Saunders protested.

Jax shrugged. "Different mainframe."

A shrill squeal and shriek from Nos grabbed their attention again. The Skraawl had been watching their exchange through the displayed image of the Station, and Jax glanced down at the corner counter.

"Saunders, that counter...it's our casualties..." she said, suddenly nervous again.

Saunders leaned forward and barked an inquisitive sounding screech while pointing to the counter.

Nos, from their new position on the slab, leaned forward and passed an obsidian banded claw through the counter, which stopped scrolling. Twenty-two. That was how many survivors they had left on the Foliage Prime planet.

Jax watched the glow of the holographics illuminate the chamber and the faces of those within. Saunders screeched her own absurd replies, as the Skraawl cycled through various phrases pulled from Station surveillance and memory banks. Another, smaller Skraawl, less than half the size of Nos, lumbered over toward Jax who instinctually shied away, remembering the press of an obsidian blade.

But the smaller creature, still larger than Jax, only reached out to press a clawed aft-leg into the slab and depress the surface. A segment of the stone pushed open and Jax realized it wasn't actually stone anymore. Clearly, they had manipulated it to form the casing of what was actually a large internal machine. It wasn't gears that moved inside, but lines of light and surging masses, as if the internal structure were alive.

The smallest Skraawl chortled some sort of guttural warble, and fixed most of its eyes on Jax, who looked the creature up and down in tentative wonder before stepping closer to the revealed mechanism.

Another warbled chirp and Jax felt the press of the blade at her calf again. She danced aside.

"Easy Vamp, I was still somewhat kidding about the leg!"

Saunders slipped over to her and slid her hand in Jax's.

"Jax," she said, drawing Jax's attention. "They want to team up. They think we might be the answer to get them out of Pentagram's oversight. *Jax, they want to help!*" Saunders' voice strained with tentative optimism.

"Okay, that's great, but why do they keep trying to cut my leg off? Not a great first handshake. They *do* know we can't regenerate them, right?"

Saunders turned to the slab center again, and this time, Jax realized she hadn't quite been watching how things were progressing. Saunders reached over the hard surface to let her hand immerse in the holographics and immediately several characters emerged. They were not human alphabet, but Saunders cascaded through them seeking the right ones for her needs and returned with a message she displayed for Nos.

The lead Skraawl considered the question presented to them, and then slid from the place they were resting. The creature picked up its large obsidian blade-spear again and slowly lumbered closer to Jax and Saunders. Jax didn't like the look of their approach. She reached out to grab Saunders' shoulder and put some space between them again. But Nos stopped a not uncomfortable distance from where they stood and only reached out with the spear to point to Jax's leg.

Nos screeched something, and the lights behind them on the slab flickered.

Saunders cocked her head and studied the holographics and the alien for longer than Jax might have expected. She then waved her hand to craft a new message and kneeled down next to Jax.

"Ah, what the hell Jillian?" Jax stammered uneasily as the other woman lifted the leg of Jax's pants.

"Nothing, they just seem to think you had something wrong with your leg. Their standard operating procedures when they have a problem with a limb is to just remove it. But...there's nothing wrong with your leg..." Saunders replied, and even emphasized it to the alien who flickered at least two sets of eyes down along Jax's calf.

"Certainly wasn't expecting to be showing it off on this excursion," Jax mumbled and pulled her limb from Saunders' grasp. The blond stood up again.

"So now what?" Jax asked, as they stood regarding the creatures who hosted them. Nos was still studying them. Saunders shifted, weighing her stance and how it might be interpreted by aliens that walked on their hands and killed with their feet.

"Now, we figure out if we stage a rescue, or an attack," Saunders replied with a grin.

Nos attempted to mimic the gesture, instead displaying rows of needle-sharp teeth and a dead-eyed expression.

"Uh, maybe let's not teach them to smile," Jax muttered. The holographics rearranged.

"IM SORRY I LET THE ASSHOLES LIVING DOWN THERE MESS WITH YOU"

"What the *fuck* are you saying in that Station core?" Saunders barked and Jax felt a scandalized look cross her face.

Nos lumbered forward again this time pressing them outward to the cavernous exit.

As they let the Skraawl escort them, Jax glanced back over her shoulder.

"Do they *know* what they are saying when they copy my little inner dialog like that?"

"At least they have your charm," Saunders replied, and she reached out for Jax's hand as they were led deeper into the chasms of Skraawl citadel.

5.2.1

The sideways fun-house dynamics of the tilted station didn't particularly put Saunders off. She had seen worse during zero-grav transport flights with the TSF. And besides, she liked a challenge. Jax, on the other hand, had spent so many years on this blasted station that she knew each bolt and rivet by heart—Saunders suspected, on occasion, intimately—which made it all the more entertaining to watch the mechanic trip her way across the new surface they had to call the floor.

Right on cue, Jax nearly face planted over the conduit box sitting proud of the wall they were walking on.

"You should probably tie your boots babe," Saunders provided, helpfully.

Jax flailed to upright herself, arms windmilling, and when she finally got herself steady again, she glared around at the small group tailing her.

Ged soldiered onward, with Corine, Lowery, and Rhyse in tow, letting Saunders catch up to where Jax stood nursing her ego. And her ankle. Obah brought up the rear, also limping, and carrying a bag for collected stock.

"I *like* my boots just fine," Jax grumbled.

Saunders threw her hands up in defense. "I mean, no complaints, happy to knock them a bit with you later even, but figured, for safety's sake..."

Jax cocked her head in an expression that clearly said "are you serious?" without the mechanic needing to say anything at all. Obah delicately picked her way past, avoiding participating in the conversation with a polite distance. Saunders gave her own sheepish grin and ducked her head to continue on their rounds. Jax followed at her side.

"Why the jokes, Jillian?" Jax asked, as she stumbled again over another uneven wall panel.

"Hey, no one calls me that outside the bedroom!" Saunders snipped. Well, okay, maybe Obah could call her that. And her dad had called her that. But that still left a pretty short list.

The mechanic paused and turned toward Saunders.

"So, you can make jokes about our sex life under the sea, in front of all the residents for that matter, but I can't call you by your first name in normal conversation?"

Saunders felt her face flush. Then she, too, tripped.

"Maybe you should tie *your* laces..." Jax grumbled.

Saunders righted herself and jabbed a gentle elbow at Jax's side. "*You* can call me whatever you like—within reason..." she amended.

Jax tripped again, and swung a hand out in balance, grabbing Saunders' wrist in the process. Saunders flexed her arm to provide the mechanic a solid object to steady against. When Jax rearranged herself, she slid her fingers down to grasp Saunders by the hand.

They followed after the others, Jax's hand flexing as she nearly tripped again. She gained her footing and then helped Saunders down the bulkhead that divided the Supply ring at the two-seventy-degree mark.

"Security, I think this one is still accessible!" Rhyse called.

"Copy that," Saunders replied, and flashed her light to indicate where they were on the ring.

Jax let go of her as they arrived where Lowery was kneeling on the entrance to a storage bay. The one overhead dripped ominously, so none of them would be trying their hand at busting that one open, but the one beneath their feet was promising.

"This should be...ah good, food stores," Saunders piped up, checking a hand-written manifest. Her tablet was toast, and the computers never worked, but Saunders had learned early on that paper and pencil could save your ass. Just, maybe not the ass of anyone else.

Obah was shaking out the carrying sacks she brought and Jax was already hammering away at the door mechanism to crank the storage bay open.

"I have a spare power pack, would that be easier?" Rhyse offered.

Jax looked up, scandalized. "And fry us all? We're sitting in a bathtub!"

"Jax," Saunders hissed, as Rhyse gave her a look of alarm. "It's not a bad idea..."

"If you have a power pack, we probably want to save it for something real, not risk it like this," Jax grumbled, amending her outburst. "I can open this manually."

"If it isn't too much then," Lowery interjected, "I'm going to keep looking. This place gives me the creeps, I'd rather get this over and done with."

Saunders didn't like the idea of anyone wandering off alone. They were still unsure of the structural status of the majority of the station, and there had already been so many failures already.

"I'll go with him," Ged replied, putting a hand on his wife's shoulder reassuringly. Lowery nodded and continued to pick his way down the warped corridor. Corine cast a tepid glance at Saunders as well and turned to leave.

"We'll meet you guys at the tug hanger with Andee, okay?" Saunders called after them. Only Ged looked back with a weak smile. The TSF teammates kept walking.

Losing Bracken hurt those two. And they were missing half their squad still. More than five Terrestrial Surface Force squadmates just vanished within the rings of this behemoth. And they didn't trust her. Saunders wanted them to, but they were a team, and not *her* team. Her team was gone. Or, well, her team was now Jax.

The Mechanical Engineer was grunting seductively at the gear box she was manhandling in a way that made Saunders feel complicated about a few things. Shaking the departing TSF Sentinels from her mind, Saunders returned to where Rhyse was desperately trying to find a way to help Jax without getting her fingers bitten.

"I can put force on the wrench while you crank the lever—"

"I don't need anyone touching my wrench!" Jax barked.

"Jax isn't a fan of sharing her toys," Saunders stated genially, as she surveyed the action.

"Look, if I get it cracked open, you can help by bracing the gap," Jax offered, in what Saunders considered a very amicable compromise.

As the Mechanical Engineer strained against the sluggish gears another sound picked up at the edge of Saunders' hearing. It sounded like dragging, but echoed weirdly. Then a large thud nearly knocked Saunders from her feet.

"What was that??" Rhyse shouted.

Saunders whirled on the woman. "You heard that too?"

The settler looked up at the storage units overhead. Outside those units, some of which were certainly flooded, was the exterior of the station and the abyss beyond. And what lurked in that beyond gave birth to the shivers Saunders felt.

Another slam against the station echoed dully around them.

"Jax," Saunders called, through gritted teeth, and she scanned the overhead. "Are you hearing this?"

But the mechanic only barked in reply. "I thought you guys were going to brace this gap, I can't keep it open forever!"

Rhyse dropped to her knees to wedge a crowbar into the gap.

Saunders remained standing, waiting for the sound to come again, but it was quiet beyond their walls. She had heard that noise before though. Jax may have slept through it, but it had kept her awake that first night trapped in here. Her imagination conjured up some phantom creature, abyssal and ancient, seeking a weakness in the station's compromised exterior, and their fragile lives within. No matter where Saunders went, there would always be monsters.

A bark of triumph dragged Saunders' attention back to the group beside her. Jax and Rhyse managed to trip the door manual release from inside, and the storage compartment rolled open. Rhyse dropped inside and started handing items to Obah and Jax.

Silence enveloped them, beyond the scuffle of the mechanic and the residents. Saunders let her attention return to the dark corridors around them. A faint flicker of light indicated how far around the bend Ged, Corine, and Lowery had gotten. Saunders at least could feel relieved that Tess hadn't accompanied them on this trip. It was creepy enough without her shadowing them, silently.

"Look, just hand me whatever you see, you don't need to sift through them as you go," Jax grumbled at Rhyse, head and shoulders proud of the wall they stood on.

Saunders rolled her eyes at the prickly mechanic. Jax needed to work on her people skills. It would probably be hard down here, with so few people.

Then, the echoing started up again. It began about twenty degrees back toward common access and swept overhead, as if massive feelers of the unseen entity were grasping for a way inside.

"Seeker," Saunders whispered to herself. As if giving a name to it made it less daunting, less terrifying.

Something splashed in a nearby drip pool from one of the flooded lockers. Saunders tore her gaze from watching the dark surface above her to looking in the small divot of water.

A flash. Another of the things she had given to Dorian. He hadn't gotten back to her, but there were more. Saunders wondered how many had already found their way inside.

The weight of the behemoth beyond them shifted overhead and then passed. Saunders looked down the corridor, but Gedry's light had since disappeared around the bend. It was as if whatever stalked outside the station followed the three who had departed. Behind Saunders, Jax was still barking orders at poor Rhyse.

"I mean the storage locker is deeper than this, you're probably standing on a container, let me see!"

Saunders turned back to find Rhyse kneeling, only the top of her head emerging, and Jax, in all her svelte glory, hanging hips and ass out of the recessed locker, with the top half of her torso sunken beneath the propped open door. The image sparked a tight panic in Saunders' gut, and her imagination flared uncomfortably.

"Hey guys, lets maybe rethink this—"

A massive smashing sound resonated the entire station.

Then the station *moved*. The unsteady surface beneath their feet shifted as if the entirety of the station had lost its static equilibrium on the sea floor.

Another smashing sound and Obah fell over, unable to support herself on her busted ankle. Saunders pitched forward, slamming a kneecap to the wall panel and gritting her teeth against the pain.

In the height of the assault, Jax had made the good decision to extricate herself from the storage bay, but Rhyse had not. The settler braced on the edges of the open bay door, still supported within.

Another smashing sound, this time directly overhead, as if the behemoth had returned for them, rattled the entirety of the station around them. A grinding sound echoed out in answer and Saunders heard a shout.

Rhyse was struggling to her feet, slipping on the slick surface within the cargo hold. Jax had regained her footing, lunging to pull the settler to safety, but the storage bay door was grinding closed. Rhyse had limited range of motion to work with and she slipped again, pulling Jax's shoulder into the closing gap.

Saunders saw the entire event in slow motion. She wanted to move, but her treacherous feet simply wouldn't respond. Why would they? They had never responded before.

Jax managed to yank her arm free of the tightening gap, and Rhyse surged upward again, trying to get her head and shoulder through the narrow opening. Saunders wanted to scream. Then the microcosm they existed in sped to catch up with her. She scrabbled to her feet and dove to pull Rhyse to safety, but Jax blocked her path.

The mechanic had braced on her palms and one heel and squarely kicked Rhyse in the face. The settler reeled and crumpled under the assault, but she tried standing back up again.

"I said, get *down*!" Jax snarled and aimed another kick. She connected squarely with Rhyse in the jaw and the settler dropped through a gap narrower than the space between her ears. The woman disappeared, but as the gap squeezed further shut, she thrust her hand up again. Saunders wanted to grab at her, but Jax was howling at the woman.

"Stay down!! What the hell is wrong with you? STAY DOWN!" Jax kicked out at the questing hand again but the gap was too small. The mechanic flipped herself over and scrabbled at the exposed mechanism she had used to wind the door open.

Saunders surged forward to grasp at Rhyse' outstretched fingertips.

"Saunders!" squealed the resident.

"Rhyse, no!" Saunders managed to get out as the doors ground shut, cutting off a feral scream.

The hand Saunders held no longer held her back. She released it and stared in horror at the barricade entombing Rhyse. Obah had also managed to regain her footing and hobbled over. The older woman dropped to her knees to hammer on the door.

Saunders felt rooted to the spot. Beneath the storage doors was silence. What had happened to Rhyse?

"Don't they fucking tell these idiots to hunker down and pick the safe side?" Jax was spewing an endless stream of rage as she slammed her tools into the gear box again. "All she had to do was get down and I can get her out, why did she have to keep *trying?*"

"Rhyse? *Rhyse!* We're trying to get you out!" Obah was calling.

Saunders knelt there, looking at the motionless hand, then at the fraught tension of the Mechanical Engineer as she worked, then at the distress of Obah hammering at the storage bay door. Somewhere down along the ring another smashing sound echoed, with more screams. Her people were still suffering.

She glanced in the direction the trio had departed in and saw that Tess had arrived, right on time. She was standing, just at the apex of the curved ceiling. Another step, and she would fade into the darkness beyond. The look on her face was almost taunting. A reminder that Saunders couldn't save anyone, even if she tried.

"Saunders get *over* here!" Jax shouted, and Saunders snapped her attention back around. Tess Jacoby wanted to haunt these halls and remind Saunders of her failures, but Saunders would spend her life fighting off these ghosts.

"I need your muscle!" Jax howled again.

Saunders managed to make her feet react. Casting a withering glare at the ghost, she hurdled over Obah and grabbed that absurd wrench.

"Jax, why did it close? I thought the power was off?" Saunders snarled as she threw her hips into restraining the wrench.

Below her Jax's back strained at the effort to dislodge the gears.

"Whatever hit the station, it tripped the mechanical fail safe. That woman—Rhyse, she could have reopened it from inside, but she just *had* to panic."

The side of Jax's face looked sweaty as if, despite the chill, she was perspiring from effort.

"Okay I think I have it. I need you to leverage that gear connection and let me in there to pop out the failsafe," Jax stated.

"I'm not letting you in anywhere," Saunders said, weakly.

Jax glared over her shoulder.

"*Jillian, just do it!*" the mechanic ordered.

Saunders flung her weight into the wrench and felt a slight give. Jax disappeared from her line of sight, and she could hear the mechanic grunting again. Then the wrench gave entirely and behind her, the storage door clunked open.

Obah was already down in the tight space, regardless of her messed up ankle. Saunders threw herself back on the wall near the open door and shone her light in to see the damage.

Rhyse was unconscious. Her arm was crushed beyond saving, holding on by whatever tissue had not been severed completely.

"We need to get her to medical," Obah called up urgently.

"Is she alive?" Jax asked.

"She's in shock," Obah replied.

Both Jax and Saunders leaned over to help pull the older woman up. Jax dropped into the storage bay alongside Obah.

"The door isn't going to close again, is it?" Saunders asked, in worry.

"I removed the lead gear. It can't. I also left my screwdriver in there, so unless it wants to defy static physics..." Jax trailed off to kneel down under Rhyse and hoist.

"All the same I'd rather see you all out of there," Saunders remarked, reaching over to help pull up.

Saunders glanced back at where Tess had stood, but the Sentinel had faded into the gloom.

They managed to get Rhyse to the surface, and the settler came to with a howl of pain. An echoing scream came from around the bend and Saunders shot to her feet to watch after it.

"Go, I can help get her to Medical with Obah," Jax yelled after her.

As if hearing the mechanic say it, Tess re-emerged from the bend and walked off toward the distant lament. Saunders looked at Obah and Jax, who were wrestling with the miserable Rhyse, and turned to follow.

"I'll find you, on Three," Saunders called over her shoulder, but Rhyse's screams were probably too loud for Jax to hear her.

Saunders picked her way across the uneven surface, her own pale flashlight a pitiful glow to see by. Tess stayed several meters ahead, moving in an awkward zigzag, as if she knew where to put her footfalls for even ground.

"Why can't you leave me be, Jacoby?" Saunders whispered under the breath, frustrated at the woman proceeding her. "This has nothing to do with you. I tried—I'm *trying*." Saunders felt a lump in her throat and she swallowed it back. There was still anguish ahead of her.

They rounded the bend, slowly, endlessly to the left, the degree tick-marks on the ceiling the best indicator of progress. The screams ahead continued, but Saunders couldn't make them out. For all she knew she was chasing even more ghosts.

Another several degrees and Saunders rounded the corner to see a faint glow. It was pale, but enough to wash Tess out in shadow. As Saunders stumbled over, she saw the hulking outline of Andee, illuminated by the light blue of her back-mounted arc welder.

Andee stood over the hunched figures of Ged and Corine, but Lowery wasn't anywhere to be seen.

"I was right next to him, I was *right there!*" Corine howled.

Ged was restraining her. The Base Sentinel flailed in his grasp and Andee stepped in to grab her by the scruff of her disheveled cropped red hair.

"Easy, killer, easy," the welder muttered.

"Don't *call* me that," Corine snarled and she wheeled around as if trying to return to Ged's side.

It was then Saunders realized Lowery *was* still there. Just whatever was left of him. His body lay, partially submerged in another drip pool, and what could be seen of him looked like he had been...chewed on. Large round welts covered his body, chunks ripped from his flesh as if something had latched on and then torn free. His face was a mangled mess.

"What happened?" Saunders released a shuddering breath. She sank to her knees next to Gedry.

"I'm...not sure, Security," Ged answered. His shoulders slumped as he reached over to prod at one of the marks.

"Don't *touch* him!" Corine spat, where she scrabbled at Andee's grip like a feral badger. "I was right *next* to him. Then that...*thing* hit the outside of the station!"

Saunders' blood ran cold. "What 'thing'?" But she knew. It was the Seeker; more real than the shadow of Tess Jacoby haunting her still.

Corine managed to extricate herself from Andee's restraint and dropped down next to Saunders and Ged. She grabbed Lowery by the collar to hoist him up from the shallow pool he lay on.

"Just, that noise, whatever hit the station, the whole place *moved*. Then he just, vanished, like something grabbed him." Corine replied, voice wavering now that she was closer to her teammate.

"Did he slip into this water?" Saunders asked, looking down at where her knees were submerged. There may have been another flash of something, but it was small. Had those creatures done this? Saunders discretely pulled her knees from the water and backed up a few inches.

"No, he didn't *slip*." Corine glared at the three of them. "Something *grabbed* him, didn't you hear me?"

"How is that even possible, dude?" Andee asked.

"What she means," Saunders interjected, putting a hand up to pause Corine's onslaught, "is, could it be possible he did slip and it *seemed* like something grabbed him?"

"No..." Corine growled, "I know he didn't slip because when he was right next to me, he was ten degrees *that* way," she punctuated the statement by punching her finger further around the ring.

"She's right, we had already passed this segment. It's how Andee heard us," Ged replied.

Saunders put her head in her hands and squeezed it.

"This doesn't make sense, we're in a sealed space station, under water, and now we think something is *grabbing* people?"

"Sorry, Security, was that a question?" Andee replied. "Because I think we've gone straight past making sense to somewhere clean off the map."

Saunders took a few deep breaths. They weren't going to be safe here, isolated on this level. They needed to reunite the group, get back to Medical, and figure a way out of here.

"Andee, I need you to help us move him, we're getting out of here," Saunders barked.

"But I have work to do—"

"Not alone, not down here. We'll re-gather our group and make sure everyone has a backup plan. But right now, we need to get out of here."

In medical, the screams of Rhyse beckoned them like a beacon toward the rest of the group. Obah set to work on her the best she could, but as Saunders walked up, she could see they were at a disadvantage. A limb amputation down here was only asking for infection and illness.

Saunders directed the others around the ring toward where they were storing the other bodies and stepped into the makeshift medical bay.

"I've done the best we can with what we have— Oh pipe *down* Rhyse!" Obah barked at the woman who wailed unintelligibly. "What happened with them? Was that...Lowery?" Obah caught sight of the group receding.

Saunders rested her weight on the metal table. She looked down at the remains of Rhyse's arm where it terminated just below the elbow.

"There's more happening on this station that any of us are ready for," Saunders replied. She glanced back up at Obah. "We need to regroup and re-strategize this."

"We didn't get the supplies we needed, did we?" Obah responded. And no, they hadn't. If Lowery hadn't been in a rush, if they had all stuck together, maybe they could have avoided this. Maybe they could have carried out the supplies they needed and not lost life and limb.

Just beyond the corner of the med bay, Tess adjusted her TEx gear in a shrug, and Saunders scowled.

"Where's Jax?" she asked, suddenly realizing the mechanic wasn't in the area.

"I let Engineering head back up to Five. She kept offering to knock Rhyse out with her wrench," Obah replied.

Saunders squeezed her fingers to her temples and exhaled. She could only partially assume Jax had been kidding.

"Okay, when you get Rhyse calmed down enough, get her back over to Four. I'll tag up with the others and round the group up. If I'm late getting there, we need to tell everyone: no more solo groups. We need to stay contained to Three, Four and Five, and the group fixing the tug needs to be bigger. No more digging in potentially flooded rooms. If we can access it, we can use it, but we can't go prying any more doors open."

"Shouldn't that mean you would need someone to go with you right now? To not be solo?"

Saunders gave a low chuckle. In the corridor space beyond, Tess was checking the settings on her weapon.

"I won't be alone," Saunders flashed Obah a grin, in hopes it would spark some rogue confidence. "I'll grab Engineering and keep her with me."

Saunders stepped outside of the Med-Bay. Rhyse had quieted to soft whimpers. Obah had clearly found some of the anesthetic stashed in one of the localized storage lockers.

"Okay Jillian, see you soon," Obah replied.

Saunders set off around the medical ring, Tess her only company. This time, the ghost didn't take the lead, but fell into step some distance behind her.

"I don't need you shadowing me everywhere," Saunders grumbled, well aware that despite her new orders for the group, she *was* walking alone.

Forty degrees from the few, working, makeshift med-bays they had managed to set up, Jax had arranged a space for the bodies they had collected. There were more than a dozen.

And Saunders knew there were even more, never to be found.

She couldn't look too long at the rows of bodies. Tizik, Bergan, Collins, Lowery, Paul, half of another settler's group...it was too much. As if sensing the unease, Tess walked past her and into the morgue, circumventing where Gedry stood over Lowery. Tess walked along a few of the rows, stopping at the feet of Tizik Bracken.

"Fucking twist the knife," Saunders grumbled, aggravated she had finally sunk to the level of talking to the shadow across from her. It had been years since these nightmares had echoed around her. Before the Drop, she had wondered if the hallucinations were new, or just her past coming back to haunt her.

Saunders took a deep breath. The chill masked any decay, but it still wasn't a great taste in the air. The inhale was mostly to calm the twitching, itching feeling she knew would grow the longer she let herself focus on the group of dead residents she had failed, and the vision of her past failures that taunted her from across the morgue. Time to go.

"Meet us on Level Four when you are done in here!" she called to Gedry, Andee and Corine. The last one ignored her entirely. "Don't leave anyone down here alone."

There was a new threat to their survival in this nightmare. They needed a plan, a way out of here. She needed to gather her people. She needed to find Jax.

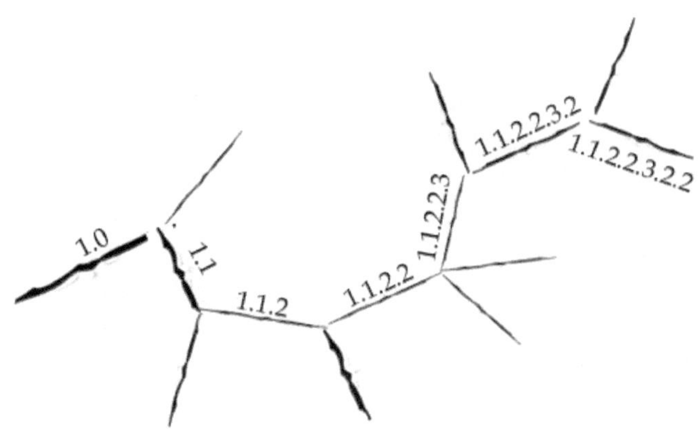

1.1.2.2.3.2.2

"Andee, come on I *know* you're in there!" Jax bellowed and hammered on the door frame again, then paced the corridor outside the tug hanger a few times before jabbing at the outer-lock door with her wrench.

She couldn't be sure when she had started carrying the damned thing so regularly, but the shifty nature of the residents put her on edge. Sure, some of them had seemed reasonable enough, but they had all simply vanished into their respective rooms, and those who emerged these days were typically faces Jax didn't care to see much of. In fact, maybe it had been one too many run-ins with someone from Zick's crew that made her grip her ridiculous weapon of choice so tightly.

Jax strode back up to the door and raised a fist to hammer on it once again. It rolled back before her blow could land and Jax had to restrain herself from socking Andee in the tits on accident.

"Engineering, you have access to the whole fucking station, why the fuck are you *knocking*?" Andee growled. She wore her goggles, the lenses flipped upward to sit over her head like ridiculous, round antennae. The grimy dark rings of weld particulate around Andee's eyes confirmed that the woman probably hadn't left the space in nearly ten day-cycles.

Jax paused, her mouth hanging open, caught in a righteously valid logic argument.

"I...uh...didn't want to interrupt," Jax sputtered.

"Ah, yes, this interrupts me *far* less." Andee nodded sagely.

"Oh come on, I don't know if you have Eave in there or something!" Jax protested, and jutted her hand inward toward the tug hanger interior.

"Is that a subtle grant of permission for me fuck people in this hanger? Because I am all about opportunity." Andee raised a challenging eyebrow.

"For fucks sake!" Jax stormed inside.

The interior was free of anyone other than Andee. Bits of metal were strewn about the cramped hanger, the decrepit tug centered in the middle.

It looked *less* decrepit though. Jax nudged the clean weld marks on the outside of the docking ring. Her hand came back covered in metal grit, and she wiped it on her shirt.

"Careful, that stuff itches like crazy," Andee said offhandedly, as the door slid closed behind her.

"This looks good. But aren't you done with this yet?" Jax commented, leaning close to look at the smooth metallic sheen of the patch job, and nearly inhaling too much particulate.

Andee shrugged back into her weld pack and slunk around the far side of the tug. A bright blue flash meant she had resumed her work without answer. Jax sidled around to follow, shielding her eyes as she went.

"You'll go blind if you keep doing that," Andee called out, her tone sounding dangerously close to scolding.

"What, have you just started patching anything you can find on this thing?" Jax squinted against the sparks.

The weld pack snapped off and Andee leveled Jax with a stare.

"What, exactly, am I supposed to do otherwise? Wait to die? Might as well keep busy while I'm waiting." The weld goggles snapped back into place and the sparks started to fly again.

Jax hung her head and leaned against the hull of the tug. Then pulled away and strained to look at the buildup of ground metal shavings she had collected. She was going to need a new shirt. And Andee had made yet another reasonable argument. Jax was just sick of the suck from all this depression.

"Alright, fine Andee. Keep working on it." There wasn't much else to add to this conversation. Jax turned to meander out of the hanger.

"Did you need something, Jax?" Andee's voice called after her.

Jax paused, feeling spiteful.

"Nah, just wait here to die, you're doing great!" she called, her voice a strain above too chipper for her own liking.

There was a thud, a curse and the hulking form of the welder jostled out from behind the tug to glare at Jax again.

"What the fuck, dude?"

"Or, yeah, you can come look at something for me," Jax snapped back, grumpily. She turned and strode out of the tug hanger.

Andee had long legs, so she caught up with Jax easily enough in the corridor.

"Security sure has a thing for assholes huh?" the welder stated casually.

"I've been told I'm an 'acquired taste'." Jax strode onward to lead the route down to Level 1.

"And here I had to go, acquiring you and all," Andee grumbled.

"I'm sure glad you didn't say 'tasting me' just now," Jax mused, ignoring the funny feeling of anyone being interested in her company.

"No, that's Saunders' job. She's small, but she could beat the shit out of me. No thanks."

They continued on in silence, which Jax took to mean that the welder was in a particularly shitty headspace. Jax allowed the quiet. If Andee wanted to talk she usually had no reservations about it.

Jax's target was the Level 1 back ring airlocks. She had been subtly tracking the various actuation cycles and it had been anomalous at first. She couldn't be certain it wasn't a computing error. But then the pattern became consistent enough that she needed to get ahead of a real tragedy.

"What are we looking at?" Andee finally spoke up as Jax lead them toward one of the worst culprits. This was just a transitory airlock for exterior maintenance. It didn't require a failsafe registering a docked craft, so Jax suspected it was easier to manipulate.

"I want you to weld this shut," Jax stated simply.

"Come again?"

"I don't want it to work." Jax jabbed at the buttons on the control panel.

"So just...yank the plug or whatever. You own this place yeah?" Andee replied, sounding confused.

Jax sighed, and resigned to the whole conversation.

"I did. Someone is overriding it. I can think of a few really shitty reasons we don't want that to happen." And one of the reasons Jax enjoyed Andee's company would be how quickly the welder could pick up and roll with the idea. She was already crouching and examining the airlock door contact points.

"It can't just be this one then," Andee said, after a few minutes.

"No, we need all of them, but these are the ones that freak me out the most." Jax scanned the corridor to ensure there were no eavesdroppers.

Andee didn't comment further. She prodded at the framework and craned her neck upward to look at the contact to the Station ceiling. Then she sighed deeply and rose back to her feet.

"I haven't seen Eave in weeks now. I just assume she isn't interested."

Jax inclined her head toward the welder as she, too, looked over the airlock in front of her.

"She's certainly interested in the fucking nav readouts," Jax stated absentmindedly.

"Well, yeah, it's all we have to look forward to!" Andee barked.

Jax groaned. "You are starting to sound like Saunders with the fucking word play."

Andee looked at her with an expression of extreme innocence.

"That wasn't even wordplay dude, it was the truth—hey, did you do this?"

Jax did a double take and spun her head around to look at where Andee was suddenly indicating. The welder was gesturing to the wall behind them. In large block letters, in a paint that Jax couldn't fathom the source of, someone had written a question.

"Are you hungry yet?"

"I, what? No!" Jax stammered. She strode over to the graffiti and picked at it with a finger. It was dry. It had been there a while.

"Engineering!"

The voice made Jax jump in her work boots. She whirled around to see who was calling her. That lanky, persnickety man who Saunders had introduced to the biofiltration room was striding up to her. Jax startled at his close proximity as he came to a stop in front of both her and Andee.

"...Yes?"

"Security tells me you managed to salvage a sample from the biofiltration room?"

"A sample?" Jax asked, confused. She glanced back at Andee, who shrugged.

All the equipment was still up there, and all the dead stuff had long been ejected or incinerated. The only thing left was—

"Yes, a sample of plant life? Security tells me it's in your berthing?" The man's voice carried a growing aggravation that Jax was willing to match.

"Ralph?" she spat out, incredulous.

"Who?" both Andee and Dr. Dorian Bezley replied in confused unison.

Just in time, Saunders jogged up from behind Bezley.

"She's named it 'Ralph'," Saunders huffed, from her exertion.

Dr. Bezley assessed the group of them impatiently.

"If something survived in there, then it's prudent that we use it as a baseline for germinating new samples." The Doc regarded Jax through his spectacles. "I have not had any luck so far with my current sources."

"Ralph isn't edible." Jax gave a dismissive wave, as if it would clear the whole matter up. But Bezley just shook his head.

"That is irrelevant, the sample is only a baseline, it can be used to graft other sources for propagation."

Jax stood, staring at him, entirely confused about what was being asked of her. She looked from Saunders to Andee, then back at the Doc, as if waiting for them to supply some crucial added quantity of information. Bezley, in turn, was looking at her expectantly.

"So, you..." Jax prodded, hoping it would spur the man to provide an actual useable statement.

"Can you please bring the sample to the biofiltration room so I can use it to graft new samples?" the horrible man replied.

"Absolutely not!" Jax barked, and Bezley stepped back in alarm. Saunders put out an arm across Jax's front.

"Jax, babe, if it means more food...so we can *survive*..."

Jax glared at the woman she loved in the face of this betrayal.

"I'm gonna...go. Do that *thing*. The thing we talked about, yeah, Engineering?" Andee drawled, taking a massive step aside. Jax looked plaintively after her, as if the welder might be able to help. "Good luck with, er...Ralph."

With that, Andee strode off, leaving Jax to look fervently between Doctor Weed Eater and the woman she was supposed to trust with her most intimate secrets. It was painful, realizing what was being asked of her. They wanted to take her plant away.

"Jax, c'mon, *look* at this!" Saunders implored, gesturing to the newly discovered graffiti. Jax scowled as if this had all been an elaborate plan to divest her of her longest roommate, and stormed off toward Common Access.

Saunders followed Jax up to their quarters on Level 5. Jax jabbed at the door latch and stalked through into the cramped space. She stood there, surveying the stringy green crisscrossing her room.

"This is *not* what I meant by 'try your hand at interior decorating'," Jax snarled over her shoulder as Saunders entered.

"Jax it's just a plant, you can go visit it in biofiltration anytime you want!" Saunders protested, hands open as if to placate, or sprout-nap.

Jax turned to sweep schematics off the desk, sending a rain of dry leaves down with them. She braced her arms on the edge of the desk, growing mane of hair cascading in front of her eyes and she scanned the edges of her room. Her shirt itched, probably from the metal shavings Andee had warned about, and Jax ripped it off over her head to toss along with the leaves.

"Ralph is *not* just a plant!" she countered, seeking wherever the questing end of the tendrils had gotten to.

"Right, got it. Throw pillows: no, personified weed: yes," Saunders grumbled to herself.

Jax glared over her bare shoulder, through the curtain of her hair.

"Look, it's just been part of my space here for so long, it's been"—Jax felt a surge of discomfort and looked away—"company."

But instead of seeing Saunders' reaction, Jax saw the battered tablet Saunders so frequently had been clutching, now laying on the floor, near several printed manifests, all partially buried under the layers of schematics Jax had just swept aside. Jax leaned forward to look closer, the plant forgotten.

"Come, on, not this still?" Jax stooped to pick up the manifest.

Saunders surged forward and snagged them from her fingers.

"We are still *missing* people!" Saunders replied, her voice in a rush of exhalation. "And the last one we found wasn't even supposed to *be* here!"

"Yeah, but that was *months* ago!" Jax protested.

"So?" Saunders rounded on her with a glare. "These are still *real* people we are missing! I can't just forget about them!" She looked almost hurt.

Jax felt the argument shift around her.

"Look, why can't we just accept that something awful and unheard of happened to us? We fell through a rip in space and things happened. People didn't survive it. Some of them wound up in places they shouldn't have any right in physics to be, and others never turned up at all! If anything, we get to live longer out here because of them!"

"That's really fucking callous of you," Saunders snapped, her voice sounding heated.

"But what else are we supposed to do about it? The records are just not something we can rely on—"

"Look, we were here to fetch your twig, not talk about my fucked-up record keeping."

Jax stood upright and shot her hands out in front of her.

"Hey, I didn't *say* you had fucked up record keeping. Just noticed is all."

"It's absurd, sometimes, the things you notice and the things you don't," Saunders muttered, almost to herself.

Jax wasn't sure what to make of that comment. She had noticed Saunders stressing about her newfound role of leadership on Station. She had noticed everyone reacting as badly as expected to the discovery of numerous dead bodies, often by violent means. She had noticed the airlocks cycling, and the ever-present loom of depression that hung over their heads like an axe. That alone was plenty.

And right now, she noticed Saunders standing in her— their—quarters; face flushed with indignation and something else more primal. There was hurt there as well, and Jax was over any desire to be the one to hurt Saunders ever again.

"You have done a *hell* of a job here, in the middle of purgatory with us all," Jax stated softly, sweeping the hair out of her face so she could get a clearer look at Saunders where she stood.

"Flattery is not going to get you out of handing over this plant," Saunders shot back.

Probably not. But there wasn't anything wrong with a distraction. They had been out here for nearly eight month-cycles, spinning into the cosmic abyss. Their distractions were all they had left.

"What if I just feel like flattering you anyway?" Jax asked quietly, tentatively, pressing her luck.

Saunders growled in distaste, but the corner of her mouth had quirked just enough for Jax to know it was working. The Security Officer stepped back over to the wall near the doorframe and leaned against it. Her head was tilted back to rest on the metal behind her and she surveyed Jax from half lidded eyes.

Jax turned and let her weight rest on the desk to study Saunders back.

"Look, are you going to get this plant pulled together?" Saunders asked from where she appraised Jax in her mess of a quarters.

"Probably not," Jax growled.

"Are you at least going to put a shirt on?" Saunders replied, her mouth twitching in the slightest hint of a smile again.

Jax smirked.

"Probably not."

"You're insufferable, you know that?" Saunders replied, her voice sounding less strained with every minute.

"Me? Are you going to tell me why you are so obsessed over these stupid rosters?" Jax shot back in a challenge.

Saunders broke eye contact and sought some spot on the curved ceiling. She sighed, impatiently.

"No, Jax, I honestly don't want to think about it right now. I'd much rather you just come over here and help me forget about it."

This probably wasn't the most productive course of action. Jax had a distant, fleeting thought that it would be more important to understand what Saunders had meant about the rosters, or why Jax herself was resistant to letting Ralph go. The dread and discomfort were ever-present and growing; accompanied by the unease of their future and the plans they had started putting in place.

But Saunders' green eyes glinted and she bit her lip as she stared Jax down.

Jax surged forward from the desk as if propelled by some motivation other than her consciousness. Her right hand braced hard against the door frame as she let her added height over Saunders confine her against the wall. Her other hand laced into the soft hair growing uncontained down Saunders' neck, and she captured Saunders' lips with her own forceful energy.

Saunders responded in kind. Her hands grasped almost desperately at the bare skin on Jax's back, pulling Jax's weight almost entirely against her. Jax switched from assaulting Saunders' mouth to trailing her lips over Saunders' jaw to the space just below her ear.

"You're not getting that plant," she growled slow.

Saunders' hands had traversed from Jax's back down beneath the waistband of the back of Jax's utility pants.

"Would you stop talking about the fucking plant already," she murmured as she reached back up and grabbed Jax's face to pull their mouths back together. Jax grabbed her around the waist and, while Saunders had the muscle mass, Jax had the height. It was easier than she expected to pivot them both away from the wall to the floor full of scattered schematics, resident rosters, and the dead leaves of a long ignored and stubborn plant.

Afterward, they remained on the floor, sprawled across the detritus of loose schematics and discarded clothing.

"I probably need to clean this place," Jax mused to the arc of ceiling above them.

"You know a good way to start, right?" Saunders replied. She was also laying on her back, head still pillowed on Jax's inner thigh, perpendicular to Jax on the floor. "You can start by cleaning up that damned plant."

Jax reacted by clamping down her other leg that was tossed across Saunders chest, trapping her briefly.

"I thought you said to stop talking about the fucking plant?" Jax huffed out, then her energy dissipated. She relaxed her leg.

"The plant is all there's left to talk about once we're done with the—"

"Okay just *don't*," Jax interrupted and squeezed her legs again.

"You know that is entirely not helping the matter," Saunders growled. She wrapped her hands around Jax's left calf where it lay across her lower torso and used the opportunity to trace delicate fingers up Jax's skin. Jax squirmed.

"That *tickles*," she growled at the blond between her knees. The delicate questing fingers continued as if Saunders had hardly heard her. "I *said*—"

"This scratch of yours looks like its healed pretty well, it's only a few months old...faded." The fingers traced the ghost of a mark on Jax's calf again, then Saunders twisted in place and crawled up from where she lay. She settled her weight entirely on top of Jax, save for propping herself up on her elbows.

"I honestly forgot about it, we've had so much else to think about," Jax replied, putting her own arms behind her head for lack of a pillow on the hard flooring. "Those were hallucinations we were fighting. Now there's threats that are real...and it's just become another scar on this tapestry." Jax punctuated the comment with a gesture that indicated the whole length of her.

But Saunders had busied herself with tracing her fingers across Jax's collarbone. She looked to be deep in thought, or potentially deciphering an even worse double entendre than plant themed innuendo.

"Jax, if we let Dorian work, we might survive longer than what we have before us currently. I don't really understand your resistance. What else are we going to eat? Don't *answer* that!" Saunders read the words on Jax's face before she could even speak them.

"Not fair," Jax pouted.

"Not having enough food for the whole station is not fair!" Saunders replied indignantly.

Jax shifted uneasily, then settled again, craning her head from where she lay to see Ralph's vines. The stupid greenery had been a wilted leaf, limp in its hydro-gel pack and buried under the husks of its brethren. Jax had nearly tossed it out with the rest but had dropped the gel pack in her insistence to carry them all at once. On return she noticed that the contents were green rather than crisp and dead, so she moved it to an open container and packed in some fresh growth medium. And then she had stuck it on a corner shelf of her berthing, expecting it to wither.

Eight years later Ralph was still slinking along. It was a long time with a plant. But Saunders was right. Ralph could be destined for greater things than the ambiance of her quarters.

"I guess I'm just worried that it's been doing so well for so long that moving it...would kill it. I might not be emotionally ready for that loss."

Saunders moved her hands to lay folded flat on Jax's chest, and she rested her chin on them to look Jax in the eye.

"It doesn't have to be forever, Jax. Just long enough for Dorian to get the samples he needs. Then Ralph can come back."

Jax filled her lungs to capacity, as best she could with the weight of Saunders on her chest, then let out a long exhale.

"Fine. He can have my plant."

Saunders grinned. She pushed herself forward to kiss Jax then hopped up to her feet.

"Right, then let's get this vine untangled."

And thus, Jax found herself in the center of the Level 5 corridor, clutching the small container that held Ralph, stringy green foliage bundled in one hand, small plastic containment pot in the other. Jax braced herself before the biofiltration room entrance, Saunders conveniently at her back, blocking any last-ditch escape.

Dorian Bezley was puttering around the space that had killed so many of Ralph's fellow vegetation. The hydroponic racks had been reset, the hydrogel had been spread out, and a lab table had several trays of what looked like leaf clippings.

"What took you so long? I can't leave these grafts waiting like this!" Bezley called, ever impatient.

"Got tangled up," Jax muttered, then shoved the potted plant in Dorian's hands to avoid any further questions. She watched as he set the foliage down and started combing through the stringy leaves that had crawled forth from the container through Jax's quarters for the better part of a decade.

"Good luck in there, Ralph," Jax called, quietly.

Dorian Bezley glanced up, confused.

"Do you expect this plant to respond?" he asked, concerned.

Jax slouched, and shrugged her shoulders, refusing to give a verbal response. She didn't need sentient plants in her life, just the company of something green.

"Security?"

The source of yet another unfamiliar voice in the hallowed corridors of Level 5 drew Jax's attention from the fate of her leafy friend. She spun around to see Ged's wife entering the corridor through the wide-open door frame to Common Access.

"Hi Obah!" Saunders replied cheerfully. The positive tone evaporated as Obah came forward, her face a look of despair. "What's wrong?"

"It's my nephew, Bergan."

Jax raised a hand to rub at her temples. So many names she had never bothered to learn, had never thought she needed to care about. Saunders on the other hand, immediately knew who Obah was speaking about.

"Of course, is he okay?"

"He's missing."

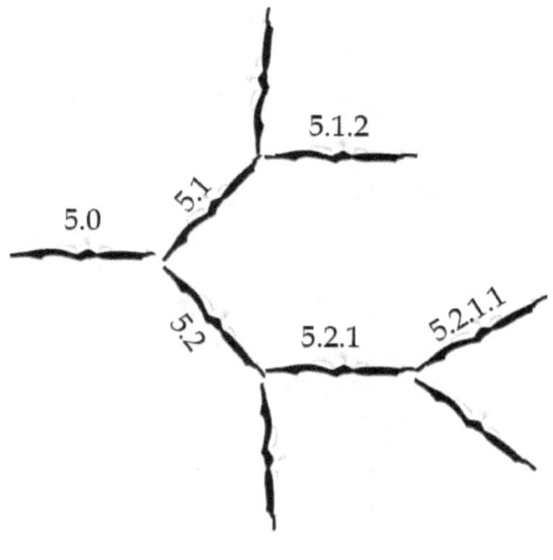

5.2.1.1

Employee Access was only partially flooded below Level 2, so Saunders took that route up to Level 5. Tess stayed on Level 3 with the bodies. Saunders figured it was better to not think about it. On Five she stopped by the biofiltration room.

Dorian Bezley was curled around a sample dish, with a meager table lamp illuminating a small circle of gloom around him and the wriggling thing in front of him.

"Bez, are you okay in here?" Saunders asked, quietly.

The man startled.

"Okay? Why would I not be okay?" he snipped.

"Sorry, just a turn of phrase." Saunders put a hand up to placate the prickly doctorate.

Bezley went back to his studying as if he hardly had registered Saunders' presence. Saunders inched toward the small ring of light. The sample flashed as it squirmed.

"Did you need something, Security?" a soft voice asked at her shoulder, and Saunders jumped. Kivan emerged from where he had been perched in the shadows.

"Fuck, didn't see you there Kiv," Saunders exhaled. The man only blinked at her in reply, and an awkward silence fell in the space between them all.

"Have you been able to identify that sample?" Saunders finally managed to ask as she dragged her vision from the unwavering eye contact Kivan held with her, back to the studious Bezley at the table.

"No," the man replied, curtly.

Extended awkward silence. Jax was better at these. The mechanic could just exist, waiting quietly, as if it were a challenge to see who would lose comfort in it first. Saunders hated these silences. It was why she usually got along better with the trade settlers and TSF squads on station, than the researchers who passed through.

Bezley eventually looked up again, and sighed, as if Saunders' presence was frustrating to him.

"It's some cephalopod adjacent subspecies, but none I can identify in this form. Invertebrate."

Saunders understood some of those words. She wasn't sure what else she might expect from the man.

"Will it...grow?"

Bezley quirked an eyebrow at her.

"It does have indications of being a juvenile. I cannot say for sure what it might develop into," he replied.

Kiv had circled the bench and leaned shoulder to shoulder with Bezley. The researcher seemed unphased by this.

"I'm seeing them everywhere now," Saunders posited. "They are getting inside. I'm worried they are not the only things getting inside."

Bezley regarded her in genuine interest. "You think there are other samples?"

"I hope there aren't," Saunders chuckled, almost to herself. The look Bezley gave her was one of passive frustration. "Okay, look, I need to gather everyone on Level 4. Glad you two are together, since no one should be wandering solo, but we have had a few incidents and we need to discuss a new strategy."

"I cannot leave my work," Bezley stated with forced calm.

"Yes, but—"

"Kiv is here, we will be fine." The statement was concise. Saunders gave up. At least these two had each other. At least

Kiv was doing something other than moping alone in the wake of his former long-haul partner going insane and stab-happy before the Drop.

"Just, be careful." Saunders turned to leave.

"Of course, Security," Bezley replied, but he was already engrossed in his study of the sample beneath him.

Back in the corridor, Saunders found herself alone. Tess was nowhere to be seen, and Saunders hoped to avoid any action that might draw the phantom back to her presence. Level 5 was the shortest level, and Saunders still didn't feel like wandering it. She instead opted to see how her voice carried in the gloom.

"Jax, where are you?" she barked into the darkness.

A thud and soft cursing directed her around the bend to the defunct Power and Life Support central control room. Two work boots dangling from overheard told her the mechanic was sitting just inside the horizontal room.

"Jax? What are you doing up there?" Saunders squinted into the darkness. The mechanic's feet swung and then her face appeared just beyond them.

"I was trying to see if I could use Rhyse's power pack to at least spark the backup computers. But it's useless," Jax responded.

She twisted and lowered herself down into the corridor. She let go of the door frame and dropped the last couple feet to the opposite wall. Jax hissed and stumbled with the landing, and had to fling her hands out to catch herself on what was once the floor.

Saunders shot a hand out to help, but the mechanic waved her off.

"How is Rhyse?" she asked.

"She'll live. About as long as the rest of us at least. I heard you offered to put her out of her misery though," Saunders replied.

Jax snorted a gruff laugh. "Would have put the rest of us out of our misery too. Obah said she'd have to take the arm off, right?" The Mechanical Engineer peeked over at

Saunders through her absurd curtain of hair, and Saunders saw unease and apprehension in the question.

"Yes, it's gone," Saunders admitted.

Silence settled between them as Jax nodded and turned away, adjusting to the answer, or simply preferring the quiet. It was hard to tell sometimes. But Saunders needed answers.

"Jax, why didn't you secure the door better?"

The mechanic spun back around, alarmed.

"I thought I *had*," Jax growled, but the frustration was aimed at herself, not Saunders. "You think I haven't been trying to walk back through the steps?"

"We don't really have the ability to throw away lives here," Saunders replied, unsure who she was telling this to.

"I didn't exactly suspect we did. I had my own head down there too, you know. It's not like I thought she was expendable," Jax snipped. And she was right.

Saunders had seen them both hard at work, and then she had seen Jax try to save Rhyse.

"Sorry, I didn't think you were treating her like she was expendable," Saunders replied quietly. A soft noise alerted her that Tess had finally tailed her over to Level 5. The Sentinel was examining the dark control rooms overhead. Saunders shivered in the cold, and squeezed her eyes shut, hoping it might make Tess evaporate.

"What did Ged and the others find? Uh, Corine and Lowery, right?" Jax asked, clearly trying to show she was learning who people were. And Saunders felt her heart soar for a moment, before it crashed to pieces at her feet. She opened her eyes to see Jax, standing before her as her future, and Tess standing beside her as her past.

A sudden and uncontrollable urge to sob boiled up inside of her. It felt like a rising pressure burning in her ears and twisting at her throat. Either she could let it free and wail, or she could crank the past life of a soldier past ten and laugh callously about it. Saunders didn't want to do either. There was no use in crying, and there was pain in laughter. Instead she let out a strange, half bark, half sigh that, at least to her ears, sounded like she had been punched in the gut.

"What?" Jax asked, looking concerned. Tess simply wore the same judgmental expression she always carried.

Tess' eyes had once been blue. They were opaque now. Saunders didn't want to focus on them, so she forced herself to study Jax instead. The mechanic's eyes weren't black. Saunders knew that from the numerous times in the well-lit Station she caught Jax staring. They were dark brown with *just* enough light to see a clear shape around the pupil. In this gloom, they were simply shadowed. And in these shadows, Saunders knew her own expression reflected.

"Lowery is dead," she managed to say.

Jax's expression shifted from concern over Saunders' outburst to outright distress, and her skin paled even further.

"How is that even possible? All they did was walk ahead!" Jax cried out and leaned her weight against the floor panels behind her.

"We don't know," Saunders began.

"Did he fall? He was being such a jackass—"

"I said we don't *know*," Saunders hissed, and then the ability to hold on to her rising panic broke. She heaved a shuddering sob and sank to the wall panels beneath her. Below these panels were server rooms, with long-dead circuitry. Now all the purpose they served were as a platform for her to fall to pieces on. And she *could not* fall to pieces. Not with this many lives relying on her. Again.

"Okay, it's okay," Jax was saying, and Saunders found the mechanic on the panels next to her, wincing as she landed on her ass so she could look Saunders in the eye. "I'm sorry Saunders, I know you are close to a lot of these guys."

"I'm not *close* to any of them, not really," Saunders barked. She loved meeting the new residents, but it was always knowing they would depart. And they should depart happy and rested on the next leg of their journey, not in a body bag.

"There's something going on, isn't there?"

"I already told you, no one knows. The marks on his body, they were strange but—"

"I don't mean that, I mean with you," Jax interrupted. Saunders shot a glare at her.

"The only thing wrong with me is that my people keep dying and we're still stuck down here," she heard herself spit back. And she couldn't help but cast a glance over Jax's shoulder at where Tess leaned against the flooring, watching them.

Jax didn't miss it. The mechanic looked over her shoulder to study the empty corridor and then she narrowed her brow and adjusted her seat so she was a little more stable. Saunders swallowed hard, waiting for questions about what she might be seeing in such an abandoned corridor that keeps drawing her attention.

"That's...a not insignificant issue," the mechanic admitted, instead. "But the thing is, there's something you aren't telling me."

"What exactly do you think there's left to tell you Jax? You're in here with us," Saunders argued, her voice sounding a half octave too high. She didn't want this. She wanted to be on sturdy ground, and even footing. She felt her brain seeking the cracks in the conversation to lay down the seeds of some absurd joke to break the mechanic's concentration. They needed to get out of here and back to Four.

"I'm not going to know unless you start talking to me," Jax shrugged. Across the corridor, Tess smirked.

Saunders cast her vision upward at the dark windows of Power and Life support and glared at the abyss beyond. She knew if she started talking the well would open and swallow her whole. And then it would be all about her. Her pain, her weakness, everyone's worthless sympathy. She didn't need it. Not in this mess. She needed them all on their game, or they would get hurt. Saunders hadn't come to this station, dropped through that rift and come to settle on the bottom of this otherworldly ocean just to talk about stupid things she couldn't change any more than their current predicament.

But Jax wasn't budging. The mechanic was sitting resolute beside her, boring into her with that shaded glare that made Saunders want to sling back a barb that would put the issue to bed for good.

"*Fine*," Saunders hissed, narrowing her eyes at Jax, who, for once, looked truly taken aback. A previous version of Saunders would have relished the win, but she loved this woman. It wasn't a game any longer. "If talking about my bad memories of losing my crew helps, I'll just go ahead and regale you. Hell, we can get the whole gang in on it, how's that sound?"

Jax looked as instantly uncomfortable as everyone Saunders said the first thing about this to. The mechanic winced and pulled away from Saunders' view.

"Or maybe not. It's never really a *fun* conversation," Saunders replied, leveling Tess with a challenging look. She hoisted herself to her feet, and the Sentinel took a step backward into the shadows. Now the ghost looked like nothing more than a silhouette.

"Jillian wait, hang on," Jax twisted to stand, as if to chase her down. The idea of the mechanic chasing *her* down was tantalizing in its own way, but then Saunders would be using this pain of hers for something fake. Why did it have to have anything to do with her at all?

"Come on, we need to get back to Four—" Saunders growled.

"No, this is—"

Jax had turned to put her weight on her leg to stand and instead made a sharp, pain-laced intake of breath, and gripped her calf with both hands, knuckles shining white against the dingy black of her work pants. The motion sucked the courage and the story right out of Saunders' lungs as she surged forward to touch the woman across from her.

"Jax? Jax! What's wrong?"

Jax was waving Saunders back, wincing, but deflecting her.

"I'm fine, don't worry about it, please, Saunders, keep telling me. It's important!" Jax protested, through gritted teeth. But Saunders was singularly focused now.

Her hands had dropped to where Jax still gripped her leg tight, wrapping gently around the flexing wrists.

"Jax, let me see, please."

"I said, it's nothing—"

Saunders took advantage of her crouched position over Jax to tip the other woman off balance. Jax pulled a hand from her leg to keep from toppling over, and Saunders moved into the newly opened space between them. She reached an arm out to steady Jax, and with the other, calmly, but firmly, pulled the mechanic's hand from her own leg.

"You matter more than the past Jax, let me see." Saunders calmly rested her hand on the bottom of Jax's pant leg. The mechanic returned her look with an unreadable expression at first, that then relented into something that looked like trust.

"Okay."

Saunders gently lifted Jax's pants leg to expose the bare skin underneath. It wasn't like Saunders hadn't had the chance to see all of Jax yet in their time since the Drop. But that had all been done in the oppressive darkness of their modified quarters, and, admittedly, Saunders' attention had been disproportionately drawn to other parts of Jax. Now, as she pulled back the stiff fabric, Saunders bestowed some long overdue attention to Jax's left calf.

A long and gruesome gash stretched from the back of Jax's calf to the shin. It was dark in the lack of light, but it also betrayed signs of advancing infection. The edges were ragged, open lines of skin. It looked nothing like the simple red scratch they had inspected just before the Drop. Saunders sucked in her breath.

"Jax, how long has this been like this?" She pitched downward to better inspect it. Above her, Jax made a sharp intake of air, betraying more of the pain that Saunders had thought was simply discomfort at the topic they had been discussing.

"I don't know, it's just been getting worse, but it wasn't that bad, it just has been bothering me lately."

Once again, Saunders had been utterly careless. But then her own shoulder had been mending perfectly fine since she had sustained that injury. That had been a full-on stab wound. Jax had just been scratched, so Saunders had let it go from her mind in lieu of larger problems.

Had it only been a week ago? Had it only been a scratch? They had both wanted to badly to agree that was the case. Just a clumsy brush with a wayward rivet, a scrape of metal, a vicious, pointy wrench being swung blindly at a horde of swarming insectoids, borne of their imagination...

That scratch could not have been from the bug that bit Jax. The hallucinations had faded, and the injury had remained. Saunders' stab wound had not been from a cannibalistic butcher, but from a resident gone psycho from deep-space insanity. Jax's injury could not have been from the horrific nightmares they had fought off, because those were *not real*.

Unless they *had* been real. This dark and ominous gash, with blue veins of infection snaking and radiating from its center across previously unmarred skin, had only been a slight surface injury before. Something was very, very wrong with it.

"Jax, we need to get you to Medical, this is not okay." Saunders felt panic in her own words.

"There are more important things, really, it can wait," Jax groaned. But Saunders could tell the pain was intensifying.

"No, this might be tetanus, or blood poisoning. I should have kept an eye on it." Saunders scrambled to her feet, her deep, dark, stories of the past blissfully forgotten in the impending crisis of Jax's pain.

Saunders planted her boots, feet set as wide as her hips and flexed her strength to hoist the mechanic upward. Jax bounced on her right leg, not putting pressure on her left. It seemed like the pain was magnifying with each passing moment.

"Obah!" Saunders shouted through the overhead opening to Level 4. The galley they met in was roughly ninety degrees from Common Access, but with the station this quiet,

Saunders hoped the woman would hear. She contemplated leaving Jax behind in the stairwell to go and get the nurse, but then Jax howled in unintelligible pain.

"Obah! I need you on Medical!" Saunders roared through the opening again. Then she shouldered the mechanic's complete weight and dragged Jax onward to Level 3.

Saunders slammed through the propped open gap in Medical's doorframe and dragged Jax through the dark corridor, past the upended med-bays.

"Ow, Saunders, easy!" Jax squealed. "Otherwise, I'll *really* need medical help by the time you find her."

Saunders ignored the joke, and tightened her grip around Jax's slight waist, and slender forearm.

"Obah, are you on this level?" Saunders roared again. Perhaps it had taken longer to get Rhyse ready to move and Obah hadn't made it to Level 4 yet. A drip of water echoed forebodingly down the corridor. Tess walked a few degrees ahead, as if clearing the way for them.

"Oh my god, would you just fucking leave us alone?" Saunders snarled.

"What? Who are you talking to?" Jax groaned.

"No one. There's no one here, I need Obah," Saunders replied quickly.

"I mean, she can't go far, she's in the lame leg club, right?" Jax asked, through gritted teeth.

"I sent her to Berthing with everyone else." Saunders kicked herself for slipping up. "I'll check you over without her, I'm the medical expert after all." That last part was mostly a reminder for herself. Tess might be taunting her, but Saunders still had the skills. Let her at least save Jax.

She dragged Jax's hopping form around to the sparse med-bays that had been converted after the Drop. Neither Rhyse nor Obah were there, but they hadn't been gone long. The surgical tables were both empty, but the one Rhyse had been on had not yet been cleaned. Saunders glanced away from the bloody mess and dragged Jax to the other table. The least they could do is avoid cross-contamination.

Saunders hoisted Jax's arm off her shoulders and guided Jax's hips to the table. Jax hopped twice on her good leg, then hoisted herself on to the sleek, cold surface.

"You and I have got to stop meeting here. I'm starting to think its serendipitous," Jax grumbled weakly, a sheen of sweat glinting in the pale light of a portable lamp stuck to the side of the bay.

Saunders looked up from where she rummaged through the bin full of gauze and sterile packaging. Ah, right, this was the same section of medical where Jax had once kept her from dying. If Saunders wasn't feeling so consumed by the energy of a new crisis she might have thought the concept was romantic.

"Hell of a meet cute. We could have had Level 1, but you had to be a shit about it." Saunders resumed her scavenging through the meager supplies.

"I'm so sorry about that, Saunders," Jax moaned, gritting her teeth and screwing her eyes shut.

Saunders popped up from her excavation and returned to the table. The lighting was atrocious, but she could see Jax's complexion was not just the gloom. The mechanic was ill.

"We can wander down memory lane about our first date after I figure out what the fuck is wrong with your leg," Saunders growled, and switched on a backup triage lamp she had prized from a nearby locker. At least its battery still had a charge.

The brighter light cast more ominous shadows, but Saunders could get a clear look at the discoloration on the wound. It was tinged black, blue and grey at the edges, and it was weeping from some internal infection. Saunders gently touched it and Jax threw her head back, howling in pain.

"What is going *on* here?"

Saunders jumped, both from Jax's cry, and from Obah appearing at her side. The older woman limped into the awkward space, reaching out to steady herself on the metal table.

"Obah, I need your help—" Saunders started. Jax had yanked her leg away from Saunders' caress, and was gripping it with both hands, just below her knee, as if squeezing there would stop the pain from spreading.

Obah took one look at the injury and hopped over to the other side of the table.

"Jax, Jax, listen to me, I know it hurts, but you need to let Saunders work." The woman put her hands out to Jax's shoulders. Jax shrugged them off.

"Its FINE!" roared the mechanic.

"Jax, I love you, but I will tie you down to make this go easier," Saunders growled.

"Jax, she's not kidding. You need to relax!" Obah reached out and grabbed Jax with what looked like a vice grip. The mechanic shook from her grimace of pain to look up at the older woman, then over to Saunders.

Saunders let her face soften in sympathy. It was easier because looking at Jax always made her soften.

"Let us look at this. It's going to hurt, but it will have to hurt before it gets better. Please, babe, trust me." Saunders reached out her hand to Jax's face, brushing under the excess of dark mane that fell over to one side.

Jax grit her teeth in momentary resistance, but then Saunders felt her jaw relax, and her expression calmed.

"Be forewarned, I'm going to make this up to you later," Jax stated. Saunders smirked.

"Whatever pleases you. Now, take off your pants and let me work."

"I said *later*!" But Jax let Obah push her back to the hard surface of the surgical table.

Saunders pulled the never-laced work boots off of Jax, while Jax pushed her utility pants down past her hips. The pain in her leg must have spiked because she let go with a hiss and squeezed her eyes shut. Saunders pulled the filthy garment the rest of the way off, leaving Jax in just her underwear and a t-shirt.

Now, without the slouching excess fabric in the way, Saunders could see the extent of the wound. From the other side of the table Obah exhaled.

"How did this happen?" the older woman asked, concern rising in her voice.

Saunders looked up at Jax, who took that moment to open her screwed-shut eyes and stare back at her. A message passed, unspoken, between them. The truth probably was not going to help.

"Jax, scratched herself. While we were fighting to save the station. Before." Saunders kept her eyes pinned on the mechanic. Jax relaxed as Saunders spoke, as if to show her relief that the truth was safe.

"But that was days ago. I find it hard to believe it could get this bad without either of you noticing. Jax currently has the most regularly attentive medical care on this station," Obah remarked, in disbelief.

"Lady, I don't think we know each other well enough for you to be commenting on my sex life like this," Jax growled, through pain, and what seemed to be embarrassment. Saunders' face flushed too.

"It's been dark, and we've all been preoccupied. Besides, I checked it right before the drop, and it was not nearly this bad." Saunders chose to busy herself with the nature of the problem than explore the fact that she may have, once again, done a poor job taking care of her people, her Jax in particular. As if to emphasize this, Tess glared at her from outside the bay. Saunders winced and looked back at Jax who was also glaring, but at Obah.

"Dear, believe me when I say this, I'm beyond relieved you two sorted yourselves out. But this looks like some advanced infection." Obah pushed roughly on Jax's shoulder to stifle whatever retort the mechanic might dream up.

Saunders ripped open some sterilization wipes and proceeded to attempt the clean the area. Obah busied herself with restraining Jax, who chose to flail in retaliation and pain.

"FUCK THAT HURTS!" Jax roared. Saunders ignored her. The whole wound area would need to be disinfected, cleaned, and dressed.

"Obah, you were organizing this area, can you find me the pain meds, and a sterilizer?" Saunders called over the squirming bare legs of her favorite surly mechanic.

Obah let go of Jax to retrieve the supplies. Jax, to her credit, only relaxed, heavily on the table, panting at the exertion.

"What are you *doing* to me, babe?" Jax groaned from where she lay.

"That was just me cleaning it, Jax," Saunders stated. "But I think I need to get in there and clean it deeper. That's what the field sterilizer is for. That won't be fun, I'm afraid."

"You tease," Jax said in resignation.

"Well, then I need to dress it, and we need to get you to bed, to rest," Saunders continued. "I think we have some decent pain meds you can take, if we didn't give them all to Rhyse yet—"

"I *knew* I should have knocked her out instead," Jax grumbled.

"—And the anti-microbial cleanser gel has a numbing agent in it. But the cleaning will suck." Saunders pressed onward, ignoring the subtle threats of violence.

"Maybe you could just...knock *me* out?" Jax offered. Obah had come back with the supplies Saunders had asked for.

"We're not hitting you over the head, dear," the older nurse interjected.

"C'mon, my wrench is just over on Level 5, one good swing—"

Saunders gave Jax a look that was enough to silence her.

"Sadist," the mechanic wheezed.

Saunders leaned forward and kissed Jax, brushing a hand over her clammy forehead. Jax had broken out in a sweat again, further igniting Saunders fears of a mounting infection.

"Squeeze Obah's hand, grit your teeth, but let me work, so I can make it better," she whispered. As if on cue, Obah gripped Jax's right hand, pulling the mechanic's attention from where Saunders was already applying the sterilizer.

Jax knocked her head back and cried out in pain to the dark, echoing halls of the submerged Level 3.

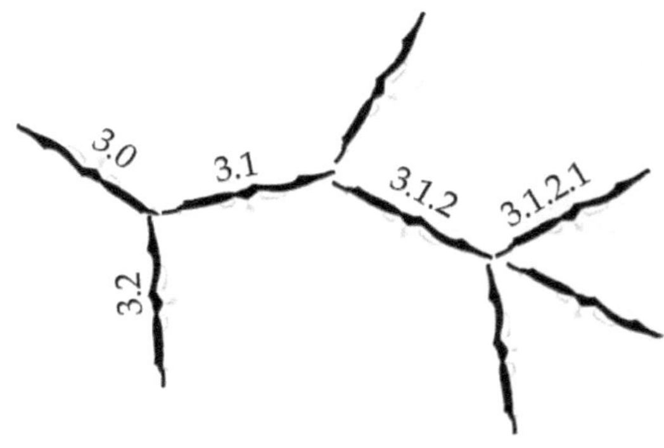

3.1.2.1

Jax awakened, uncomfortable in the chill air. She should be sleeping, but her most base-level instincts reminded her she was on an alien planet in a cavernous room, where she could only assume the intention was to keep her and Saunders as "guests" and nothing more. Whatever internal rhythm dictated her waking cycle was being piloted by a feeling of general unease. It was cold. She stirred and the continued chill on her skin told her Saunders was not where she should be, keeping her warm. Instead, there was an emptiness beside her that drove her more awake with every moment.

Just as Jax felt she needed to open her eyes and see where Saunders, or at the very least, the bedding, had gone to, she felt the feather light brush of something soft. Warmth flowed over her and a weight settled on her back.

"Where did you go?" Jax murmured sleepily to Saunders. The other woman didn't answer, just drew the blankets up around Jax and pressed her weight close.

Despite the dread of their surroundings, Jax started to drift off again in the comfortable presence of the woman she loved. Saunders, apparently, had other ideas. Jax felt a soft nuzzling at the base of her neck. It tickled and she stirred. Then the barest hint of teeth grazing at the space between her shoulder blades.

"Babe, not with all the aliens around," Jax chuckled and squirmed. But it was a lot harder to move than she expected. A strange weight was pinning her arm where it lay outstretched under the fluttering blanket.

A feeling of revulsion shot through Jax, and her eyes flew open with the sharp pain at the nape of her neck. She screamed and flailed as the fine fur of the Cloak wrapped around her. Needle-like teeth bore into her neck and dewclaws sliced at her wrists. Jax rolled onto her back, arching her spine to try to pry herself from the parasite, but it clung fast. She may have continued screaming though she couldn't hear it over the thundering sound of her own heartbeat.

A flash of light shot through the darkness and a new weight landed on Jax. She had a vision of herself, entirely cocooned in alien parasites, found by Saunders, hanging from the rafters, drained of blood. But the new weight grabbed Jax's forearm before the hot pain in her wrist released and her arm fell free. Someone rolled Jax on her side and with a slicing shock of heat in her neck, the repulsive warmth of the Cloak disappeared.

Jax rolled onto her back in time to see the Cloak flap off into the oppressive darkness beyond the chamber. She could only see its barest hint of an outline in the pitiful beam of Saunders' flashlight.

Saunders dropped to her knees next to Jax, who managed to sit up, her hand pressed to the back of her neck. It felt raw, and when she pulled her hand back, there was blood.

"Let me see," Saunders stated.

"Where did you go?" Jax shuddered with panic as she batted away Saunders' hands.

"Let me *see*," Saunders repeated insistently, and she grabbed Jax by the bare shoulders, twisting her to the side so she could examine the damage.

Jax realized she was hyperventilating and gripped the real bedding beneath her to try to ground herself. It was mostly the bedding they had brought from the tug, which meant it had come from her Station. She squeezed the rough and nearly threadbare blankets trying to regain her senses, and get them under control.

"It didn't fully latch," Saunders was muttering around the flashlight in her teeth as she prodded the raw spot at the back of Jax's neck.

"Well, it certainly felt like second base at least," Jax hissed as Saunders touched a particularly tender spot. "What was it *doing* here?" She hadn't recalled sharing her bedroom with parasitic flying batwings before bedding down for the night.

"I'm more concerned with what it was trying to do, I thought Cloaks only paired with Skraawl leadership or honored elites. At least that was the impression I got." Saunders let go of Jax's shoulders and Jax slumped back to the bedding to face her.

"Have I been promoted then? They shouldn't have," Jax grumbled.

"I'll have to ask them about it," Saunders mused, lost in thought. Jax could hardly make out her face in the dim light.

"Where were you?" Jax asked again, now Saunders wasn't desperately trying to save her neck.

Saunders glanced up and Jax caught a glint of deepest jade in the gloom of their alien quarters.

"I couldn't sleep. I went for a walk."

"*Alone?*" Jax hissed. Saunders dropped her gaze. "We still don't know what they want from us, and you just left me here? We both could have been slaughtered," Jax hissed. "Or worse, made *fashion* victims..."

"I *know* that, Jax," Saunders hissed back, her voice a strained whisper. "That's been the noose around our necks for nearly a year now. Every decision we make, every branching choice that occurs, we always have this hammer waiting to drop."

At this, Saunders leaned forward, slowly, closing the space between them and resting her forehead on Jax's shoulder. Then Saunders pushed forward further, forcing Jax to lay back again on the floor they had claimed as a bed. Saunders curled up with her face in the crook of Jax's neck and wrapped an arm around her, almost possessively.

"Don't fault me then, for feeling the safest I have felt in a while here, with you, with the Skraawl. Right now, danger-blankets notwithstanding, this is the first time I haven't felt the noose. It feels like we might be...alright?"

Jax didn't reply. She wrapped her arms around Saunders in kind and held on tight, staring into the intense darkness above. And she understood. This might be what home needed to be from now on.

* * *

A day on the Skraawl home planet was longer than a human day cycle. Light poured in through strategically placed openings in the Citadel, reflecting off the shiny surfaces within, and illuminated the interior for well over thirty hours. The nights were equally as long, leaving Jax and Saunders to struggle to keep up with a circadian rhythm that was not their own. The Skraawl seemed at once both nocturnal and diurnal, with an obvious lull in activity at the terminus between their long night and day, and again at dusk.

Most of their activity, aside from their dalliances with sentient garments, had been occurring on the long days, leaving the long nights to sleep, and whatever more private matters the Skraawl wanted to address without them. Jax had a distinct feeling they were missing half the conversation. But as of yet they still lacked the tools to ask what else they might need to know.

Saunders had taken up residence in a room tangential to the large cavern they started in. This smaller space had another slab projector which she became more adept at manipulating. Jax spent most of the time on her back, head under the rock, trying to understand what technology they were working with. They hadn't gotten far in the three Skraawl nights they had been on planet.

"If I had to guess, the rock generates a particulate field on the near-molecular level, then it uses an alternating magnetic field to manipulate light patterns reflected off the particulate. So it's the light moving, not the dust," Jax muttered mostly to herself, as the cold, hard rock pressed into her back.

"Mmhmm," Saunders mummed in return, clearly focused elsewhere. Jax slid herself out from under the smaller slab surface in their work room and glanced up at the other woman. She was engrossed in the symbols flickering in front of her, and passing her hand through them to manipulate and change them.

It was Skraawl habit to lay physically on the slab to reach the projections. Saunders, with her short stature, had done the same, laying prone on the surface, her boots hanging off the edge as she reached forward to shift through the changing light patterns. Jax hadn't quite adapted so easily so she hoisted her ass onto the slab, her legs dangling off the edge.

"How's the alphabet coming along?" Jax asked nonchalantly, as she scrubbed at the raw spot at the back of her neck where the Cloak's lamprey-like teeth had done their damage.

"It's progressing, mostly because of the work they already did—stop scratching!" Saunders barked, and Jax saw the glint of her glaring past the glowing display.

Jax sheepishly retracted her hand from her neck.

"Sorry, I don't have disinfectant here, and I'm not sure what they'll think of last night," Saunders replied, apologetically. She returned to cycling through the characters which Jax noticed were starting to line up with segments of recorded dialog from the Station core.

A quiet, almost hypersonic screech sounded from the entry way and Jax looked up.

"Ah, yeah it's Vamp," she noted and slid off the stone surface.

The small Skraawl tilted its head inquisitively, almost like a dog, and lumbered toward Jax. Vamp didn't carry an obsidian blade, which made Jax instantly more cheerful to see them, but the Cloak shrouding its form, clinging to its neck and arms, made Jax shudder in revulsion, especially as it fluttered of its own accord. This Skraawl, however, seemed intent on sharing the details of its species' technology with Jax, so she was generally receptive to its company. The creature ducked its head down as if peering under the slab where Jax had been laying and gave an inquisitive sounding snarl.

"Right, I was taking another look," Jax replied nervously, still unsure of the boundaries. She consciously had to pull her hand back from her neck again. Vamp blinked at her, each of its eyes winking in a staccato order, covering the grey sclera and white pupil slit with the vertical lids in a seemingly random order. Jax took it as another question, but she wasn't sure how to answer with only two eyes.

Vamp turned and pressed a taloned aft leg to the obsidian wall on the side of the chamber and Jax watched as a depression formed around the appendage as if the obsidian stone was wet sand. The Skraawl pulled its claws back and the depression remained, then split down the middle to open up. Inside there were rows of items.

"Heh, auxiliary storage locker," Jax chuckled. The Skraawl returned with what looked like a dark-grey boulder held in its grip, and sidled up right next to Jax's shoulder. So much for boundaries. Vamp held the rock in front of Jax, then rotated its aft appendage to show how its claws fit into the underside. Then Vamp held its other appendage aloft and wiggled the claws as an example.

The stony surface of the rock flickered and the same symbols Saunders was pouring over streamed across the surface.

"Oh shit," Jax noted, sagely.

Saunders glanced up from where she lay. "What is it?"

"It's a Skraawl tablet." Jax watched as Vamp manipulated the symbols on the surface. They emanated a flashing light as they moved.

Saunders slid from her perch to see what the fuss was about. Vamp held out the object and Saunders took it in her hand.

"SkreEEk," Vamp instructed. Saunders must have understood, as she slipped her hand into the space the creature's claws had occupied and turned the object back over.

The symbols flashed again.

"Jax." Saunders' voice was hushed. "It's how they communicate with the Malacost. This is their translator!" she held the object up and it caught the light. Jax had a brief glimpse of the light reflecting off layers of the interior. If there was a mechanism in there, it wasn't visible. It looked like infinite layers of obsidian all the way down.

Saunders was fidgeting with the object more, and the patterns were flashing past rapidly.

"Jax, do you think you could find a way to patch in the limited vocabulary we have into this translator and have it also add human speech?" Saunders asked, awe struck.

"Uh, sure, just after I send a quick email back to Earth to tell them I'm gonna be home late for dinner," Jax grumbled. Saunders had an expression of impatience.

"You retrofitted a busted station service tug with alien organic propulsive technology that runs on sunlight and photosynthesis. I didn't think it was out of the question to ask if you could handle something like this."

Jax pursed her lips and tilted her head in consideration. Saunders wasn't wrong.

"Here, hand it over." Jax reached out her hand. Saunders relinquished the translator. "Do you have a verified set of alphabet/ vocalizations/ lettering?"

Saunders nodded, glancing back over to the large slab in the room.

Jax left the other woman to her work as she found a corner and sank into it to study the hunk of technology that Vamp had procured. Vamp took the opportunity to study Jax. She endured the uneasy feeling as long as she could before glancing up at the creature.

"Yeah Vamp?"

The creature chirped a reply. Jax glanced at Saunders for an assist but she was scribbling something down on a notepad. Jax couldn't for the life of her remember where she might have gotten it from.

Vamp chirped again. Jax looked back at the creature. It took a step forward and thrust a claw at Jax.

"Not sure what you want," Jax replied, squinting upward.

Chirp.

"It's an inquisitive sound. It means they want you to clarify," Saunders called from her work.

"Clarify what, Vamp?"

"AAaap," the Skraawl replied. Jax exhaled in frustration. It was impressive enough that Saunders had been able to learn a few words.

Jax thrust a finger at the creature. "Vamp."

The Skraawl beat its chest with a fisted aft appendage and replied "AAaap."

"Would you rather I call you AAaap?" Jax asked, unsure if she was even carrying a correct conversation. Vamp instead took a heavy step forward and thrust its claws toward Jax.

Jax regarded the creature from where she sat. Then slowly poked her own chest.

"Jax."

"What?" Saunders called, sounding partially distracted and mostly confused.

Vamp poked the space between Jax and itself again.

"Jax," she repeated.

"What are you talking about over there?" Saunders called again.

"AAak," Vamp replied.

"Introductions," Jax answered.

Saunders didn't have time to reply before Nos entered the room. Vamp spun and unfurled its spine, bringing the aft appendages back down and forward, emphasizing the act of standing on its hands. The Cloak followed, creating a sort of furred curtain beneath the creature. It was an odd stance, but Jax had started to associate it with some form of call to attention. It was also not a comfortable looking stance, as it seemed to strain the flexible spine of the creatures in a way they had to force.

None of this mattered as Nos pointedly ignored the small Skraawl to bear down on Saunders. Jax flinched at the direct movement, but Saunders merely rolled to the side to show the Skraawl leader the work she was doing.

Vamp relaxed and returned the aft legs to their position over its shoulders. It extended a claw again toward Nos and chirped at Jax.

"Uh, Nos?" Jax tried. Vamp quirked its head again. "Nosferatu if you want to get formal, I dunno. What's their name?" Jax asked, not really caring if it was too many words. These creatures actually did have names, she was sure of it. It wasn't like Legs who they could only address via flashes of light. Skraawl had speech. Just speech that absolutely shredded the vocal chords. Jax's little nicknames had helped.

"SkIIrEk AH!" Vamp barked.

"Skiirek Ah," Jax replied.

Nos snapped their attention upward and regarded Jax with all six eyes at once. Jax wanted to sink into the hard stone floor. The creature maneuvered around where Saunders lay and lumbered toward Jax's position. A clawed appendage grabbed Jax by the collar of her coveralls and before she knew it, she was hoisted to her feet next to Vamp.

The Skraawl leader was half again as tall as Jax, and even standing she still felt shrunken in comparison. Two sets of aft appendages reached out and grabbed Jax by the shoulders, just as a bark of alarm resonated from Saunders on the slab. Jax tried fighting but Nos was mostly muscle and claw. She was roughly turned to look at Vamp while a scramble sounded from across the room, indicating Saunders' efforts to extricate herself from the holographics.

"What did you say?" Saunders cried as Jax was forced to regard Vamp across from her. The smaller Skrawwl gave away no details in its expression. Jax took a shuddering deep breath, ready for the killing blow, imagining the sharp obsidian daggers usually adorning the claws of each of Nos' aft appendages.

Instead, a single, cold, sharp talon traced the mark left by the Cloak the night before. Jax shivered both from the repulsive memory, as well as the feeling of barely there razor sharp claws.

A bird-like warble sounded from the throat of the creature who restrained her. Vamp replied with a chirp, and Saunders skidded to a space at their side, screeching like a banshee and probably not making sense in *any* language. Nos replied by removing a single aft appendage and grabbing Saunders by the neck. The shorter woman scrabbled in response, trying to break free, but Nos only turned her to the side and also looked at the back of Saunders' neck.

Then suddenly both Jax and Saunders were released.

Nos strode over to the holographics again, leaving Saunders to rub at her bruised neck and Jax to shrug the feeling of helplessness from her shoulders. From the slab Nos barked and Saunders spun to follow.

"Not even going to buy me dinner first?" Jax snarled after receding pair.

"Not *now* Jax, just be glad you still have your head!" Saunders replied over her own shoulder.

Nos had taken a place at the head of the slab and slammed a clawed fist on the surface. The lights spun up to generate numerous characters. The Skraawl swung an aft appendage wide, causing the Cloak affixed to the ankle joint with a formidable dewclaw to flutter around the forelegs.

"Awwk," Nos barked.

Saunders had taken a place to Nos' left, but conveniently out of arms reach. Nos flapped the Cloak again and Jax squirmed as it writhed down the length of the Skraawl's body.

"AWWK," Nos barked, louder.

Saunders lifted a finger to indicate the living garment. "Cloak," she replied.

Nos nodded, a gesture Jax had gathered it had learned from Saunders and stepped forward to the holographics. With a wave of the claws, several symbols came up. With another wave, segmented words from the Station records also appeared.

"SELECTED."

Saunders cast a discrete glance at Jax and turned back to the graphics. The object in Jax's hand warmed suddenly and she glanced down to see it also reflecting the symbols from the center of the large slab.

"Why?" Saunders asked, as she sent a series of symbols back toward Nos. The symbols again reflected on the object in Jax's hand, flickering as they went.

Nos tensed and in an instant the Skraawl leader launched themselves upward, landing massive forelegs on the obsidian platform that generated the holographics. Saunders flinched away from the explosive action and the leader of the Skraawl enveloped themselves in shifting, glowing holographics that reflected off the mottled surface of its skin.

A screech. Characters, both alien and human, cycled through the graphics that surrounded Nos.

"HOW ARRIVE"

Saunders shot Jax a quizzical look. Jax shrugged, bewildered.

Nos shrieked again, this time drawing Vamp toward the platform as well. The smaller Skraawl approached, head bowed as if being chastised. The words repeated again, shining across Nos' frame, the ripples of the living Cloak, and the surface of the object in Jax's hand.

"HOW ARRIVE"

The words and characters dissolved in the display and instead, another image appeared. It was non-descript, looking more like chaos patterns and fractals than anything the Skraawl had shown them before. A jagged edged shape spread across the visual space, looking like a vicious scar adorning the Skraawl leader's features.

Saunders had shifted to the side, and stood at Jax's shoulder.

"Jax," she whispered cautiously.

"The Rift," Jax breathed, voice low and conspiratorial.

"That's what I thought," Saunders replied. "Nos is asking us how we got here."

The Leader of the Skraawl bellowed again, slicing its claws through the holographics of the massive tear in space that had brought the humans to their doorstep. It was exactly as Jax recalled, though seeing the image reduced in front of her was jarring. It had been a massive tear, spreading from one end of her vision to the other, bleeding chaos through the fabric of space before transporting them somewhere that represented the opposite of humanity.

"Do you know what the Rift it?" Jax heard herself call out.

Nos cocked its head, then replied with an aggressive roar.

"HOW ARRIVE"

Vamp turned and warbled to Jax, a chirp that created the same inquisitive sound from earlier.

"They aren't telling us, Jax..." Saunders muttered, low and under her breath. Nos snarled and slammed a fore-foot into the slab surface directly in front of them, towering over where they stood and baring its teeth aggressively. Jax instinctually grabbed at Saunders and stepped backward from the threatening display.

"We don't *know*!" Saunders barked in return.

Nos snarled again. Vamp chirped: a far friendlier sound than what bore down on Jax and Saunders where they stood.

"Jax, they are *asking us*. They want to know how we got here! What do we tell them??" Saunders hissed in Jax's ear. Jax could see their tentative safe haven crumbling around them, reduced to their own mystery of arrival, and the threat of their existence.

Vamp chortled again and Jax cashed in on her odds.

"We have no idea what that was that brought us here, Vamp." Jax spoke hurriedly, imploring the smaller creature to understand. A bright spark of hope that these creatures understood the anomaly, that they might have answers, faded into a dull panic that drove Jax's need to explain how truly lost they were.

"Our arrival, it surprised us too!" Saunders tried to add.

Nos drew back from its menacing stance and waved a foreleg through the image of the rift and elicited another shriek.

"MORE"

"More rifts?" Jax heard herself reply. The thought terrified her with both the possibility, and the potential of a route home.

"MORE HUMAN"

"They want to know if more of us are coming," Saunders stated, resigned. "They want to know if we really are a threat."

Nos turned to glare down at Vamp who chirped in reply to an un-shrieked request. Then the leader of the Skraawl slashed its appendage through the image of the rift, dissolving it, before sweeping its Cloak around itself and launching itself from the slab surface. Nos landed hard on the stone flooring and strode from the room. The holographics went dark. Vamp chirped and turned its body to block Jax and Saunders from any other path but to follow Nos from the chamber.

"What the ever-loving *fuck* is happening?" Jax hissed. Saunders grasped her upper arm as if it were a life preserver and clung to Jax's side.

"I'm as lost out here as you are, Jax."

"So now what? We can't tell them how we got here, but they clearly *know* what that rift looked like..."

"They saw it, but they don't know what it is," Saunders amended.

"Well, great, that makes two of us," Jax scoffed, as she was pushed along after the massive form of Nos, Vamp marching at her back. "They don't trust us at all then. For all we know we're being led to a new prison."

"I don't think that's what happening," Saunders replied, as they passed Skraawl guards standing post along the massive passageway.

"Ah, didn't realize you had managed to translate more screeching sounds so quickly," Jax hissed.

"I *think*," Saunders continued, through clenched teeth, "and this is just a stretch, but the fact that one of those *things*," she indicated the Cloak fluttering in Nos' wake, "tried to latch on one of us tells the Skraawl we've been accepted. Which, I guess, good?"

"Oh, lovely, I always wanted my bathrobe to pick me rather than the other way around. I hate non-consensual clothes," Jax growled.

"Easy Jax, you're already calling Nos by its title, what were you and Vamp *doing* over there?" Saunders hissed as they maneuvered the corridor behind Nos, past more sentry Skraawl who regarded them with the curiosity due a pair of alien creatures in their midst.

"Aak," Vamp replied from behind them.

"I told, you, introductions." Jax glanced behind her at the Skraawl bringing up the rear. Saunders wheeled around to look at the smaller Skraawl who accompanied them. Jax took the gamble that they were still in good graces and gestured pointedly at the Security Officer.

"Saunders," she stated to the creature.

"SAAwwS," Vamp replied enthusiastically. Saunders opened her mouth but no reply came out. Instead, she looked back at Jax in what appeared to be a mix of shocked and impressed.

"Yep, Saaws," Jax affirmed. She looked back down at Saunders. "Maybe we're still on their good side after all."

Nos had barked orders ahead of them and massive hidden doors rolled aside. A crack of light appeared, reaching from the floor to so far over their heads that it seemed to go on forever. Jax squinted as the gap widened, and she saw it was instead reflecting off the layers of obsidian hundreds of feet overhead, as if it were some form of infinity mirror.

The crack in the doors was wide enough for three of Nos to fit through abreast. The leader of the Skraawl strode through on heavy handfalls, and Vamp escorted Jax and Saunders to follow. If Jax had thought the first room they had been shown was massive she needed to recalibrate her sense of size. This cavernous ceiling looked to be a hundred meters high, with a width to match. Furthermore, the light came from a massive crystal window overlooking an expansive plane beyond the rim of the cavern they were recessed into. They were high enough up off the planet's surface to allow for a view that reached almost to the curvature if not for the dense forest surrounding the Citadel.

A massive stone-looking ring sat at the center of the room. It slanted upward before reaching a horizontal surface and every few degrees along the ring a Skraawl lay manipulating imagery and screeching softly to its neighbors. Holographics appeared in small segments around the ring before various sets of participants. It was the largest gathering of Skraawl Jax had ever seen in one place, even as Saunders' concubine (or consort?).

There was a notch in the ring and Nos strode through to the center. Vamp halted, and taloned appendages grabbed at Jax and Saunders to keep them from following. The holographics closed and Nos ascended a platform so it could be seen by all.

Nos gestured to the room at large, accompanied by commentary Jax couldn't comprehend. As it spoke, the holographics converged overhead in a large display, showing formations and shapes that made little sense to her. What she did recognize were the images of her Station, in ruins, and the overlaid image of the Rift, appearing like a slash across the Station representation. Next to her, Saunders inhaled.

"Jax, it's an invasion!"

Jax squinted at the lights again. The patterns started to make more sense. She looked past the glowing forms to the crystal window and realized the planes beyond were not simply ground, but assembled spacecraft awaiting action.

"Look outside," Jax muttered back, nudging Saunders in the side. The sharp breath told Jax she, too, noticed the fleet. "They were planning this for a while."

Jax scanned the room, glancing upward at the shapes and images overhead. A picture was worth a thousand words in any language. The husk of the Station, the shape of the

Skraawl spacecraft on approach, the outline of a clear human form. The lines indicating the positions of Malacost and Foliage, highlighting points on anatomy. Jax no longer needed translation. The visuals were enough. Around the massive ring, Skraawl were replying and calling out to Nos' statements.

"They think we were brought here to help them fight the Pentagram system," Saunders whispered.

"Better than thinking we're here to invade *them*," Jax replied, voice as low as she could make it. At the far side Jax caught sight of two forms she was not prepared to see in this space.

"If they want to fight the pentagram, what the *fuck* are they doing here," Jax hissed, instinctually stepping closer to Saunders. The two Foliage were present at the ring, not laying prone like the rest, but standing statuesque, as if they were common house plants. Jax may have considered them to be dead if it wasn't for the parted gap in the carnivorous petals at the top, showing the pink-tinged interior and the teeth-like spines that lined the vertical slit. The interior fluttered and flickered as if responding to the images, and Jax caught the tell-tale responding light fluctuation in the holographics.

"I suppose every revolution needs a few traitors," Saunders replied, following Jax's line of sight. The Foliage seemed to shuffle in place, as if replying in the affirmative.

"Just like that, huh?" Jax replied, her nerves still singing in apprehension.

Saunders didn't reply. She was watching the display with renewed interest. Jax returned her own view to the holographics as well, though the flickering display apparently told her less than it did the woman at her side. A heavy, clawed appendage landed on her shoulder nearly throwing her off balance. But it was only Vamp, standing at her other side, also watching the images flash past.

Nos finished with a roar, a sound Jax had not heard before emanating from the creatures they called host. The surrounding ring of Skraawl replied in kind and the cacophony reverberated off the towering walls of obsidian. The flashing holographic lights ceased and the roaring continued until abruptly it cut off. Nos was looking at Jax and Saunders.

"We're going to fight," Saunders stated, simply.

"Wait, what?" Jax stuttered.

* * *

Saunders shrugged in the pressure suit, as if it would get it to fit her in the shoulders better.

"Stop squirming," Jax snapped, then bit her lip to hold back her temper. "Sorry, just, integrating this isn't exactly straight forward."

"That's not why you're pissed," Saunders countered, and Jax knew she was right.

"We already talked about why I'm pissed, what's the point in talking about it more?" Jax replied, then stuck the screwdriver in her teeth so she could get both hands into the life support pack.

"I'm allowed to want you to not be pissed at me before I leave," Saunders stated. "But I can't leave them to fight our battles for us, you know that."

"*Bullschip,*" Jax spat around the screwdriver, before pulling it from her teeth and continuing. "I'm pissed because I know for a fact that you wearing an old Station pressure suit, with a haphazard weapon I made from spare parts is not the advantage that an elite warrior species needs to buck the local regime. I still don't understand why *you* have to go!"

Saunders turned, despite Jax's squeak of protest, so she could look Jax in the face better.

"I'm *going,* because we don't have an answer for them when they ask us how we got here. Because we are asking them to take us on faith, and we understand *very* little of their faith. All we *do* know is that they are an elite warrior species, and they value that trait. If I can show them we are just as willing to get our hands dirty, maybe they'll think less of cutting them off." Saunders' green eyes bore into Jax as if she was begging for her to relent. But Jax was feeling selfish.

"I doubt that a pint-sized human is the strategic edge they have been missing to oust themselves from alien assholes. Jillian, you're a *combat medic*, not special ops," Jax proclaimed to the glassy, rock-like walls of the Skraawl cross-system transport they were currently riding on. She grasped Saunders by the shoulders and turned her about face so she could continue patching the translator through the suit comms.

"*Standard issued*, not *pint sized*. Just because you possess some stretched dimensions doesn't make everyone else short, Jax," Saunders quipped, as she picked up the hedger. The sight of the mismatched weapon only made Jax feel more uneasy. This was not a good plan.

"I'm more than a medic, Jax," Saunders continued, "I still had all the basic combat training of any other person in the TSF, I just also had a specialization. My skills are rusty, but they are still there." Her voice resounded with the aggravation of repeating conversation. Jax was intent to have it again.

"Is that why you're doing this? To brush up on your warrior skillsets? Because if that's all you need, we can just call this whole plan off and go wrestle or something."

"Tempting," Saunders replied, tilting her head to the side. "I'd say we should do that any way, but we're a bit committed to this at the moment. Drop is in an hour."

"Hence my commitment to changing your mind," Jax grumbled.

The lead wire to the Comms port was still being stubborn and she craned her neck to see its contact point. Saunders shifted again as she tried to check the charge on the Hedger. The wire pulled from Jax's fingertips again.

"Saunders, if you keep wiggling, this life support system is going to explode on you, mid-mission."

"I thought you liked it when I wiggled," Saunders replied, deadpan.

"Not helping!"

Saunders managed to hold still for a critical few moments longer, allowing Jax to re-pin the lead wire and check its continuity. Then Jax re-installed the enable plug, and snapped the external cover back in place.

"Fine. That should hold," Jax stated. "You won't have the flashes, but you'll have the HUD showing you the minimal amount of translated speech we have. If only you had, I dunno, waited for us to figure out more translations so this wasn't just you running in with a battle cry." It was her last dig, but she knew it wouldn't stick. Saunders was going.

From where Jax stood she viewed the back of the shorter woman, whose shoulders were squared up in the bulky pressure suit. It made her look even more buff. Saunders was flexing and shifting her arms and legs, making sure the cumbersome gear didn't restrict her movement too much. Jax swallowed a lump in her throat. And picked up the helmet to make sure the HUD would carry over the translator feed.

"Jax," a soft voice said. Jax turned her head to the side and masked her face with her focus on the helmet.

"Jax," Saunders said again, and a stiff glove reached out and tapped her on the chin. It was too much and Jax had to screw her face up to keep from breaking down. Saunders grabbed her waist with her other arm, pulling her roughly to the bulky pressure suit.

Jax heaved a sob and swallowed the next so she wouldn't be the weirdo bawling her eyes out on an alien spaceship.

"I'm not ready for this," she managed shakily. "I'm not ready to just say goodbye and watch you leave; to wait for your return that might not happen." At this she bit her lip to not lose her composure again.

"Even if it means bringing back the rest of our people?" Saunders whispered.

"Not to be callous, Jillian, but I would absolutely give up twenty-two residents to keep you safe," Jax barked, feeling a bit more in control of her emotions.

"And the fact that I know that is secretly not really true, is one of the reasons I love you," Saunders replied.

Unintelligible screeching echoed through the hallways. Jax wasn't able to decipher it, but with a sinking feeling of dread, she assumed its purpose. Of course, Saunders understood the call.

"That's the muster. Time to get to the drop deck," she said, arcing her head to glance down a corridor that echoed with responding screeches. She turned back to look at Jax, who had been stalling with her study of the smaller woman.

"Let's go, Jax." Saunders' voice was warm and comforting. It did nothing to calm the roiling terror in Jax's gut. Jax wondered if Saunders felt it too, as part of the calm before battle.

Jax grabbed the rim of Saunders' suit, where the helmet attached. It was a solid metal ring, and it made for a perfect handle. Jax pulled Saunders close, and up, to press her lips to Saunders' in the dark, inhuman hallways of an alien battleship.

"Return to me, Space Marine Saunders," Jax said quietly to the space between their lips as they broke apart.

"Jax, there's no such thing as 'Space Marines.' There's just the TSF and the ANF—"

"Jillian, just, please. I need you. Come home to me." Jax had to swallow hard to not break her stoic nature twice. The last thing Saunders needed was an emotional sendoff.

Saunders, her movement restricted by Jax's grip on the ring of her suit, reached out gloved and armored hands to Jax's hips and pulled her as close as the suit would allow.

"You are my home. I have no other plans," Saunders replied, and kissed Jax again. The screeching echo repeated, and they parted. Jax picked the helmet up off the floor and tucked it under her arm.

"Alright, let's get you to war. Don't want to be late," Jax declared, mustering all the bravado she could. They both clomped off down the hallway, toward the drop deck.

* * *

Twenty-one human lives existed in this corner of the universe.

Jax didn't care.

She sat in that dark, obsidian-walled room set aside as quarters for her and Saunders. In an oppressive quiet she felt the weight of her own existence heavy on her shoulders. She would remain alone in this room. She would remain alone, again, forever.

Jax was not a soldier. She wasn't a warrior. She was a space station mechanic without a space station. And now she was without the Station Security Officer.

The panic, the fear, the disbelief, all worked up again in an effort to suffocate her. It couldn't be real. This was a terrible dream she was having, and she would wake up the next morning, with Saunders snug in her arms, begging to be kissed awake. There could be no universe where Jax had to go on existing and Saunders could not.

But reality was sharp and painful. So painful that Jax screamed. Her voice echoed off the walls of the chamber she confined herself to. Jax let herself scream until her voice could no longer take it. She didn't know what words she was saying in her own language, or the language of the species they had claimed allegiance too, she only knew that she screamed as if that alone might bring Saunders back.

And when she was done screaming, she cried. Unbridled, uncontrolled, and unashamed, she let herself cry through to exhaustion. And when she couldn't cry anymore, she lay there, encircling a tattered helmet. Her body felt numb to the universe around her, her head fuzzy in disbelief.

A fluttering at the edge of her vision shifted in the swallowing darkness. A familiar heavy warmth slid across her, and Jax did not have the energy, or the care to fight off the pressure nuzzling her neck again. When the Cloak latched on, she welcomed the pain. She wanted its sharp sting as the creature sank its teeth and claws into her. But instead a numb feeling spread across her, blocking out the surroundings and zeroing in on the aching void left in her heart. It made her curl closer, aggressively around the relic in her grasp, seeking the bite of the hard cracked metal and glass to etch the reminder of her loss even deeper into her memory.

Jax let herself drown in the eternity that was her grief, wrapped in an alien parasite, and choking on the realization that eventually she would need to pick herself up, and find a way to live on, without Saunders. Jax would need to find a way to see the next morning without the woman she had never known would mean so much to her.

Only one thought helped in this expanse of terrible grief. Jax could only imagine, in some other, distant universe, there was a version of herself that didn't have to face this loss. That perhaps, when they had fallen through an inexplicable rift in deep space, that they had come out through more than one exit. She hoped that on one of those possible other paths, there was some version of Jax where Saunders returned, victorious, to live another day.

So this Jax, this poor, distraught, heartbroken Jax, wrapped in a Cloak, clinging to a broken pressure suit helmet and the memory of someone she loved, might hope that this was only her nightmare to live, and her's alone.

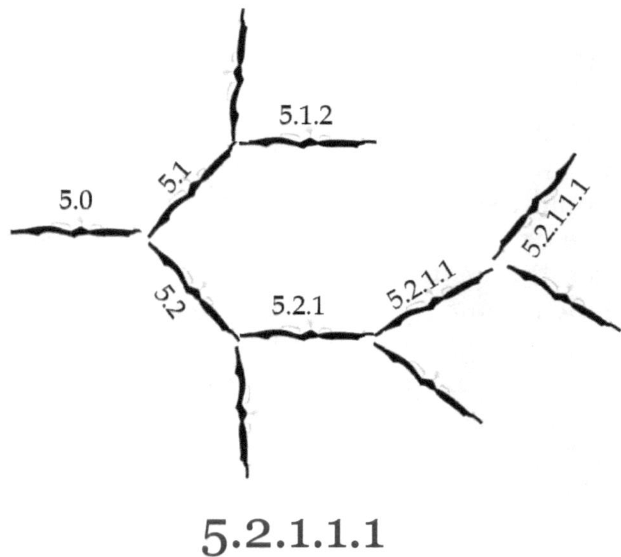

5.2.1.1.1

Saunders didn't consider herself a gear-head, or anyone obsessed with machinery. She was quite content to leave that to Jax in this relationship. But she could at least appreciate good hardware. She walked through the tug that Andee had been outfitting, admiring the progress she pretended to recognize. In honesty, it still looked like a hunk of junk, more so now that it had all this extra crap tacked onto it. But she wasn't about to question the process.

The welder was grinding away at some patch Jax had directed from her confinement for recovery over on Level 5. Saunders hoped she had translated the repair correctly, since it seemed to relate to water-tightness. The jokes wrote themselves sometimes, but in reality, she was pretty invested in this thing being seaworthy.

Saunders looked at the silhouette of Andee, her eyes obscured by the round goggles, her hands steady on the smooth equipment that hummed as it vibrated away on the surface of her most recent weld.

"So how does it...go?" Saunders struggled with the right word. The welder paused, dropped her arms and lifted the goggles. Her face was smudged by whatever fine metallic particles escaped her magnetic filter, but the warm tan of her skin still showed through.

"Go?" Andee asked.

"You know, through the water?" Saunders squinted her eyes up awkwardly.

"You mean propel? What gives it thrust?" Ged's voice wafted up from the engine well where he was still working a patch.

"Yes, we could all use a little thrust in the process," Saunders responded, feeling a little more in control.

"We're using compressed air, mixed with a propeller system Andee rigged up to run off the existing engines," the older man replied from where he was busy cranking a wrench. It was never as satisfying when no one called her out on it. "Engineering drew out the schematics for us, I trust her." Oh well, Saunders would have to find a way to bring it up in conversation next time she saw Jax. The mechanic knew just how to be the right level of upset over the bad jokes.

"And Jax can pilot this, right?" Saunders asked tentatively, choosing to stay on topic.

Not that she wanted Jax to go. In fact, Saunders couldn't understand *what* she wanted. But their options were limited.

"She designed it. And we kept the interface the same, so yep, either of you should be okay to drive her," Andee replied.

A loud groaning sound echoed through the station. They had been coming more frequently, as if the Seeker sensed their eminent departure. Saunders hoped that when Jax departed, it didn't invite the Seeker to fill the void she would leave.

"Have we still not found out what that is?" Andee looked up and around the confined space of the tug storage compartment.

"No. Bezley is still running tests on the samples I gave him," Saunders grumbled, as the groaning of the station died around them. "It's not like he's had a lot of time. Or resources."

"Kivan told me at dinner last night that Dorian thinks it's a giant squid," Ged suggested from where only his legs were visible hanging out of the engine well.

Saunders felt her face pale, and was glad no one would be able to see in the gloom. The idea of the Seeker as an intelligent, malevolent creature on a mission to infiltrate their fragile safe haven, was her own imagination. The idea of something real out there was almost too much to handle. She took a deep breath to steady herself.

"Well, could always find a use for the tentacles." She smirked, seeking an outlet.

"Whoa, maybe we're on Earth after all!" Andee barked out, flipping her welder mask back down.

"Wouldn't that be *hilarious,*" Saunders said flatly.

The weld equipment humming started back up again as Andee returned to her task, and Saunders walked from the tug to the opening in the floor leading down to the corridor below.

Bezley was glued to the samples in the small room he had been corralled in. He hardly looked up when Saunders lowered herself into the space from the corridor above.

"So, I hear you have a theory it's a giant squid?"

Bezley *did* glance up at that. Then over at Kiv who was clearly a permanent fixture in this dark space. Kiv shrugged but said nothing.

"That was a joke," Bezley replied, before peering back down at the wriggling sample before him.

"Or...normal sized squid?"

"I think something is trying to get into the station," he stated simply.

It was disconcerting to hear from someone who had all the flights of fancy of a medical textbook.

"Ah, the Kraken then," Saunders stated, sagely.

"I'm serious, Security. All I see out there are these small things flitting past. I can't catch anything else long enough to get a solid look at it. I've never seen anything like this, but its larval in form. They will grow. I can't tell if its final form is Earth-life-like, or something entirely new. The sounds we are hearing are deliberate though. I did time in a deep-sea observatory on Titan. There's a difference when it's just a structure settling, versus something prodding the exterior, searching for weakness."

"Well, we did have two more compartments flood, thankfully this time without casualties."

Saunders wasn't sure why she was unloading on Bezley. Normally she would muse to Jax about these sorts of statuses, but Jax was off recovering still.

"I sure hope, for all our sakes, that I'm wrong. But it would be nice to get that tug moving so we can at least feel like we are taking some action instead of waiting for whatever is out there to come and get us," Bezley replied. In response, another aching groan sounded on the exterior of the station.

"Hold your horses, Kraken," Saunders grumbled to the noises.

"Saunders!" Jax's voice called from the dark corridor above. Saunders jumped, having not expected to hear the mechanic's voice. Jax should be in bed. *Healing*.

"Jax, what are you *doing* here?" she hissed upward. "You were supposed to be resting, not wandering all over the station. Your leg—"

"Just come up here, please," Jax called back up.

Saunders bid Bezley goodbye and carefully climbed out of the room back into the shadows of the corridor. Jax took a stuttered limping step back to give her room to stand.

"You called?" she replied to the mechanic once she had her feet firmly on the flooring.

"I need you," Jax replied.

"I mean, the feeling is mutual, and I *know* it's been a while since, again, *you should be healing*, but you can't wait until we go to bed tonight? I at least want to shower," Saunders replied genially.

"That's not what—I mean, yes, but... Saunders, just, follow me," Jax exclaimed, exasperated.

She was placing more weight on her left leg, and Saunders felt relieved at the sight. It could have been worse. Then she remembered it would only make it easier for Jax to leave her behind. Saunders swallowed hard at the thought and relapsed to her comfort zone.

"Right now, it is!" she replied in a chipper voice, to the dripping darkness around them. Jax groaned in response as she turned and limped off down the sideways corridor to the Common Access shaft. Saunders followed.

Jax led her silently to Level 5. Saunders really did start to wonder if the mechanic was, in fact, hatching a plot for mid-day sex. Not that she would entirely complain. But instead of leading them to their quarters, Jax took a turn toward the core access strut.

"I mean, I'm down to try, but I don't know if we'll fit in there." Saunders strode up beside Jax.

She knew it was probably a serious matter, but the endless stress of their predicament had worn Saunders' nerves thin. And Jax made the innuendo so easy sometimes.

"I was checking the core out, making sure it would last with me gone—"

"Jax, that's the last place you should have been! We could have sent Ged, or someone else to go in there. You were *crawling?—*"

"Station is my keep, and my leg is fine, thanks to you," Jax interjected.

"I'm the medical specialist here, Jax, I told you to take it easy, we are going to need you to pilot that tug—"

"We don't have time. There's something wrong in there," Jax insisted, shining her flashlight at the tight, dark tunnel that was the crawl access to the Core. Saunders felt her blood chill.

"What do you mean?" She rather hoped that Jax was not about to lead her down the dark access route. For some reason the narrow spoke ladder seemed less terrifying when it was nearly weightless, and led to the lit stationary core.

Jax hung her head. She didn't look like she was going to crawl through.

"The reactor is running, but I think it's breaking down. I was in there pulling whatever diagnostics I could, and I don't think the reactor can handle the lack of recharge from the rotation." Jax sounded resigned.

"So, what does this mean?" Saunders asked.

"It means the Station will break down entirely, and all life support will be dead. Anyone left behind is going to suffocate. I'd say they would have three days after reactor failure."

Saunders' legs wobbled and she braced herself against the smooth floor that acted as a wall.

"We can't...we can't get everyone off station..." she stammered. Jax was toeing the access route with her boot, where it recessed into the floor.

"No. We can't." Jax looked up at her.

There was that overwhelming, sinking despair again. Whatever was swimming around the station chose the moment to slam against the exterior. Saunders snapped her eyes up. It reverberated, almost like blaster fire. She winced and averted her eyes from the shadows.

Tess lurched from a dark corner, her blaster raised as if providing cover, but another groan knocked the vision from her feet and Saunders winced. She didn't want to watch this. She didn't want to watch Jax leave.

When she finally drummed up the courage to look the mechanic in the eyes, Jax was studying Saunders carefully.

"I can't leave on that tug, Saunders," said the mechanic, glancing over Saunders shoulder in the direction she had watched Tess take cover in.

Saunders shrank under the distress of Jax knowing she was seeing things again. But Jax had kept talking, without comment of the shadows that echoed around Saunders in this moment.

"I can't get on that tug, and take it up to the surface, knowing that you are down here, at the mercy of the fate of my Station."

Saunders looked at Jax in full. She had a sinking feeling about what the mechanic was telling her.

"Then we'll both stay. Andee can—"

"Andee is a hell of a welder, and she's smart, but that tug needs at least one trained operator or else we are sending it out for nothing," Jax stated firmly.

"Jax. Do not. *Please.*"

"Saunders, we didn't even think I would heal enough to take it in the first place. It was always going to be like this," Jax insisted.

Saunders squeezed her eyes shut in realization and knocked her head against the metal panels behind her. She felt Jax's presence move from the access strut to directly in front of her. Wirey arms wrapped around her shoulders, and she was pulled into the chest of the Mechanical Engineer.

"I know you don't want to leave them." Jax's voice echoed around her, enveloped her from where she was pressed against Jax's breast. "But I need you to think about this differently. I need you to think of this as you leaving to do everything you can to save them. You aren't leaving them behind, you are the one getting the help."

"I can't—" Saunders objected into the pockets on the front of Jax's coveralls. She couldn't leave them, Jax included, while the shade of Tess followed her.

"And I need you to also know that you aren't leaving them alone. You're leaving them with me. You are trusting me to stay here and keep them alive, keep the Station alive, so that they will be here when you come back."

Something snapped. Deep down, inside the space Saunders had been keeping her darkest feelings locked into place, something raw broke free. She would endure a thousand stations under siege, a million lifetimes branching from one drop through a rift in deep space. Once, a millennia ago, she had wanted to put distance between her and the Mechanical Engineer, but she could no longer find the strength to leave Jax behind.

"I can't leave *you.*" She gripped Jax by the front of her coveralls and shook her. "I can't, *I can't!*" and she found herself sobbing.

She shook, involuntarily, uncontrollably, as if the creeping cold that had seeped into the eerie, dark halls of the sunken station chose this moment to thoroughly chill her. The echoes of her lament had driven any vision of Tess from the area, but it only left room for more darkness to press inward. Jax pushed Saunders back, unzipped the front of her coveralls and then pulled Saunders in close again. Jax wrapped her coveralls around Saunders' shoulders and held her to the thin shirt against her warm chest.

Saunders sobbed into the warmth between Jax's breasts and held on tight. Jax ran her fingers through Saunders' hair and rubbed her back. Every time Saunders felt herself calming, the magnitude of what they faced dragged her sobs back to the surface.

How was it that the first person that Saunders felt was worth pursuing, after all her loss, had this much more to offer her back? And Saunders had never *really* believed this love might come to fruition until she had suddenly found Jax, naked in her bed, amid the mounting mystery of an ailing station. She had certainly never expected Jax to come back after that first night together.

Somehow, out of all scenarios that Saunders perceived to be possible, in all the universe's possible paths, they had found each other again. And now either she stayed in these wiry arms, or she left to save the people she had sworn to protect. Two sides of what she considered her whole, at odds in this dark wet void.

"I never told you why I became an engineer," Jax's voice echoed again around Saunders from where her face was still pressed to her chest. Saunders wasn't sure if that was a question and pulled back, seeking out Jax's face in the gloom of the dark Level 5. Somewhere around the curve, the ominous dripping told her those doomed to stay behind probably had even less time than they thought.

"I suppose it really came from when I was very young," Jax continued, as she pulled Saunders to her side with an arm around her shoulders. "I think I really just wanted to be an inventor. I loved taking things apart and putting them back together again—not that they actually worked afterward." Jax flashed the half grin she had apparently been perfecting since it made Saunders a bit weaker in the knees than whatever scowl the mechanic used to wear.

"I think what really did it for me was the fact that I also wanted to explore." Jax had started leading them back around the curve of the level, putting a bit of her weight on Saunders' shoulder to offset her leg. "I wanted to create, but I also wanted to go somewhere with it, you know? I wanted the stars. I wanted to know that I found a way to get us there." Jax winced and paused. Saunders put a hand up to grasp at Jax's neck, and feel for any signs of a fever. But Jax kept talking, glancing back down at her.

"I put so much of myself into achieving that dream, and then I lost so much of myself. And it's what brought me to you, so far out here, wherever we are. My plans may not have gone the way I expected, but I still think I achieved what I set out to do," Jax whispered.

"And what was that then?" Saunders finally found the ability to keep her voice from cracking.

"Well, isn't it obvious?"

Jax's face was hard to read in the darkness, but Saunders thought she could make out a look of concern, that maybe she had missed something. It wasn't as if Jax had spun off on one of her technical rants. She had some romantic notion of engineering and science. Easy enough to understand.

"I really just wanted to find myself amongst the heavenly bodies. And I sure did manage to find myself one of those," Jax replied.

Saunders blinked. She blinked again. The fog lifted. Jax's face came into sharper focus. The Mechanical Engineer's eyes were dark, but they sparkled in the glint of the tiny flashlight. Saunders' demeanor shifted into something familiar. A rivulet of water dripped down next to them.

"Okay we're going to have to dive into that one a little deeper," Saunders replied.

"Not your best."

"Yeah, I'm a little off my game, but I know what can turn it back on," Saunders quipped, and grabbed Jax's hand. She turned and hauled them down the sideways corridor.

"Easy, still healing remember?" Jax called, but Saunders wasn't paying attention.

"If I have one night left with you before I need to leave, I'm making it count," she grumbled.

"What was that? I can't hear you over the sound of my own victory," Jax responded from behind her.

"I said I need to fuck you senseless until it's time for me to leave!" Saunders barked over her shoulder and dropped them both down the access hatch to their quarters.

* * *

"Okay, ten minutes to blow this joint!" Andee called over the noise of the tug hanger.

Saunders suppressed a shiver and looked at the small band of residents departing. There would be six of them, chosen by skillsets, with the excuse of seeking rescue, and returning. It wasn't like leaving felt any better than staying behind.

Bezley peered into his samples in a hand-held container, holding it up to the dim light in the hanger. Saunders was hoping he would have a better idea of what waited for them out in the deep, but having him next to her would probably be the closest they would get to answers.

Rose had unfurled herself from her grief and offered her mastery of orbital physics. Saunders would have wanted a navigator, but getting a pinpoint on their celestial location had to fall to *someone.*

Saunders suspected Kivan mostly wanted to just follow wherever Bezley went, and she couldn't fault him. It was rough giving a seat to someone who barely talked, but at least as a transport pilot Kiv could help operate the tug.

Corine was the last to show up in the hanger. She shouldered her grey TSF duffle with a glare at the group. Saunders wanted to feel good about having her along, but the hostility had only grown since Lowery died.

"Thought you were a grunt, not a sailor," Andee chuckled.

"Thought you were a welder, not a diver," Corine snapped.

"I can dive all day baby," Andee shrugged and walked off before Corine could retaliate.

Great, so it would be an antagonistic rise to the surface. Saunders already wished there was a seat for Jax on this shit-can. At least she could rely on Jax's stellar personality to alleviate the arguments between the others.

"You guys have food and supplies for maybe two weeks," Obah read off a checklist. "Hopefully that is enough to get you somewhere," she continued.

"And the power banks are charged?" Rose asked from where she was reviewing the supply stores back to her.

"Yeah, I pulled them from the core yesterday. They are charged," Jax replied, strolling in between them both.

Saunders didn't want to be obvious about hanging back, but the moment she set foot on that tug this all became real.

"Time to go, kid." Gedry had walked up next to her. Saunders let her shoulders slump.

"I wanted to drag this out as long as possible, but you are right." She sighed.

"It's not forever. It's for now. We need you," he said in that paternal manner that Saunders cared deeply for. "She's going to keep us safe."

Saunders looked up at him.

"I love her," she said quietly.

"Yeah, and we all can tell she loves you too." He smiled back. From the tug cockpit Jax turned around and caught her eye in the dim light. Saunders squared her shoulders.

"Alright, now or never," she stated, as bravely as she could. She walked into the cockpit.

"Your seat." Jax held her hand out. Saunders looked down at the main pilot seat. Andee was strapped in next to it in the co-pilot seat. The other four were lined along the sides, waiting for her.

Saunders turned to face Jax one last time, and threw her arms around the mechanic's neck, straining her face up to kiss Jax goodbye. She felt Jax hold her tight in return. The group around them was quiet. Saunders pulled away.

"Keep the lights on for us," Saunders ordered. Jax responded by glancing around at the endless gloom, eyebrows knit together. Saunders lightly slapped her shoulder. "Wait up for me," she whispered.

Jax smiled. It was the rarest sight, but Saunders wished she could see it forever. Instead, Jax pushed her gently to the seat that awaited her. Saunders sat down.

Anyone who was not making a break for the surface retreated from the tug cabin. As she buckled the straps, Saunders looked over her shoulder and caught a sight of Jax one last time, standing just outside the door of the tug.

"I love you Jax," Saunders called.

"You know I love you too, Jillian," Jax replied. The door closed.

Saunders swallowed hard and turned to the tug controls in front of her. It was mission go-time. It was violent insurrectionists slaughtering her squad, and forcing her to fill her duty of service. It was her call to arms. She would not be effective if she was distracted.

Outside the tug they heard three clangs. That was the signal that the tug compartment was being cleared and sealed. Once the break occurred, there would be no more comms. This was it.

"Sixty seconds," Andee read out next to her. Saunders pushed the thought that it should be Jax reading out the timeline. She pulled in a lungful of air and then carefully exhaled. She flipped the prep switches to direct power to the engines.

"Twenty seconds."

"Assume crash positions," Saunders barked to the crew. "The wall breach will be violent."

"Ten, nine, eight..."

Saunders drowned out the countdown. She hated countdowns. During her squad practice drops she always chose to sing some favorite one-hit-wonder in her head, allowing the moment of drop to catch her off-guard. It always made the jolt easier for her. She hummed the opening bars to a song that had gotten Jax out of her chair, dancing, and into her bed.

There was no flash of light when the breach came. Andee had ground the station exterior to a fracture point. A carefully calculated point of weakness and the pressure outside bore down. An endless hammering of torrential flood water knocked the tug from its place. If the tug moved too much it wouldn't be able to escape the opening they had made. Saunders gritted her teeth. There wasn't a way back *inside* the station either. Not without flooding everyone.

The air trapped in the compartment escaped ahead of them. Saunders flipped the power on and jogged the updated propeller system that Andee had fabricated. The tug moved in the water.

"Alright, let's make this worth it," Saunders shouted, and punched the throttle. The tug rose from the dead station.

There was only one window in the cockpit. There were exterior cameras, but it was determined that they would not work under water, so they had been disabled to avoid a power short. As they rose from the station wreck, they had no way of looking behind them at what lay in their wake. It wouldn't have mattered. The water was as dark as the endless expanse of space.

Whatever modifications Andee had bestowed, they seemed to work. The exterior flood lights remained on, and they cast an eerie beam through the murk. Something small swam past.

"Bez, did you catch that?" Saunders asked. The biodiversity researcher unbuckled his restraints. There was no real point to remaining seated in this state.

"It moved too fast." He remained peering over Saunders' shoulder as they rose.

Time ticked by. They ascended slowly enough to avoid depressurization. Jax and Ged had estimated they were at a depth of maybe thirteen thousand feet. It meant that Saunders had to draw back on the throttle or else the whole crew would suffer painful repercussions.

Something else swam past, larger this time.

"That...could have been anything," Bezley said, resigned. Saunders was surprised they had encountered so little underwater life yet. The idea made her uneasy.

"We're past ten thousand feet, by Engineering's calculations," Andee reported.

"This isn't right," Saunders mumbled under her breath.

"What isn't?" Andee asked.

"We should see a shift in lighting," responded Rose. Saunders didn't know when she had also left her seat.

"Right, we should have better visibility," Saunders agreed.

"Maybe it's night?" Andee suggested, innocently. Saunders pushed more negative thoughts from her head. She hummed the second verse to herself.

Another endless block of time passed. The light *did* shift. The water adopted an unnaturally violet hue.

"Is...is this even water?" Saunders asked, as it became clearer that there was a distinct purple shade emerging.

"We tested the leaks in the station as best we could. It *seemed* like water," Bezley replied. In the middle distance a large shadow crossed their path.

"Bez..." Saunders trailed off.

"I saw it. It could be whales, or this planet's equivalent..."

The shadow dissipated, as if it had never been there before. Saunders started the song over again in her head.

"We should be at five thousand feet right now," Andee reported.

The water should definitely be lighter at this depth. Saunders peered out through the window as best she could. There were more shadows in the distance, swimming, just beyond the reach of sight. Then several glittering streaks zipped past the tug, as if they were shooting stars: more of the creatures Saunders had found for Bezley to examine.

The engines stuttered.

"Andee, what—" Saunders felt the controls shake in her hands. The welder next to her was running her hands over the controls in front of her as well.

"I don't know, it's like they aren't...propelling well enough..."

"Like it's not water anymore?" Rose probed.

"I—I guess, yeah," Andee admitted.

Saunders pushed the tug controls as far as they would respond. The tug started to shake more notably. Above them there was no clear surface in view.

"We should be at three thousand feet right now," Andee reported.

"Where is the surface?" Corine asked.

"There isn't a surface."

Saunders didn't realize her eyes were closed. She was busy singing the bridge; the moment she knew Jax would spend the night with her for the first time, as they had shuffled, flailed and spun in her quarters. It felt like years ago in time, but had maybe only been weeks. She opened her eyes. Rose had spoken.

"What?" asked Kivan, who had also joined them in the cockpit.

"There will not be a surface," Rose repeated and Saunders knew, without asking for clarification, that Rose was right.

"How?" Andee asked, fighting the tug controls still.

"It is some form of gas giant. Like Jupiter perhaps, or Neptune, yet not as massive...not as dense. There will never be a surface. Pressure will simply reduce until it dissipates into the atmosphere. There will not be land, and there will not be a surface to the water."

The crew was quiet, considering the answer. Something massive knocked into the side of the tug.

Since four of them were not strapped in, they were knocked violently to the side. Kivan struck the tug interior wall headfirst and went nonresponsive. Rose hit the wall back first and cried out in pain but remained conscious. Corine had been gripping the co-pilot chair which only knocked her into Bezley.

"What the fuck was that?" shouted Andee. Saunders had already unbuckled her own seat to tend to Kiv, who was bleeding from several places in his face. She went to move him but realized the fatal angle of his neck.

Something smashed into the tug again from the other side, sending Saunders sprawled down between the back seats. The crew was shouting, un-intelligible and panicked.

"Get strapped in!"

"It's trying to break open the tug!"

"He's dead, leave him!"

Saunders was dazed, but she managed to pull herself up from where she had fallen. She tripped over Kivan's body, and hauled herself back into the pilot seat, grasping at the restraints.

"WHAT'S OUR DEPTH?"

"Does it matter? There's no surface."

"WHAT'S OUR DEPTH?" Saunders shouted over the chaos. Andee looked at the clock that they were timing themselves with.

"One thousand feet, but—"

The tug shuttered to a stop. The controls no longer responsive. The chaos silenced.

"Neutral buoyancy," Rose said.

"And I cut the deep-space engines. They're useless now," Andee whispered.

A sense of quiet apprehension settled, as if they were waiting for a deathblow. It came.

The impact was harder than any of the previous impacts, warping the exterior. A leak sprang. Instead of water pouring in, thick, dense, moist, water-vapor fog poured in. In front of the cockpit window a massive, dark shape swam into view. The Seeker was real and it had found them at last.

Large, almost endless shadowy appendages emerged from the central form. They writhed as if they had a consciousness of their own, undulating outward, too many to count.

"If this isn't liquid, how is that swimming?" Andee asked quietly next to Saunders, her voice full of terror. Saunders chose to look death in the eye.

"I don't think it is swimming."

An impossibly massive, armored, sinuous limb snaked around the exterior of their only vessel. The interior of the tug fogged with the thick, soupy vapor. Saunders coughed on the imposing atmosphere, and knew she was going to drown.

"Dorian, Rose, get the pressure suits on!" she ordered, coughing as she tried to get the words out. She was only vaguely aware of the movement behind her. She reached for the oxygen mask under her seat, and only managed to get it on before she realized Andee had already passed out.

Saunders reached over to try to outfit the welder with another mask, and saw darkness from the corner of her eye. She nearly missed seeing the head-on impact. The tip of an unfathomably long tentacle, as thick around as Saunders herself, smashed into the cockpit glass. The soupy atmosphere poured in.

Saunders struggled, twisting in the tug wreckage. She tried opening her eyes and they stung. They watered and blurred the destruction around her. She thought she could make out someone in a pressure suit before something long and grasping from the depths snaked around them, pulling them down below.

The neutral buoyancy of the planet's atmosphere held Saunders stationary. She couldn't swim, she couldn't sink, she could barely see save for the shadow of the Seeker filling half her vision as it loomed.

It wanted her.

She wanted to fight. But instead, she let her last moments spiral. She would never see Jax again. Her people were doomed. There would be no rescue. The universe did not want them to survive. If it wasn't her watching Tess die, it would be her watching the residents, the station, her Jax, die.

"Jax," she managed to say. She coughed on the thick atmosphere as it breached her oxygen mask. Something curled, unforgiving around her leg and pulled.

Saunders' world went dark.

7.0

"Aw hell naw," Andee groaned as she steadied herself in the station corridor. She kicked off the mass obscuring a portion of the wall and felt her foot sink into the soft material. Damned these massive work boots. With her foot stuck as it was in the gunk, every kick just caused the rest of her floating body to sway in the lack of gravity. She couldn't reach another surface and so, she was stuck.

The corridor was clogged with more masses, preventing any clear line of sight. The only fact Andee could be certain of was the station was no longer spinning.

"Andee?" a voice called from the other side of the wedge of trypophobia inducing blockage.

"Yeah! Yeah, I'm here!" Andee called out, not entirely caring who it might be that was seeking her. Alright, maybe there were a few faces she would rather see than others, but given the current predicament, she wasn't about to be choosey.

Ah, score. A gloved hand reached out and grasped the wax-like substance surrounding Andee's location and the station Security Officer hoisted herself into view. Saunders was good people: solid, able to take a joke. And this whole situation was fucking hilarious.

"Hey, Security! Just in time for the fun and games!" Andee chuckled dryly. Saunders was wearing one of the station pressure suits, helmet clipped to the side of a harness that drew a tether from somewhere back behind her.

"How long have you *been* here Andoria?" Saunders asked, reaching to grab her forearm. Andee batted her away.

"I'll stay here longer if you're gonna call me that," she snorted. Saunders rolled her eyes and wrapped her arms around Andee's arm to pull. The stupid work boot came unstuck and Andee floated free.

"Grab on, we can wind back toward the anchor."

"Don't have to tell me twice," Andee chuffed. She looped a hand into the back of the harness as Security navigated them through the slices of material bocking the path.

"I've never seen anything like this before," Saunders stated as they pulled the tether from the gunk where it had embedded itself like a cutting wire.

"I have," Andee replied.

Saunders shifted in her suit to glance back at her.

Andee shrugged.

"I used to keep bees back when I lived on Pacifica. They use them for pollination on the floating base. This looks like the inside of a beehive. Or a wasp nest," she added. She kicked at a mound of soft material as they passed. "See the shape here. Like comb."

"Bees? In space," Saunders mused, as they maneuvered back the way she had come. "At this point I guess I can say I've seen weirder."

"Don't forget the 'or wasps' part," Andee added, genially.

"I was purposely forgetting that part," Saunders grumbled.

They squeezed through two slices of comb that barely left enough room for them to pass through sideways, but on the other side a few other faces waited to greet them.

Predictably, there was that socially awkward Mechanical Engineer that ran the station. Made sense: Security was sweet on her. Not that Andee saw the appeal, though that wrench was choice. A few of the Terrestrial Surface Force guys were nearby, wearing whatever of their gear they probably had on hand. They wouldn't have weapons with them though. The entirely alluring Navigator Eave was also in the group. That certainly piqued Andee's interest.

"Who's that?" the mechanic grumbled. Andee smirked.

"Everyone's favorite arc welder, dude, I thought you all were waiting for me!"

The mechanic looked taken aback and reverted to her signature glower. Saunders only chuckled.

"Jax, this is Andee. Actually, she says she's seen this kind of material before." Saunders kicked at the wax substance.

"As a welder?" Jax asked, confused.

"Nah, as a debutant," Andee snorted. Jax the Engineer gave her a scowling look. "I was just saying it looked an awful lot like a hive."

"A hive for *what?*" Eave replied. She bore a similar prickly nature to the mechanic, but for whatever reason it worked on Andee. She grinned.

"Whatever we can imagine," she replied with a wink. Eave gave her an impassive look. Yikes, swing and miss.

"If this is a hive, I'm not particularly interested in what lives in it," the mechanic was saying. "Look at the size of these openings. Whatever made this is not your ordinary sized insect." Andee caught the look Jax was giving to Saunders. Damned they had it bad for each other, but that wasn't a suggestive glance.

"What aren't you two telling us?" Andee took no issue slamming herself right in the middle of that little moment. They could cope.

It was Saunders who looked resistant to saying anything. But she replied anyway.

"Right before...that, uh—"

"Drop," Jax interrupted, helpfully. Andee nodded at her in due appreciation.

"—Right, 'Drop', were any of you also, uh...seeing things?" Saunders finished.

Yeah. Andee had seen things. Not great things. Bad things. Down right fucked-in-the-head things. Best not dwell on those.

"Let's just go with yes," Andee replied, and figured she could keep it at that.

"Any of them crawling?" Jax asked.

"On occasion," Andee barked, narrowing her eyes at the group. No one wanted to really make eye contact at the moment.

"Okay well, Engineering and I found ourselves fighting off a swarm of...something insectoid. And large," Saunders added.

"It was the best, really," Jax grumbled. Andee chuckled. Okay, Engineering might be good for a laugh.

"So you are saying these *things* you were seeing, *hallucinating*, have come to life?" Eave asked, incredulously.

"Boy that sounds like a bad day," Andee sighed.

"But I didn't see any insectoids...before," Eave argued. "I only saw my bunk mate lose her shit, then start scratching her face off. Maybe *she* saw bug things?"

Saunders was shrugging in her bulky suit. "I don't know if there are hard and fast rules happening right now, not after...whatever that 'Drop' was."

"Did anyone feel like smuggling a can of bug-spray on Station? I promise I won't get pissed this time." Jax shot a furtive glance around the group.

"Nah, none of that, but if I can get to my arc welder pack, I can maybe cut a better path for us," Andee piped up. Not that she wanted to be the avant-garde for this excursion, but she couldn't think of a better way out.

"Path to where?" Jax asked.

Andee shrugged. "You tell me. I'm just the muscle."

"Are there any other survivors?" Eave asked. The thought dredged up some uncomfortable thoughts so Andee scrubbed at her face and looked away.

"We just haven't found anyone," Saunders was replying.

"Ah, yeah, well, maybe that's the task, right?" Andee piped up. "Finding the others."

"Sure..." Saunders responded, as if she was entirely unsure. But Andee needed action. This floating in a brood comb, talking old business and new business wasn't her vibe.

"Look, my gear is stacked up on Four. If we can get to it, maybe find a few more? Those are some solid steps I can take. You all don't even have to come with me!" Not that going alone sounded great either.

"We can go with," Saunders replied.

"Excellent!" Andee grinned. "Got any more of those shnazzy pressure suits?" They looked bulky, but protective. Andee could still remember a few too many stings.

"Uh, maybe not in your size," Jax replied, cautious. Andee chuckled.

"Wouldn't be the first time. Oh well, the weld pack probably wouldn't fit over it anyway. Wanna lead the way, Security?" Andee wasn't sure where, exactly, they were, anyway.

"Actually, follow me," the mechanic replied. Sure, whoever wanted to get this bus moving.

Jax led the group to a wall panel partially obscured by the comb. The engineer aimed a grungy boot at the substance and kicked, breaking the pieces away in chunks. As the blockage cleared, Andee could see that the panel was on hinges. Clever.

The passage was narrow, but still wide enough for Saunders to enter while in the pressure suit. The group followed the Mechanical Engineer inside.

"This route goes straight to Four," Jax explained.

"Is this standard on *every* station?" Andee asked, looking at the padding covering what appeared to be thermal control lines. It looked hazardous to the health.

"Nah, custom job," Jax grumbled.

"Nice!" Andee quipped. Nothing like some unregulated passage to add to this adventure.

"We're going to have a problem," Eave interrupted.

"Naw don't say it like that babe," Andee sighed. The Navigator shot her an impatient look, with only a hint of a smile at the tail end. Score.

"What? Where?" Jax had turned to look at her.

Eave poked a thumb over her shoulder to the passage ahead of them. Even in this narrow route, there were chunks of tightly packed comb.

"Fucking hell, it's like we just...appeared. Inside some space-bee hive," the TSF guy spat. His shirt read "Bracken, T." on it.

"That's a good take on it, Brackent," Andee observed.

"Alright, well, we'll just have to kick our way through." Jax lunged off toward what must be Level 4, pointy-looking wrench-monster aimed like a lance for whatever blocked their path. Nothing like a can-do attitude in the face of guaranteed anaphylactic shock. They all hauled after the mechanic.

Brackent pulled up alongside Andee in their ascent, and she jabbed out a hand. "Andee, you?"

"Tizik," he replied, and shook her hand briefly with a nod.

The hardest part of their passage was forcing Saunders in that suit through the waxy blockages. Andee almost told her to leave it behind at least twice, but even then, someone needed to be bee-proof.

Level 4 wasn't any better. Scratch that, it was worse. The group emerged in a tightly packed maze of comb that made it look like the corridors were entirely blocked. The lighting dipped low and cast the entire space into deep shadow. Jax swore.

"Lights burning out?" Andee asked, trying to figure out where on the ring they were situated.

"No, the Core is dying. If we aren't rotating, we're running out of power," Jax replied, her voice sounding strained. "Saunders and I killed the rotation for hours before the Drop, so we were already eating up stored energy. Who knows how long this has been still now. For all we know we're about to lose power all together."

"If we lose power doesn't that mean we lose air too?" Tizik asked.

"Well spotted, Brackent," Andee muttered to herself. Ah, there, on the ceiling: the number twenty-eight. They were roughly fifteen degrees from her room. She took Jax's lead and aimed her boots through the wax, busting a hole as they went.

"Is anyone else offput by the fact that we haven't encountered one of *them* yet?" Eave asked the group behind Andee as she worked.

"One of what?" Andee called over her shoulder as she kicked again, widening the opening.

"The"—Eave sounded so resigned to stoop to this level, but she committed anyway—"space-bees."

"Oh man, sweets, I was hoping our luck would hold," Andee replied, as she stuck her head boldly into the next section of comb to see what awaited her. Thankfully nothing. She pulled herself through and offered her hand back to Eave. This side of the comb was far more open.

"If we're losing atmosphere and life support, do we have enough suits for everyone?" Tizik was asking, as they punched through the waxy blockages.

"There's ox masks, and temp suits in each berthing," Saunders reported. "But not like this one. Theres only a couple, and they're elsewhere on station."

"Aren't those temp ones only good for a couple hours?" Eave asked, quietly.

"Better than nothing, babe," Andee replied from where they were working side by side to pop through another wax wall.

"You're being pretty bold with your terms of endearment there, Dory."

"Ah, but see, Eave, *you* called me Dory. Which means the terms of endearment are working!" Andee grinned to mask a grimace as she exerted effort to break through the barrier.

At Andee's berthing door the group waited outside while she pulled on her weld kit. The pack used a solid-state power source to generate an arc, which was supposed to be flame-free, but it was at least a working cattle prod. It took special permits to get this stuff on a station like this, and Andee wasn't about to just leave it behind, wherever they were.

As Andee emerged from her berthing, kit in hand the group was, predictably, bickering, as some are want to do in a cosmically inexplicable crisis.

"Should we just...keep pushing through the whole level?" Tizik was asking, as he peered at the full blockage of wax that partitioned off the next segment of corridor.

"Nah, I think we need to get down to Level 1 and see where we've landed," Jax replied.

"Landed?" Eave snipped, sounding impatient. "We were hundreds of parsecs from anyone's destination, hence our even *being* on this trash heap in the first place. Where the hell could we have *landed?*"

Jax looked like she might pop a gasket.

"First off, whoever you are—"

"Her name's Eave," Andee replied helpfully.

"—we could be trillions of parsecs from where we started. And second off, this *trash heap* kept us alive while taking us here, so show some respect!"

"Sorry, it's a *lovely* trash heap," Eave sneered.

"*Thank you,*" Jax growled. Man, this group was a riot.

"Hey, do you hear that?" Tizik interrupted.

The banter ceased. A faint knocking emanated from the other side of the wax wall Tizik was leaning toward.

"Oh, I don't like that sound," Jax breathed. She clutched that absurd wrench closer to her chest.

Andee clicked the restraints on the pack. It cost more than she might very well make in a lifetime. But hey, it was supposed to be her lifeline for lifetime, *if* they made it out of this mess.

"I wouldn't do that," she suggested. But Tizik didn't seem like the kinda guy who took orders from random welders. He kicked at the wax, breaking through a portion of the thin looking wall, then the layer behind it. One more kick and a hideous face greeted them.

That was *not* a honeybee.

A gnashing maw, twitching feelers the length of a human arm, and far too many segmented legs appeared in the small gap and made quick work of Tizik's initial effort. The wax fell away as whatever they had disturbed sought to ensconce itself in the cozy little nest they were housed in.

"Shit, is it too late to say I told you so?" Andee roared, sparking her welder pack. Jax also swore something creatively colorful and slashed with the pointy end of the massive wrench.

Andee added an arc of electricity hot enough to melt space-grade metal and the creature shrieked something awful.

"Great, now its friends know where to find us," Andee grunted as she grabbed a handhold in the nearby wax and kicked. The critter gave a death rattle and shrank from the opening.

Nothing followed...yet. But Andee wasn't about to just go sticking her head into fun new places. That much couldn't be said for Tizik who clearly hadn't gotten the message the first time. Now he was head and shoulders through the opening the bug-thing had made.

"Corine? Corine!" He shouted and wriggled his way through. Great, that meant the rest of them needed to go. Andee let the others through, taking a post as rear guard. Mostly so she didn't have to squeeze her bulk through the narrow wax opening. But the sounds from the other side were not encouraging.

"What *did* this?" That was never a good thing to hear when surrounded by space-wasps in an alternate dimension. Andee didn't need many data points to know that.

But she did the unadvisable and poked her head in anyway.

Across from them were absolutely massive hexagonal tubes of comb. Thus far they had mostly been passing through the comb from the side, or through less developed sections. But here they were facing a series of comb tubes head-on. Usually there would be baby bees, or larva, or food in these. Well, the food was probably accurate. Food for these *things*.

Tizik was busy wringing his hands in front of a woman Andee vague recalled seeing around the common area. She wasn't that recognizable wrapped up in a hundred thousand silk strands, cocooned in a corner of the wax capsule. Whatever they had just squashed must have been prepping her for preservation.

"Right," Andee barked from the opening. "Who votes for hanging out a bit with Corine here and who votes for getting the *fuck* out of here ASAP?"

Tizik shot her a glare, which was certainly earned. That was his dead teammate, and Andee was not taking the time to say her respects. But it was Saunders' look of apprehension that made her swallow her words a bit quicker than expected.

"I can't just leave everyone else in here with *this*," Saunders replied, subdued.

Andee swallowed hard, unsure how to respond. She knew for a fact she wasn't sticking around to find out who else was wrapped up like a lunch to go.

And behold, it was the surly mechanic, in the lead with the reason.

"Saunders, we don't even know where to look. This bullshit is everywhere and we are on *borrowed time*. The best thing we can do is get our group out and see what the status is beyond these walls. Maybe we can buy some time from the outside, draw people out with us?"

Saunders didn't seem to buy it, though it sounded pretty damned good to Andee. The mechanic was an ass, but she wasn't a dumbass. Andee watched from her little wax hole as Tizik tried to extricate the husk of Corine. The other TSF guy, Flick, looked on helplessly, and Jax pushed herself over to Saunders to try to keep reasoning with her. It was Eave returning to the wax portal to push her way back through that caught Andee by surprise.

"Come on. If they want to debate the ethics of leaving everyone behind, let them. I'm down for getting the hell out of here," she grumbled.

"Knew I liked you!" Andee made a space for the woman to pass. "But I do think we need them. At least to make it out alive."

"Fine, but we can wait for them to figure that out while we find those spacesuits the Security Officer was talking about," Eave replied as she re-entered Andee's bunk.

"Come on in, why don't ya," Andee chortled.

There were four bunks in the single berthing Andee had been occupying, mostly, on her own. That meant four emergency suits, if this place was being run by regulation. Probably a good thing Saunders cared about her work so much, because all four were stashed in a pop-out panel near the lavatory.

"Great, that's enough for the lot of us," Eave muttered, unfolding the nearest and holding it against her angular shoulders.

"Not sure I'm gonna fit in that," Andee chuckled. Eave shot her an impatient look, but Andee was learning it meant she was calculating a snarky reply.

"They're one size fits all. If I can fit, so can you."

"Are you inviting me to share?" Andee asked, innocently. Eave dropped the suit from her shoulders.

"It doesn't even phase you, does it?" she asked.

"What, the bugs? Nah, we had a really bad infestation this one time, when some off-world transport docked...was cleaning webs off my shit for ages." Andee shrugged.

Eave sighed and shook her head. She handed the suit to Andee. "You're something else, you know that?"

"Hey, you're the one who ran into *my* bunk to hide when things got all creepy," Andee grinned.

Eave looked mildly panicked at the comment and Andee felt a tiny pang of regret.

"That was because I was looking for Quinn after I had to watch her rip her face off. Sorry for being a bit unnerved at that, but I doubt I'll ever see her again—"

"Are we interrupting?" Saunders said from the door frame. At least Jax had stayed in the corridor.

"Yeah, actually," Andee started, but Eave cut her off.

"We're getting out of here. If you guys want to stick around that's great and all, but I don't feel like getting trussed up like a lunch sack."

"We're waiting on *you guys*," Jax barked from the corridor.

Andee wanted to argue, but an unsettling sound reverberated from out in the corridor.

"Well, why didn't you say something sooner, mate!" she rumbled instead, and, suit snagged from Eave, shoved past Saunders back to the corridor.

Outside Jax, Tizik, and Flick had set up a perimeter. Beyond the waxy walls the hive residents were coming home for dinner. Flickering shadows and chittering told Andee they might be surrounded.

"Okay, suits on gang, let's get the hell going!" Andee charged.

Jax figured the best path to lead them down was back the way they came. Judging by the size of what had eaten Corine, Andee could see the benefit. It had been hard enough for them, as squishy humans, to pass through. That didn't stop the walls from crawling with the echoes of the swarm as they pushed back down toward Level 1.

"The only way out is going to be an airlock. It can still open even if we are on a planet or something," Jax was saying up ahead.

"I still don't understand how we wound up on a planet after all this," Eave hissed at Andee's side.

Some commotion from up ahead, announced by the string of expletives from the station mechanic and her Security Officer, told Andee something had breached their route. In the tight order of passage Andee could hardly see what was ahead. Saunders scrambled her way forward into a dim segment of passage and Andee shoved after. She was met with a slimy glob of bug viscera and smashed husk of whatever had crossed their paths. That wrench was wicked.

Flick screamed. Andee twisted just in time to see him grasping at the soft wax surrounding him. Tizik grabbed at him, but the wax crumbled and Flick disappeared, screaming, back up the way they had come.

"Time to *go!*" Andee shouted and shoved Eave past the dead bug Jax had skewered. Tizik was still shouting after his squadmate until Andee heard the sound of whatever was after them breaking past. Then she heard Tizik fighting for his life. And theirs. It wasn't a great sound.

Jax busted through the wax near the entrance like a linebacker and tossed herself into the corridor, wrench first. Andee waited for Saunders and Eave to push past as well before she rocketed herself after. The section of corridor was still empty, but the noise of the hive was rising around them in an incessant hum. Tizik didn't follow.

"Quick, get the damned suits on, we can use this airlock!" Jax barked from behind Andee. She was at the far wall hammering at an access panel that looked like it barely had enough juice to power the red LED that said it was sealed.

Andee shrugged out of the weld pack and wriggled into the suit Eave had passed her. It was thin, and felt like she might stick a foot through it. Saunders was clipping her own helmet in place and trying to suit Jax up where she was busy fucking with the airlock panel.

With the suit on, the weld pack didn't want to reseat against Andee's back like it should, and she wrassled with it to avoid ripping anything. Eave—already suited and masked—came up behind her and, feet planted in some waxy goo, leveraged the weld pack mass so Andee could settle it. Eave pulled herself free of the muck by holding onto Andee's shoulders and swung herself around to the front of the pack straps.

"Let's hope we get out of this alive, Dory. Then we can learn a little more about each other," Eave stated, pulling the mask down over Andee's face.

"Everything I know already, I like," Andee chuckled. Eave just rolled her eyes.

The airlock opened.

"Everyone get in!" Jax shouted, just as something started gnawing its way through a nearby wall of wax.

"Don't have to tell me twice!" Andee replied, and planted her suited hand on Eave's ass to push her toward the airlock entry.

"Has anyone bothered looking *outside* yet?" Eave protested.

"What, did you change your mind about leaving?" Jax snarled in reply. This was a goddamned vaudeville routine.

Andee would be entertained with the spicy attitudes if there were considerably less spinnerets, stingers, and gaping maws trying to drain them of their soft innards.

The airlock cycled. The outer door clicked green and hissed open weakly, as the station power died.

Andee wasn't sure who was so eager to eject them all into the beyond, but they tumbled out in a ball of cheap pressure suited limbs, wrench, and weld pack. Some mild gravity existed beyond the Station, which struck Andee as strange, but she was too busy extricating herself from the wax she became stuck in.

Rage and impatience took hold and Andee thrashed to yank herself free. She scrambled to her feet in time to see the other three huddled just beyond the open airlock.

The halls of comb stretched in every direction. Narrow gaps crisscrossed to show an endless latticework of wax and hexagonal chambers filled with moving inhuman shapes or stationary, possibly human shapes. In at least two orthogonal directions, snippets of dark universe could be seen. Along the halls those *things* crawled, swarming closer now that they had made such a disturbing entrance.

Andee pushed herself over to the other three to stand at their backs. They weren't arguing anymore.

All halls of comb led to a common center. The station must have appeared in the middle of all of it, so suddenly it could have intersected the structure in a thousand ways. And right in front of them the central hub of the hive pulsed.

Or, well, the massive egg sack of the queen was pulsing. And the drones, there for her protection, the workers, there to do her bidding, were swarming closer and closer.

"Ah, fuck," Andee said.

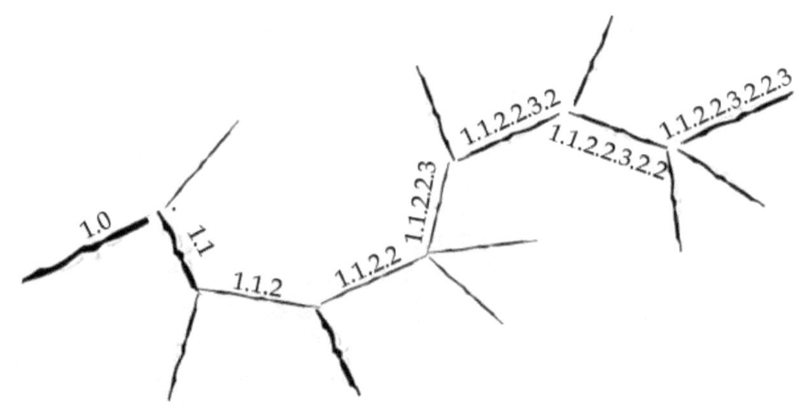

1.1.2.2.3.2.2.3

"You all should be ashamed of yourselves!"

Jax certainly *felt* ashamed when it was put that way, but she wasn't particularly the one getting yelled at. Obah stood with her back against an airlock, as if blocking someone's path. The congregation of residents they had found gathered near it had, in turn, been attempting to block Andee's path, as the welder stood with weld pack mounted, goggles in place.

"You want to control us?" someone shouted. Jax took a slinking step back to find herself even with Andee.

"Didn't sign up for this, boss," Andee grumbled.

"Not your boss?" Jax glanced up the mountainside that was Andee's shoulder and reveled in the illusion of safety that standing in her shadow gave her with this irate crowd surrounding them. Saunders was nowhere to be seen.

"We have been adrift out here for nearly a year now!" Obah snarled. "We have found the bodies of our lost friends, and mourned our fates, but here you all are, celebrating a *suicide*!"

The words echoed as a hush fell. It was as if the truth needed to be aired out in order for the magnitude to settle on them all.

"If someone was willing to give their life so that the rest of us may live longer, that absolutely *should* be celebrated." Zick's whisper was sinister.

Obah rounded on him.

"You, Rogle, are so young to find yourself in the respected role of foreman—"

"—Hey, I earned my post just like anyone here—"

"I'm not *finished!*" Obah snarled. Jax flinched. It had been decades since she had felt the wrath of a parent, but it stung just the same. Obah looked back at the rest of the gathering, then glanced over her shoulder through the porthole to the body that drifted in their wake. They would find out who it was, eventually. Jax was not looking forward to that conversation with Saunders.

"My *nephew* is gone. The only family Gedry and I had, and all we could carry with us across the stars. And for all I know it's because of you lot putting stupid ideas in his head. Did you all forget?" She scanned the group, but so many had chosen to avoid her eye contact. "The distances we choose to travel? We were *never* coming back. We may have tricked ourselves into thinking we might. Maybe we could have, in time. But our paths? They are almost *always* one-way."

Obah glared at Zick once again.

"Your team would have settled so far from Earth that it would have been stupid to ever return, Rogle. *How* is this different?"

Rogle opened his mouth to object, but Obah had already moved on.

"None of our futures were guaranteed at our destinations. We could have tricked ourselves; lulled into the false safety of being in proximity to humanity, but the universe had a different idea."

Obah pushed herself off the airlock door frame and strode through the group, forcing as many to look at her as possible. At Jax's side, Andee shifted slightly toward the abandoned airlock, but Gedry slipped in beside her and put an arm out to pause the effort.

"What we have all been faced with, is the most raw and unfiltered form of the universe's indifference," Obah continued, her voice echoing off the walls. "And some of us have proven that we cannot handle it. Are you afraid of your mortality? You!" she rounded on Corine and Pento, who had so boldly split from the rest of their squad. They shrank under her scrutiny. "Your team was headed back to Earth. But you were returning from combat. Your return was never promised. How is this different?"

Neither Sentinel bothered to reply

"We see the end before us, but we can make a different outcome. Our choices, every moment we take to decide between one direction or another: do we walk the ring clockwise or counterclockwise? Each of these changes can impact the outcome."

"And every outcome has a different universe," Jax whispered, almost as an afterthought.

"What?" Andee flinched and peered down past her shoulder.

Jax shook her head to clear it and looked back up.

"What?" she replied, equally confused.

"But why do we just let one group make the choices for the rest of us?" Enith barked. He sounded impatient, as if this lecture bored him. He shoved forward from where he flanked Zick and strode up to Obah, thrusting an accusatory finger in Jax's direction. *Now* Jax was the guilty party.

"Engineering and Security have been making choices that affect *all* of us this entire time. Directing our lives as if it's still their station!"

"It *is* my St—" Jax coughed around Andee's massive hand as it blocked the rest of her retort from escaping.

"First, they make the choice to send us on this stupid trip, when we could have been rescued by now if we stayed put! And now Engineering is getting her goon to weld the airlocks shut, taking away even our choice of how we die!"

"Look, we're more like platonic goon friends, I wouldn't particularly say I'm *her's*," Andee protested, hand still smothering Jax like a calloused dinner plate. Jax nearly bit her in retaliation. The hand dropped and Jax reveled in her newfound fresh air to load her retort in the chamber.

"So, would you all rather vote on who gets to live or die?" Saunders strode into the group, canceling any snarling response Jax had saved up.

The Security Officer had given up on any semblance of a uniform at this point. She wore faded sweats that just barely showed the outline of "TSF" on the leg, and a sweatshirt that...said "Engineering" on the sleeve. She looked exhausted: the strain of their trip and the food rations taking a toll on the burly figure she usually presented. She glared expectantly around the group.

"Sure, *Security—*"

"If you hate me doing my job so much you can dispense with the title," Saunders interrupted Zick, immediately taking the vitriol in his reply down a peg.

"Fine, *Jillian—*"

"Oh *no*, we are not *that* good of friends." Saunders leveled him with her heated glare. Then brushed right past anything further Zick might have had to say.

"But fine. Let's vote. Who here thinks we should leave the airlocks open so people can pick and choose when they get off this ride, and who thinks we should take a precaution against the stress of this journey?"

Obah looked like she wanted to interject but Saunders had drawn even with her in the group and reached down to grasp her hand. The older woman held her peace for the time being.

"Okay? So let's vote. Who wants precaution?" Saunders called out. Several hands tentatively started to rise. Not enough.

"And who wants a coward's way out?" Saunders growled. More hands. More tentative, embarrassed hands than Jax was comfortable with.

"*Fine.* We'll leave this one unwelded." Saunders raised her chin as if in defiance.

"But!" Obah released Saunders hand and stepped forward again.

"We have a choice. Right here, and right now. Work to survive, or give in and give up. And right now, I see a group of people giving up." She glared at them all. "I refuse. We are here now. No further from home than we had already sent ourselves when it comes to the rest of humanity. Those of you who want to give up? I'm ashamed *for* you." Obah scanned the crowd again.

"Those of you who have the spirit, the willingness to look at the heart of the universe and fight back? Those who want to make this work? I will work *with you.*"

A deafening silence fell on the crowd like ash. Jax saw parties and pairs start to drift away from the back. Slowly the group began to dissipate.

Ged departed Andee's side for where Obah stood, her eyes burning fierce, her face looking ready to crumple with emotion.

"Whelp, guess I'm not needed here anymore," Andee chirped, good naturedly.

"Back to your bat-cave?" Jax growled, keeping her eyes on Saunders who stood with her head hung, off to the side from where Gedry comforted his wife.

"Nah, I think I'll go check in with Eave. See if we can defile Level 5 for you," Andee replied offhandedly. Jax snapped her head up with a glare.

"Don't you fucking dare—"

"Hey, 'Spirit and willingness' and all that, right?" Andee grinned, the goggles making her look like a six-and-a-half-foot tall, deranged owl. She then shrugged. "Look, I was supposed to be a year into my contract in the Outer Bands by now, working off my debt. There wasn't an *end* to my contract. If we're being honest, this whole little excursion is probably the better outcome for me. At least I got a date out of it."

With that, the welder gave a hearty wave and strode off back toward Common Access. Jax watched Andee's massive form disappear before she found the courage to look back at where Saunders remained.

Gedry and Obah had also departed, along with any stragglers. Now Saunders was the only figure filling the corridor, her hands pressed to the airlock door, her eyes keenly tracking the distant figure in their wake.

"Hey," Jax started.

"Who was it?"

"Jillian—"

"Not *here*. Who *was* it?"

"We don't know," Jax replied dejectedly.

Saunders hung her head again, breaking her line of sight with whoever they had lost. There would be no way to tell if they had been alive before they had been ejected, or already dead. Jax didn't want to think about it *or* the fact that their death had, in some ways, extended their survival odds. Their numbers were dwindling in uncomfortable ways.

"I'm going back up to Five," Saunders replied eventually, as she turned from the porthole.

Jax watched her walk away, unsure of where she herself should go next.

"Are you coming?"

Their quarters were still disheveled, but they bore a distinct amount of change that Jax could just barely put her finger on. The bedding was still rumpled, her tools still discarded in a corner. There was still a pile of laundry, and a few remaining crunchy leaves from Ralph. But Saunders' duffel had found a neat corner to reside, and Jax had cleared out part of her locker to make space. Some slight sense of order had come to the small berthing, accompanied by a single, menacing, yellow throw pillow, placed challengingly on one of the two chairs.

Jax picked it up and tossed it, as was habit, back onto the duffel, and hoisted herself up on the desk, work boots resting on the pillow-less chair. Saunders had infiltrated Jax's space, and it had become a mashup of their own ways of occupying a room: chaotic and orderly, in rapid succession.

Now the shorter woman stood almost dejectedly in their shared quarters, as if unsure what steps to take next.

"If you want to take a look through the records on who was on Station, I can go down to two and check the morgue..." Jax had started. But Saunders cut her off.

"I don't want to think about that right now."

Jax quieted and waited for Saunders to offer up her own plan. The woman nudged her duffel with a work boot and then turned on Jax.

"Maybe you should take that tool belt off," she stated, suggestively.

Jax felt it like a slap to the face.

"Sorry, that...just doesn't seem like the best plan at the moment..."

But Saunders closed the distance between them, squeezing between Jax's knees to splay questing fingertips along the zipper to Jax's coveralls.

"Oh come on, we can celebrate the spirit of livelihood that Obah is asking for!" She leaned in closer, her lips grazing the base of Jax's neck. "Or at the very least, take our minds off the fact they all want to jettison early from this cruise—"

Jax pushed Saunders' shoulders back to put space between them.

"Jillian, someone is *dead*, don't you fucking *care* about that?"

Saunders glared at her.

"Oh no, Jax, I'm *over* all that," she sneered.

"What the *fuck*, Jillian?" Jax pushed herself off the desk to put more distance between them.

"Oh come on, that's what you want isn't it? To get past any issues I have with the fact that I, once again, can't keep a single damned person alive when it's literally my only job?" Saunders rounded after Jax to keep the fight going.

"I didn't *say* that!" Jax objected.

"No, this is great! You get to keep thinking everything is fine, and I get to escape my nightmares between your legs! It's perfect—"

Jax felt it like a punch to the gut.

"Is *that* what this has been to you? An escape?" Jax's voice fell quiet with anticipation and dread, as she gestured between the two of them.

The air had shifted, and Saunders had frozen, green eyes locked on Jax like a homing beacon.

"What? No—"

"You *literally* just said that!" Jax pointed at a spot on the floor between them is if it were evidence of the past statement.

Saunders thawed into motion and took a step away, tossing her hands up.

"Well, okay yes, but that's not all!"

"No, that's *not* all," Jax growled, rounding on the Security Officer to address her. "Something is going on, with *you*." Jax felt a sickly swirl in her gut, as if she had missed a significant detail in a calculation, and it was far too late to fix her work.

"Nothing is *going on*, besides, apparently, this argument," Saunders shot back.

Jax felt her face flush. "But there *is*. And you won't tell me about it. Instead, you'll just drag us back to bed together, like it'll make me forget...Or make you forget?" The words falling from her own lips made things feel very real. Jax had admitted she had fallen in love with Saunders for all the things she had always known were worth loving about the woman, but maybe Saunders had really just needed the warmth.

"You've certainly seemed like an enthusiastic participant." Saunders was standing with her back to the door again. "And something tells me you don't *really* want to know these things about me."

"Why *wouldn't* I want to know?" Jax cried out. "I told you I love you. I mean *all* of you!"

"Oh you don't know that. Look we both have shitty backgrounds. We can use a little secre—"

"I told you, ages ago, before all this! I don't want to be *used*!" Jax shouted now, and she wasn't sure if it was anxiety or heartache that burned in her chest. This was building to a pain she had thought was long since left behind.

There was a beat, a moment between them, in which Jax felt the Drop all over again. This time as the conclusion of a delusion she realized she had been entertaining; that she and Saunders could just ignore their past. Then Saunders, at least, had the good decency to flash a look of absolute panic before she surged forward, hands out to try to stop the avalanche.

"Jax, why would you say that? I *love* you, I'm not *using* you!" And she absolutely sounded like she was trying to convince herself as well. Jax squirmed away. It all just felt too out of place.

"I think that a decent argument could be made that you are!"

Saunders was relentless. She pushed onward, closing the gap between them again to put an arm around Jax's waist, her other hand reaching up to Jax's face. But Jax wasn't having it. Not now. She dodged the contact, leaving Saunders' hand hovering between them. Jax needed the breathing room, but Saunders stood between her and the door, and any mechanical malady she could use as an excuse to not face this head-on.

The space yawned between them; the Rift, reimagined. All of spacetime seemed to be sucked into this void now, dragging the last several months in with it.

"So, is that it?" Saunders' voice was soft and full of anguish.

The overwhelming feeling of addressing the challenge before them had swept Jax up in its torrential flow, but Saunder's words breathed life into something Jax had not actually even considered. She narrowed her eyes and cocked her head, allowing the possible path forward to flash before her, showing a future without Saunders by her side. It followed with a feeling of panic.

"Is what?—No! That's not—" and then she backed up, a hand raised between them to keep Saunders at bay. No, she didn't want this conclusion. Not now. Not after all they had shared together. "No that's *not*...'*it*.' I just don't want to feel like the entirety of our time together is you escaping something that needs to be dealt with."

Saunders looked like she was trying to reason with herself as well as the situation. Her eyes shot from one side of the room to the other as she hunted for answers.

"So, you *don't* want to be the place I turn to when I need to forget about everything bad that's going on? You don't want to be the good thing in my life?"

"Oh don't fucking even start that," Jax snarled, squirming at the ugly feeling those words evoked. "That's a low blow and you know it! Manipulative doesn't look good on you."

Saunders immediately reversed, wearing a look of increasing distress. She thrust her face down into her hands and stifled a scream of frustration. Jax could see this burning her up inside, and the pain it was causing Saunders was starting to eclipse Jax's own hurt. She sighed and hung her head, squeezing her eyes shut to shed the weight of her discomfort. She still loved this woman. Jax reached out and grasped Saunders by the elbow. She pulled gently until Saunders' forehead bumped into the spot just below Jax's chin.

"Jax, tell me what I can do to make this right, please!" came the choked and muffled voice from down around Jax's collarbone. "I can't do this without you."

"I just want you to stop." Jax spoke, without finishing the thought train in her head. Even she didn't have the answers, just the knowledge that it still felt right to hold Saunders like this.

"You want me to stop having sex with you?" Saunders asked, tone muted.

"No, I don't want you to stop having sex with me," Jax interjected, hoping it wasn't too forceful sounding. "I want you to stop having sex with me instead of telling me what is wrong, and keeping me from being able to help you with it," Jax corrected. "I don't think that's too absurd to ask of the person I love."

"I do love you, Jax, I fucking swear," Saunders nearly sobbed, "I love how much you care for this Station, and how that genuinely flows down to the people within it. I love how even at your most distant you are always there to do exactly what needs to be done. I love your commitment to the needs of everyone, even when it's at the expense of this place you have called your own for so long."

"I...don't need a list, Saunders," Jax mumbled. But, the list was kinda nice. "I just need to know you feel like you can tell me more about yourself other than the most effective way to...uh..."

Saunders coughed a wet laugh and then let out a shuddering breath.

"Look," Jax switched tracks. "Can we just start from scratch here? Please Saunders. People have died. More are *going* to die, that's the nature of the nightmare we live in. And every time you withdraw into some headspace that I can't follow, blocked by your tendency to distract me with your legs wrapped around my neck. I don't *want* that. Well, not *just* that," Jax stuck a hand up to stop Saunders' reply before she could make it. This statement was long overdue.

"Jillian, I want you to take me with you when you fall into that well. I want you to share what's bothering you, not shield it from me. Please. Tell me everything. It can't make me love you any less."

From somewhere below Jax's chin, muffled in the faded black shirt Jax wore, Saunders' voice carried upward.

"Yeah, okay."

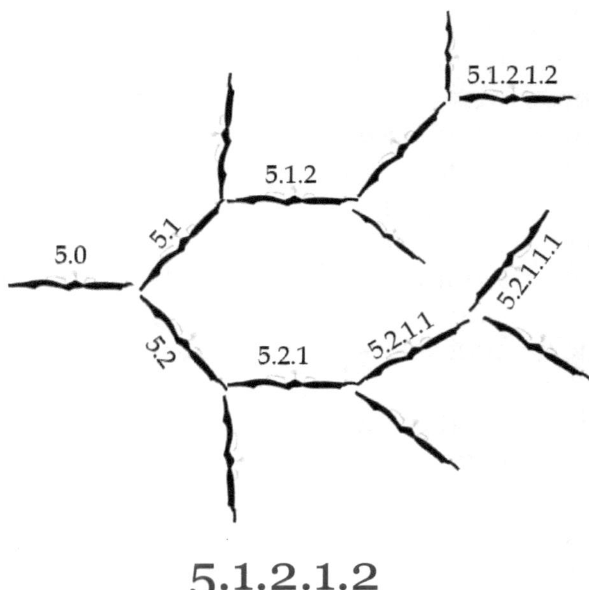

5.1.2.1.2

Saunders stood in the fridged gloom of Level 5, her body tense, her senses on alert. The Seeker had been slamming into the exterior of the station at regular intervals now, dragging some questing appendage along the outer hull. The noise faded again, for what felt like the fifth time in as many hours, leaving Saunders alone with her thoughts. And Tess.

The Sentinel was looking worse for wear, her multi-surface utility uniform shredded below the knees, the flesh there looking damaged or lost altogether. Saunders gave the vision a withering glare.

"Why are you here Tess?" she finally asked. The shadow didn't reply. Tess never had replied in all the instances of Saunders seeing her. But the taunting sight of the Sentinel had finally gotten to Saunders.

"Why can't you just leave us alone?" she begged. The opening to her and Jax's quarters lay some half a meter away, with Jax resting, recovering below. "I have Jax now. She keeps me tethered. I don't need this reminder, not anymore!"

Tess simply shrugged, and mirrored Saunders' withering glare. It was always a look of judgement, of disappointment, that told Saunders she was as much a failure as she felt she was. But Jax needed her. These residents needed her. And the presence of the specter was finally reaching a limit Saunders didn't know she had.

"I said LEAVE ME ALONE!" Saunders roared. Tess responded by taking a step toward her, sending a terrifying shiver down Saunders' spine. The ghost had never made any effort to get closer to her.

"Jillian?" Jax's voice waivered upward from the dark hole. Saunders flinched toward the sound, not wanting to take her eyes off the sight of Tess in front of her.

"Jillian are you up there? Who's up there with you?"

"Jax, you're supposed to be resting, your leg is still fighting infection!" Saunders protested. Tess had not moved any more, just stood frozen, her blank eyes trained on where Saunders stood. "Please," Saunders pleaded, unsure of whether it was aimed at Jax, Tess, or herself.

"Yeah, but you don't sound okay, I'm coming up!" Jax called.

"No!" Saunders barked, and tore her eyes off of Tess to look at the entrance to their quarters. In that instant the sentinel disappeared again. Saunders scanned the dark shadows, panicky and unsure of her own thoughts. Then a clunking sound from below told her Jax was serious about climbing with an injury.

"Jax," she hissed and she strode over to the opening. Looking up at her was the pale face of the mechanic, her dark eyes looking concerned and her expression masking the discomfort of her injury.

"Who was up there?" Jax pressed, as Saunders lowered herself down into the snug berthing, pushing Jax back toward the bedding. In the wake of her adrenaline passing, the cold surged into Saunders' bones, and she shivered violently. The bedding was still warm from where Jax had been sleeping, and Saunders pulled off her damp outer clothes to wrap herself in the blankets.

Jax had slumped back down next to her, still favoring her injured leg. Saunders pulled the blankets back and grabbed at the mechanic to pull her close. In the warmer dark of their private space together, pressed snug against her Mechanical Engineer, the pressure of the fear which gripped her broke through. Saunders felt her shaking evolve from a reaction to the cold, to a release of tears. It was too much: their submerged prison, the threat of the Seeker, their limited resources, the vision of Tess haunting her. Saunders broke down.

"Jillian, please, talk to me," Jax was repeating, her arms tight around her, hands rubbing her back, stroking her hair. It wasn't helping. The tears ran harder, the shaking intensified.

"Please, Jillian, I'm here."

Saunders bawled into the darkness until she fell, fitfully asleep.

* * *

Saunders rolled over in her bunk to look at the ceiling of her squad's barracks. The grey of the metal panels overhead was the same, flat grey of the asteroid rock they were surrounding themselves with. Saunders made a quiet mental note to wear nothing but bright, cheerful colors once she made it off this infernal rock.

"Saunders, just because you aren't TExxing with us, doesn't mean you can just lay there."

Saunders didn't feel like making eye contact with Tess. She knew what the woman looked like, strapping on her chest plate to the contact points on her hivewear.

"Look Jacoby, you never cared when I just lay here before, I'm not in any rush to get reamed right now."

"Whatever Med, we'll all just get to work without you."

Saunders decided to not give Tess the satisfaction. If she wanted them to take a break, she could chill the fuck out when Saunders wasn't chasing after her like some lovesick teenager following her to battle.

"I need to lay off the operatives, you guys are all about the fast fuck, and nothing about the slow burn," Saunders grumbled to the barracks walls. Tess was thankfully already out of earshot, roaring with the rest of her squad as they pumped each other up for their training exercise. Whatever. She'd be back later, full of adrenaline from the training and looking for an outlet to burn through. And Saunders wouldn't have the willpower to say no. It would be the closest she might ever get to the fight.

Five years of wasted potential, and Saunders couldn't even join in on the fun stuff. No, she had a damned summons to the CO's office.

"Don't worry Med, I won't fuck them up too much."

The base of Saunders' bunk shook. She finally turned her head to look down at the hulking mass of Sentinel grinning back up at her.

"That's bullshit LaPont, you'd fuck them all if you had enough time," Saunders snapped back at him.

He snorted.

"Just the ones you let me, right?"

"Fuck *off*." But Saunders wasn't really mad at him. He pumped his weapon excitedly and gave the edge of the bunk another rough shove before he bounced back to the center aisle of the barracks.

"Good luck with that asshat paper pusher," LaPont called as he turned to the barracks exit. He hoisted his bulk up just enough to slam his gloved fist into the top of the door jam, adding a new dent to the busted metal sign that had the word "Rock Raiders" painted on it in chipped tarmac paint.

"To gravel we go!" he chanted down the hall, after the rest of her squad.

Saunders gave herself another moment to stew in her own bullshit before pulling herself out of the thin covers and dropping down to the cold floor. The barracks were empty. Her team was off without her.

She placated her bitterness with ten rapid pushups before hefting herself to her feet in her own attempt to pump herself up. It was futile. Saunders popped open her own locker, and ran her hand through her short, shorn hair, looking in the mirror inside the door. Then she reached past the muted grey on black of her unpowered multi-surface utility uniform for the crisp inspection whites. Today would not be a workday in her hivewear, along-side her teammates.

Today, she needed to get ripped to shreds by some power-hungry bitch of an officer, who didn't know the meaning of a workday. That meant some show-pony bullshit, in a uniform she hadn't worn seriously since boot. She had packed on enough muscle since then she probably wouldn't even fit in it, which was even better. Now she could get written up for poor uniform management along with whatever mess she had gotten herself into with her fucked up record keeping.

She pulled out the pristine uniform and glowered at it as if it embodied the bullshit recruiter who had lied to her.

"You'll be on a settlement planet, providing medical support. You'll get your hours done in no time, and leave with full ride to medical school. Less time if you wind up in some front lines action!"

Saunders wouldn't have had a problem with that outcome. Some deep-space security posting or field medic work for a squad fighting the Astral Rights insurrectionists would have been a term of service she could be proud of. But nothing happened on this infernal rock. And those hours she needed for her medical license were worthless. She would barely be qualified to manage a bus station after this, much less an emergency ward.

Whites on, hair slicked down as tame is it could get, Saunders exited the barracks ten minutes after her team. She glanced off down the corridor to where they had all traipsed off to their training exercise. She should be there with them, armored up, med kit strapped in place, ready to step in when one of them played a little too rough. But duty called elsewhere.

Saunders knocked once on Commander Elmhower's office door and waited, body frozen in attention.

"Enter."

The door rolled open, and Saunders stepped through efficiently. She stopped in front of the Commander's desk, saluting.

Of course, he took his time staring her down before saluting her back. She held her arm as motionless as the rocks surrounding them, intent to not give him a single reason to think he had another thing to mark against her. He finally graced her with a responding salute and she dropped her arm with a snap.

"Medical Sentinel Second Class, Jillian Saunders," he drawled. She made a point of staring at a space just two inches over his head. He refused to rise, nor did he indicate she should relax. Instead, she busied herself with finding the infinite void just beyond the room they were residing in, willing her expression to not betray how badly she thought this was a waste of her time.

Commander Elmhower obviously thought this was not a waste of time.

"Do you know why the Unified Earth's Terrestrial Surface Forces are out here?" he inquired. Saunders flinched internally, and bit the inside of her lip to keep it from showing. Five years in and she shouldn't have to put up with this boot level fuckery.

"To provide security and support in humanity's pursuit of planetary surface expansion, Sir!" she barked. Textbook.

"But do you know what that *means*, MS2?"

From her peripheral, Saunders could see him lean back in his plush desk chair, twirling a pen casually in front of him. He was purposely trying to make her squirm, asking these lofty, open-ended questions.

"Would the Commander like a more in-depth explanation, or this soldier's personal opinion?" Saunders willfully pulled the snark from her voice with every syllable. She wanted to make it out of this meeting alive.

Commander Elmhower considered this for a moment before changing his approach.

"We keep records out here, MS2. These records are important. You have been entrusted with the health and safety of your team, and the other teams out here. How useful do you expect to be to them if you cannot keep your inventories in order?" he admonished. This time the flinch showed on her face.

She was here to keep them alive and keep them healthy. But five years on a rock, where no one knew you were even there, meant her job was all about keeping a track record on every bandage, every cotton swab, and every moist towelette. They may as well ask her to track the condoms used on leave. That, at least, was a more dynamic inventory.

"Permission to speak freely, Sir?"

"Denied. I don't want to hear your excuses, MS2, I want solutions."

It was probably a prerequisite requirement that all TSF commanding officers be jackasses with a hardon for spreadsheets. Saunders wanted to do her job so perfectly that when this asshat finally came to her with a papercut she could revel in the bureaucratic schadenfreude of forcing him to fill out an outtake form for the singular bandage she would issue him.

"I want this place to run like clockwork. I want everything in order and everything in its place, do you understand MS2? Your services are best spent seeing to it that our inventory is spotless, and tracked. If I so much as get even the slightest impression that our valuable and critical medical supplies are not in balanced order with the purchasing intake, you might find yourself busted back down to MS3, or finding a new rating, do I make myself clear?"

For fucks sake, these assholes really liked listening to themselves speak. Saunders clenched her jaw.

"Yes. Sir," she gritted out.

"I should hope so. With how little your services are needed elsewhere I would think it would be easy to keep track—"

The room rocked violently to the side. Saunders had been standing stiffly, taking the barrage of insults as they were hurled, which left her sorely off-balance. She snapped from her position of attention and crumpled to the side. The wall next to her imploded, sending a cascade of dust over them both.

Commander Elmhower had gotten knocked over in his cozy desk chair and he scrambled up from behind his desk, grasping out at the comms panel just out of his reach.

From the hallway there were several shouts and the sound of blaster fire. A siren blared over the speakers indicating a rapid oxygen depressurization. Saunders scrambled from the floor, coughing through the dust.

The commander was shouting something panicked, or something distraught, but Saunders couldn't hear it anymore. Her line of sight was on the corridor, visible through the damaged doorframe and wall.

Her team was out there. They were out there, without her. Something was happening to them, and she wasn't there for them. The shouts of the commander fell on her ears, soundless as she pushed through the remains of the door. She looked down the corridor toward the entrance to the flight deck where the training exercise was happening. A few soldiers were running down the length, some were injured.

Saunders pushed down the hall, limping from where she had hit the flooring. With each step, she pressed herself to move faster. Her vision narrowed in on the exit ahead, leading to the training field. She passed the door to her barracks, where her medical gear was located, uselessly stashed next to her MSUUs and her own armor, her own weapon.

She grabbed an emergency ox mask off the wall, pressed it over her face and shoved her way through the exit to the open dome of the asteroid surface.

The lighting shift blinded her and her vision swam until she was able to take it in. Then it was only a sea of blood.

The dome of the atmosphere bell covering the rock surface was fractured. She could see the barrier knitting itself back together to limit the air leakage, but instead she was gazing over the field of remains.

This had been her team. She had seen them not half an hour ago. They had been alive, excited to do something other than janitorial duty. She had sent them off with a sharp biting retort, as they had left her behind to be subjected to her lashings.

Saunders waded into the sea. It was a wash of gore, mixed with the shifting pattern response of the hivewear uniforms working to match the muted grey of the asteroid surface. Clearly the camouflage hadn't worked well enough, because someone had seen them.

She passed the lower half of someone's body, ending violently mid-torso, tripped over a leg, and fell to her knees. Her crisp, inspection-ready white uniform was covered in the dark grey ash of the asteroid, and the crimson streaks of her team's remains.

She was empty-handed. She was supposed to be out here with them. If she had only been here, with her supplies, she could have saved them, she could have done something. She tried rising, turning to find the voices that cried out in anguish. There were survivors, she needed to find them.

Saunders slipped again, tripped over the prone figure of someone in her path. She looked down at the smashed and mostly headless figure of LaPort, the man who had so gamely challenged her before embarking on his last course of action, calling out their team's motto like a battle cry.

A heat surged through her, pushing Saunders onto her back. She scrambled away, seeking out across the sea, wondering who was even alive anymore.

"S-Saunders?"

She whirled around, spinning, swimming in the mess. Her team. She was here now, she could help them. She scanned the sea of bodies. She was vaguely aware more blaster fire was erupting, though she could not tell if it was coming through the broken atmosphere bell or from the cover fire of those still left alive.

"Jillian..."

Saunders spun again and saw her, prone, under an outcrop of grey, cratered rock.

"Jacoby...Tess..." Saunders dove under some close-range blaster fire and scrambled over to the woman who, until a week ago, had still been crawling into her bunk every night. Though she may never be crawling again missing that much of her lower body.

"Saunders, you're here…" Tess trailed off, her vision seeming to phase in and out of focus.

Saunders ripped her service coat off, followed by her belt. She needed her medic kit—that was where she had tourniquets—why didn't she have her medic kit? Why was she dressed like she was in some stupid parade?

The belt wasn't stopping the bleeding.

"Jacoby, I need to get my kit, I can't—"

"Jillian, Jillian don't leave me!" Tess grabbed for her with what remained of her arm. Saunders froze in place, staring down at the person she thought had been her future at one point, who she knew might still have been. She looked up, at the lives winking out of existence around her. If she had only been here earlier, ready.

"I need to save you—"

"Please."

The scene spun around her, filling, louder and louder with the screams of those dying. Saunders felt the grip on her arm weakening, saw the woman dying, saw her team liquifying around her, felt the air leaving her lungs as she screamed.

"Saunders! SAUNDERS!"

She felt the shaking quake through her and the dark and bloody surface of the asteroid faded to be replaced by a different darkness.

Saunders sat up violently, clutching her chest, and throwing the blankets off. Even the damp cold of the Engineering quarters was more welcoming than that suffocating feeling. She scrambled in the tangle of bedding, and felt the Seeker's long, questing coils wrap around her.

She screamed, and thrashed, pushing herself away, holding her head, still hearing the echoing screams of her dead team.

Jax's firm arms wrapped around her again and pulled Saunders roughly back into her chest. Saunders struggled, but felt the arms tighten around her. Her face pressed into the crook of Jax's neck and the screams died down.

Saunders breathed steadily for a few moments and let her head clear. The mechanic held on tight to her. The moments ticked by and Saunders felt the dream fade around her. The echoing blaster noise was replaced by the steady drip of water, somewhere in the room. The horrors of her past were replaced with the pressing horrors of their present. Saunders gripped Jax tight to her.

"It's okay," Jax said softly above her. "I'm here. You don't have to tell me about it, just, let me hold you."

Saunders rested, willing her tightly coiled muscles to relax. She had kept these stories to herself for so long. She had been haunted by the ghosts of Tess and her team, reminding her of every failure she ever had. With the real nightmares mounting around them, she couldn't shoulder this load any longer. She wanted the shadows to cease, like they only did in the arms of the woman holding her.

"Jax," Saunders whispered to the darkness between them.

"Yeah?"

"I need to tell you."

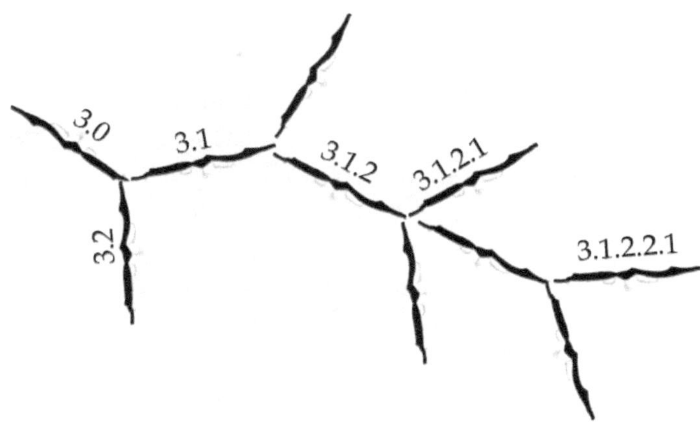

3.1.2.2.1

The barbed tongue snaked toward Jax, pausing just inside her peripheral vision range. It hovered as if calculating its next move.

"Vamp, if you don't pull that back in, I'll cut it off in a way it won't grow back!" Jax snarled as she worked a screwdriver into the interior of the translator. It didn't have screws, but the screwdriver was long and pointy enough to give her the reach.

The alien sitting adjacent to her reeled in the tentacle-like appendage, and the reach *it* granted, and Jax swore she heard the Skraawl chuckle. Jax put the screwdriver down and glared at the creature. Then she powered up the contraption and dragged her hand over the surface, selecting several symbols and letting the hemisphere vibrate with corresponding Skraawl speech.

Vamp stopped chuckling.

"No tongues!" Jax growled. The Skraawl warbled a bird-like sound and Jax had only a moment to put down the translator before the smallest Skraawl alien tackled her.

Jax scrambled out from under the appendages in too many places, felt the threat of the barbed tongue again and grabbed a foreleg to knock the creature over.

"Stop flirting, Cul is coming," Saunders stated as she entered the room.

Vamp broke free from Jax's lock hold and crawled on all four limbs to a vantage point that let it assess Jax, who was sprawled on her ass glaring up at the departing alien.

"I'm not flirting babe, it just keeps sticking its tongue out at me."

"Flirting," Saunders repeated. Jax rolled her eyes and got to her feet, casting a glare at Vamp who was warbling again, in a very self-satisfied way.

Jax strode over to where Saunders had pulled up the main display again.

"You know you're the only person I let stick their tongue out at me," Jax argued. Saunders glanced up from where she was scrutinizing the symbols.

"Funny, the result always includes you rolling around on the floor."

Jax felt her face flush. Saunders went back to her task.

"Is that translator working now?"

"Worked enough to get that message across to Vamp," Jax offered.

Saunders turned to sit on the slab.

"Jax, I told you, Cul is coming. If there's anyone we need to convince that fighting the Malacost and their little Foliage army is a bad idea, its Cul. They already don't trust us because we aren't warriors." Saunders sighed, sounding exhausted.

"Cul doesn't trust us because you won't let him cut off my leg. Thank you, by the way," Jax replied.

"I like your legs. Both of them—" Saunders bit back her reply as Cul swept into the room, Cloak fluttering more from the sure nature of the creature's stride than from its own ability. The alien wasn't as imposing as Nos, but it was a close second. With only a normal single set of aft appendages, Cul bore a menacing obsidian weapon that seemed charged with the same energy powering the slabs and translation devices. Its eyes had a more metallic sheen to them than most of the other Skraawl. The creature's body was marred by scars and gouges that looked too brutal to have regenerated completely. More to the point, Cul didn't seem fond of either of them.

"EEikkaa," Saunders stated, addressing the Skraawl second-in command. It was a muted word, and Jax wasn't sure it had the same meaning if it wasn't intoned in a vocal cord shredding pitch.

Cul strode past to the slab. Large and formidable talons strummed through various symbol combinations before Cul waved almost impatiently at the holographics.

"WHERE IS TRANSLATION"

Jax wasn't sure if the creature meant to ask it as a question, or if it was an error in the programming. She ducked her head down to the handheld terminal to see if it fared better, and Cul roared with impatience.

Saunders replied back with another word in Skraawl that still didn't sound right coming from a small blond, but Cul refrained from another outburst.

Jax held the translator out and swiped at several glowing characters. The human words appeared the same time the translator screeched and flashed.

"WE MAKE PROGRESS"

Cul bore down on them, and Jax had the fleeting desire to step in front of Saunders to protect her. Then she remembered Saunders was less breakable. As if reading her mind, Saunders shoved Jax aside, and stepping in front of Cul, who shrieked in protest.

"What do you want?" Saunders barked. Jax struggled to program the question, but Cul hissed as if they understood.

"SkIIrEk AH hEIIKAy kIIReeek Ikaii," Cul snarled.

"NOS FIGHT, YOU AFRAID"

"How many times do we need to tell him we're a bit more fragile?" Jax grumbled.

The translator lit up with some combination of shrieks and Jax had no way to tell if they were correct. What she could tell was Cul's eyes narrowed as if under threat and the creature bared its pin-like teeth, growling deep in its chest. Before Jax could register the threat, Cul aimed a powerful foreleg at her chest and kicked, knocking her backward into the stone.

Winded, and unable to breath, Jax shook the stars from her eyes in time to see Vamp scurry into Cul's path. The Senior Skraawl gave the smaller one only a passing glance before grabbing it with one hand and ripping its right arm off with its other. Cul then tossed both Vamp and its departed limb as if they were refuse and pulled out the charged obsidian weapon it held.

"Wait!" Jax wheezed, holding her stomach. "Bad translation!"

Saunders dove in from the side, slipping on the blood from Vamp's arm, and landed across Cul's path to Jax. There was a horrific moment where Jax saw Saunders killed for a simple calculation error, but Cul snarled and went to pass her. Saunders threw her hand out just as the obsidian blade got too close to Jax for comfort.

Jax winced, but it was Saunders shouting in pain. Eyes open, panic surging in her chest, Jax scrambled on the floor with Saunders at her feet, trying to see what had happened. Saunders clutched her hand, clearly coated in human blood and not the yellow tinged Skraawl blood.

"What happened?! What *happened?!*" Jax barked, reaching out and grabbing Saunders by the shoulders. She glanced up to make sure a killing blow wasn't coming, but Cul had stepped back as if studying them. Even Vamp had picked itself up and was creeping closer, arm stub already no longer bleeding.

Saunders was hissing in pain on the floor and refusing to release her hand. Jax didn't know where to put her own hands, as she wanted to see what was wrong, but not make it worse. She scanned the area as if the answers might be written on the floor, but instead found a finger. Saunders' finger.

"Holy shit," Jax snarled, and shot a glare up at the creatures crowding them. At some point Nos had also entered the room. Saunders was gritting her teeth and wincing as she squeezed her hand. The bleeding wasn't excessive, but it was obvious.

"Are you satisfied now?" Saunders shouted at Cul who hissed in return.

"We need to get you cleaned up," Jax muttered, trying to rise to her feet. There were medical supplies back at the room they shared, and more on the tug if they were allowed to leave.

Nos strode forward, shoving Cul aside, who snarled in response. The Skraawl leader roughly snagged Saunders by the arm with an aft appendage. Saunders cried out in pain as the creature hoisted her wounded hand up to its face to scrutinize it. Her pinky was cut clean off at the second knuckle. Better than a whole leg, but Jax wasn't thrilled about Saunders losing anything, much less a finger.

Saunders trembled in the grasp of the Skraawl leader and Jax made a motion to reach out to her, but Nos snarled and pulled Saunders further from reach, which only made her groan louder through gritted teeth.

The barbed tongue probed outward and nearly came in contact with the wound, but then withdrew. Nos snarled something over its shoulder, and Cul replied with a shriek and a roar.

"NOT FIGHT, THEY DIE" spelled itself out on the large holographic.

Followed by Cul's response:

"USELESS"

Nos released Saunders and she dropped back to her knees, holding her hand. The two lead Skraawl turned shoulder to shoulder and lumbered out of the room.

"YOU COULDN'T TELL THAT FROM HOW EASILY THOSE SHRIMP BASTARDS WERE SLAUGHTERING US??" Saunders roared at their receding forms, before she crumpled in pain.

Jax rushed back to Saunders' side and reached for her hand. Saunders pulled it away, but Jax reached again.

"Let me see it. I need to see it," she argued. Saunders relented and let Jax pull her hand toward her. It wouldn't make a difference. There would be no way to reattach it.

"I need to get you to the med kit we brought with us," Jax replied. Saunders nodded, mutely. She was green in the face.

Jax hoisted them both to their feet and turned to drag Saunders from the room. Vamp strode up, one arm short, and extended its remaining talons. Jax recoiled for a split second before realizing the small Skraawl was trying to help.

"KoOOm," the creature barked, turning to leave, and Jax was almost certain she understood the word. She led Saunders out of the room, following Vamp's lead.

Saunders winced as Jax cleaned the remains of her finger. Vamp held out a canister of what Jax assumed was water, but was leery of using for medical purposes. Saunders was more interested in getting answers.

"What *happened* back there? Vamp?" She looked at the creature. They hadn't brought the translator with them, but Vamp regarded them like it was considering an answer. It made the same warbling sound it made when it was mulling over its next steps. This shouldn't surprise Jax, she had been talking at the small Skraawl for the better part of the last ten day-cycles. Maybe it had picked up on things.

"Skiirik Ah eEik kaaah, eRIEsK sKeek," Vamp paused and made a violent motion at its own missing arm, then continued. "KooOOskraaA, keereeIIk aAukEEi."

Jax stared at the creature as if on pause, a bandage hovering over Saunder's hand. She shook her head and looked back at Saunders who was contemplating the creature.

"Don't tell me you understand each other," Jax stated, to both.

Vamp trilled a warble again. Saunders turned to look back at Jax then nodded resignedly at the bandage.

"Vamp says Nos realizes we don't have the same warrior capability as they do. They didn't realize until this happened, and regeneration didn't start." She weakly emphasized her hand, where Jax suddenly remembered to wrap the bandage.

Jax cast a glance at Vamp's arm. It was already fully sealed. It would probably start to reform in the next day cycle.

"Right, so maybe they didn't see how easily we were mowed down on Station when we got here."

"It's not like they were part of that attack. They know we can die, just not how...easily."

"Okay, so what happens now?" Jax worked carefully to not cause Saunders added pain, as she bound and wrapped the remains of her finger. The other woman winced and sucked in a breath anyway.

"SkoOOrkIIah," Vamp replied.

Jax glanced up at Saunders again, who chuffed out a breath as if laughing through the pain.

"Great, we're going to try a more 'diplomatic approach'."

"That's all it took? Some light dismemberment?" Jax replied, incredulously. "What would we have gotten for my leg, the honeymoon suite?"

Saunders examined the patch job Jax had done, then held up her disfigured hand and grimaced a smile. "Worth it, I guess."

Jax scoffed. "There is no universe in which I am going to be happy about you having *fewer* fingers."

Saunders studied her, head cocked to the side. "Is there an upper limit to the number of fingers?"

"Ten," Jax growled.

"I'm impressed," Saunders replied with an eyebrow raise.

Jax scowled and waved Saunders off. "You're impossible sometimes."

Saunders hoisted herself back to standing and paced the room they called their quarters.

"Nothing's impossible without a little prep. Okay Vamp, what do I need to do next?"

* * *

"Nevermind, I'll pass," Saunders squeaked out. Jax didn't blame her.

Nos, apparently, didn't have any patience that day. It roared at them again, and pounded a fist on the nearby slab.

"REPRESENT SKRAAWL"

The Cloak flapped aggressively against its restraint. It looked hungry, for something with no eyes, or facial features. But the effort to latch onto something made it seem ravenous.

Saunders took a tentative step toward the parasite. It sensed her movement and strained toward her, its dewclaws grasping, and its suction-like mouth, rimmed in tiny sharp teeth, made a wet sound at her as she drew close.

"Jillian..." Jax trailed off. She rubbed at the back of her neck where a Cloak had tried seizing her. It had healed fine, but the repulsive feeling remained: the fluttering, fine fur, the pain in the wrist and elbow joint as the dewclaws sought purchase, the disconcerting nuzzling at the neck preceding the pain...

"Nope, sorry, can't do this!" Saunders took a massive step back and put her hands up. The Cloak shuddered in proximity to its target so suddenly removed from its reach. Saunders grabbed Jax by the hand and hauled her from the chamber.

As they passed, Nos screeched something at her and Saunders turned and screeched something back, unintelligible or not. Jax would have found it funny if not for the fact the last miscommunication cost them a body part. She merely jutted her chin down and avoided eye contact with the creatures as Saunders led her out.

"So you're okay with them taking pieces of your hand for the sake of peace, but you won't get a little cozy with a nice, furry, blood sucking parasite?" Jax asked casually as she was dragged back to their own chamber.

Saunders finally released Jax's hand, rooted to the spot. She full-body shivered.

"Sorry that was just...too weird," she replied and stomped over to throw herself down on the bedding.

Jax sat on the edge of the non-living blankets to look over her shoulder at Saunders.

"Okay, so now what?"

"THREE DAY" clipped a truncated phrase from the translator held in Vamp's hand.

Jax nodded as the creature limped into the room. It looked like it had gotten the short end of another squabble. But Vamp's stubby leg already featured a lengthening appendage, and Jax swore she saw claws already.

"Yeah, yeah, I know, three days till we talk to them," Saunders grumbled. She absentmindedly rubbed her neck.

"I'm not exactly complaining here," Jax piped up. Saunders glanced over at her. "If you have that thing wrapped around you, where exactly am I supposed to sleep?"

Saunders rolled her eyes and glanced at Vamp.

"HOW ARRIVE" the creature manipulated the translator.

Saunders sighed and slumped back again.

"We already told you, Vamp, we don't know," she spoke to the room at large.

Jax looked between the woman on the bedding and their surprising alien ally.

"You keep asking us, and we can't tell you. What do *you* know about that Rift?" Jax pressed in return. It was the same exchange they always had. Nos had clearly given Vamp the task of getting answers out of them.

"RIFT KNOWN"

That reply was *different*. Saunders sat up at Jax's side.

"You've *seen* them before?" Jax hissed, her voice full of disbelief.

"RIFT KNOWN" Vamp repeated.

"Vamp," Saunders said quietly, carefully. "If I do this. If I bond with this Cloak, will Nos trust us more? Can you help them believe us when we say we don't know how we got here?"

At this the Skraawl chirped in reply.

"And can you tell us more about these rifts?" Jax pressed.

Vamp merely chortled, birdlike from the corner: an inconclusive response. But Jax was filled with a new wonder. If they lasted out here, there might be more answers to the darkest secrets they had encountered in this universe.

The long twilight was setting in at the planet's horizon, and the chamber light was dimming. Saunders had remained where she lay, propped on her elbows studying Vamp where it crouched, its own Cloak swished around its forelegs

"Vamp, do you like your Cloak?" Saunders finally called out. The alien regarded her then fiddled with the translator.

"NOT UNDERSTAND"

Saunders laboriously rose to her feet and strolled over to where Vamp perched. The alien eyed her in partial suspicion. When she got close enough, Saunders circled the Skraawl, reaching a hand out and almost touching the Cloak. Vamp pulled back with a low trill in its throat.

"It's important to you, isn't it?" Saunders asked.

Well, of course the alien symbiotic parasite was important to the alien hosts. Jax thought the question was a bit redundant. But Saunders tilted her head as if examining Vamp's reaction.

"HONORED"

"But *why?*" Saunders' frustration resounded in the strain of her voice. Vamp cocked its head again, quizzically, and Jax was certain the creature hadn't fully grasped the question. The Cloak fluttered again.

Then, as if being driven by a force exterior to their own will, Vamp unfurled their uninjured aft leg over its shoulder and grasped the Cloak by its...neck? The parasite writhed grotesquely and shuddered as if in revulsion, before pulling away from the raw wound on its host's neck. The thick Skraawl blood oozed from where it was feeding.

Jax froze in horror as she watched her inhuman friend start to wail. The stump of their other aft leg began to bleed, as if the wound were opening up again, Vamp's mottled skin paled as if it were washed in pain.

"Vamp, STOP!" Saunders barked. The Skraawl elicited a weak warble and jammed the questing Cloak back into its neck. The effect was near instant. The wound stopped bleeding, and Vamp's energy returned. The Cloak fluttered smugly about Vamp's sturdy forelegs.

Saunders stepped forward and put out a hand, tentatively brushing the fine fur of the Cloak. Vamp didn't recoil this time. Instead, it chirped and good naturedly snaked out the barbed tongue to lap at the closing wound on their leg stump.

"It helps the pain, helps to heal you, doesn't it?" Saunders spoke. Jax shifted uneasily, as she watched the shorter woman regard the remnant of her smallest finger. Vamp chortled again.

"STRONGER WARRIOR"

Saunders nodded as if deep in thought. She sighed and turned to walk back toward Jax. "Alright Vamp, you can tell them, at next light, I'll try again. And maybe we can talk further about the rift that brought us here."

Vamp shook its head, almost like a dog shaking off water, as it resituated the re-attached Cloak. It them regarded them both with its silvery eyes, as if expecting more. Jax watched as Saunders returned to the bedding.

"But not right now. I know you don't get this part Vamp, but it's time for the humans to sleep. Sorta," Saunders called over her shoulder.

Jax felt her eyebrows skyrocket, and inadvertently made awkward eye contact with all six of Vamp's eyes. The alien just gave a confused chirp and slid from its precipice.

"THREE DAYS"

The translator repeated. Vamp limped from the chamber. Jax watched it go.

"They've seen those rifts before, Jillian," Jax breathed, her voice hushed in apprehension. If these creatures knew what a rift was, there were answers, facts, data to study. Maybe, even, a way home.

"We need to get them to trust us first," Saunders replied, sinking down on the bedding beside Jax. "They still think we have answers for *them*, I don't think they are going to have answers for *us*."

"But they saw it. They have an image of the whole thing...that's...that's *data*. And if they say it's a known variable...then there's an answer on the other end of the equal sign," Jax mused, her voice hushed.

"Which makes this alliance even more valuable," Saunders replied, her hand tracing over Jax's knee where it pressed against her side. The act was mildly suggestive, but Jax's thoughts were elsewhere.

"Why do you think Vamp is different?" Jax mused from the bedding.

"Different?"

"Yeah, they aren't as violent at Nos, or Cul. They want to help. They want to communicate. They're smaller too," Jax recounted.

Saunders shrugged and lay back on the blankets.

"I guess there's weirdos in every species, Jax. You would know."

"Hey!" Jax barked in objection, twisting to glare at the other woman.

The former Security Officer had a glint in her eye.

"Lucky for you, I'm into your kind of weird. Now, if I need to shroud myself in those things to save the human race, give me one night to wrap myself in you first. Clothes off Jax, it's not like we have all thirty hours of night here."

* * *

"Showtime," Saunders announced, under her breath to Jax. Her shoulders were squared, her chin lowered. Her gaze was set determinedly on the large drop deck doors of the Skraawl transport. But Jax could only stare at the awful furry parasite latched onto Saunders' neck and joints. The Cloak's mouth pulsed gently where it attached, and the bottom of it fluttered.

"How's it feeling?" Jax asked tentatively, trying to not shudder in revulsion.

"Feels like I can fight these fuckers off singlehanded," Saunders snarled quietly, as the cloak fluttered around her. Those Danger Blankets must be a hell of a drug.

"Hoo boy, that's not a great idea..." Jax exhaled. She swung her shoulders awkwardly in her worn coveralls. They still had the faded patch on the chest that read

"ENGINEERING." She would be the only representative without a Cloak, but she wasn't about to drum up hard feelings about it.

"Just remember. We paid our ticket with the Station. *My* Station. Gave them nearly *all* our resources. All we are asking in return is they let us go," Jax hissed, low to avoid their Skraawl counterparts picking it up.

"Yes, but then they can't *study* us. That's what they really want."

"Then they shouldn't have been such assholes about it," Jax griped. The heavy footfalls of Nos echoed down the sleek glasslike form of the Skraawl transport.

"READY" sounded the robotic voice of the translator.

"Ready," Saunders replied, looking resolute, if not spurred by the furry stage-five clinger on her neck.

Large bay doors of the transport opened slowly to reveal a pillar of light from the innermost planet of the Pentagram system. Massive spires of twisted coral, braided with organic plant life, streaked toward the sky. The dense and humid hanging gardens of the Prime Planet nearly blocked out the binary starlight as Jax and Saunders followed the vanguard of hulking Skraawl into the cavernous maw of the system's main governance assembly.

"Why does every entrance on this world make me feel like I'm getting eaten by something?" Jax grumbled, eyeing the creature feeding on Saunders.

Saunders, however, stormed forward like she was on a warpath, her head bowed low, shoulders tensed, jaw set. She didn't respond.

"What song do you have playing in your head this time, babe?" Jax asked, in hopes that it would distract her from roiling masses of Malacost and Foliage, like a garden full of giant centipedes.

"You wouldn't like it," Saunders growled.

"What? I love your music, what are you talking about?" Jax asked, trying to keep the hysteria out of her voice as they passed a brigade of moldy psychic Foliage.

Saunders didn't respond.

"Jax!" Of all the things Jax had expected to hear and see, her own name, shouted from the warped corridors of vegetation and coral, was not one of them. Even Saunders paused in her march and looked around bewildered. It was Rose.

The deep-space gravitational theory research scientist broke from a dark corner, running toward the group. Jax had a fleeting sight of Foliage moving to intercept, pursuing from wherever Rose had been standing. This entire endeavor was already fixing to end in violent bloodshed. Jax could see the situation deteriorating in a matter of seconds.

Rose, for all her small stature, and scientific nature, was fast enough to reach their delegation before the Foliage could intercept. Vamp closed the space behind Rose as she arrived, even if Cul looked as scandalized as an alien could look at the sudden arrival. Saunders looked like she might bite a second finger off to keep from embracing the other woman. Jax felt ecstatic.

"You are alive!" Rose hissed to Saunders, falling in step with her as they continued along the downward sloping tunnel toward the main chambers. She looked up with trepidation at the lumbering forms of Nos, Cul and Vamp.

"I'm sorry we took so long. This needed a lot of work," Saunders whispered back.

Rose let out a hardly audible sound that might have been another comment, but it was thoroughly squashed by the sight of the Cloak around Saunders' shoulders. Or maybe it was the tightly bandaged hand missing a valuable finger.

Jax scanned the roiling masses as they walked. She had a creeping feeling their Pentagram hosts had not expected them in such company. Which, fair point: this hadn't exactly been top ten on Jax's list either.

"Why are you here?" Saunders was asking Rose.

"I think they assumed you both were dead. We assumed that too, unfortunately," Rose responded, a tinge of regret in her voice.

"No, we agreed on it, if Jax and I ever left, to just assume the worst."

"It's bad, Saunders," Rose admitted. "They took Zick last nightfall. They aren't even hiding the fact that they want us for...testing." Rose coughed over the last word.

"'*Took Zick*'?" Saunders clarified, bewildered, breaking her line of focus to assault the researcher with a sharp green stare of bewilderment.

"*Testing?!*" Jax hissed from where she strode between them, a step behind, like some sort of sentient flag pole. She barely remembered who Zick was. But the other word freaked her out more.

"Is that not what they wanted all along? They want to know more about us, so they can be ready when more of us arrive," Rose stated grimly.

"Do they *really* think more of us will show up?" Jax was scanning the surroundings in growing unease. "The Skraawl keep asking us how we got here. But Rose, the Skraawl know about the rifts!"

Rose spun to look at Jax in surging academic curiosity, but Saunders interrupted.

"Rose, if they kill him...this is a delicate situation already!"

"I do not think they killed him," Rose replied, a lingering glance remaining on Jax before she redirected her words at Saunders. "I think that is the point is it not? To see what keeps us alive."

"Okay that's worse. You all understand that's worse right?" Jax felt a bit of anxiety jump in her chest. This tunnel was so long, and the portal ahead opened like yet another maw of a massive, deep-space, ravenous beast.

"*SKRAAWL FIGHT*" came a robotic voice, nearly drowned out by a piercing screech from Cul.

Rose looked up, alarmed, as did Saunders.

"*No!*" Saunders hissed, and Jax wondered if the woman simply misjudged that Cul might be a poorly behaved pet and not a twelve-foot-tall bat-lizard-alien monster with blood lust.

Nos saved the moment by screeching directly in Cul's face, as friends do.

"Rose, meet Nos, leader of the Skraawl. They are here to help us argue for human extraction," Saunders stated, low and precise, but loud enough for the translator to pipe the words back to Nos in a strange shrieking echo. "In exchange for our support, and possibly a better understanding of deep-space inter-dimensional rift mechanics. That might be where you come in."

Rose smiled an *enormously* gracious smile up at the large creature, considering this was the first time the small researcher had ever seen a Skraawl.

Saunders grabbed Jax, who startled and glanced down at the white, four-knuckle grip clenching the frayed sleeve of her coveralls. Jax took in the sharp dewclaw embedded in the tender skin of Saunders' wrist, followed the arm up to where a second dewclaw punctured just at the crease of the elbow, and finally all the way up to where it was attached to a very intense looking Saunders.

"Jax," she hissed, this time even lower to avoid the translator, "go find them, *please.*"

It was such a genuinely imploring request. It was a plea, directly at odds with Jax—a curmudgeonly waste of space who preferred the company of behemoth space stations to humanity. But the genuine fear in Saunders' features propelled Jax. She could go. She could be a hero.

"But what about you, your translator—"

"I'll be fine. You did great with this thing. I'll manage," Saunders interjected.

Jax felt some form of gravity holding her still as she grappled with the realization of what Saunders was asking her. She was asking her to leave, and find what had always been most important to Saunders: people. And it was why Jax loved her.

"Okay," Jax stuttered. It was bardic poetry in this instance.

"I will go with you—" Rose started.

"No. Stick with Saunders. Don't give them any more reason to suspect something is up," Jax managed, more coherently. Her head was starting to wrap around the mission, analyzing it, looking for courses of action she could take, engineering it like any other problem she had ever encountered in the weight of endless space aboard her Station. She might not be good at people, but she had always been good at keeping them alive.

"If they ask where I am, tell them you lost me," Jax stated. Saunders flinched. Jax wanted to kiss her, but that would invite more flagella than was preferable.

"*SaAUW,*" Vamp called. The Skraawl had stopped for Jax and Saunders. Jax took a deep breath, coughed inelegantly on the heavy, moist air, and took a bounding step back. She looked fleetingly over each shoulder before nodding curtly to Saunders, Rose, and Vamp.

"*AAaak?*" Jax heard the smaller Skraawl question, but Saunders was already pulling Vamp onward after Nos and Cul, through the ominous beckoning coral archway to the main chambers.

Jax tailed them, keeping her head low. As their group edged closer to the chamber entrance, the writhing crowd of locals dispersed to tubed pathways through the floor of the cavernous meeting hall. Jax took the first opportunity she could.

There wouldn't have been time to say goodbye. Saunders needed to stand her ground to their captors, millions of glittering eyes, or light sensors (or *whatever* the mold used for sight) would be watching her ascend to state their case, shadowed by a species that for all its fight, still was at a loss to these Pentagram nightmares. And Jax, she needed to slip out of sight and haunt the eerie coral tubes surrounding them in search of whatever humanity they had left.

As Saunders slipped through the archway, Jax eased off to the side and held her breath, more from fear of taking a risk than the lack of oxygen. She bolted for a nearby tube. Once inside she flattened herself to the wall, holding as stock still as she could. She waited for flailing plant appendages to seek her out, or the lightning-fast whip-flash of deadly claws to snap her in half, but moments ticked by and nothing sought after her.

The coral entry to the main chamber constricted closed like a massive orifice, sealing Saunders and the Skraawl inside. Jax took a deep breath and immediately regretted it. The air was, if possible, even more damp in the tube than out in the massive corridor.

Suppressing the urge to eject a lung, Jax turned and felt her way deeper down the tube. The light started to fail her. She would be forced to resort to touch. The dreaded thought of being in a lightless alien tube, feeling her way along until something slimy and inhuman bit her arm off was less than invigorating, but Jax didn't dare break out a light. Nothing worse than telling some wayward Malacost to "fuck-off" with the brightest light possible to their sensitive peepers, especially when on a rescue mission. Instead Jax bit her lip and edged forward.

At half a dozen dark paces, the tube opened up into a branch, and a pale light re-illuminated the coral surface faintly enough for Jax to get a better feel for her surroundings. She was blessedly still alone. One branch of the tube angled upward, the other downward into darkness. Either way, the illuminated direction led to a massive room full of pissy aliens, and the other direction probably led to death or dismemberment. Jax edged down and away from the faint glow.

The tube wound down like a lazy spiral, and Jax suspected it would lead her deeper into the massive city structure of Prime. If the curve of this coral tube continued, Jax would be under the main hall floor soon. Not that she knew where she *really* needed to go. For all she knew, the Station survivors were on a different planet or moon all together, but it was too late to turn back now. As if Jax could just saunter up through that massive sphincter of a door frame, and sidle on up to Saunders empty handed, as the other woman bartered for their livelihoods.

Jax continued to follow the tube, her hand held firm to its rough and damp surface. The backlighting had long since dissipated, but faint bioluminescence showed various tube branches at irregular intervals. Every branch signified a passed opportunity; an alternative reality in which Jax could have followed that branch to whatever destiny it may have led to. Rather, she kept her hand on the wall and followed its course, leaving all those infinite possibilities in her wake.

They could have led anywhere, or nowhere. But this tube led somewhere. Jax rounded a curve again, and saw the shift in lighting to tell her that there may be a change ahead of her. Above her there was the congregation of a hostile alien star system, and their single possible link to an alliance. Before her, the tunnel tube opened up on a small dim chamber.

There were machines down here. Organic and inorganic mixed together in the common practice of their inhospitable hosts. Low flickering light probably communicated some message Jax would never be able to understand. An otherwise ominous hum of some mechanism at work filled the cramped space.

Jax's eyes tried to adjust. The light was brighter than the previous dark tube, but still too dim to distinguish any real objects. It may have been a utility room, or an auxiliary maintenance locker. It may also contain hidden denizens of the local planet, simply waiting to dissolve her feet from underneath her. Jax could turn and try a different tube, try a different fate, but her eye caught on something.

It was a human hand. Real, ghostly in the lack of lighting, and also very dismembered.

Jax crept further into the room. The hand was stretched out, removed cleanly from its arm, fingers held extended by spindles of organic looking machinery. It had the distinct visage of something on display. Jax tore her eyes from it to the surface beside it and bit a hole in her lip to keep from making a noise.

It was a human torso. It had been divested of its limbs and was spread apart; its chest cavity held open by more mechanisms. Within, Jax could make out movement. She dreaded the idea of some larval creature burrowed inside, making a meal of this unfortunate soul, but as her eyes continued to adjust, she saw it was the motion of living organs.

"The fuck."

Jax knew enough about basic human anatomy to know that had to be impossible. Especially considering the notable lack of head.

This was a resident. This was a former Station transient, who suffered the Drop, and now would never live to tell about it. Was this Zick?

Jax retched, her vision of the Meat Market swimming into view, and she backed up into a display of various limbs against the far wall. This was more than one wretched soul. This was several of her people, now little more than a science experiment in hell.

"Skraawl, we warned you of human threat. There are many things we do not know about these creatures, why would you choose them over Sciiraak alliance?"

Jax couldn't contain the shout of surprise that escaped her. The voice had come from within the room, speaking clear language she knew and understood. It hadn't quite been normal sounding, but echoed as vaguely human. She spun in place, quick to avoid eye contact with the eviscerated parts surrounding her, and cautious her shout could have attracted unwanted attention.

Her eyes had fully adjusted now. In the center of the grisly display, too easy to dismiss as another piece of machinery or alien technology, was a human head. It was suspended by more spindly organic machinery penetrating it through the ears, eyes, and gaping wound below the neck.

Jax retched again.

The head moved.

Its mouth opened, eyes devoid of life.

"Should Sciiraak consider Skraawl a threat now too?"

That was the voice. They were using this head to speak. They were using the head of one of Jax's Station residents to communicate with the above congregation.

A subtle clicking sound emanated from across the room. There were flickers in the low light and the shadows elongated, as if pinched by invisible fingers and dragged upward into towering forms that pressed closer. Despite the warm, humid air of this hell hole, a cold drop of sweat trailed down Jax's neck.

Something moved behind her just as the head in front of her spoke again.

"Humans are a threat," it bellowed.

The shadows loomed, surrounding her. Sounds came from behind her, closing in, blocking her way out. There were flickers, a rustle, a flutter, a warble?

"AAaak?"

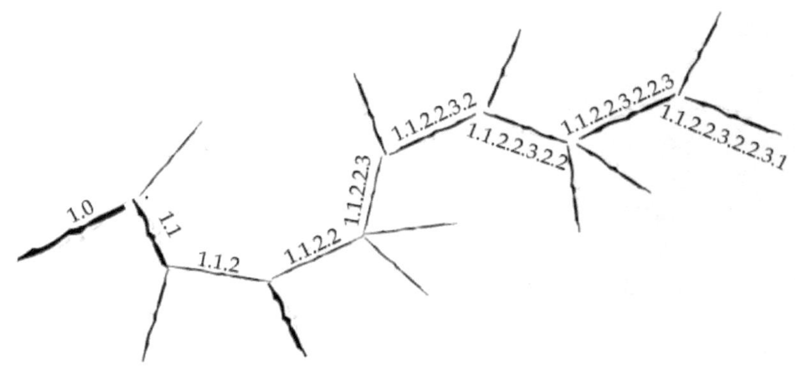

1.1.2.2.3.2.2.3.1

"He's such a vindictive *fuck*," Saunders growled, storming into Power and Life Support.

Jax was halfway through an argument with Eave about star tracker data caches, and she looked up with alarm.

"Who are you fucking?" Eave drawled in annoyance. She had become far too comfortable calling the navigation hub her own domain. Jax had been making an effort to reclaim her space.

"Don't even make a *joke*," Saunders hissed, and grabbed Jax by the collar to aggressively hammer her point home with a kiss.

"Yeah, yeah, we all know *that*," Eave grumbled with a dismissive wave, her knees pulled up to her chest, station lounge robe pulled tight around her broad shoulders.

Saunders had wound her arms possessively around Jax's middle and hidden her face in the thin knit of Jax's shirt.

"If I drag you to bed right now, will it still count as me handling high stress situations with sex?" Saunders grumbled.

"Not if we talk about it first," Jax replied, distinctly not making eye contact with Eave.

"I don't want to talk about it." Saunders' voice was muffled in Jax's chest.

"Is this Zick again?" Jax didn't really need the answer.

"I should have never suggested democracy." Saunders came up for air now. "He found his fucking footing with that one. Now he wants to vote on *everything* from the distribution of every cracker to the color of the damned hazard lights. If anyone wanted to take a trip through the airlocks, why couldn't it be him? If he's going to be so smugly magnanimous about that..."

"Feeling murderous? I like that," Eave quipped, and returned to cycling through the endless data readouts.

"Like what?" Andee was standing in the door frame now, her weld pack slung over a shoulder casually. Jax distantly remembered a time when this place was hallowed, only graced by herself and Saunders whenever the former Security Officer saw fit to drag Jax from her haven. At least now it seemed limited to their friends.

"Are you done with the tug finally?" Saunders asked, glancing up.

"Never," Andee replied.

"You love that machine more than anything else," Eave grumbled.

"I can relate," Saunders sighed as she hoisted herself onto the counter.

"They're making fun of us." Andee jabbed an elbow at Jax. It never ceased to knock the wind from her, but Jax had simply adapted to the blows. "I take it lunch rations were a jovial affair again? Everyone getting along?" The welder dropped herself casually on top of Eave, who sputtered in indignation and lashed out with her slippered feet to kick the welder off of her. Andee chuckled and shifted to a spot behind the irate woman, allowing Eave to tilt her head back against the welder's massive form.

Saunders sighed from her perch, tossing her shoulder length sandy hair over her shoulder and out of her face. "As well as can be expected, given the continuing food shortages. I need to check in with Bezley again about his samples. I'd take a salad any day now over another fight with those assholes."

"So much for 'friendly and courteous to all station residents'," Jax muttered under her breath.

"*That* was the job description? Where can I voice my complaints?" Eave retorted.

"Would you only give this place a *'one star'* review?" Andee offered helpfully.

"For fucks sake will you all just *get out*? This is supposed to be a controlled space!" Jax growled.

"On the contrary, I am quite pleased to find you all in here at this moment," Rose piped up from the entry. Collins followed closely behind her, ducking to enter the incredibly close-packed secured room dedicated to the primary control and operation of the Station.

"Come on in," Jax grumbled, admitting defeat.

"We wanted to discuss something with the collection of you all," Collins rumbled in his deep voice. He made Andee look stunted, and Jax could only imagine how such a timbre could reverberate throughout a lecture hall.

"Did you finally figure out what that bullshit was that we dropped through to get into this mess?" Andee called from her lean against the far wall.

"Why fucking bother, that's behind us," Eave growled.

Rose glanced at Jax with a calculated smile, then handed a digital readout to the navigator.

"Miss Idenah, could you enter these data points into the main navigation computer construct?"

"Now hold on a fucking second!" Jax sputtered and surged forward to stand at Eave's shoulder as she entered the data. But Rose placed a calm hand on Jax's shoulder and handed her a different digital readout. "Here is another one for you to look over, Engineering. Similar to the one I had showed you last month."

Jax glowered at the researcher and then shifted to perusing the data in front of her.

"Well, that complicates things," Jax muttered, glancing over the gravity patterns spelled out in data points.

"What does?" Eave was still entering the content into the computer, but Jax had shifted to glance over her shoulder again.

"There." Jax jabbed a finger at a line of inputs. "There's a conflicting gravity signature."

Eave craned her neck around to scrutinize Jax.

"And how exactly can *you* tell just from looking at that?"

"Oh, she is correct. It is beneficial to obtain a peer review, but Collins and I have also confirmed this." Rose glanced back up at Collins as if to ensure she was accurate. The man nodded his head once and returned to the readout on his own portable screen.

"Anyone care to bring the jarhead up to speed?" Saunders interrupted.

"Welder too, please and thanks," Andee added.

"They think they found a more viable target for us," Eave translated, giving the new data a closer read after Jax had so helpfully jabbed her finger at the relevant line of code.

"Sorry, what?" Andee scrunched her face as she peered over Eave's shoulder.

"Like, a better planet, or...?"

"We'd need to change direction, wouldn't we?" Saunders stated softly.

Jax glanced over at the look of unease on her face.

"Well, if we need to make a course correction, we need to make it fast. We are pretty much at our maximum speed before we need to start reversing thrust for approach."

"I did specifically *avoid* saying we need to course correct, I just wanted to verify you both understood the parameters," Collins spoke from on high.

"Oh, enough with the pedantic academics already," Eave huffed. "There's a reason I went into the workforce trades, you lot are ridiculous. What are you *saying?*"

Rose sighed. "Of course, if a new location were to be selected, we would need to be prudent in our execution. Time is certainly in short supply, and if we get this wrong, there are severe outcomes we may not want to face."

"Well, I appreciate you letting us know the *gravity* of the situation," Saunders replied. Jax, Eave and Rose, turned in slow unison to look at her.

"Okay, sorry, I couldn't let that one go. But yes, serious matter." Saunders clearly was trying to refit her face to look studious and concerned, but the edges of her mouth were failing at not curling into a self-satisfied smile.

"Right, well, are we sure this other target is worth changing course for? It may be nothing, or maybe we're already aimed at nothing. These aren't some mild decisions," Jax responded, slowly, turning back to Collins, but fixing Saunders with a side eye.

"I can only provide you data," Collins sighed. He looked tired. Jax could tell this mission had been his driving force for nearly two years. "We knew that we were headed into a target-rich sector. There would be opportunities to adjust as needed. This target appears to be viable."

"And besides, Engineering, you already verified our analysis of these alternative targets," Rose interjected.

Jax rounded fully on the researcher, brow narrowed and face incredulous.

"Since when?"

Rose smiled benignly. "I have been running data post-processing review past you for the past year. Collins and I would never have pursued it without your gravity signature assessments."

"You made course analysis decisions based on the input of a space station mechanic?" Eave retorted. "No offense, *Engineering*."

"None taken. What the *fuck?*" Jax also scrutinized Rose.

"No, of course we would not do *that*," Rose replied with a smile that made Jax feel an uncomfortable lump in her chest. It was reminiscent of a past that Jax had been damned certain she had buried behind her.

"I ask you all now. Given the increased odds of this option, what course should we consider taking? Even selecting this high percentage region, there still remains the chance that there were a million other options closer in range. We will never know." Collins assessed them all in the wake of his request.

Jax felt an involuntary shudder up her spine. The idea there may have always been a better way terrified her. It was something they would all just have to learn to live with. It haunted her more that she may have already influenced the path, but she *did* know what a gravity signature looked like.

"We may offer the decision via a vote," Collins suggested. Saunders threw her head back and groaned, loud and long, next to them all, causing Collins to jump a bit.

"Did I say something wrong?" he asked, alarmed.

"No, just, Saunders has grown a bit tired of the democratic process," Jax replied, absentmindedly reaching out and placing her palm over Saunders' face, muting the guttural complaint. Saunders shook her face and shrank from Jax's hand.

"I mean, you are right," Saunders replied, ceasing her audible objection and swatting Jax's seeking hand away. "It probably should be voted on, something of this magnitude. I'm just not looking forward to it."

They all stood quietly for a moment.

"Why even fucking tell them?" Eave finally broke the silence, her voice cracking down an octave.

The group turned to regard her again. She cleared her throat, pitch returning to normal.

"I'm just saying, do we really need some shitty foreman to have input on something he doesn't know fuck-all about? If this is the group the Jahars trusted with this, why involve anyone else? Either we make it or we all fucking die. What's the difference?"

The group was quiet, but Jax couldn't think of a counter argument. If they missed, and the group found out, well...there were worse problems to deal with. And if they made it? They could be pissy for a bit, but Jax figured it would be lost in the grand scheme of their impossible survival.

"Okay, but what's our window to make a decision?" Saunders replied, finally.

"I mean, at our current speeds, the sooner we act the better, we can switch at any time, but it adds time on an exponential level the longer we wait," Jax explained. Saunders seemed to mull on this, as a tense quiet grew in their midst.

"Fuck if we ever make it back to humanity, I am suing Westin for *so* much back pay..." Eave sighed, breaking the silence.

"Westin?" Andee cocked her head down, confused.

"Waypoint Station Transit Network," Saunders replied, distractedly. She chewed at her lip as she stewed over their course of action.

Andee locked eyes with Jax, who rolled her own and jabbed at the faded WSTN icon on the sweatshirt Saunders had stolen from her.

"Fuck, don't ask *them*, Engineering probably still thinks this whole adventure is a perk! Time and a half times infinity—"

Saunders snapped from her reverie and whirled on the group, cutting off whatever other snide remarks Eave could drum up.

"Okay, as the least sciencey person here, I say we do it."

"Do what? Sue the station?" Andee barked.

"She means change direction, Dory..."

"Security, are you sure of this course?"

"Hey! *I'm* the navigator, 'course' is my whole—"

"Babe, you're a certified *medic*," Jax reminded Saunders, amidst the distracted chatter. "That's science..." Saunders replied with an aggressive shrug.

"Fuck it. As the *really* least sciencey person here, I say 'hell yeah!'" Andee roared. Saunders cracked a grin and whirled back on Jax.

"Outstanding. Now, *that* counts as talking. Jax, quarters, now!" Saunders grabbed Jax by the hand and dragged her from the scene of their illicit crimes.

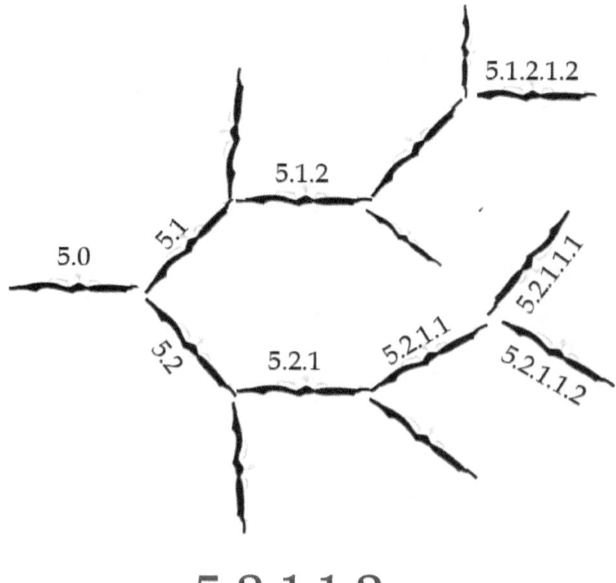

5.2.1.1.2

With Jax's leg sluggish to heal, Saunders had relegated her to their quarters. The mechanic wanted to put up a fight about it, but it was an easy fight to win when Saunders merely had to gently push the woman and she would tip over in pain. It was nothing a threat of leaving her locked in Medical couldn't fix. It did leave them to divide up the rest of Jax's workload.

Ged was puzzling over the task at hand.

"So you're taking over loading the power banks?" Saunders asked.

"I'm trying, Jillian. I know Engineering has been out of commission lately, but she didn't quite get a chance to walk me through it," Ged sighed. He hoisted one of the power banks and positioned it near the Common Access opening.

"I'll check in with her and see if she can relay any better details. I thought it was just a matter of pulling them from the core when the time comes."

Ged nodded and struck off to give it his best shot. Saunders figured it was as good a time as any to check on the mechanic.

Down in their quarters Jax was grumpy.

"I can still function, Saunders. Why can't you at least prop me up on Level 4 so I can help Rose with the inventory?" Jax grumbled as Saunders dropped herself on the horizontal surface near their bedding.

In the dim glow of the single light, Saunders could make out the sheen of sweat on Jax's forehead. The infection in her leg was not yet under control. Saunders had been checking it periodically, but the wet, dark nature of their surroundings was not helping.

"The more you exert yourself, the sicker you are going to get."

"Yeah, well I'm sick of being stuck down in this dungeon," Jax growled, and rubbed her leg.

"*Jax*! Don't fuck with it!" Saunders dropped to her knees and grabbed at Jax's wrist.

"Ow, okay, okay, sorry, I didn't even realize—"

Something large, heavy, and *angry* sounding slammed against the curved ceiling panels that made the far wall. Both women froze, Jax panting heavily in her fever.

"Has Bezley figured out what the fuck that is yet?" Jax stammered, after a few quiet moments had passed. Saunders released her grip on Jax's hand and sat next to her on the blankets.

"He has some ideas, but I doubt he believes any of them," Saunders said to the surrounding walls. She then looked back at Jax's pale face. She couldn't bring herself to mention her thoughts of the Seeker. Not since admitting that she was constantly haunted by the ghost of dead girlfriends. The mysteries of the deep would just have to wait.

"You don't look so well, babe," she said, instead.

"Well, you're going to take the tug to the surface and snag us some rescue, and then I'll look way better in some genuine sunlight, trust me," Jax wheezed out.

"Jax, I'm not leaving on that tug, I can't leave you behind like this!"

"That's bullshit, who the fuck is going to fly that thing?" Jax furrowed her brow. Saunders supposed it would be a challenging glare were the mechanic in better health.

"Andee can figure it out. Kivan can help her."

"That's a stupid fucking risk, they could blow the whole operation!"

"Kivan is a professional transport pilot, and you trusted Andee to make that thing seaworthy, why can't you trust her to fly it?" Saunders snapped.

"It's just a risk, when it's all we've got—"

"Yeah, well you're all I've got, and I'm not leaving you behind. They can do it, babe. We don't have to leave just yet. I can take a week to get them up to speed," Saunders said, softly.

Jax looked like she was about to have a rage fit at the idea of Saunders letting anyone but the two of them touch the controls of that precious cargo tug. Saunders readied her retort, telling Jax to settle down, and then she realized, it was not a shake of rage that was wracking the Mechanical Engineer. Jax was seizing.

"Jax!" Saunders jumped into action, grabbing the shoulders of the mechanic and trying to steady her. But Jax had screwed her eyes up and was convulsing violently on the tangle of blankets.

"Fuck—" Saunders jumped up and scrambled up the pile of junk to the door hatch.

"OBAH! ROSE!" she screamed down the echoing corridor. She hoped someone from the nearby Level 4 could hear her, she didn't want to have to leave Jax behind.

Saunders stormed through the doors of medical, followed closely by two TSF Sentinels carrying Jax's limp body.

Obah had managed to get ahead of her and had swept the space around the single med-bay clean, turning on the lights as she went. Rose followed close behind them all.

"Quick, here, put her down," Obah motioned to the clear metal surface of the surgical table. Avery and Flick placed

Jax's body on the hard surface and stepped back, Saunders swept in, Rose at her side.

"Where are the scissors, we need to get these sweats off her," Saunders stuttered out. Obah had spun to the storage cabinets.

Saunders' hand shot to Jax's face. The mechanic had gone unresponsive in the time it took for Saunders to get help hauling her body out of their quarters. Saunders shook Jax and brushed the dark curtain of hair back.

Behind her, Obah had handed the trauma shears to Rose and instructed the research scientist to cut the station-issued sweatpants off of Jax. Saunders slapped the mechanic, hoping to get her conscious again.

Jax's eyes fluttered and she groaned.

"Jax! Love, stay awake, please!" Saunders pleaded with the other woman. A sharp intake of breath from behind her made her spin around.

Rose had cut back the thin fabric of Jax's pants, exposing the extent of the damage to Jax's leg.

The dark, discolored stretch of infection spread up, and out from the necrotic stretch of damaged flesh. It had been nothing but a small scrape. Deep purple spider veins spread viciously up and away from the damage, carrying toxic, dead tissue into what still remained alive on Jax's leg.

"That leg needs to come off."

Even in all the years of medical training, and in all the heat of traumatic combat, that statement always hit like a sledgehammer. Saunders felt the wind knock out of her.

"Did you hear me, Jillian?" Obah asked, shoving a pack of sterile wipes across Jax's limp body, and into Saunders' chest. "She won't make it another night if we don't take it, that's blood poisoning, and necrosis."

Saunders grasped numbly at the pack of wipes, swallowed heavily, and reached, blindly for Jax's limp hand beside her.

"I, don't know if I can do that, not just with the three of us..." Saunders' mouth felt full of spit and she had to swallow hard again, this time to keep the feeling of hurling from rising up. Rhyse had been different. That had been an accident.

"You two, go get my husband, and Bezley," Obah ordered at Flick where he stood at the edge of the med-bay. He turned, wordless, Avery in tow, and left. Obah turned back to Saunders.

"What haven't you told us Jillian," Obah pressed. Saunders tore her eyes away from the damaged flesh in front of her. She swore she saw something inside it move.

"What?"

"This is not just an infection." The older woman was pressed against the surgical table. Saunders dropped her stare to Jax's face, but this time the mechanic wasn't imploring her to lie.

"Before the Drop...we were all hallucinating... Jax and I kept having to fight off swarms of just atrocious, monstruous bugs. Things that just do not exist in nature. We knew they were hallucinations, but they felt so...real. Jax got...bit by one." Saunders screwed her eyes up at the madness of the memory.

"Bit?" Rose asked, incredulous.

"I don't know, we fought them off and then they disappeared. The bite was still there so we assumed it was just a scratch from her work, or our fight, that maybe we had imagined it being a bug bite," Saunders stammered, losing control of the line of thought.

"Okay, whatever it is, it's gotten bad enough that we need to take action," Obah interjected.

"Okay. Okay, okay, okay." Saunders felt her mind racing and forced a deep breath. "Obah what do we have?"

She needed to regain control. She was trained for this. She was trained in the fires of combat. She wanted nothing more than to prove herself capable of saving her people, of saving her person, and here was her time.

"Scalpel, saw, disinfectant..."

"Sssaunders?" Jax groaned weakly.

Saunders bolted to her side.

"Shh, stay awake, please Jax."

"What's going on?"

"Jax, I'm so sorry, we...we need to remove your leg...it's killing you—"

Jax surged up from the table.

"NO!"

Saunders and Rose combined hauled her back to the cold metal surface.

"No, Saunders, please, please don't!" Jax's eyes were wild, and unfocused, suppressing the intense pain that Saunders knew she was experiencing.

"Babe, if we don't you're going to die. I'm not ready to lose you like that, please!" Saunders wasn't ready to cry, not in the middle of this crucial of a moment.

A slam from somewhere in the corridor echoed throughout the room, and Ged swept in with Bezley in tow. Obah wasted no time in briefing them.

"But you were fixing it, I was okay..." Jax was drifting off again. Gedry pushed over and grabbed Jax by the shoulders, holding her down. This woke Jax back up again. She thrashed against the restraint.

"Babe, please! Please, let me save you!" Saunders pleaded. Tess hadn't shown up since the nightmare that had driven Saunders to confess her whole story to Jax, but this moment threatened to bring the ghost back.

"Saunders, listen to me!" Ged barked. Saunders looked at the settler's bulk, securing the mechanic to the surgical table.

"You are the medical authority here. I've been through this before, so I'm here to walk you through it, but you need to clear your head. We need to move fast."

Saunders took a step back and inhaled. She looked from the earnest, warm face of Gedry, to the grim, serious lines of his wife Obah. She looked over at the ashen, yet determined look on Rose's face, and the tired, yet familiar expression of Dorian Bezley. Then she looked at the pale, sweat-drenched, anguished pain on Jax's face. These were all real faces. Not ghosts. Not yet.

Saunders stepped forward and grabbed Jax by the face. The mechanic's eyes rolled in her head before focusing on Saunders. She leaned in and kissed Jax.

"Jax, I'm so, so sorry. But please know, we are here to save you." She kissed Jax's stilled lips again, and stepped back.

Jax had stopped thrashing. She watched Saunders step back, and then her eyes circled the group, before landing again on Saunders. A look of resignation fell across her and she dropped her head weakly back to the table.

"I love you," she said.

Outside the station the Seeker assaulted the exterior again. But deep in Medical there was nothing else for Saunders to focus on but doing the best job she could do.

"I love you too, Jax," Saunders replied, hotly. She placed her hand once again against Jax's face. The mechanic went limp.

"Okay." Saunders took several deep breaths to steady her heartrate. "Scalpel."

* * *

"Jax, I'm just here to check on you—" Saunders paused.

She dropped the rest of the way down into the Mechanical Engineering quarters. The light was just as dim when she left Jax there a few hours ago. But Saunders was just able to make out the shift in shadow; the lack of volume to the nest of blankets that had become their bed. Jax wasn't there.

Her blood ran cold. Jax had not been in any condition to move.

Saunders swept the cramped space, seeking out the dark corners of the lavatory, the upturned bunk against the wall, the dark spaces under the storage lockers. She willed the small emergency light to do a better job showing her the confining space.

As if mocking her, the Seeker slammed something large and heavy into the station exterior. Saunders jumped back, looking up through the layers to the station wall that stood as the lone barrier between her and the fathoms of aquatic pressure surrounding them. Whatever was out there was getting more and more intent on getting in.

Saunders was starting to panic. Jax would be suffering from shock, and blood loss. Maybe the operation had gone poorly, maybe she was already gone.

Something on the converted flooring caught Saunders' eye in the dim glint of the tiny, pitiful light she held like a beacon. She crouched.

It was blood.

"JAX!" Saunders screamed to the emotionless walls of the station as if it had, itself, betrayed her. She threw herself to the floor to search the surrounding area. With a deep, sinking feeling, she noticed additional red gore very clearly marking a path.

It was a path she had already traveled, leading up, and out of the Engineering quarters.

Saunders jammed the light between her teeth and scrambled back up the makeshift stairs of lockers and tables, to push back through the hatch. Her head emerged into the damp, dripping corridor of Level 5.

Again, the Seeker chose that moment to grip the station in a vice and squeeze. Saunders flinched at the sound, and wondered how many more compartments would flood under its assault. Something alive was out there; something with intelligence. Saunders wished she could get a clearer view out of the station, but it was a fleeting wish. What she really wanted was to find her Jax.

The assault on the station exterior subsided and Saunders reemerged from her hideout in the off-center quarters. She stuck out a hand and felt the wetness that had accumulated while they sat so confined at the bottom this infernal ocean hellscape.

But it wasn't water. The weak light shone on crimson. How had Saunders missed this? She had just climbed down this hatch not a moment ago. Nevermind that, how could someone who just had their leg removed manage so easily to just...wander off...while leaving such a distinct gory trail?

Another sound accosted Saunders as she pulled herself out of the hatch into a combative crouch, ready to pivot and move in whichever direction she needed. This sound echoed off the walls and floor, and Saunders couldn't quite pinpoint it.

"JAX!" Saunders cried out again to the gloom, feeling loss and panic simultaneously. "Where are you?" Her voice echoed strangely down the shrouded corridor.

She shouldn't have left her. It was only for a moment, it was only so she could make sure everyone else was okay, but it was too long. She should have stayed with her.

The sound came again, this time reverberating, like the sound of nails on a chalkboard. Saunders stood up, spinning back and forth trying to pinpoint its source. Was Jax stranded somewhere? Was she hurting? Of course she was, but was this her call for help?

A loud, metallic THUNK sounded, different from the creature gripping the station exterior, different from the echoing scrape. Saunders whipped around toward where she had heard it and took several steps in its direction.

"Jax—" She cried out again.

The scraping resumed. It was the unmistakable sound of metal scraping on metal. Underlying the scraping sound there fell the heavy sound of impossible footsteps.

"What?" Saunders managed weakly, the rest of the air leaving her body in an instant.

The dim glow emanating from the tiny flashlight was barely enough to cast shadows, but it managed to frame the sideways corridor in stark contrast. The uneven surface of the wall panels beneath their feet showed a minefield of rivets and obstacles rising and cresting from the wall support struts. A halo of barely there light rimmed a void of darkness ahead, so close Saunders could not see the sharp curve of the station's shortest level.

From this void stepped Jax.

But it wasn't Jax, not anymore. Her long, unkempt mane of dark hair was blood matted, and hanging in front of her face. Her normally sharp, glittering, dark eyes were obscured, as if they were not even there. She stepped forward, her right leg emerging from the shadows.

She should not be walking. She had not been able to walk prior to the emergency amputation. Now Jax was upright, and moving, where she had been nearly comatose in the hours beforehand. Saunders took a step toward her out of instinct, out of relief, and froze.

Jax's other leg emerged from the creeping dark. Where the body of Jax ended, a new body emerged. Long, sinuous, coils of flesh curled out from the remains of Jax's leg. They dropped downward in a heavy pillar, restoring Jax to her full height, and then they swept outward, coiling and writhing around her as she moved.

Saunders couldn't scream. The love of her life was being replaced by something...else. She stepped back, away from the approaching monstrosity, and tripped over a raised lip in the wall.

Jax took another step forward, her re-grown, re-imagined appendage following. Saunders saw it grow in real time. The flesh elongated and flexed, reaching up the walls and behind the approaching figure of the Mechanical Engineer. They seemed to move of their own volition, seeking something unknown as they stretched outward from their host.

A radiating scrape of metal tore Saunders from the sight of the mass approaching and, with a sinking finality of dread, she noticed that Jax dragged her wrench along with her, the battered head ringing off the metal panels. The wrench's wicked, blunt point was aimed upward, gripped tight in the greying and unnaturally damp hand of Jax as she continued forward.

Saunders felt her scream finally rising in her chest, knew she would not be able to stop once she started, and scrambled further backward.

Jax was haloed now, entirely in the poor circle of light emanating from Saunders' tired and spent flashlight. In this last visage, Saunders could not tell where Jax, the creature from within Jax, or the shadows cast about from the two might end. It seemed the whole of the damned corridor was filled with the writhing, coiled, and hungry abomination that stood before her.

The shadows moved as if they, too, reached out to grab her. From the exterior of the station, the Seeker desperately wanted inside, and gripped the walls with finality. The structure shuddered, and somewhere Saunders heard what sounded like a rupture, but she couldn't be sure. She wasn't paying attention to anything but the remains of the woman in front of her.

Jax took a final heavy footfall with her renewed and horrific limb and paused. Saunders had somehow managed to get both her feet underneath her and she crouched, wanting desperately to spring away, but finding herself rooted to the spot.

This was her Jax. This was the surly Space Station Mechanic, who had taken her for a wild ride of a chase, fought bloody to keep them all safe, thrown herself at any threat that had offered to take Saunders from this universe, and still had found a way back to her. Saunders had found loyalty, honesty, and selflessness, in spite of the grumpiness. And Saunders loved Jax for it. But was this even Jax anymore?

Saunders would not leave. She would not leave her Jax, no matter what fate befell them. She would stand and face this unfathomable horror before her and accept it for whoever and whatever it was, because it was *Jax* and in this abhorrent and atrocious rut of a universe they had found themselves in, Jax was all Saunders wanted to keep her life meaningful.

The silence was oppressive. It was peppered with the increased frequency of dripping and running water. The shadows seemed to breathe about them both in the space of time around a single, dying light.

Then, Jax spoke.

"Saunders."

Her heart flipped, soared, sank into a well of despair. Jax's voice came from everywhere and directly in front of her all at once. It sounded like it was strained through more than a single mouth. It rang off the walls and dripped down around Saunders like the imposing moisture that increased with every passing day-cycle.

"Jax, I'm here," Saunders whispered, still unable to move.

"Saunders. Run."

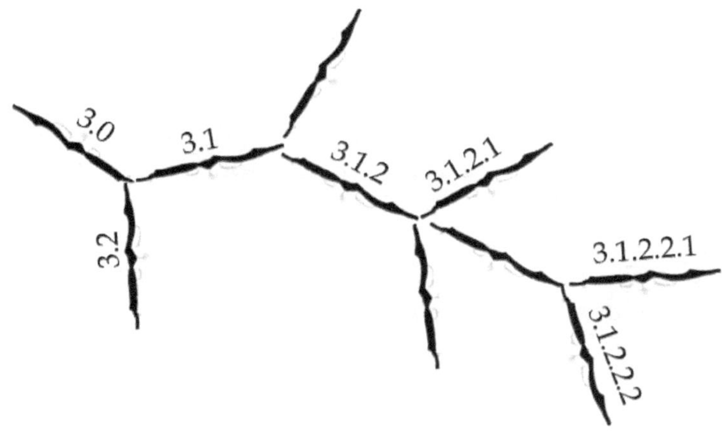

3.1.2.2.2

Nos led Saunders and the rest of the group through the massive coral aperture to the main chamber. Jax trailed behind, wary of the crowding Foliage, and realized Rose had also dropped back.

"It looks like you both made friends," the researcher commented.

"It seemed the better option," Jax huffed, as they were pulled into the hall and the entryway constricted behind them.

"Assessing our current options to consist of 'die now, or die later', I am inclined to agree," Rose whispered. She cast a sidelong glance at Vamp who had lumbered up next to them, as if she wasn't sure the third option was as inviting as she made it seem.

The chamber they all occupied was darker than any other spaces Jax had seen in the Pentagram, most likely to amplify the light wave patterns. She caught sight of a roiling mass of sleek shells and writhing vines, and knew it was not a place she wanted to linger. In front of her, Nos and Cul swept a wide berth. Standing in their wake, Saunders looked impossibly small in her new Cloak.

"What, precisely, might Security be wearing?" Rose squinted into the gloom. Jax could almost get away with lying but figured against it.

"It's a long story, and you probably don't want to know right now." Just as Jax said it, the Cloak fluttered and Rose made a noise Jax knew was not one of confidence in a secure and *normal* future.

Vamp shifted its position and Jax became aware of a ring of Foliage encircling them. They had entered this chamber, led by blood thirsty warriors still in debt to the ruling class, then let themselves be surrounded. The stupidity of the situation coated Jax's thoughts in a syrupy sheen of panic, and she subconsciously shifted to ensure Vamp was fully at her back.

It wasn't silent in the room. An unsettling, constant, almost *overwhelming* sound of rustling, fluttering, shuffling and snapping could be heard. Each light flash was produced by the rapid flicks of Malacost appendages. The whip-like flagella of the Foliage cracked the thick and humid air. The endless flutter of what sounded like insect wings make Jax itch.

Nos apparently also had limited patience for it. Or it was just fed up with whatever the Pentagram argument was, because it reared back and roared, which, despite the din of general noise in the chamber, still promptly scared the shit out of Jax. The fluttering subsided, and the Skraawl leader barked out another series of screeches and snarls, waving the translator in the thick air like a beacon.

Jax inched toward Saunders' shoulder, making an effort to not touch the Cloak.

"Do you have *any* idea what's going on?" Jax asked, realizing Rose was right at her elbow, listening in.

"I do...sorta," Saunders whispered to the side, without breaking her line of sight. "I can read some of the symbols showing up on Nos' translator. It looks like the Malacost *really* want to focus on the fact that we literally showed up out of nowhere; that we're a threat. They keep bring up how we got here."

"Well fuck, I want to know the answer to that riddle too," Jax grumbled.

"Have we not shared our theories with them numerous times?" Rose hazarded from Jax's side.

"Of course we have. But it's not like any of our answers are satisfactory, are they?" Jax mused. Then, "Not *now*, Vamp!" as she batted away the extended barbed tongue.

Rose looked around with a surreal expression of alarm and horror.

"Sorry, it's Vamp's favorite topic too, they're just less murderous about it," Jax muttered dismissively. She nodded at the creature. "Vamp, this is Rose."

Vamp warbled quietly in response and turned to hiss delicately at some nearby Foliage.

"Will you knock it the fuck off back there? This isn't a joke!" Saunders hissed from her spot in front of them all.

Nos was screeching again. The translator in its hand spat out a word.

"SUPPORT"

Then,

"HUMANS"

The succession of light show paused. Nos turned aggressively to Saunders and reached out a taloned appendage to haul her forward. Jax wanted to protest at the rough treatment, but it wasn't particularly the place, and Saunders looked like she was ready to dive into whatever Nos had to throw her toward.

Another screech.

Saunders reached out tentatively for the translator and tapped out a few symbols herself, which communicated *something* but then Nos pulled the translator away and gestured aggressively to the roiling masses. They wanted Saunders to speak.

Saunders glanced back at Jax in apprehension. They had gone over symbols, cross-translational meanings, and basic correlated phrases that could communicate their needs, but not a speech to be directly mistranslated.

"Just, say it like you would to me," Jax responded, unsure why she felt so confident to give such an answer. "Worst case, they'll fall in love with you like I did."

Saunders rolled her eyes, but the look of strain on her face lightened. She turned back to the audience.

"We're grateful for the patience you all have had with us, as we find our way. We found ourselves so far from home. *Something* brought us here, outside our control, and now we are stuck here. We only want a home. The Skraawl have offered that to us. I'm asking that you please let us go." Saunders' voice rang across the alien chamber, sounding like music to Jax's ears in comparison to the endless cacophony of restless creatures that filled the space.

"HOLD A SECRET"

The translator had picked up some of the flashes and translated them.

"MUST PROTECT OURSELVES"

It was enough for Saunders to get the message and formulate a dignified response.

"Bullshit," Saunders swore, loud enough for the translators to pick up. There was a horrific accompanying flash. *Something* had been translated and Saunders didn't seem to care.

"We are *lost*. Helpless. *You* chose to murder us first. We have paid, in blood, *over twenty lives*. We gave you the only home we had and all the information we knew of, all in exchange for food and shelter. But it wasn't enough. Now you are taking our people!"

Saunders was mad. Jax could appreciate it, but she could also feel the impending cranial crack of a Malacost whip. At least Cul looked impressed for a massive Bat-Lizard-Alien.

A flittering, chittering ruckus sounded throughout.

"STOLEN"

"Stolen? What have we taken? You stole from *us!* We have given you *everything!*"

Then, quite suddenly, there was a vocal response, in human words.

"You have taken technology from Sciiraack alliance. First you appear, without warning. Then you take from us. Skraawl, we have warned of human threat!"

"Son of a fucking bitch—*Jax* they know how to speak our *language!*" Saunders said it *way* too loud. Jax was busy feeling the prickle of shame one could only associate with grand theft of alien technology.

"Look I was gonna return it—"

"Oh fucking forget about that, this means that I don't have to do this damned chitter chatter, I can tell them exactly what I think," Saunders spat, determinedly, shoving the translator into Cul's startled appendages while still ignoring Jax's weak protests.

"Well, good luck. It was nice loving you while I still had a head," Jax mused. But Saunders was already on her march.

"*You* were murdering us. We are scientists, and settlers, and tradespeople. We are not *dangerous*, we are not *thieves*! We never wanted to be here, but we *are,* so why can't we share our knowledge?" Saunders called out emphasizing her point.

"Humans have nothing to offer us?" barked the speaker.

"Then why are you taking us for experimentation?" Saunders howled, the Cloak fluttering around her ankles, flooding her with suicidal adrenaline. Jax wondered if she could yank the damn thing off, and save some tiny moment of humanity before they were all flayed alive.

"Has Saunders always been this...aggressive?" Rose inquired, looking more and more alarmed as this circus proceeded.

"Not in public, no," Jax replied, feeling like a limp balloon.

Nos took the opportunity to bellow something nondescript out over the audience again.

"ABOMINABLE HEATHENS" chirped the translator in hand.

"Whoops," Jax winced, feeling the glare on her shoulders from Saunders like the bite of a Cloak. She hadn't ironed all the translation kinks out, but hadn't exactly assumed their captors would be able to translate in real time. Then again, it's not like Nos *hadn't* called the Malacost and Foliage abominable heathens.

"Sciiraak should reconsider our peaceful alliance with Skraawl," echoed the voice again.

"How the fuck are they *doing* that?" Jax hissed. "Did you know they could do that?"

Rose furtively shook her head, trying to shake off the accusation. From over Jax's head the Skraawl were bellowing their opinions.

"LEARN, PARTNER, HUMAN FRIENDS"

At that same moment, Vamp landed a heavy aft appendage on Jax's shoulder. It wasn't particularly reassuring, but coupled with the admission that the Skraawl might help them even if Jax *couldn't* answer all their questions about their arrival, the gesture was the most comfort Jax had felt in nearly a full cycle.

"LEAVE MALACOST, TAKE HUMANS"

"Humans are a threat."

"Why are we a threat?" Saunders challenged, a sweat breaking out across her neck where the Cloak latched.

"Different. Inside. There will be more. How did they get here?"

"We don't know how we got here, but if we knew, I can tell you we would go back," Saunders hissed.

"Lies."

"So, is your plan to keep us here, pull us apart, study us, and hold us hostage? Because you can't trust us?"

"Yes."

"Well at least they are honest," Jax chirped, amicably.

"SKRAAWL TRUST HUMANS," Nos roared. Cul screeched something that sounded like disagreement, but the Skraawl leader slashed at their second in command with an obsidian clad talon and Cul shut up.

"Sciiraak trust Skraawl less."

"You all have evolved together, for such a long time. Your species, Sciiraak system, and Skraawl, have known of each other for so long. Did you never think there would be others out there? Why choose *this* moment to tear apart what you have built? Let the humans go to Creea. And then let us work *with* you to understand what mystery brought us here," Saunders urged.

The room was quiet. Small flickers of light snapped at short intervals across the dark chamber. Sidebar conversations.

"If we let humans go, how can we be sure they will not put Sciiraak under threat?" It was another challenge. Defiant. This voice sounded so strangely human.

"Think of this as your first opportunity to show you are capable of expanding your diplomacy beyond just what's familiar to you. We have had to put blind faith and trust in the Sciiraak. Now show that you can extend a similar capability."

Oh Saunders. Jax was more and more in love with the woman every day that passed. She sure thrived on a challenge. Trust her to throw one right back in their non-faces.

More quiet. More flickers. Jax exhaled, realizing she may have been holding her breath longer than medically encouraged.

The communication system barked again.

"The delegation from the Sciiraak committee chooses to recognize human request for release from Sciiraak hospitality."

"Pssshh, 'hospitality' is one way of putting it" Jax scoffed. Saunders shot a withering side eye from over an alien parasite clad shoulder. It shut Jax back up.

"Sciiraak will release all human obligation to the Skraawl."

Jax exhaled audibly but saw Saunders tense at the translator voice relenting around them.

"In exchange…"

Jax scanned the room, taking in the crowd of whips and flagella, and creepy acidic mold colonies, keen on hearing what their next evolution of intergalactic partnership may bring.

"Only if you give us the one called Jax."

A slimy, sludge-fill cold swept over Jax from the top of her head to her feet. Next to her, Saunders turned to look up at Jax, who stared pitifully down, rooted to the spot.

"*What?*" Jax hissed.

Saunders wheeled around to the cavernous chambers.

"Absolutely not," she shouted, far louder than necessary.

A skittering series of flashes cycled through.

"*Then humans are threat. Give Jax, take humans.*"

"Why?" Saunders called out. She stepped back, seeking contact with Jax, reaching to touch her.

"Does...does it fucking matter?" Jax squeaked as Saunders connected with her.

"*We know what she is.*"

"What am I?" Jax snapped her head back to the room. What were these alien assholes getting at? "I'm human too."

"*We know what's inside.*"

"This is bullshit." Saunders swore again, answered by a chorus of light flashes skittering around the room. She turned, quickly rotating on the spot to put her own body against Jax and not that of an alien parasite. "They are making shit up now. They have been playing us from the start." She looked up, plaintively into Jax's face.

"*Then, we will keep humans. Study humans.*"

Cul roared something and reached for Jax.

"Back off!" Saunders snarled, and shoved her shoulder in between them. It was comical considering Cul's massive bulk. The Skraawl tried again and Saunders roared something unintelligible and animalistic right back.

Jax's head was swimming with the gloom, flashes of light, and the slithering tendrils, or tongues, or vines, or anything inhuman crowding her vision. She was vaguely aware of Vamp snarling in the fray with Cul, and Nos barking definitive orders she didn't recognize. All she could really understand was the possessive grip Saunders maintained on the front of her worn coveralls.

"*Jax. Threat.*"

"I just want us all safe..." Saunders said quietly, so that the translators wouldn't pick it up. She turned and laboriously lowered her forehead to Jax's chest as the Skraawl turned to snarl replies to the masses.

"Okay," Jax whispered.

Saunders jerked her head up violently to scrutinize her.

"*What*?" she asked.

"I said, 'okay.' Let them have me." Jax shrugged. Saunders squinted at her.

"What the fuck are you talking about?" she asked, gripping her closer.

"We need to get our people off here. That's what this whole mess was about. So, let them have me. Take *our* people, and let them have me in return."

"Not on my life," Saunders growled.

"I'm serious, babe. You can work at getting me back, but if that's what they need right now, let's go with it," Jax pressed.

Saunders turned from her, swung her face up to look at the bulk of Nos and Cul, who were screaming in their own language at the surrounding aliens, then out across the dim room full of murderous aliens. Jax's heart sank, overloaded with the dread that the Pentagram might just find enough ways to torture her before Saunders could come back.

But instead, Saunders pushed her back, letting Jax land in the gripping claws of Vamp, who warbled a chuckle. Saunders then wheeled around and *shoved* her way through Nos and Cul, *elbowing* Cul hard, in what looked like where a spleen might be. The two Senior Skraawl parted in surprise as Saunders snapped out her night stick from a security belt she insisted on still wearing and smashed it into the coral surface in front of her.

"Your threats are worthless. Your fear of humans is clear. We are not a danger to you. Let them all go. You cannot have any of us!" she shouted to the group.

"*Threat! Danger! Destroy!*" whatever voice the Malacost, or Sciiraak, or whatever, were using, it started to chant, backed by a repetitive strobe of flashes.

"Well, this has gone exceptionally well," Rose piped up.

"AaaK" Vamp screeched. Jax had extricated herself from the talons and glanced at the creature. Rose renewed her alarmed interest.

"Did this...Skraawl...just address you by your name?"

"Aaak, Aauss eEEIIkAAIIsKAAwwl!" Nos bellowed over them all. Vamp chittered as if it thought it was a clever reveal the Skraawl leaders *also* knew how to say their names. Saunders was looking upward, bewildered. Jax focused on the translator barking out a sentence pulled straight from one of her worst days in the core.

"FIGHT ME, BITCH"

That had to be a *direct* translation.

The chambers fell to a cacophony and an endless strobe of light flashes. Jax closed her eyes to try to block it out. She needed to clear her head, but vivid visions of alien vivisection swam back up to her forethought.

A loud blast, like a foghorn, echoed throughout the chamber. It rattled Jax's teeth and she snapped her eyes open. In the quieting echo of the blast's wake, a silence fell around them, accompanied by a distinct lack of flashes from the Pentagram crowd. Saunders used the moment to edge closer to Jax, seeking contact again. Jax reached out to grab Rose and also pull her in. Vamp eschewed all personal boundaries and wrapped them in their Cloaked aft appendages, and...sure. They needed all the help they could get.

Finally, the translator sparked up again.

"You ask difficult things. Trust will need to be built. The Sciiraak accept that all Humans can leave in partnership with the Skraawl. Sciiraak expect efforts to be made on behalf of human representative Saunders to further build human and Sciiraak trust and partnership."

"Oh, so now they feel reasonable," Jax hissed. Saunders let go of the death grip she had maintained on Jax and stepped forward.

"On behalf of humans, I accept this proposed partnership," she stated.

Nos bellowed something aggressive sounding at the chamber. Behind them, the wall of militants evaporated, and the coral orifice enclosing them cycled open.

Cul stormed past the group but refrained from assaulting Saunders in passing. Instead, it was Vamp who made a delighted sounding screech and sank a set of claws into Saunders' shoulder to swing her around after the looming senior Skraawl.

"Ow, okay, thanks Vamp," Saunders winced through gritted teeth. Jax felt herself similarly handled and shoved through the chamber entrance. Rose was allowed to move on her own, blessedly. Nos bore down on them as they took up the rear. It was clearly a tactical move, putting the weak in the middle of the strong. But Jax welcomed the sudden feeling of security it brought her.

Out on the transport landing strip they finally were able to pause. Cul had already left for the Skrawwl transport to signal their cohorts to land and escort the rest of the stranded Station residents off planet. Saunders turned to Nos, hands wandering over the translator as if she was unsure she needed it.

"SkIIrEk AH" she screeched. Then, "Thank you."

Nos blinked each of their eyes in a staccato sequence, then tilted their head in the same birdlike fashion Vamp did.

"oOO TAaak, EElp SkrAAwL," the Skraawl leader replied.

The translator wouldn't pick that up. It was Nos showing it had also worked at trying to learn human speech. Vamp chirped approvingly.

Saunders grinned at the massive creature, which wasn't entirely advisable, as Jax was certain that would be interpreted as an act of aggression. Nos returned the gesture in an unsettling row of needle-sharp, long teeth, since their species *adored* aggression.

And, speaking of aggression, Saunders took the following moment to wheel around on Jax, making the lanky mechanic jump behind Rose.

"Please, do not involve me in this!" The researcher threw her hands up in defense and scooted to the side next to

Vamp, choosing a brand-new alien creature robed in another living alien creature over getting caught in the crosshairs of Saunders' wrath.

Jax squirmed under the sharp green stare of her better half.

"What the *fuck* was that 'oh, let them take me, save yourselves' melodramatic bullshit in there Jax?" Saunders hissed, interjecting the inquiry with her best dramatic overture impression.

"Okay I didn't sound like that—" Jax protested. Saunders punched her in the arm. "Ow."

Vamp chittered.

"I would drop through another rip in space just to keep you, and you are an antisocial *recluse*, what the *fuck*?" Saunders hissed. Jax stood there mutely. Then she glanced back up at Rose and Vamp standing shoulder to hulking, inverted, creepy, living danger-blanket clad shoulder.

"These are our people. My people. My friends. We've gone through so much. I...care about them. They are home to us. And I want us to be safe. I want you to be safe. If that meant taking one for the team, then I'm ready," Jax admitted.

Saunders fixed her with a probing stare. Jax felt that the Malacost alone would never be able to study her as thoroughly as the woman in front of her did. Then Saunders stepped forward, wrapped her arms scandalously around Jax's neck and pressed their lips together again.

A shadow fell over them all. Jax froze, and Saunders turned around, disengaging from their embrace. The looming figure of Legs, defacto Malacost leader, threw their relief into sharp contrast.

"You make bold assumptions of our leniency, human," barked a translator, from somewhere within the multitudinous feelers down the middle of the standing creature. Jax gulped. Of all the Malacost Jax had seen, Legs earned the name for looking the *most* like a massive centipede rather than some bastardized shrimp. The grasping, numerous appendages looked foreboding.

"You make fast assumptions about our innocence. Maybe it will be best to learn about us through partnership rather than confinement," Saunders replied.

"We are sincere in our warning. We do not understand your arrival, but we do know: there is something inside this one." Then Legs turned to regard Jax.

Jax had a sudden vision of Legs cracking out, snapping Saunders in half, and revoking all agreements. But Saunders stood her ground, facing down any threat with a bold, challenging jut of her chin. So Jax also drew herself to her own, full height, still nowhere near the height of the creature before her, and presented her own challenging stare. A shudder told her Nos had also stepped forward.

Legs regarded them all, through eyespots, feelers or whatever senses the creatures possessed, and then unfolded its length to a low-slung form and scurried off without a response. Jax exhaled what felt like all the available oxygen in the soupy atmosphere.

"Any more of this and *I'm* going to start questioning who I am and where I belong." Jax groaned.

"I know where you belong. You're sticking with me." Saunders' voice bit through the fog of Jax's bewilderment. "*I* know who you are, not them. There's nothing *inside* you," Saunders growled, making eye contact that Jax felt in her soul. "Other than me. Sometimes."

"Seriously?" Jax squeaked. "*Here??*"

"Pardon, if you two are done saving humanity, shall we proceed in escaping this hell hole?" Rose suggested over the bustle of the landing pad. Cul had returned from calling in the calvary.

Saunders regarded the group, still gripping Jax at her side.

"Excellent. Let's go round up our people and get Zick back. It's time to go to our new home."

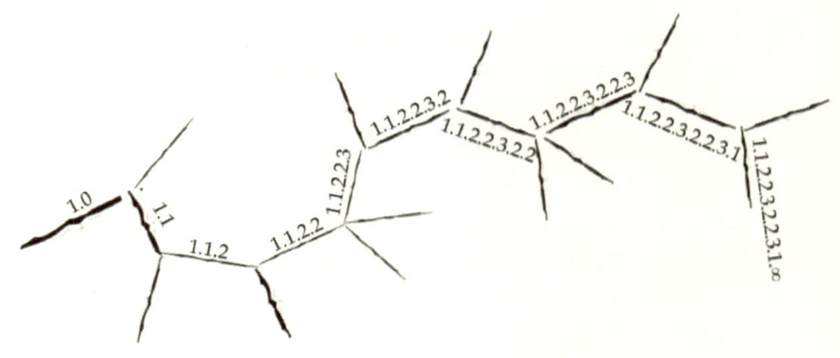

1.1.2.2.3.2.2.3.1.1.∞

Jax pressed her back to the cramped space behind a discrete panel on Level 3. She willed her breathing to calm, but her heart was hammering too heavily in her chest. Across from her, Saunders was curled in a tight ball, her eyes glazed over as she stared into the middle distance. It was more than a thousand-yard stare. It was the stare of a gallows walker.

Around them, the Station groaned. It was a pressing reminder of their predicament. There was no escape. They were pinned down like animals, awaiting their dissection.

Jax hauled her spud wrench up and across her chest to inspect it. It had incurred damage, forever ago, as they had fought off what seemed to be hallucinations of nightmares. The variable head no longer worked, leaving the teeth gapped at a permanent distance. Now it had further scars to tell of their dissent to madness.

Madness that came from the inevitable last few grains of sand, drifting from an hourglass. Their time was up.

"Saunders. Saunders wake up." Jax reached out and prodded the woman gently with her boot.

Saunders didn't respond at first, then jolted violently as if she had suddenly woken from a nightmare. Jax lunged to throw a hand over her mouth and pull her close. They couldn't risk being heard.

"Shhh, shhh, just, come here." Jax made sure Saunders was pressed against her in the tight space.

She hoisted the wrench over between them. The tapered end had been ground down to a nastier point. Gouges along its length carried bloody residue from past encounters. A scrap of an old utility belt had been bolted to it in two places, creating a shoulder strap of sorts so Jax could sling it over her back for easier carrying.

Saunders said nothing as she looked numbly down at the space between them where Jax fiddled uselessly with the variable head and its new damage. It broke off in her hand, the bottom jaw tumbling from Jax's fingers and clattering on the floor. They both jumped, skittish, and froze, listening.

Moments sludged passed as they trained their ears for any sounds from the outside corridor. Nothing.

Saunders slowly moved again, reaching down to her side and drawing out the worn and nicked kitchen knife she had stashed to her hip. She numbly turned it in her hands, looking over its damaged form.

"We can't stay here, Jax," she said quietly. Jax nodded, next to her. They couldn't stay, but there was also nowhere to go. Well, other than to the end.

The Station was dying, and this time for good. Their supplies had dwindled, and their resources were gone. There was a certain layer of hell associated with the inevitable end of their survival. Jax had long since stopped letting herself think of whatever alternatives they had missed to avoid this. Maybe this was the conclusion all along. To slowly go mad in the crushing reality of exactly how trapped they were.

To be honest, Jax wasn't even quite sure what they were hiding from. Whether they were found now, or lasted just a little bit longer, the end was the same. She just felt like she wasn't ready yet. She wasn't ready to be separated from the woman next to her. And she knew Saunders wasn't ready either. They clung to each other. Jax let herself still again, her brain firing off some fantastical sequence in which her and Saunders had been able to survive, been able to have a life together. It was unobtainable. It was heartbreaking.

Jax's stomach stabbed her with a grueling pain of hunger. Her thoughts drifted like the trash they had left in their wake so many millions of miles ago. Had it been Koty Higgs' body? Or had that been a ruse? Had anyone truly left them all through the airlock? The empty morgue downstairs begged the question: how long had Zick and his crew been feasting on the dead?

Saunders shifted beside her, drawing closer. She no longer had her firm muscular build, instead looking haggard and drawn out. Jax had already been lanky, and now she felt like she might snap in half if she couldn't keep her feet under herself. Neither of them had been willing to give in to their hunger enough to sacrifice their friends.

But they had no more friends.

"We can't stay here, but I don't want to keep going either," Jax mumbled next to her. Saunders looked over at her. "Why can't you just let me head them off, you could—"

"Because I'm not ready to exist where you do not," Saunders replied. Jax understood this. It was why they had run. They were at an impasse, neither willing to let other go. And Jax was so exhausted.

"You won't have to exist long," Jax replied. It wasn't a joke, but she felt like it was. Next to her Saunders shook. Jax couldn't tell if it was from fear, or laughter, or exhaustion. It was probably a mix of all three. Saunders looked over at her, eyes wet, terror on her face, and the edges of her mouth curling up.

"You don't want to be in that situation either, otherwise you wouldn't be asking," Saunders replied. Jax nodded. Saunders was right.

"I suppose it's the nature of humanity, to cling to the very last strand of hope in survival," Jax said thoughtfully to the wall across from them.

"I would cling to every possible moment I could ever have with you, Jax," Saunders responded. Jax looked back at Saunders, saw the pain in her face. She leaned in and kissed her, probably for the last time.

Out in the corridor a crash sounded. They pulled apart. The sound of a sharp object dragged across the corridor wall panels echoed, getting closer and closer to their hideout.

Footsteps followed, less than before, but more than just the one pair. They were outnumbered. Jax felt her pulse quicken, the adrenaline surge. She eyed the gap under the power conduit that may be their only way out if they chose to keep running. Or they could always give in and return. Return to the Meat Market.

"I know you're in here, Security," called Zick, tauntingly.

He would never give up control. Perhaps he had held it all along...planning, plotting. And as it became clear there would be no salvation across the stars, Zick Rogle would be their ending.

"Your number is up, Saunders, it's only fair. Stop hiding, it's a waste of energy to have to keep hunting you down," he called.

Next to Jax, Saunders gave a sharp inhalation of breath. She locked eyes with Jax. They didn't need to speak to know what the other was thinking. They both stared at the liminal space between them, as the scraping and footsteps got closer.

There was only one place to go. Only one airlock was left, unwelded, down on Level 1. Their run was over.

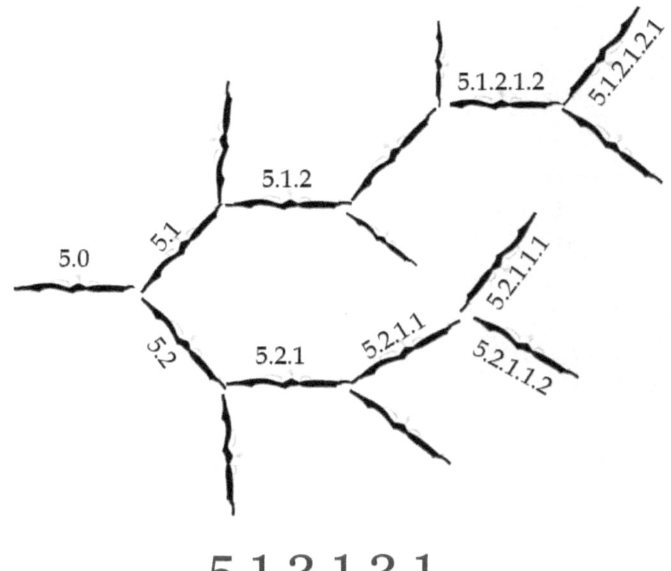

5.1.2.1.2.1

"I can't leave them," Saunders stated aggressively. It wasn't a shout, but it was close. The timbre of her voice echoed strangely in the sunken, sideways station. Across from her stood Jax, who looked distinctly aggravated. The look was familiar, but Saunders hadn't seen it directed at her since before the Drop.

"You aren't leaving them. You're *saving* them," Jax argued back. Saunders put her hands on her hips, resting on her security belt she mostly wore out of habit these days.

"I *told* you how much this is affecting me, I can't do it."

"So you'll leave your ghosts behind with me. *Someone* needs to pilot the tug," Jax insisted. She shifted her weight off her left leg.

"And that is going to be you," Saunders stated factually. "You're the one who squirreled it away in the first place. I've never even flown it before!"

In the dim light of the Level 5 corridor, Saunders saw Jax's face fall. She felt a pang of guilt, and understanding. But if she left on that tug she could be damned sure it would be Tess in the co-pilot seat, judging her the whole way.

"Do you really think staying here is going to be less difficult than leaving?" Jax argued. Her brow was furrowed in an added layer of concern Saunders appreciated. "I can keep this place safe, you *know* that."

"You can brief Gedry on the core problems. Brief me on it. Or train Andee on the tug, and stay here with me, just please don't ask me to go," she pleaded with Jax. The mechanic looked exhausted.

Jax hung her head, then moved forward. She kissed Saunders on the top of the head and stepped past her.

"I'll talk to Gedry," she said, as her shoulders found themselves even with Saunders. She inclined her head toward Jax, but the mechanic continued on her way back to the Common Access point, limping slightly.

* * *

Saunders found Rose in the Level 4 Galley. The research scientist remained subdued in her grief. Saunders had not pressed the matter. She recognized the feeling, and Rose seemed adrift in the absence of her brother.

"Coffee?" the researcher asked quietly. She indicated the dented coffee pot on the weak, underpowered heat spot. A few dehydrated food packets were laid out as well. They would be...crunchy.

"Is it coffee, or is it some monstrosity Jax created?" Saunders inquired, cautious.

"You may not like the answer." Rose gave a slight smile. Saunders rolled her eyes and took the cold cup. It tasted like sludge from the kitchen sink mixed with coffee grounds. But they had no hot water, so she figured it was the best they could get.

"That was horrible," Saunders coughed.

"The coffee, or telling Engineering you want her to leave?"

Saunders froze. She looked up at Rose as if she was seeing the woman for the first time.

"What do you mean?"

"I mean, I am aware you are struggling with the concept of leaving us here when you depart for help," Rose replied, insightfully.

Saunders sat quietly, enjoying that the couches had been correctly oriented. It felt good to sit on an actual chair for a change.

"Are you just very perceptive, or is it obvious how much of a problem I'm having?" Saunders asked tentatively.

"My job has been interpreting data. In this instance of review, it is a little of column A, and little of column B. Maybe a lot of column A, depending on who you talk to," replied Rose. "But you and Engineering have been prime entertainment for those of us bored and in desperate need of distraction from our fate."

Saunders felt herself flush.

"Are we that obvious?"

"Oh, it was obvious prior to this predicament, and my team was only present on the station for a few days. It has been fascinating." Rose broke out in the first real smile Saunders had seen on her since the Drop. The researcher leaned forward across her knees, staring off into the middle distance as if recalling a thrilling idea.

"If I were to have been an anthropologist, as opposed to a physicist, I may, in actuality, have described this experience as a mission success, for its observation potential," Rose replied, positively grinning.

"Ouch," Saunders mused, and gave a snort. "Don't tell Jax, she'll sulk for days."

Rose inclined her head gently, letting her conspiratorial moment pass. They sat quietly.

"So tomorrow, Jax departs in the craft to the surface and you remain behind to administer to those who we must leave down here?" Rose asked, exploratorily. Saunders' shoulders dropped.

"Yes. I need to stay. Really."

"Really?"

"Yes, I can't... It won't go well if I leave," Saunders insisted. Rose took a deep breath that made her shoulders rise and then drop again.

"What does Jax need?"

Saunders didn't have an answer. She mused over the silence. Rose nudged Saunders in the knee with her own, and returned to prepping some of the dried food with lukewarm water as best she could. Saunders watched the process, dreading the taste for later.

"I need to help load the tug supplies. Thank you for the coffee, er, whatever this is, Rose," she eventually said.

"Oh, trust me, you should not thank me for that," the researcher replied. Saunders snorted a laugh in response and returned to Level 2 where the tug was staged.

* * *

"Ten minutes till we go for a swim!" Andee called to the group. Saunders looked over her shoulder at the welder who was doing a last hull inspection and then at Jax who was standing in front of her, hands thrust roughly in the front pockets of her coveralls, shoulders hunched.

"Don't have too much fun out there without me, okay?" she insisted. She wanted to demand that Jax commit to returning, but that was just *asking* for bad luck, and they already had the odds stacked against them.

"I mean, there's only so much fun to be had," grumbled the mechanic, glancing at Gedry who had taken responsibility of the core. The look of unease on Jax's face meant she still wasn't comfortable with the arrangement.

Worse of all, Saunders knew Jax wanted to ask her to go with them, and she feared that she wouldn't be able to say no, now that the moment was staring them in the face. Her place was here, with her people. Saunders found herself suddenly busy with the front of Jax's coveralls, moving her hands furtively, as if she needed to be contributing to something. Instead, she found herself smoothing out the grungy outfit, and double checking the zipper.

"You should...probably get strapped in," Saunders stuttered out. Jax gave her a long, lingering look. Then she sighed and leaned forward to kiss her.

"I'll let that one pass," Jax whispered over Saunders' head, before stepping back. She clasped Saunders' hand one last time, and then she turned to the tug cockpit.

Saunders retreated from the tug access door, and picked her way over to the compartment access hatch that dropped down to the corridor below. There, against the wall, Gedry rested, waiting for the go ahead to seal the room.

"Are they ready?" he asked.

"As they'll ever be," Saunders replied. She set her jaw as she saw the tug's headlights run through a test cycle, the door preparing to be closed.

"Are *you* alright?"

"Don't ask me that." Saunders hated how young her voice sounded as she said it. "I need to be here."

"Do you really?"

Saunders turned to the senior foreman beside her and looked up at him. He gave her a warm smile.

"I have this unresolved need to be responsible for those who I am charged with caring for. It's tearing me apart," she admitted, glancing over his shoulder to where Tess haunted a dark corner.

"Have you ever thought that you do better caring for others when you put yourself first?" he proposed. Saunders rolled her eyes.

"Yeah, I get it. Just...you don't understand—"

"I do."

"No, I mean...my TSF service contract...what happened—"

"Saunders. I understand," he said again, gently, and she turned to him again to really see his face. Oh, it clicked.

"You too?"

"Look. We're all grownups here. We've done pretty good at keeping ourselves alive. Jax showed me the core maintenance. Just think. If she can trust me, someone she barely knows, with the life of her precious station, you can trust a bunch of us adults to care for ourselves for a bit down here," Gedry said, putting two large, rough hands on Saunders' shoulders. In that instant, she hated being so short. She felt like a child. But...a comforted child.

"Saunders, you belong on that tug. You belong with that woman. And you know it. We all know it."

Over their shoulders she heard the sound of the tug access door clanging shut. They would need to leave the room and seal it off soon. Saunders felt a lump in her chest pinch painfully.

"I can't—"

"Yes, you can."

"No, I mean, there's only six seats. I can't kick someone off..."

"You are not 'kicking' anyone off," said Rose, who was standing next to them both. Saunders jumped. The research scientist was even shorter than Saunders.

"Rose, what are you doing here, we have maybe two minutes to breach!" Saunders stammered.

"I am here so you can get your ass on that tug. Jax needs you. And I shall stay here and maintain operations while you seek us rescue," Rose replied matter-of-factly.

Saunders paused, looking between Gedry and Rose, and back again.

"Obah and I will keep the place warm for you guys when you get back. And Rose will keep them in line," Ged stated with finality.

Saunders wanted to fight, to argue. But when she glanced back at Tess in her dark corner, the ghost smiled and nodded, before fading from view. And there was nothing more to be done.

With a glance over her shoulder back at the tug, Saunders expected to see it in its final steps of departure. But the tug wasn't departing. Its door was still open, and Jax was leaning, long and lanky, against the door frame, arms crossed over her coveralls. She was waiting for Saunders to make up her mind.

She took one last look back at Rose and Ged. Saunders hoped to say something truly expressing her gratitude, but all that came out was, "damn it's weird when you Martians swear." Rose smiled benignly in response.

Then, Saunders was running before she realized it. She crossed the short distance from the container port access to the woman waiting for her and found herself jumping, throwing her arms around Jax's neck, wrapping her legs around Jax's waist, coming to rest with her forehead pressed to the other woman's.

Jax stumbled under the added weight, but managed to catch Saunders and hold her there.

"Well?" breathed the mechanic.

"I had to watch you leave once in my life," Saunders murmured through whatever tears wanted to escape. "I can't watch you leave again."

"So, you're going with me?"

"I'm going with you."

* * *

"Depth is three thousand feet," Saunders read off from the co-pilot seat. Next to her Jax peered through the dark water.

"I would have expected more light at this depth," Jax muttered. Bezley had undone his restraints and was leaning between them, also peering into the murky depths. There had been little sea life to witness in their ascent. No Kraken, no Seeker, nothing at all really. Some small fish-like creatures wriggled by, almost similar to the samples they had found, but the tug glass was thick, and the lighting poor enough that details were hard to come by.

"You still glad you took the Security Officer and not the planetary gravitational expert?" Saunders asked. Jax looked over at her.

"Well, I certainly *feel* more secure."

Saunders wanted to shove her. And kiss her.

The tug ascended.

"Two thousand feet," Saunders read off. The water was clearer now, though still devoid of life. A small glint of light sparkled in the distance. It gave Saunders a spark of hope.

"Oh, please be a terrestrial planet. I want to see sunlight," Jax grumbled.

"Finally sick of deep space?"

"Babe, I've been sick of deep space since four weeks ago."

"Huh. Wonder what changed that," Saunders mused.

The water's surface rippled gently as if in a breeze. There were no storm cells in the distance, even near this part of the ocean. The sun rose in the early morning sky, first grey, then pink, then a cold, early blue at the edges.

The tug craft broke the surface with a gentle splash, and bobbed in the water. The engine sputtered, unable to really propel them further, but the dawn of a bright day peeked through the thick glass of the deep-space vehicle that, until a month ago, had never even seen the surface of Earth before.

Yet here they were, bobbing in the ocean of a planet that Jax had left so many years ago, intent to never return. Down in the cockpit, the Mechanical Engineer and the Security Officer, accompanied by their crew of four others, stared out at the Pacifica settlement structure just off the bow of their small craft.

"How, in the FUCK? I'm *home??*" Andee broke the silence first. Saunders looked around at her alarmed. Then back at Jax.

Jax was frozen, as if paused in time. The woman was six years older than Saunders, but the lack of Earth environment had drawn out her youth, making her look younger. The only giveaway was the echo of age reflecting in Jax's eyes as they took in the early morning sunlight.

"Jax," Saunders whispered. She didn't know what else to say, but it seemed to snap the mechanic out of it because Jax turned to look at her, face struck full of bewilderment. It was a bewilderment Saunders shared.

Then Jax laughed. It was a chuckle. Then a giggle, then she was in hysterical stitches, holding her sides. Saunders looked at Jax like she was insane, then she heard another laugh from beside her. Dorian Bezley was also barking a loud chuckle. And suddenly the whole tug was in on it, cheering, shouting, laughing.

Jax reached out to grab ahold of Saunders by the shirt and pull her close. Saunders felt the laughing, shaking body of the woman she loved surround her. And finally, Saunders joined in.

Amid the elation, Saunders was only passingly aware of Jax absentmindedly rubbing her left leg.

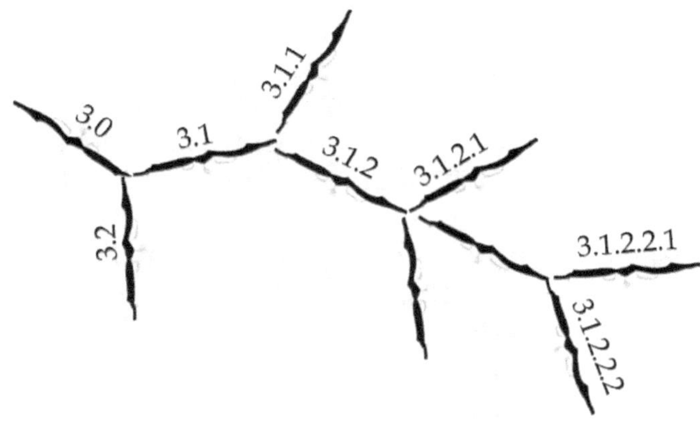

3.1.1

"RUN!" Saunders shouted, as Jax backed away from the snarling Skraawl fighters. Jax stumbled backward, eyes trained on a gnarly obsidian spearhead pointed her way.

Somewhere over her shoulder she heard Saunders moving through the dense vegetation. Jax scrambled to her feet, hoped to all hell that she wouldn't feel a laser spear in her back, turned and vaulted some alien shrubbery in pursuit of the other woman.

They clearly hadn't made it far since landing on Creea, as Jax could see the glint of light off the parked tug. But they had made it far enough, and Jax was struggling in the planet's gravity. Their pursuers were gaining on her. Jax tripped again, and tucked her shoulder in her fall to keep from eating a face-full of foreign-planet dirt.

Living in deep space for a whole third of her life kept Jax looking pretty damn young, younger looking than Saunders even, who was at least five or six years her junior. It was the weak and variable gravity, the lack of natural sunlight, and the endless cycle of re-purified and scrubbed air that kept age off Jax's face. But all of that had wreaked havoc on her body's ability to maintain proper structure and fitness when she returned to actual, rock-and-dirt planet surfaces.

Suddenly Jax was regretting not working out more. Her chest burned with the exertion as she dragged herself back to her feet, and forced a lungful of over-saturated air through her system. Jax's boot hit a snaking vine and she pitched forward again. She twisted to see the shapes of the Skraawl advance party emerge from the surrounding shrubbery and had a brief thought that she was well and truly fucked.

A blast rang out from somewhere just beyond Jax's shoulder, as Saunders re-emerged from the tug, placing herself between Jax and the door, and aimed the hedger squarely at the creatures baring down on them.

"Jax, get in here!" she shouted, and she fired another warning shot for coverage, launching a saw blade close enough to start a new cycle of hair as Jax scrambled back to her feet and booked it for the tug entrance. Saunders backed up into the tail end of the vehicle and slammed the door latch closed.

Jax had already hit the cockpit to immediately set the launch sequence and get them off the surface. Saunders stomped down the short corridor to the co-pilot seat, even as Jax was already lifting them off the surface.

The tug pivoted above the clearing of trees to show that the advancing party of Skraawl had halted at the perimeter, either by command or by Saunders' cover fire. Emerging from the group was Cul, an insidious looking second-in-command. The massive bat-lizard-alien unfolded its hind legs from where they rested over its shoulders to plant them firmly in the ground. Cul reared up, swiping the massive tree-trunk sized forelegs toward the ascending craft, roaring a threatening-sounding call.

"Well, they don't look happy to see us at *all*," Jax muttered, and swung the craft around.

It would have been nice to break to orbit and reassess their situation, but once the tug passed the gravity well of the planet, two Skraawl transports emerged to cross their path.

"Shit I do NOT have dogfight training—Saunders GET STRAPPED IN!" Jax shouted, hauling her own shoulder straps down against the shift in gravity. Jax punched the synth-drive and heard a pop from behind her.

"Don't tell me that was our ticket out of here," Saunders moaned from next to Jax. But Jax was already scrambling out of her seat.

"You drive!" she barked as she hauled herself by hand back down the corridor to her tools. A blast rocked the craft, knocking Jax into the storage locker at the back, which burst open to release its horde of tools and supplies. Saunders roared something unintelligible and a string of expletives were the only reply Jax could manage.

Another blast.

"Are they firing at us?" Jax finally managed to bellow from where she was swatting her way through the mass of tools, to get to the failing synth drive.

"Warning shots, but they'll be real shots if you take any longer back there!" Saunders snarled.

Jax had made it to the hatch that housed the converter connected to the external synth drive. It was her finest engineering yet, considering she didn't have the intelligence of a sentient carnivorous plant. She pulled herself down into the engine well. Another blast shook through the cruiser.

"Jax, I love you and all, but for fucks sake if you don't hurry up, I *will* murder you."

"Okay fuck the niceties, I mean business," Jax spat at the engine converter connecting the alien tech to the still-very-human controls system. She swung her wrench at it in an echoing clang.

The wrench bounced off the converted engine and nearly knocked Jax over into a back spin, but Jax had wedged her boots in the grating for stability and went in for another swing. The converter gave another pop, and spun back up again.

"Saunders! Saunders, hit the Synth!" Jax called from her anchor point by the engine well.

Saunders didn't wait for Jax to return to her seat, but punched the throttle, dropping them into synth-space. Jax got caught in the instantaneous acceleration vector and was hauled sideways, her left knee popping at an agonizing angle where she had it still hooked in the floor grating. She toppled over sideways with a rage-filled howl of pain, her shoulder bashing into the edge of the storage locker near the engine access well.

The battered tug dropped into synth-space, leaving the exterior dark, and the Skraawl fighters blind to their direction. A weightless environment returned. Jax let herself float there, mid-corridor, her left knee on fire, her shoulder bruised, staring up at the ceiling of the tug, debating all her past life decisions. She hung, suspended in the lack of gravity for as long as she felt she could avoid returning to the cockpit, but eventually Saunders would need help.

Jax grabbed her wrench, used it to push herself around to a better position, and hauled herself back to the pilot seat. She winced as she pulled herself back down into the seat restraints, letting her wrench float off to the side.

"Where are we going?" she managed through gritted teeth. Saunders had white knuckles on the attitude control system, though it wouldn't work while in Synth. She punched the computer readout as Jax managed to clip the restraints over her shoulders again.

"I modified some of the coordinates back to Pentagram to kick us out tangential to both systems."

"What? Why?" Jax wheezed out.

"Because we're fugitives"

"We're what?" Jax's knee felt like it was being eaten off with acid. She gripped it in an attempt to quell the pain and understand their predicament.

"Skraawl got the message from Legs. Judging from their reaction, we are not welcome there, and based on the violent send off, I can hazard we aren't welcome back in the Pentagram either."

Jax squeezed her eyes shut to think through the pain.

"Wait, wait, so what about everyone we left back on Prime Planet?" Jax had a horrible idea what the answer might be.

"If they are still alive, the best thing we can do right now is avoid them," Saunders replied.

"How do you figure?" Jax coughed out. Saunders had finally taken her hands off the controls and was assessing the pain that Jax was in. She unbuckled her restraints and floated out so she could examine Jax's leg.

"Because *if* they are still alive, even if they are going to be abused and suffering, us showing up will only make things worse," Saunders said, almost dismissively. She was already pulling Jax's coverall leg up so she could examine the damage. Her fingers passed a faded scar from a battle waged in a different universe altogether, then traveled up to the swollen and misshapen knee.

"Ow, dammit!" Jax swore, "Careful! Or were you serious about murdering me?"

"Take it easy, you may have broken it. I don't have to murder you if that is your go-to method to fix the engine converter under threat of fire. I see you have reunited with your favorite wrench."

"It worked, didn't it?" Jax gritted through her teeth as Saunders inspected her knee.

"Come on, I need these coveralls off you."

"I may not actually be in the mood at the moment."

"I need to look at your *knee,* Jax, come on, they can't track us in Synth-space right now, we have some time."

Jax's knee was not broken, but it was terribly sprained and possibly torn. Saunders managed to bind it as best as possible, and they hung in the lack of gravity near the storage lockers.

"They'll find us as soon as we drop out of Synth-space," Jax insisted. "As soon as we emerge and pick up a light signal. My guess is they'll calculate a probable sphere of range, scan the vicinity, and tag us as soon as we drop out. Gives us maybe an hour once we stop."

"So we'll have to keep moving," Saunders replied. She was re-packaging the sparse first aid supplies they had on board.

"Keep moving *where?*"

As far as corners of space were concerned, this one wasn't all bad. It could have been desolate and empty, devoid of resources. Instead, it had multiple viable systems in it. All of which just happened to be ruled or controlled by murderous, slaughtering alien Bat-Lizards, Foliage, and giant Death-Shrimp. There were *tons* of possibilities.

"I swiped a bunch of coordinates from the Prime Planet database, I think we can use some of the outlying systems and just stick to the shadows. See if things blow over, or I dunno, become space pirates, or something, for the rest of our miserable lives," Saunders grumbled.

Jax stared at her in near disbelief until Saunders noticed. "What?"

"Just, all of that—swiping coordinates, planning to be space pirates...my knee hurts like a bitch, but I'm so strangely turned on by you right now."

"You're absurd, Jax."

"I'm not the one who just said 'Space Pirates' as a sincere potential career move for us," Jax countered.

"We are also facing the very real fact that we are being hunted for the sole reason of just...showing up, unannounced," Saunders bemoaned, forlornly.

"That's what this is really about, isn't it? We just showed up suddenly, in the midst of their little empire, and they can't explain us."

"Do you really think humans would be much better if the Skraawl, or, heaven forbid, the Malacost, showed up in *our* galaxy suddenly?"

Jax hummed noncommittally in reply. Saunders had a point. But it was irrelevant. They weren't *in* humanity's galaxy. They were far off that map.

"Well, at least I'm getting hunted *with* you. Not *by* you. Silver linings."

Saunders squinted her eyes at Jax, a reluctant smile at the edges of her mouth.

"You're weird sometimes, you know that? We better get back to the cockpit, we're going to drop out of Synth-Space and we need to pick another destination if we only have an hour between hops."

* * *

The tug dropped out of the sky in a rapid approach. It flared at the last moment, kicking up a dust cloud around its base. The Foliage and lower caste Skraawl in the area scurried from its halo, taking cover. The spacecraft landed hard on the packed soil of the outlying Pentagram settled system.

A sense of apprehension settled over the waiting craft. The creatures in the area poked their heads and vines out in cautious interest. From the settlement's center a contingency of Foliage surged forward, tendrils questing, psychic connections seeking to bend the very metal of the machine in their midst.

The side door opened up with a snap and Jax stepped out, back kept flush to the exterior. She hefted an awkward looking collection of mechanisms toward the approaching Foliage and fired a single shot, blasting the creature off its flagella in a burst of gelatinous, plant-based goo.

"Go!" Jax shouted. Saunders broke from the cover of the vehicle while Jax took aim and lobbed another shot at a second approaching Pentagram militant.

Jax adjusted the armor she had manufactured who knows how many planet hops ago. It fit awkwardly over her, now shredded, coveralls that were tied across her waist still. The armor did its job of blocking a laser spear from the incoming Skraawl pawn.

From her vantage point under cover of the tug stabilizer, Jax could see Saunders hurdling barriers around the side of the settlement. She watched as Saunders took cover around the corner of a building and fired her hedger in response to another assault. Jax took aim and provided the cover fire that let Saunders keep moving.

A blast knocked too close to Jax's head and drew her attention back to the additional Foliage streaming from the settlement center. Jax adjusted the repurposed pressure helmet she was using for head protection. The responding aliens had gotten too close, so Jax dropped the blaster to her side and raised her right arm to swing the heavy, clunky end of her battle wrench, smashing the head of the Foliage closest to her.

"Any day now, babe," Jax hissed under her breath. She let off another three volleys of blaster, aiming contained solar energy from the synth drive, taking out the next few sentient carnivorous plants that appeared. Fewer were emerging now, and Jax hoped they might be in limited supply. The Skraawl would be another issue though. They were never done fighting. There must not be that many of them on-planet then.

Five minutes went by. Jax pulled herself back into the body of the tug, emerging once to fire a warning shot at a bold Skraawl, smaller than the usual imposing beasts. Saunders had five more minutes before Jax needed to pull the tug from the surface and hunt her down.

A blast smacked the side of the craft. Jax poked her head back out again. Great. The Foliage had just been taking their time rolling out their cannon. Or...it could be a cannon. It mostly looked like a massive lotus pod, but given enough time around these creatures Jax had learned there were few limits to what could be accomplished with sentient vines, psychic mold, and a can-do attitude. Jax swore and lobbed a return volley at the group, splattering one and knocking another over. She needed to keep them from getting too close or they would just phase through the tug walls and she would be toast.

The Foliage cannon looked to be charging again and Jax was unsure if the vehicles outer shell would survive it. She took careful aim at the base of the pod and took a chance. Blasting it might take the whole settlement out. Or it might just super charge the cannon for more efficient human destruction. Or it might short circuit it and take out the Foliage surrounding it.

Turned out that last one was the case, which left Jax looking at her garbled mess of a blaster with awe and reverence. A blast echoed from somewhere deeper in the settlement.

"That's my cue!" Jax shouted at the remaining settlers who were still in hiding. Jax pulled into the tug, slammed the door shut, and jumped into the pilot seat. The craft rose smoothly on its alien tech upgrades.

Jax leaned on the responsive controls and set off at a low altitude across the surface of the settlement, heading toward the blast.

In the middle of what probably passed for a town square Jax found her target. Saunders was posted up in a corner, a stolen sack slung over her shoulder, busy with a shootout against several militants. Jax circled once overhead, caught the signal from Saunders on the ground and dropped the tug down right in between the contest. The armor upgrades would have to hold. The door opened, and Jax swaggered out. She didn't really have a choice; her leg had never healed properly, so swaggering was all Jax could really do. A blast knocked into the tug door just inches from her face, but Jax aimed and took out the perpetrator.

Saunders bolted from her hideout for the open door. Jax aimed another cover shot as Saunders streaked past, giving Jax a quick kiss on the cheek as she got close enough, before disappearing into the hollow of the craft.

"And that's my exit. It's been a blast everyone!" Jax called, and hauled herself back inside. Saunders was already in the copilot seat, dragging the tug back up into the sky.

"Well, did we have any luck?" Jax asked as she dropped herself in the other seat before they hit low gravity.

"Pulled in a few food stores, some extra power packs," Saunders said as she focused on dodging some heavier ground fire. Her hair was falling in her eyes, and Jax could tell she would ask her to shave it off again to keep it from getting in the way.

"Well, that's good, we were running low," Jax hummed as she helped punch the coordinates for the next hop. "Should I bother asking about the main objective?"

Saunders didn't reply. She was busy hauling the shoulder straps down over the discarded Malacost shells she wore as armor. Jax waited patiently.

The tug broke orbit and dropped into synth-space. Jax wasn't sure which section of the galaxy they would drop into next, but chances were they had already been there. Maybe it would be one less they would have to slink through before their run would come to an end. She let herself relax a bit in the seat against the restraints and waited for Saunders to reply to her last question.

Saunders finished crunching the navigation numbers and finally looked over at Jax.

"I got the message off: electromagnetic coordinates that we think correlate to the Rift, with hope that Rose can process it and barter our existence."

Jax looked over.

"And we think she has the tools to process that still?"

"I sure fucking hope so," Saunders replied. "You processed the data first, and you are both brilliant, it's the best hope we have."

Jax felt elated. Strokes of luck, months of tracking movements, intercepting data packets, and deciphering communications between aliens they hardly knew how to communicate with in the first place, might just all pay off.

"So now what?"

"Now we hope Rose is still alive to get it, and then, we wait," Saunders answered.

Jax sighed and relaxed back in the seat. Saunders reached out and grasped her hand. The dark depths of synth-space enveloped them.

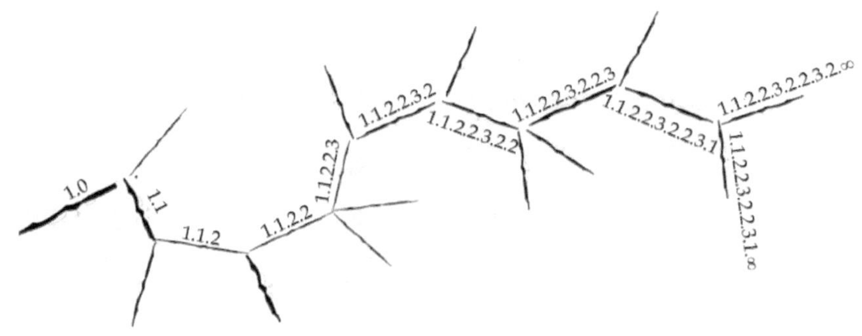

1.1.2.2.3.2.2.3.1.2.∞

"Hey, you know what would be *perfect* right about now?" Andee asked.

Jax peeled her vision from the porthole to the tug secured outside the Station for the first time in nearly a decade.

"What...?" she replied, cautious.

Andee grinned and pulled out a canister shaking it as she went. "Racing stripes!"

Jax made a lunge for the can but Andee held it over her head out of reach.

"Give it!" Jax growled, to no avail.

"Nah," Andee rumbled. "Rhyse gave it to me, it's mine now." She strode off down the corridor of Level 1. Jax hiked her toolbelt around her waist and followed.

"Don't you dare go outside to spray that. You had your chance while it was still in the hanger!" Jax noted.

Andee paused in her stride to think it over. Then she shrugged.

"Then I'm gonna paint some sweet flames on her when we land."

"Okay yeah, well, we have to *land* first, that's a critical step."

Andee had pocketed the paint canister and continued along the ring toward Common Access. Jax remained in step, but was already lost in thought on the obstacles ahead. Outside the Station, a faint glow of a nearby planet illuminated the exterior, the tug in its new placement on Docking. The steady spin of the Station as it approached caused a slow rotation of shadow as the reflected light arced with the turn of the engines.

System checks, failsafe procedures, redundancy in execution, abort steps, contingency plans... Jax could be busy for the next ten week-cycles, which was about how long they had to reach an orbit around their target. It would take longer to fathom the fact this insane jaunt across the stars had worked.

So lost in her thoughts was Jax that she missed the wiry, compact frame of the Security Officer blocking her path, and Jax nearly tackled Saunders.

"Whoa, almost stepped on you there Jill," Andee chuckled.

"No one, and I mean absolutely *no one* calls me 'Jill'," Saunders seethed, glaring at the welder.

Jax aggressively shook her head. She hadn't even bothered to try: she valued her assets too much. Andee merely chuckled and raised her hands in innocence.

"That's for telling everyone my full name at dinner," Andee shrugged.

"That was *last year*," Saunders objected.

Andee put her broad hand over her heart and mimed a sad face.

"Still feels fresh. Anyway, were you looking to be a speed bump or do I need to kick rocks and leave you two be?"

Right on cue, Saunders shot Jax a look that very much made her wish Andee would *not* kick rocks. It was a look that warned her not to be alone with the shorter woman.

"I'll see you at dinner, *Andoria*," Saunders replied, not breaking eye contact with Jax.

"Oh man, I'm going to paint so many things on these walls," Andee whined as she strode off toward Common Access, shaking the paint as she went. Jax wanted to object, but she felt pinned to the spot by Saunders.

"Yes, babe?" Jax winced. Saunders softened her glare and stepped up to wrap her arms around Jax's waist, placing her head on Jax's chest, just under her chin. Jax hesitantly wrapped her arms around Saunders' back, now in sharper contrast after years of rationing.

"Did you two get the tug outside to the docking port okay?" Saunders asked, muffled.

"Yeah," Jax replied. "That was Andee threatening to paint flames on it when we land."

At that comment, Saunders flinched.

"Can we talk about that, please?" she asked softly.

Whatever sarcastic remark Jax had chambered about Andee's artistic plans dissipated. She felt her eyebrows automatically knit with concern, and she dropped her arms to her sides.

"Yeah, sure Saunders, what's up?"

Saunders turned slowly, contemplative as she angled herself to walk down the Level 1 corridor. Her shoulder remained tilted as an invite for Jax to join her.

They walked in silence for a few moments. Jax couldn't really complain. It was only her curiosity that piqued her interest in Saunders talking more, but four years in each others' company, and not much else, made it a comfortable silence to exist in.

"Why do you have to be the one who leaves?" Saunders finally asked. They were past the research office and around the back half of the ring near the abandoned couches.

Jax felt the familiar unease of being put on the spot when she felt the answer was obvious, but she also knew Saunders would stomp right around any deflection. So instead Jax strode over to the windows offering a view of the approaching planet.

It was vaguely purple. But some of the analysis equipment indicated water in the atmosphere, and a terrestrial surface. It was a one in a hundred trillion shot in the dark, but there it was. If only they could get to the surface safely.

"You know how I always used to say 'one for people, one for parts'?" Jax asked, still looking out at the quarry they thought they may never find.

Saunders followed her to the windows to watch the planet rotate around the edge of the view. If they looked too long it might make them nauseous, but they were the most experienced in this life on a ring. Saunders slipped under Jax's shoulder to wrap herself in Jax's arms, back to her chest, as they both looked out.

"I used to hate that you said that."

"Yeah, well, I'm certainly not gifted in *people*," Jax replied. Saunders huffed a laugh, and laid her head back on Jax's shoulder.

"But, okay, yes. Where are you going with this?"

Jax adjusted a bit so she could rest her temple on the top of Saunders' head.

"We, as individuals, as a pair, as a team, have given everything we can for what this Station is. And not just what it was, but what it became," Jax started. "So, think about how much you felt a duty to your people, and how I felt my duty to this Station? Well, this Station has done its job. My time serving it has come to an end." Jax felt a slight lump in her chest at that realization. Thirteen years on this tin can, and it had done so much for them. It had gotten them here.

Saunders turned where she rested so she could look up at Jax, rather than through their reflection. She was waiting for Jax to finish.

"With that service complete, all that remains are our people. And they are *ours* now. And how can I serve them, but to take the risk in the hardware I helped build?" Jax asked.

"I know where you're going with this, love," Saunders interjected. It wasn't aggressive, but it was decisive. She sighed and turned to look back outside again. "But it is a moment of weakness in me. We have given so much. This time, I want to be selfish and keep you here, for me. Why can't we let anyone else take this risk? Why can't our work be over, finally?"

Jax stewed in thought. She compensated by hugging Saunders closer and realized the woman had once again stolen her Engineering sweatshirt. It wasn't like Jax had ever really worn it, Saunders had simply moved in and claimed it, much like so many other parts of Jax.

"Saunders, would you be satisfied if your work was suddenly over? Would you *really* be satisfied?" Jax asked, saving any questions about the garment for later.

Saunders paused a moment, before answering. "I suppose I would just find other things to work on. You can do so many other things."

Jax huffed in frustration. All these years and this woman knew the right cards to play.

"I cannot, in good conscience, ask anyone we care about —and we care about them all, even Zick—to pilot that tug onto an alien surface. I couldn't live with myself knowing I had sent them on something I wouldn't fly first," Jax insisted.

Quiet. Saunders tried to wrap herself tighter in Jax's arms.

"But what if you don't come back?"

Jax sighed.

"Did I tell you? That Rose and I have been trying to understand what happened to us, years ago, when we Dropped?"

Saunders went still, listening.

"There isn't much for us to go off of. It's something no one has ever experienced before...at least not in so much as they survived to tell about it." Jax took a deep breath to prepare herself for the best way to explain this.

"But you and Rose have an idea?"

"Well, there wasn't any way to know what might happen to us. And this is where we wound up, on the other side. Impossibly, improbably..."

"Jax..." Saunders groaned.

"Okay, okay, just...Rose has a theory...okay *we* have a theory...that maybe *everything happened*. That when we fell, a trillion possibilities expanded out from that very moment, and every single one of them were true."

Saunders twisted in Jax's arms to give her a frustrated look.

"For fucks sake Jax, what the hell does *that* bullshit have to do with me not wanting you to go on a suicide mission to the surface of a planet we had no business finding in the first place?" Green eyes flared dangerously and Jax swallowed hard.

"Look, there will always, and forever, be the possibility that one of us won't come back, but if we cling to that, then we will be crippled. If falling through that rift meant infinite outcomes, we can only hope that we get to live in a version of the universe where we can always return to each other!"

Saunders relaxed, and sank back into Jax's arms.

"And what if we're not in that universe?"

"If we don't find ourselves lucky enough to be living in *that* universe, then, well...we can take comfort that some other version of ourselves do. And that is all we *can* do." Jax swallowed hard again. There was a lump in her throat and a fear deep in her gut telling her she had no reason to believe half the shit she was saying.

But Saunders didn't reply. The planet curved past, close enough to show slight cloud cover. Even getting to the surface would only be the starting point. There would be so much more once they got there, so many opportunities for them to either make it, or not.

Then Saunders shivered.

"Okay *how* are you still cold?" Jax snorted. Saunders shot her a glare.

"First off, you're gonna tell me some bullshit fairy tale like that and then find it weird that it freaks me out? Teach me to leave you alone with Rose ever again. Besides, y*ou* routed the power to the engines for the approach, it dropped the temperature!"

"It dropped the temperature *two* degrees! And I expect that sweatshirt back!" Jax poked at the hood.

Saunders squirmed from her grasp and scuttled down the corridor.

"No, it's mine now. Don't think this little convo is over yet. There's still time to agree to disagree!" And with that she took off for the next stairwell, Jax on her heels.

8.0

The Station stretched in the new space. The distant starlight wasn't enough to warm it, but the thought occurred to it how nice it might feel.

Inside its numerous rings, several dozen lives milled about. The Station wasn't quite sure what they were doing, but in its experience it hadn't ever really mattered. What mattered more was the feeling that the Station wasn't in the best of shape. It had been fine, but something had grabbed ahold of it and shaken things up.

Some foggy swirl of memory, bearing pain, and stress, and the feeling of energy slowly leeching away, ate at the Station's consciousness. It was troubling, but as the fog lifted, it felt like the Station was awakening for the first time.

It wanted something familiar.

Deep in its rings it sought the one thing the Station could recall as a constant. All these lives passing through, coming, going, leaving things in their wake, then having those leave too, none of them were enough for the Station to recall. They added to the heady fog. But there was one thing clear in all of it. The Mechanic.

The Station didn't quite understand its feelings. They seemed new, despite the Station feeling so old. Feelings were not expected. It was simply there to turn endlessly. But the feelings were there, and the Station wanted to give meaning to them. The Mechanic had spent ages within its rings, tending so carefully to the Station's needs that there was only one word that the Station could think of: love. And so, the Station loved The Mechanic back.

Years of the Station holding The Mechanic within its rings, within its core, listening to the words The Mechanic whispered to it. And the Station had rolled onward under such devoted care. It would do anything to keep its Mechanic safe. It was the *Station's* Mechanic.

Except that wasn't quite the case anymore. No one had ever gotten between the Station and her Mechanic in the past. It reveled in the idea that there would be no one else. But something had shifted. Station suspected it had been there longer than it had realized, but even now, as it shook off the haze of its awakening, and sought its keeper within, the Mechanic was not alone.

There were always supposed to be two. Station understood this. But the two were inconsequential. Station's Mechanic had remained a constant and the second had always been fleeting; hardly worth remembering. Station had stopped bothering to recall who ever had filled the role. But this one, this one was different somehow. In the very least, Station realized the second one had a lot more of the Mechanic's attention.

The Mechanic still doted on the Station, which it appreciated. But there was something growing beneath the surface. Within the Station's walls, the Two were with each other. Focus was clearly shared between them and not on the Station, nor its other lives within. This focus was unique. The Station could feel the Mechanic's attentiveness to its needs dwindling. Something was drawing its Mechanic away.

The Station didn't like this feeling. Abandonment. Loss. Isolation. Without its Mechanic, the Station might as well be nothing more than passing dust in the cosmos. It was a crushing feeling, like it might implode, pulverizing those within.

No, the Station couldn't let that happen. It couldn't lose its Mechanic. So that meant, the Other had to go.

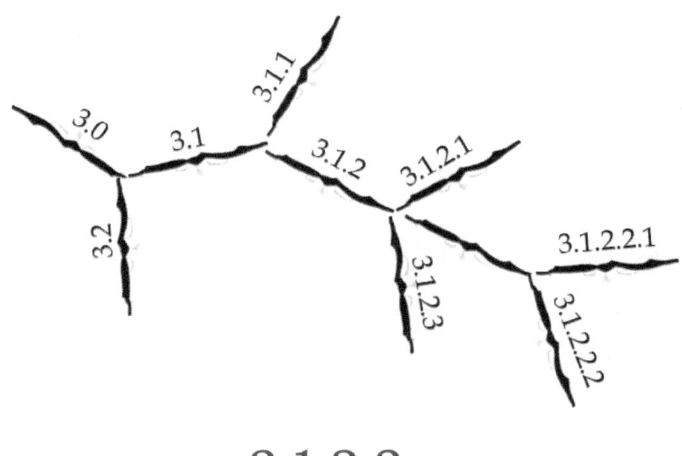

3.1.2.3

Jax stood on the open drop deck. The humid air of the Pentagram Prime Planet swept past her, blowing her long, shock of hair into her face. Her left leg ached a bit in the dense, humid atmosphere. She strained her gaze on the crowd moving toward the transport.

Cul had called them in after the initial wave, as backup. Reinforcement was needed on the surface. Skraawl warriors galloped past her to set up a perimeter as dust obscured what sounded like an ongoing battle. Screeching echoed along with the crunch and destruction of the vine-enforced coral of Prime.

Figures emerged. Human figures.

The first small groups poured passed, some reaching out to Jax in recognition and relief. Jax grasped an arm or two in passing, but her focus was drawn elsewhere, hunting, scanning, looking for any sign.

The refugees piled in now. Gedry pulled along Obah, who looked injured. Flick and Mingle were helping hoist Avery over the threshold. Then, out of the smoke walked Rose, who saw Jax and immediately ran over to embrace her.

"Jax, you returned!" Rose cried. Jax responded to the embrace distractedly. She was happy to see the researcher too, but she was still on edge.

"Rose, Rose have you seen her?" Jax couldn't hide the anxiety in her voice. Rose looked up in concern.

"Seen who?"

"Saunders! Have you seen Saunders? She was out there, she went to get you all!" Jax urged, trying to keep the hysteria from rising in her voice.

"I have not seen her, it was just these creatures." Rose looked back over her shoulder at the rest of the refugees pouring in.

Jax gripped the smaller woman's shoulder like a lifeline, unaware she was still holding on. Vamp limped down the ramp to sidle up beside Jax on her other side.

"AAus?" Vamp chirped.

Jax looked furtively at the creature and couldn't find the words. The panic constricted her throat.

She stood there, flanked by a resident and an alien as the last of the Station's surviving populace poured in from the swirling smoke and mist of the damp and industrial Prime Planet surface. A heavy weight of horror dropped in the pit of her stomach.

They should have pled their case. They should have been diplomatic. This violence was not what they needed, and Saunders was out there, maybe never coming back. Jax's knees went weak. Vamp reached out a taloned appendage, wrapped in a Cloak and gripped Jax by the upper arm, preventing a fall. Rose shot a look of alarm at the creature, but Jax only reached up and wrapped her own claws around Vamp's sinewy joint, covering the Cloak's dewclaw and hanging on for dear life.

"Jax," Rose stuttered, choosing to ignore the odd physical interaction occurring beside her. "This is Saunders. She knows how to survive, she will be back!" It was a valiant attempt at being encouraging. It hurt.

"Don't say that. Don't give me hope," Jax whispered. Cul swept menacingly out of the dust before them, as if with a sense of finality. It roared a sound of retreat and Vamp responded by lumbering back up the ramp, pulling Jax along.

An animalistic and frantic urge drove Jax to fight. She thrashed against the craws gripping her and raged against the finality that faced her.

"No! Saunders isn't back yet!"

"*AAak!*"

"You have to give her a chance to come back!" Jax shouted, as Cul stomped up the ramp. Jax caught sight of Foliage and the scurry of a Malacost through the swirling fog outside of the drop deck.

"SHE FOUGHT LIKE SKRAAWL" barked the translator.

Jax tore her eyes from the closing drop deck door to size up the Skraawl second in command. She had not yet figured out Skraawl facial expressions but she imagined this one was sympathy. It wrenched her heart. Jax gave a pitiful flail to pull herself free, twisting to see the closing door, leaving Saunders behind for good.

"WAIT!" the word rose out of the fog like a beacon. Jax froze, as did the hands and talons holding her back. The drop deck was closing still, but a figure emerged from the swirls of fog, mist, and smoke to step through the opening in the deck.

Jax knees buckled, wrenching herself from the grasp of whoever was holding her. She stumbled, regained her footing, winced at the ache in her left leg, and sprinted down the drop-deck launch ramp.

Saunders stood there, hedger dropped to her side, hand unclipping the helmet. She had just enough time to drop the smashed, and busted head gear to the metal grating on the floor before Jax slammed into her at top speed.

Jax only ever lifted anything that needed lifting: power coils, heavy HVAC equipment, massive wrenches, busted outboard rotational engines, short women in bulky pressure suits. Jax might not work out regularly, but she could still manage to hoist Saunders, suit and all, into the tightest embrace she could manage.

"Don't *ever* fucking leave me like that again, do you understand?" Jax whispered into the sweaty dark-blond hair of the other woman. Saunders didn't have much flexibility or range of motion in the suit, but she was able to feebly place a hand on either side of Jax's shoulders. As the transport took off Jax stumbled, but managed to hold on to Saunders, whose feet were barely brushing the ground in the clunky pressure suit boots.

"But we made it babe. We're all here," she whispered, as Jax managed to get her footing secure again.

"*Promise, dammit,*" Jax hissed, and placed Saunders back on the ground. Saunders looked up at her.

"Okay. I promise. Any fighting I do from now on will be in strategy planning, not field operations. There's a lot to strategize now after all. We have a new home to build." Jax flung her arms round Saunders' neck, ignoring the bite of the hard metal helmet ring and pulled her close to kiss. They then broke apart to turn toward Vamp and Rose, who watched them from the ramp.

"Let's get started then," Saunders barked, as she grabbed Jax's hand and marched them both back up into the ship.

9.0

Jax blinked. Her vision cleared. She was sitting in the corridor of Level 1, her back to the wall. Pressed warm to her side, head resting on her shoulder, was Saunders, still asleep. Jax looked out the windows of her Station, to the drifting void of space.

There was nothing out there.

Well, that wasn't true. There were stars. There were always stars drifting past with the steady roll of the Station as the outboard rotationals generated the centripetal force that simulated gravity.

What *was* missing was the massive rip in the fabric of space that had threatened them all with oblivion. Had Jax imagined it? Had Jax imagined all of it?

Then why was she sleeping in the Level 1 corridor with her coworker and half the Station residents? It couldn't have all been hallucinations.

Jax's back felt stiff, and her scraped left leg stung. She wasn't young enough to be napping on floors anymore. She had spent far too long out here in the middle of nowhere.

"Saunders. Saunders wake up," Jax whispered, her mouth brushing over the dirty-blond hair of the woman still clinging to her side even in sleep. Saunders stirred.

"Mrrrr, bottom of the fifth yard line," Saunders mumbled.

"What?"

Then Saunders shot awake.

"JAX!"

"Shhhh, I'm right here," Jax hissed, trying to not draw the attention of all the residents who were also slowly coming back around.

Saunders' eyes cleared and she took in her surroundings, the corridor, the residents strewn about, then finally Jax.

"We're alive!"

"Oh, good, so you remember it too," Jax said, only a little hysteria creeping into her voice. "I was worried I had gone insane, imagined everything. I didn't imagine everything right? You still want to kiss me, right?"

Saunders' face went through a prismatic kaleidoscope of reactions: horrified memory, relief, confusion, alarm, followed by calm recognition. She leaned forward and pressed her lips softly to Jax's for a warm moment before pulling back.

"Yes, I still want to kiss you, but I also want to know what the fuck just happened. The last thing I remember we were falling into hell."

Jax turned her face to look out of the windows across from her and pushed herself to rise to her feet. Saunders followed. They both crept slowly across the corridor until they were pressed up to the window. Some residents started to join them.

Peering out into space, everything looked…normal. Jax even caught a glimpse of a constellation she had marked in her time out here. Jax didn't stare at it long, or she would get motion sick from the spin.

A crowd had started to gather. Jax, having pulled her eyes from the stars, looked around the confused and murmuring group. Then, sudden realization struck her.

"Saunders!" Jax grabbed the shoulders of the shorter woman.

"What?" Saunders looked alarmed again.

"I need to check on the Station, check the core, make sure we are okay!" Jax felt panic growing in her.

"Okay, okay, I'll come with you," Saunders replied, placing a calming hand on Jax's shoulder, and hip. Jax faltered at the touch, then shook herself back on track.

"You need to stay with the residents!" Jax objected.

"Why? They're grown-ass adults. They'll be fine?" Saunders looked confused. Jax opened her mouth to reply and had nothing. She glanced around at the various residents stretching and greeting each other, gathering to look out into space. Saunders softened her face.

"This situation is still hot. I'm not ready to split up from you just yet. We can check on the Station and then round everyone up together. Give them updates. No one looks hurt, so let's not risk parting ways just yet."

Jax just didn't feel like arguing. Sticking together sounded perfectly fine. They pulled back from the group to head toward Common Access.

"Security!" Jax turned to see where the call came from, as Saunders twisted her head in response.

A compact little woman, with tight, dark, wavy brown curly hair pulled back in a small knot, and a sharp look in her eyes, came trotting over to them. Jax thought she recognized the resident, but she couldn't be sure. They had only just fought off a horde of hallucinations, and it might take a while for Jax to put the pieces back in place with who was who.

"Rose, are you okay?" Saunders was asking the resident who had reached where they stood.

"I am fine, but I heard you were planning to examine the Station's functionality. May I join?" she looked from Jax to Saunders and back again, expectantly.

"Oh, well Level 5 is usually locked off to residents—" Saunders started.

"You're the one who studies deep field gravitational theory," Jax stated, slowly. The veil had been pulling back, and puzzle pieces were fitting.

"That is correct, Engineering!" Rose grinned.

"Yeah, after whatever that was"—Jax flailed an extended finger out toward the Station windows—"it might not hurt to get a second opinion up there. I'm a bit rusty in my orbital mechanics after all."

Rose smiled graciously. Jax turned to continue and caught Saunders' incredulous stare.

"What?" Jax asked. Saunders just shook her head and smiled. They all three climbed to Level 5.

* * *

"What??" Saunders fixed Jax and Rose with an intense gaze. Jax felt the tips of her ears burning. She looked down at the small research scientist who had tagged along. She was their confirmation Jax wasn't going insane.

"Here is the readout of our standing coordinates from two weeks ago. These are the ones I pulled when your research team docked." Jax pointed to one screen readout for Rose to scrutinize. "And these are today's." She pointed at the parallel screen.

Rose studied them for a moment, considering. She chewed on the inside of her cheek as she crunched the numbers in her head. Then she looked back up at Jax.

"Well, I am not Eave Izina."

"Who?"

"She does waypoint navigation programing for WSTN, should I get her?" Saunders interjected.

"No, I do not think that is necessary." Rose looked back at the screens, then back at Jax, and smiled.

"Engineering is correct!" she said, glancing over at Saunders who looked incredulous.

"No fucking way!" Saunders barked.

"Hey, I resent that," Jax whined.

"You're telling me...we haven't moved? We're exactly where we were two weeks ago!?" Saunders' voice was rising, in hysteria or excitement, Jax couldn't tell.

"It would seem so, yes," Jax replied, evenly.

"So all that...mess...the hallucinations, the Station dying, the...the...*rip* in space...the *drop??* Was all a *dream?*" Saunders howled.

Jax reached out in hopes of steadying her. She was seriously worried for the woman's mental state at the moment.

"Oh, I do not think that was a dream," Rose interjected. "Everyone witnessed visions and experienced strange occurrences. We all viewed the anomalous rip in the fabric of space. But yet, here we are. Nothing has changed. I would bet my whole career on attempting to record what may or may not have happened to us recently."

And Jax believed it. The woman looked nearly giddy. In her arms, Saunders was nearly hyperventilating. Jax squeezed her close to try to calm her.

"What...what *was* that then?" Saunders croaked out. "That *thing* we fell through?"

Jax shot an uneasy glance at Rose and cleared her throat.

"I...don't know if there are words to actually describe it."

"Indeed," Rose added. "Without the correct data collection, we may never know."

"Do you think your instruments set up on Level 1 caught anything?" Jax knew the use for that equipment and had doubts, but there might always be a chance.

"Unlikely. Even if we managed, it would take decades to process such data. At this time, all we can verify is that our location has not moved. Our people seem fine, save any casualties incurred from the damage Engineering addressed in the core."

As if in emphasis, the star trackers behind Jax chimed, indicating they had completed their calibration cycle, and locked on to recognized constellations.

"But, it was so massive! That was...Jax, that was terrifying!" Saunders whispered, as if speaking any louder might summon the rift to return. Jax didn't have a reply, since Saunders was right. Her own body still hummed with the fading echoes of adrenaline as the universe opened to swallow them whole.

"So...so we're safe?" Saunders finally managed to squeak out.

"I mean, the core is still damaged. The Station is still going to need to be taken out of commission for repairs," Jax replied. Saunders looked up at her now, like she was really seeing her.

"We all have to leave?"

"I'll put a call in to Station Management and log a maintenance request. It'll halt any additional transients from heading this way, and we'll have to arrange for transport off for all current residents. Probably lock this place down in four weeks' time."

"Oh, I apologize deeply, Engineering, I understand this is your home," Rose said, sympathetically.

"Ah, it's probably past time for me to move on to the next thing anyway," Jax admitted, scratching nonchalantly at the scraggle of mane cascading down her neck. She was holding Saunders with a tight one-armed hug, and Saunders had put her arms around her waist to hold her back. Saunders' breathing had calmed and her head was resting firmly on Jax's shoulder, face pressed under Jax's chin. Jax leaned down and whispered.

"You were leaving with Rose's team, weren't you?"

Saunders looked up, surprise across her face, like recalling a memory.

"I think I can stick around and help you prep the Station for decommission," she offered. Jax kissed her on the spot.

"Actually—" interjected Rose.

Jax had a sudden regret of inviting her up to Level 5.

"I am able to arrange for our transport to delay an additional week, then you may both accompany us. From what I have heard, Jax you possess a significant amount of experience in gravitation theory yourself. If we did manage to obtain such data, you are welcome to join us to help decipher it."

"Another station?" Jax asked, cautious.

"It is a terrestrial outpost. Taurus-B. There is a station in Lagrange orbit; short tour cycles, with a surface posting," Rose replied, informatively.

Jax looked back down at Saunders and grinned.

* * *

Several hours later Jax found herself finally returned to the Level 1 corridor outside the Security Office, standing nervously before the door to Saunders' quarters. She had showered, put some disinfectant on her scratched leg, put on a clean shirt, and whatever pants she owned that were not grungy mechanic coveralls.

The residents had been briefed. The core diagnostics had been pulled. The bodies of Paul Hower and Illy Lark had been retrieved; moved to a resting place in Medical. Arrangements needed to be made: a joint report back to the WSTN Station Management department, updates on the failing core, notice of the casualties, plans for decommissioning.

Jax was sure neither she nor Saunders could think of a way to report on exactly what had happened. Sending a message across the stars that said "Station went haywire, brought nightmares to life, then dropped though a rip in space. Everyone mostly okay," would only make their lives a living hell.

But that was a tomorrow-Jax problem.

The next few weeks would be busy. Decommissioning a station took work, and planning. But now Jax stood, hesitating to raise her hand and wrap her knuckles on the door to the Station Security Officer's quarters. Tomorrow would start a whole chain of activity, but for now, there was no further work to be done, save for one thing. Jax finally knocked.

The door to Saunders' quarters opened almost immediately, as if she had also been standing there, waiting. The air stilled between them as Jax's eyes locked on the piercing green ones across from her. Saunders' face seemed at once relieved, and searching. She broke eye contact with Jax to survey the mechanic in her most presentable form. Saunders' hair was damp from a shower, her bandages freshly changed. She was wearing softer lounge pants and a clean tank top instead of the shreds of security uniform Jax had last seen her in. A scrape on her chin looked fresh, but her face flushed in Jax's presence.

"So, I was wondering," Jax stammered, running her hand through her cascading mane of hair, "would you be interested in some company tonight?"

Saunders' eyes snapped back up to look Jax in the face, and Jax saw her breath hitch. A spike of fear shot through Jax at the idea that she might be turned away. But instead, Saunders carefully took a step backward, creating a space for Jax to fill, and nodded. So Jax hesitantly stepped across the threshold, and the door rolled shut.

They were close now, the only thing between them Saunders' tentative hand placed on Jax's shirt, just below her sternum. Saunders looked up at Jax from the minute space in which they shared a breath.

"Just, tell me Jax," Saunders exhaled. "You aren't going to run out on me again, are you?"

A flood of remorse and affection threatened to spill over in an embarrassing show of emotions within Jax. Instead, she channeled it into raising her hand to brush her fingers over Saunders' chin and cup her face. Jax pushed into the space between them to close the distance for good. Her thumb brushed over Saunders' cheek, as Saunders circled her arms tightly around Jax's waist in reply. Jax leaned down and pressed her lips to Saunders'. She poured as much intent and sincerity into the contact as she felt in her heart, wrapping her other arm around Saunders' back to pull her flush to herself.

"Never again," Jax whispered, breaking apart so she could make her promise. "Not in this universe, or any other existence I can perceive."

And she couldn't explain how she was so sure of it.

* * *

The Station was dark. The core would continue to spin the wheel for a few more hours, but then it would enter a shutdown sequence. The residents had been transported off in batches over the course of a few weeks. The Station Manager had walked through the shutdown checklist and posted it up in the security office for the inevitable repair crew to find.

One transport remained, connected to the main docking port of Level 1. It was going through its departure sequence, and it was ready to leave.

Jax stood in the docking tunnel, near the internal airlock door. A single duffle bag was slung over her shoulder holding nearly everything she owned.

In her one hand, she held a thirty-six inch long, battered and damaged spud wrench; a souvenir of her service to this deep-space monstrosity. She looked back on the hauntingly dark hallways of Level 1, the void of Common Access and the layers of Station leading up to a core she would never set foot in again.

A soft hand rested on Jax's arm, making her jump. She turned to see Saunders standing next to her, holding a trimmed and contained Ralph.

"Are you ready, love?" Saunders asked quietly.

"Yeah, just, saying goodbye," Jax said, keeping her voice as even as she could. "She was a good home for so long."

Jax would miss this place. It had saved her, then destroyed her, then saved her again.

"Are you going to be okay?" Dammit if Saunders was more perceptive than Jax could ever be. Jax looked back down at her and nodded.

From behind, Rose called out to them.

"We are departing, it is time!"

Jax looked over her shoulder, down into the transport, then back to the Station again as she turned her body to go. At her side Saunders piped up.

"Come on Jax. There are new things out there for us to do."

Jax took Saunders' hand.

"Let's go."

ACKNOWLEDGEMENTS

Well here we are again. It turns out when you are left alone for too long with your own characters in your head, they just write the sequels for you. I may have vowed to never write a follow-on to Space Station X, but that was a fool's errand, so here we are. This book was not without some new challenges. What started as mini-character studies, feel-good vignettes and "fan fiction of my own work" needed to turn into a true story I was proud to share. I also decided that I couldn't simply pick one story, I needed to pick them all. Then, when it came time to finally turn this into a published work, I went and added such things as more spaceships at my day job, more teaching about spaceships on the side, and a kid, to top it all off. It's not like I ever make anything easy on myself. So once again, I need to thank several people for bolstering this behemoth and carrying me to the finish line.

First off, I want to thank Wilbur and Dad for both not only reading Space Station X, but then also asking me endless questions about it. I think it's every writer's dream to have dads let you talk about your book for hours on end. It was part of the motivation I needed to make this sequel work.

I want to thank Bill and Heather for creating this great landing place for my stories, and showing me the ropes of cons. I want to thank everyone from Space Wizard Science Fantasy who I have had the chance to meet and work alongside, as well as the numerous authors and content creators who have given me some fantastic perspective on this storytelling side quest I've found myself on.

But most of all I need to express my unfathomable gratitude to my wife. I wasn't sure who I could rely on to read this story in a raw form and understand what I was trying to do. I shouldn't have worried. She read this beast when it was forty thousand words longer than it wound up, and she was still able to help me navigate my course through to a viable revision. It's strange having someone who knows my characters as well as I do, if not better in some cases. But more than anything I am just grateful for the support, the engaging late-night chats about what the hell I'm thinking in terms of plot, and of course you (and Joselyn) keeping The Bug occupied long enough to let me finish my edits. This book would, once again, never exist without you, Nancy. Thank you the most.

ABOUT THE AUTHOR

A.Z. builds spaceships in her day job. She teaches about spaceships on the side. And now she apparently writes about spaceships in her spare time. Where she finds the spare time is still a mystery. Having been raised on a steady diet of classic science fiction and horror—consumed mostly through the staircase railing after bedtime while her father was asleep on the couch—A.Z. has always maintained a love for space travel and the unknown. This has largely fueled her career in aerospace engineering but originally fueled a passion for writing science fiction stories when she was very young. After a long quantity of months cooped up inside, A.Z. finally returned to her storytelling origins. A.Z. lives in the Mid-Atlantic region of the US with her wife and son, their dogs, several thousand honeybees, and way too many Legos.

Please take a moment to review this book at your favorite retailer's website, Goodreads, or simply tell your friends!

www.ingramcontent.com/pod-product-compliance
Lightning Source LLC
Chambersburg PA
CBHW032037050726

47590CB00001B/30